The
Seafarers

Marian Anderson Clover

Upswing Publishing
SAN DIEGO, CALIFORNIA

Upswing Publishing
San Diego, California
upswingpublishing.com

Book Layout ©2015 BookDesignTemplates.com

Book Design ©2015 Simon Mayeski

Ordering Information:
Quantity sales. Special discounts are available on quantity purchases by corporations, associations, and others. For details, contact the publisher with "Special Sales Department" in the subject line at sales@upswingpublishing.com

The Seafarers /Marian Anderson Clover. —1st ed.
ISBN 978-1-942628-00-2

Appreciation

Thanks for the technical help from my son Frank and my daughters Christine and Becky.

I appreciate Gail Golladay's encouragement and my late husband Frank's chauffeuring me to Scandinavian Viking sites.

Special thanks to Simon Mayeski of San Diego, California for his editorial skills. He transformed a manuscript into a book.

Ordering *The Seafarers*

Additional copies of *The Seafarers* may be ordered from fine bookstores everywhere.

The Seafarers is also available from online bookstores such as Amazon, Barnes and Noble and Smashwords.

And *The Seafarers* may be found at more than seventy e-book vendors as well, for a variety of e-book readers.

Visit our web site at TheSeafarers.com for more information and links to purchase the book!

Cover

Bibliography

Blum, Ralph. The New Book of Runes. St. Martin's Press, New York, NY. 1993.

Brorson, Kerstin. Sing The Cows Home. Welcome Press. 1985.

Burton, Richard. The Book of the Sword. Dover Publications, New York, NY. 1987.

Davidson, H.R. Ellis. Scandinavian Mythology. Hamlyn. 1968.

Dmytryshyn, Basil. Medieval Russia. Holt Rinehart & Winston, New York, NY. 1990.

Du Chaillu, Paul. The Viking Age (2 vol.) C. Scribner's Sons, New York, NY. 1889.

Freely, John. Blue Guide Istanbul. Blue Guides Limited of London, 2011.

Lee, Albert. Weather Wisdom. Doubleday Dolphin, New York, NY. 1977.

Magnusson, Magnus. Vikings! E. P. Dutton, New York, NY. 1980.

Martell, Hazel Mary. Food and Feasts with the Vikings. New Discovery Books, Parsippany, NJ. 1995.

Oxenstierne, Eric. The Norsemen. New York Graphic Society Publishers Ltd., Greenwich, CT. 1965.

Rosetree, Laura. I Can Read Your Face. Dell Publishing, New York, NY. 1990.

Simpson, Jacqueline. The Viking World. St. Martin's Press, New York, NY. 1980.

Tannahill, Reay, Sex in History. Stein and Day, New York, NY. 1980.

Thorsson, Edred. Runelore. Samuel Weiser Inc., San Francisco, CA. 1987.

Vernadsky, George. Kievan Russia. Yale University Press, New Haven, CT. 1973.

Glossary

Airt	Division of wind
Beitass	Long spar beneath the sail
Berserker	A very strong Viking
Bifrost	The Milky Way
Byrnie	Chain mail
Dairy	Hut where milk is made into curds
Danelaw	Northeastern part of England ruled by the Danes
Days-eye	Daisy
Diadem	Decorative forehead brooch
Ell	Measure from elbow to fingertips
Elvist	Madness
Eyrir, qurar, solidis	Denominations of money
Finespun	Fine cloth
Firestones	Amber
Freya	Goddess of love, sex, and marriage
Gardariki	Russia
Grot	Cereal
Havamal	Code of proper conduct
Highborn	Born wealthy

Kerling   Keel

Konugrad   Kiev

Lay   A poem

Loki   Trickster god

Miklagard   Istanbul

Mjolnir   Hammer of the god Thor

Ond   Energy

Quern   Grinder for grain

Runes   Twig painted with blood; used in foretelling

Runestock   Carved record of daily journey

Runestav   Used in trading; broken and divided between buyer and seller

Saxland   Germany

Skald   A poet

Taiga   Swampy forest of spruces and ferns

Thrall   Slave

Tiller   Steering oar

Touchwood belt   Made of dried mushrooms

Varangian Sea   The Black Sea

Wadmal   Tightly woven wool

Introduction

I became curious about Scandinavian Vikings on family trips to Sweden, seeing the lithe, restored ships they sailed far from home in search of new lands to settle. Or plunder.

Their voyages to Newfoundland and the New World are familiar, but not as well-known are the trips down the Russian rivers to Istanbul, the richest city in the known world. And so I set out to write it, choosing Ingeborg Andersdottir as my protagonist. Inge is a weaver and a healer, cheerfully managing her farmstead of 100 thralls (slaves). But beneath her cheer is terror. If she does not find a daughter to inherit her sacred wisdom, the mysteries essential to the Vikings' survival will be lost. Inge and Karl-Eirik, Viking captain, adopt Thora, but the maid kills a glasscaster. Their king charges Thora with Lesser Outlawry, sending her down the Russian rivers to Istanbul. Karl is killed, and Inge reluctantly inherits the boat and the command of the crew. In Istanbul, Thora is captured and put into the harem. Only Inge's skills might be able to save her.

My forebears lived in the part of Sweden where the Vikings lived. A Swedish spelman, a fiddler, told me, "The story is in your genes." I agree. Like Inge, I sailed the rivers, learned to maneuver a longship, walked the raucous streets Vikings called hel-vegr (hell-way), descended to the Cistern of a Thousand Columns, visited a harem, and found the illicit runes carved into the balustrade of St. Sophia.

I developed an admiration for these adventurers who were also artisans in wood, stone and precious metals. My research brought them to life on a journey of my own.

I

BREIDAL, SWEDEN

MARCH, 880

"Stop!" Inge shouted, racing into the weaving room.

Too late. Her stomach clenched. Only a snarled mess remained of her intricate red and green pattern on the card loom. The guilty thrall-maid was picking at the tangled strands with mucky fingers. Inge grabbed a bony arm and pulled her away. Sobbing, the girl wiggled free and threw herself on Lars standing in the door, his outstretched arm protecting her from his brother's wife.

Inge touched the tangle, her best weaving, one she could never make again. From a side table she picked up a knife. The maid peeked at it, and howled. Inge sniffed. This girl smelled of sour sweat. Looking at her straw-caked hair, Inge knew she must do it quickly or she could not do it at all.

Lars tried to fend her off with one hand on her shoulder. "Inge, do not -- "

She swallowed hard and slashed twice. The dreadful deed was done. Later there would be time to mourn. She threw the knife down, yanked the last strands of jumbled yarn from the loom and tossed the whole wad at the girl's heaving shoulders. Lars caught it.

"Inge, I know you are a healer, and would not kill her, but she has never been at Breidal before. Trying to weave was a childish thing, but she could not resist your beautiful yarns."

He handed her the wad. "And the door was open."

"Ay. Open to any at my farmstead who wish to create beauty, not destroy it."

Gently she spread the yarns apart. In truth, they were beautiful. She had dyed them herself to get the right shades to trim a tunic for her beloved Karl-Eirik. She felt again the backache from stirring the dye pot all night to get the right shade of red. She felt her fingers, pricked and stinging, from gathering nettles to make

1

the right shade of green. Her suffering had been done with a singing heart for her love, her husband Karl-Eirik.

Inge blinked back tears. Yet she was troubled by far more than a ruined weaving. When Lars sent word he was bringing a young girl as a "gift" to help her with the chores at Breidal, Inge had hoped that this would be the maid she needed to inherit her sacred, healing wisdom, only passed on from mother to daughter

She had no daughter, and if she did not adopt one, the ancient mysteries would die with her--secret knowledge the Vikings needed to thrive. Inge chided herself for trusting Lars, but she had been overeager. Not just any girl would do. But this one was not one to entrust with any kind of magical powers.

The maid was still crying, tears streaking her dirty face. Pushing the girl out of the room and closing the door, Inge told her servant Geda to seat the smelly thrall on a cross-bench at the far end of the hall.

As she and Lars walked into the longhouse, Inge took pleasure from the signs of her well-ordered farmstead. Bed covers were neatly folded on the benches for sleeping and sitting, lining the walls. At the hearth fire in the center of the dirt floor the servants stirred steaming cauldrons of meat and wild onion, and flipped over flatbread baking on stones.

"Inge," Lars said, "the walls of Breidal are covered with woven hangings already. That one was not even finished. Can not the maid and I help you weave another?"

They sat opposite each other on the High Seats decorated with fierce wooden dragon heads, and she glared at him. She fingered the gold amulet of the goddess Freya atop her blue woolen overdress. Like Karl-Eirik, Lars was a captain of a small Viking boat and cared about little else but sailing to far-off lands. He could never understand her weaving was more than pleasure.

While Karl was away, each line of weft she beat in was a hedge against her dread. What if he did not return from his yearly journey? She could not live without him. She looked up at one of her favorites, a woven waterfall in blues and greens and grays. It had helped her get through the year Karl was late returning from the Faroes.

She tucked a loose tendril of hair in her plait and began combing fleece, trying to calm herself with the familiar task. She looked at the thrall, her hair lit by torchlight. How annoying: the maid's hair glinted red-gold like her own.

But thralls walked and moved and sat with their necks stuck out like geese. Why then did this one sit upright, swinging her scrawny legs?

Before she could ask Lars, Karl-Eirik came in and kissed her hard. He smelled of the stable, and she could not help but contrast it with the subtle, perfumed scent of Lars. The two clasped arms in greeting, happy to see each other. Geda brought side tables and set mead horns down.

Anyone could see the two were brothers: the same far-seeing captain's eyes, the same lean, bearded faces, except that Karl's skin was creased by the cares of a farmstead and family. Lars wore his hair in the single man's topknot, and his clothes were fine--a leather jerkin over a tunic with flowing sleeves, while Karl wore homespun field clothes. He sat next to her.

"Kinsman," Lars said, "I brought you and Inge a thrall-maid to lighten her burdens, to repay you for saving my life when we were attacked off Frisia last year."

"Lars, my payment is that you are alive. I need naught else."

"Ah, but I should have tied this maid to my mast in the fjord, and left her. She has upset your wife."

"Upset!" Inge said. "Upset! Listen, Karl…"

Even as she told the story, she thought his beloved younger brother would far outweigh a torn and tattered weaving. Lars said he had seen the carved circle on her gate, the sign she was a kindly Mistress who did not turn down the beggar-folk if they come for a meal.

Ay. Nor would she turn down this thrall. Inge watched her tip up a bowl of grot, licking her chin, dirt and all. Did she know nothing of spoons?

"Lars, I have a hundred thralls to manage already. I need not a hundred and one. What is her name?"

"I know not. She is a mere slave. But quick."

Inge pulled apart a clot of fleece. Ay, the thrall was quick. She told him to take the maid to Estland with him on his voyage.

"Inge, I cannot. If the journey goes poorly, my men will say she brings us no weather-luck, and I must throw her to the sea draug."

Inge shuddered. The sea draug--that headless monster, that ghost of drowned seamen who sailed the seas in half a boat, who wailed when someone was about to drown. Even a dirty thrall-maid did not deserve to be thrown to the fearful sea draug.

She picked up her handspindle and began twisting fleece into yarn. "And if the journey goes well?"

"Then I must give her to every man who pulls an oar, as thanks. I will not. Though she is but a thrall, she is comely beneath the dirt. Inge, take her. Put her to work in the fields or to tend the swine. She will do more for Breidal than a goat."

Inge laughed. "From a goat I would get curds for cheese. Lars, you will pass other farmsteads on your journey. Leave her at one."

Karl fingered her silver armring set with a chunk of amber. She told him Lars had brought it. A gift always looked for a return, the Code of Havamal taught them. But no armring was worth this thrall who could not keep her hands away from a beautiful weaving. Inge looked at the tapering flames on the hearth, holding off the spring chill. The ruined pattern forgotten, the brothers began talking about going a-viking, sharing sea-talk--the only way sailors could learn.

They tipped their mead horns up to drink. These were exciting times for the Swedes, Karl said, with less ice every year so they could sail farther from home to strange lands known only through hearsay. Ay, it was a good time for the Norse, Lars said. The great Emperor Charlemagne was long dead, his Empire divided among his three quarreling grandsons. He talked of sailing east. The land across the Baltic called Kievan Rus was the largest country in the world. But the people lived in tribes, warring with each other, and though they had much wealth their land had no order in it. They had begged the Norse to come and rule over them.

"I will sail The Goldenbreast east and down the rivers of Rus to help them. Listen, Karl. No man ever has too much gold, ay? In their land we call Gardariki, there is a goddess made of gold in a sacred grove. The figure is large--with three more golden figures, each inside the other. Would not that be a treasure to capture and bring back home to Sweden? For Inge?"

"There is more. Her worshippers hang gold offerings on a nearby tree to be gathered by a sharp-eyed Swede. All I have to do is find this goddess. But if I do not--the rivers flow to the Varangian Sea, and at the end of that is the Byzantine city of Miklagard, the richest city in the world, with so much gold they cover the streets with it. There is a whole tree of gold, with golden birds that can sing, each in its voice! If there is so much gold, my men and I will bring some back. The Greeks in Miklagard will never miss it."

Inge heard the clang of a hammer on iron from the smithy outside. Could Gunnar the Smith, skilled in gold and silver as well as iron, make a golden tree with golden birds that sang? Nay. Trees were a gift of the gods, men made from the first ash, women from the first elm.

"Karl, we can sail east together," Lars said.

Inge touched her amulet. Though the brothers were close, Inge hoped each would go his own way a-viking, as usual.

"The Seafarer will sail toward the setting sun, Lars. I go to the island known as Iceland."

"You wish to see an island made of ice?" Inge asked, relieved. The brothers would not sail together. "I can show you our summer mountain pasture, still frozen, with rivers and streams of ice."

"Iceland is but one name, Inge," Karl said. "It has another name, Smorland, and smor means butter, does it not? When the ice melts, the island is covered with butter. We will not starve."

They all laughed, and Inge thought she loved these stories, as long as Karl knew them for what they were.

"Kinsman," Karl said, "I choose to sail to Iceland for one reason. It is farther north than The Seafarer has ever gone."

Inge looked at his face and saw his wide nostrils, ever the sign of a risk-taker. She knew he had a hunger to explore new lands.

She put her spindle into the split oak basket, and stood. Karl grasped her hand and held it, to stop her. She pulled free.

"I need fresh air," she said, wrinkling her nose and glancing toward the thrall, now curled up asleep on the bench. A sleeping maid could do no more mischief. It would be safe to go outside. She loved being Mistress of a fine hall, and she intended to keep it that way. She fastened her green cloak with a thistle brooch.

"Inge," Lars said, "now I see I should have dropped the maid in the Baltic to bathe her on the way up the coast, but I did not have the heart--there were too many ice chunks. She cannot help but smell--I found her hiding beneath otter skins at the burning-in. She is so slight I can bathe her in your cauldron."

"Nay, Lars."

The child would taint her cauldron. Her smell boded ill. Inge pushed open the heavy oak door, and went out through the cold trap into her courtyard. She took a deep breath of clean, unsullied air. Sickness could creep into a farmstead through the stoutest door, and steal ond, the energy needed to live. Whole farmsteads could fall apart without it. She had seen one destroyed by sickness when she was a child, the people dead where they fell, beasts found with bloated carcasses.

She touched her amulet for luck. Though she had planted a rowan at her gate and an elder in front of the cows' byre to ward off sickness, she knew not how to bar the door from it. She only knew she must keep the people in her farmstead clean, insisting on a weekly trip to the bath house. Clean and strong, so sickness could not enter their bodies. She must keep her cauldron hanging from the roof-beam and use it only for cooking.

Ah, it was a harsh land, this northern part of Sweden, where hills and dales separated one farmstead from another.

Still, there was space for men and women to stretch and spread as she and Karl had done, buying more land, more cows, until they owned four times as much as when she brought her bride-price. She loved every ell of Breidal and not least because as Mistress, she had time and ond for her beloved weaving.

Now she took a deep breath of the loamy spring smell from the Homefield. She looked at the dung pile outside the byre, and smiled. It was the biggest in this part of Sweden, and made thralls proud to be part of the farmstead, for it showed it had the most cattle. Men, and women, too, liked working at Breidal.

She heard Karl's light step, and felt his arms encircle her beneath her breasts. They had shared the same bed since their wedding twenty winters past, when first they drank their bridal ale. They had always pleased one another when he was home. Unlike other chieftains, he never toyed with the bondmaids behind her back.

"Ingeborg, Lars is sorry he brought the dirty thrall, but he meant well. If he could do it over, he would bring her in finespun, dripping jewels."

But he had not. On the morrow Lars must take her with him, she said, or they would send her to Karl's mother Halldis, who would soon teach the child to leave others' things alone.

"Inge, I know not if I want her myself. Lars says she is skilled in swordcraft, and I would not like her to best my men in swordplay. He says she is skilled in other ways. On the trip up to Breidal she twisted grass into snares each night to catch the wild hare."

"There are too many mysteries about her, Karl. How came a thrall to be skilled with the sword? They are not permitted to touch a weapon. Perchance she can weave a snare, but..."

"She can destroy a fine weaving? I am sorry for that, Inge. Then we agree. The thrall goes tomorrow, to one place or another."

Then, she told him, she could open all the doors and air the hall, though they froze.

"Good. Now, my Inge, we will put Lars's gift out of mind and enjoy the new barley sprouting in our fields."

Ay, Karl enjoyed it, when Planting was finished, and he could be off and away. Spring had come early this year, a fluke, and the barley was already in. Past their own greening fields were others all over Sweden, and beyond. The sign for men to go a-viking, as they did every year.

"Wife, I will miss you, though you know I must go. I will be back at Harvest. Do not worry about me--I am a trader. We trade when we can, only fight when we must. The Norse are the best seamen in the world, and The Seafarer is the best ship."

She tried not to shiver. But such a small ship, no bigger than her hall, to sail unknown waters.

"I am always loath to let you go each year, Karl."

This year more than most. Last night he had looked in her hand mirror and showed her his hair was graying. He had lived five and forty winters. They had both joked about his hair, and she told him he was not yet Karl Graybeard, to huddle around the hearth fire, but a strong captain, ready once again to lead his men a-viking on the wide waters. And so Karl had slept.

But she was stricken, and she lay awake, fretting. The years were fleeting, and her worry was not for Karl, nor for herself, but for her cache of sacred knowledge stored in her mind. From her mother she had learned the healing charms, the secrets in the herbs that cured sickness, that some were poisons, and a wrong dosage could kill. All this had been passed on in her family long before her mother's mother's time. But Inge had gone far beyond that wisdom. She had discovered the healing powers in the rest of her world of Breidal.

Who would believe draughts from the yew could make unwanted body growths disappear? Or waters from ground up adderstones could cure a sick stomach? Or that an armring of copper worn at the wrist could take away pain? She looked toward her Sacred Grove, and thought of the dozens of remedies that came to her while walking in the woods and fields, or in dreams.

When people marveled at the health of her family and servants and Karl's crew, even her cows, she thanked Eir, the goddess of healing.

Ah, but last night her chest had tightened with fear. She had slept poorly for good reason. The years were passing, and though she had three sons grown and gone a-viking, she had no daughter to learn the sacred wisdom.

The hard-won knowledge would die with her.

For now she must put it out of mind. Karl laughed, and she told him she would miss his laughter, almost as much as their bedplay. Their bed-closet was too big for her alone.

"Inge, you are ever full of surprises. I am remembering last year when I came home at Harvest, you had twined yellow flowers in the hair around your crotch."

This year she would have another surprise.

He told her he was beginning to see women traveling with their men on other boats. Norse families were starting to winter over in the part of England called Danelaw.

"Mayhap, Inge..."

She said they must be traveling to make a new home. Nay, her place was here- -to keep Breidal safe for him until he returned.

She whispered. "Only you and I know the trees where we buried gold. When you return, we will hide more in the dead of night this Harvest, while we gather barley by day."

Planting gold was a joyous time for them both.

"The quest for gold is one reason I go a-viking, Inge."

Ay, one.

"Now, Husband, we must go back into our hall, though I would fain stand with your arms about me, feeling your manhood swelling against me."

She took one last look at the barley sprouts pushing through the soil. Sometimes, like now, she thought of Karl seeing new sights in strange lands, while she labored at home, and she envied him.

They walked in with Karl's arm around her shoulder. To her relief the thrall-maid was still asleep. And Lars still drinking.

"Lars, I have invited a guest," Inge said. "You and your crew are welcome to stay."

"The god Frey is coming to bless your planting?"

"Nay. It is the spa-kona."

"The witch-seer!" Lars cried out, curling his hand around his sword hilt.

Like every man Inge knew, he felt safe only when his hand was on his sword. She saw he was frightened of the hag who could foretell the future with runes.

"Kinsman, she brings honor to our hearth."

"Lars, be not frightened," Karl said. "You fear no man in battle. You are a ship's captain, and she is but a hag. This casting of runes is but sport and gaming."

"Inge, she may bring news you would rather not hear."

"Lars, few spa-kona are left. I count it good fortune to have her come to our hall."

She went to their bed-closet and put on her red silk dress, and an overgarment with gold stitching. She tied on her best linen headdress. She unlocked her birch bark box and drew out the neckrings Karl brought, one from each voyage, finally choosing the pink quartz that held the sky at even. In the hand mirror she saw herself as comely, her skin clear, her eyes as blue-green as the waters of the fjord. She pinched her cheeks for color.

Back in the hall she smelled meadowsweet from the dried rushes her serving folk were spreading on the dirt floor. Pleased, she saw they had opened the smoke-vent just wide enough so the hearth-fire of birch logs burned well. Karl had put on his blue tunic, the one dyed with woad she had gathered, and sewn with her own hands. The silver brooch on his shoulder that held his cloak away from his sword was worthy of a great chieftain.

All was ready for the spa-kona's prying eyes. She would ride past the clean stone dairy and its pans of curds, the ale-vat room with its turf roof clean-scythed, the two large storehouses, the fish drying on the racks. It did no harm for the casting of runes for her to see the farmstead was well-kept.

Inge went to the hearth-fire and raked hot coals from a serving bowl, breathing in the smell of roasted meat. In the special dish for the witch-seer she had cooked the heart of the elk, the bear, the deer, the wolf and the heart of the ever-fierce wild boar. All these Karl-Eirik had brought back from the hunt.

Now she put the dish on the side table where a servant set grot made with the first milking of a goat.

All was ready. Even the dirty thrall slept on.

When they heard the horse neighing in the courtyard Karl went out to get the witch. Inge stood to greet her. The servants put their tasks aside and stood, respectfully. Though only curious, Lars and Karl's men did the same. They liked their Mistress. She never withheld ale nor mead.

The witch-seer did not stoop when she entered, but Inge saw her as shriveled, hunched, her face peering out from a fur headdress, the skin brown and wrinkled as a seed hid beneath the snow all winter. Her nose crooked down to her lips. She had outlived her teeth. Inge thought some old women had a musty smell, as though they had been closed up in the storehouse loft. But this one smelled of rain-washed air.

Beneath the thin, half-closed lids Inge saw unyielding, iron-hard gray eyes, deep-set. From them, no secrets could be concealed. There was no place to hide. Inge took a deep calming breath. The witch-seer would not withhold the truth, no matter what dangers the runes revealed.

❝Kom Heill to our hall," Inge said, leading the witch-seer to the high seat where a pillow of duck feathers would soften her brittle bones. A servant set the side table and bowls before her, and she dipped the wooden spoon again and again until they were empty.

Inge watched, wondering why Lars feared the hag. She spooned her food like other women. She was well-dressed in a fur cloak with stones down to the hem, and a touchwood belt.

When she finished eating, the side table was taken away. She stood, clasped her staff round and struck it three times on the floor. Inge gathered the women servants in a circle, and the witch began chanting. Her voice was harsh, like stone grating on stone, but the servants would follow their Mistress, so she tried to make the coarse noises.

Though she could not understand the chants, Inge knew the hag was blessing her hearth when she stopped before the fire and touched the cauldron. She led the way to the hanging herbs, the shelves with sacks and casks of food, the flat rounds of bread strung on high poles. Touching, putting her blessing forth.

Then she returned to the center of the hall, and Inge felt herself tighten. It was time to cast the runes, the lot-twigs to portend the future. The spa-kona pulled off the rune pouch on her touchwood belt.

"Mistress, what would you know?"

Inge thought the hag's voice was strong for her age. Ah, there was much she would know. Would her three sons return from Ireland with Irish brides? Would Lars find the golden goddess in Kievan Rus? And for herself, would the sacred knowledge die with her? The runes would know.

"Come, Mistress, I cannot stay till Harvest. Other women want to learn the secrets in the runes."

Inge heard Lars laugh. She must show him she was a chieftain's wife, and not one to give way to fear.

"I wish to know the fate of my farmstead, Breidal, and all who are a part of it," she said, though her voice was small.

The hag squatted down, brushed aside the rushes and drew a circle on the dirt floor. Her lips moved without a sound. Her eyes rolled up into her head. Inge felt a chill pass through the hall. The young serving women moved together, murmuring, looking to their Mistress for reassurance. When the witch-seer spoke, Inge heard a voice speaking from a far place.

"These runes are the gift of Odin, the All-father. Hear now how brave Odin hung nine nights on Yggdrasil, the World Tree, in torment from pain, from hunger, from thirst, alone, until he spied the runes, seized them and became a god."

"Hear now, the rune master Odin:

"These runes I know, unknown to kings' wives or any earthly man. 'Help' one is called, for help is the gift, and helped you will be in sickness and care and sorrow.

"Another I know, which all will read who study leechcraft. On the bark scratch them, on the boles of trees whose boughs bend to the east.

"I know a third--if my need be great in battle it dulls the sword of deadly foes. Neither wiles nor weapons wound me, and I go all unscathed."

Three times the witch-seer tapped her wooden staff on the floor.

"Choose, Mistress. For you and your hall." Inge held back. There were evil runes, and good, in the witch-seer's pouch. Mayhap she would bring evil onto her hall and herself. These runes were more than sport and gaming.

"Choose, Mistress, and learn what Odin foretells for you."

Inge felt all eyes in the hall looking at her. She felt the trust and love of the servants, depending on her, as a burden.

She wished she had not invited the witch-seer.

'Help' the first rune was named by Odin. The second for all who studied leechcraft--how to heal the sick with charms and herbs--these she knew. But the third rune would be for one whose need was great in battle.

Though she was Mistress of a great hall, wife to a great chieftain, there were battles to be won, not alone in Skotland or Frisia, but in the heart.

Inge walked to the center of the circle. The spa-kona shook the pouch, and Inge withdrew three runes. They were chips of bark, much-used, the runes writ in blood, now dried and brown. What did their foretelling bring to others who wished for their runing?

She dared not ask. One by one, she placed them in the circle, rune down.

"Turn them, Mistress, that first," the hag said, pointing her wrinkled finger.

Inge put her hand full on the floor to hide her shaking, and turned the first rune over.

"Ur is the first rune, Mistress. The rune of endings and beginnings. A rune of passage, mayhap a passage into darkness."

Inge felt a chill on her nape. It was a fearsome message. What trick of the god Loki made her ask this witch to her hall?

"Turn the second rune, Mistress. It might bring a better message, more to your liking."

Inge felt a stifling in her chest and knew it for fear. She wanted to feel Karl-Eirik's arm about her, to lean on him, but nay, it would be unseemly for a chieftain's wife to be fearful.

She turned the second rune.

"Mistress, the second rune is reidh, the rune of a journey, part of which cannot be shared. It has two elements, one above, one below. You are frighted, Mistress, but Odin's message is ever true. Turn the third and last rune."

Inge bit her lip and pushed her nails into her palms. She must not cry out, though the last lot-twig was as heavy as her cauldron.

The third rune was wyrd, the blank. The Unknowable.

"Wyrd portends death, is it not so?" Inge asked, whispering so only the witch-seer could hear.

The hag's whispered answer rasped Inge's flesh.

"Ay, Mistress, but there are many deaths--the death of dreams for one. Blank is the end, blank the beginning. You liked not the runes, Mistress, but you drew them forth."

A passage into darkness. A journey that could not be shared. And wyrd, the unknowable. Sorrow clung to Inge like a cloak she could not throw off.

"Mistress, the runes speak ever true. Now may Frey bring you good Harvest, and your sons have many sons to hold in your arms."

Karl-Eirik took a resin torch from the wall and led the hag to the courtyard. Inge sat alone on the high seat, breathing in the pine smell, aching for Karl at her side.

"Ingeborg," Lars said, "each time the runes are cast the message is different. Is it not true?"

"Ay," she answered, her voice muffled.

"Then make another runecast with some other runes. It may be happier."

Ah, there was more to the mystery of the runes than Lars knew. She had chosen the lot-twigs herself, and nothing would change the fearful foretelling. Not a second cast. Or a third, or a fourth.

Karl returned and drew her to him.

"It was but a game, Inge. Nothing can portend the future--not a toothless old hag, nor aught else. Per, bring forth the harp we brought back from Ireland. Anders, get the pipe you carved from willow reed. We will dance, and cheer Inge. She has ever loved music. Ah, but look."

She felt Karl's body stiffen with surprise, and she turned to watch. The thrall-maid stood at the hearth-fire, eyes closed. She opened her mouth and yawned, scuffing the rushes, and spoke in a voice fitting for a highborn maid:

"Karl Fairhair went forth to battle, the fire of the arm on the hawk's hand. Wound-dew, the ale-wolf, the brother of the wind touched him not. Though the spears sang, he stayed his steed of the sea and came home to Inge fair."

The hall was silent, everyone awestruck.

"Aiyiii!" Karl cried out. "The thrall-maid is a skald, a poet! How can she make a poem about me? It is the first time she is in our hall! Lars, my kinsman, I accept your gift of the thrall."

Lars smiled.

Inge knew the worth of a skald to sing a chieftain's praise from hall to hall, preserving his fame. Four marks in gold would not buy a skald, though one mark in gold bought thirty cows. "Wife," Karl said, "we can put her in the fields to work, thinking up other lays like this one, and when we have guests she can come in and spout them." "Ay," Lars said, "and when she's through, put her back out to grub in the dirt. She is yours, Karl, to do as you will. On the morrow I leave. Let us drink to a fine voyage for The Goldenbreast, and may your skald keep your name alive. Whether you or I be alive or not."

The brothers clasped arms to seal the bargain.

The maid downed a cup of milk in one greedy gulp, as Inge watched. The poem was not the best she had ever heard, but how could a thrall make one at all?

How had she learned the kennings, where one group of words meant another? How did she know 'the fire of the arm' meant the sword? Or 'wound-dew' was blood? Or that skalds often called ships, 'steeds of the sea'?

"Inge," Karl said, "we will celebrate and dance, drinking to my new skald. What say you, Ingeborg? Has not Odin smiled upon us to bring a poet to our hearth?"

She saw the brothers did not share her fears the runes revealed. They had put the witch-seer and her dread foretelling out of mind. Karl led her out to dance. She pulled his face down and kissed him.

"Of all men, Karl Fairhair, you are most worthy of a poet to grace your hearth."

She thought any woman would choose to dance with him. Sometimes, when his blood warmed like now, he looked like a man who had seen less than five and forty winters. The light from the torches on the wall flit in and out of his blue eyes.

"Inge, you are quiet. Anders, play a merrier tune."

Her thoughts ran with the faster whirling. It was one thing to know the kennings, but to make them into a poem, praising a man the thrall-maid had never seen...she had been wise enough to flatter Karl with a lay about him... shrewd enough to stand and say it in front of strangers. A maid quick with words. Who knew what other talents she possessed besides skill in swordplay...how had she learned?...a thrall was not allowed to touch a weapon. Inge looked at her chewing a crust.

As Mistress of a large farmstead Inge was used to making decisions quickly. A maid quick with words would learn the healing charms and herbs with ease. And not forget them.

The girl did not lack courage. She had dared to weave onto Inge's cherished work. Yet what was a messy, tangled piece of weaving but woolen yarn? What was dirt on a young girl but earthly mud, that could be washed away? In front of Lars and all the household Karl had declared the thrall would be a field hand, coming inside only to spout a poem about him for guests.

Nay, this thrall could be more.

Tonight when they were alone in their bed-closet she must get Karl-Eirik to change his mind. But how? He was stubborn. What she was asking was unthinkable.

The music stopped. Karl put his hands on her shoulders and steered her out of the hall.

"Wife, it has been a tiring day for you. Let us to bed."

Ay, but there would be no rest for either of them, until they talked. She knew not how to convince Karl of her plan, but she must, and now.

"Adopt the thrall? As a daughter?" Karl shouted. "Never! Inge, you have elvist, a kind of madness I have seen in battle."

He slammed the door of their bed-closet, and wrenched the key in the lock. He paced the room, covering it in two strides. Karl had not warmed to her plan of adopting the maid to learn the sacred wisdom.

She told him his ranting would unsettle the housefolk. They would think he was attacking her, and break down the door. Though no one but Lars would dare, and he was not listening. She and Karl had walked past him, tousling with one of the bondmaids on a bench. To Inge's relief, the thrall-maid slept alone, on the crossbench where Geda put her.

Slowly, to calm Karl, Inge took off her headdress and folded it. They must try to talk with sense and reason, she said.

"Sense! Your plan has no sense. We know nothing about the thrall's background, nothing of her early years, or what problems might come forth. We do not even know her name."

Inge slipped off her pink quartz neckring and put it in the birch bark chest.

"Husband, I will ask her name on the morrow. Problems come forth in the children of the most devoted parents, like ourselves."

He stopped pacing. "Our three sons are brave and fearless, the way we raised them. They sailed off to Ireland, alone, without a qualm."

"The maid was brave and fearless to stand and say a poem about a man she had never seen. Karl, tonight you said Odin brought you a skald, and you were happy."

He began pacing again. "Now I see clearer. It was not Odin, but Lars who brought her. I love my brother, but he can be faulted for being too soft-hearted about women. She would be more trouble than she's worth to take to Kievan Rus on The Goldenbreast. He wanted to leave her with you, as a thrall, not a daughter."

Karl paced faster. "Inge, if you must have a daughter to learn your womanish ways, choose a child from one of our freeborn servants, not a slave. A babe, ay, a babe. You can teach her from the cradle."

Inge sighed and pulled off her overdress.

"Karl, a babe cannot learn the herbs and the charms to make them work. We would be hard-pressed without our shipwright, Hervor. Do you remember last winter when he was felling trees, and the oak branch fell on his shoulder? It was my womanish ways that cured the break. Gunnar is forever smashing his thumbs or burning his arms in the smithy, and it is my womanish herbs that--"

"Enough! I have never been ungrateful for your healing ways, you know that."

She hung her clothes on the wall pegs and crawled beneath the fur cover in her shift, sitting up. She wiggled, and the straw tick rustled. If she was going to convince him about the adoption, she must think like Karl-Eirik. What would fright a chieftain, fearless in battle? Not another man's sword.

But a sword wielded by a maid?

Inge thought back to how quickly the girl had ruined the weaving. Ay, she was quick. Karl would not want a girl, even his skald, to be better than his men, and so shame them.

"Karl, when you are gone a-viking, the maid and I will walk the fields and woods, learning the healing herbs, and she will forget her love of swordcraft."

Of that Inge was certain. What cold, harsh metal could compare with green, healing, plants, warm from the earth? Karl stopped pacing and sat on the edge of the bed.

"Inge, years ago we decided you would take the Cup of Roots after bedplay to prevent the quickening in your womb. Our three sons are grown and gone. I am not wont to raise another child."

Inge fingered her amulet of Freya. In her wisdom the goddess had sent the maid after their three sons were off a-viking. A girl she wanted to adopt as much as she ever wanted anything.

"The maid is almost raised, Karl. She has seen fourteen winters, I trow. In one more year she will be ready to marry."

"Ingeborg, thralls breed thralls, and I am loath to have thrall blood enter my family bloodline."

Ah. This was the heart of the argument: Karl's bloodline. His father had been a great chieftain, and his father before him, and back through the generations. They died bravely in battle, but early, their fame and renown outlasting them in the poems the skalds told.

In truth, his bloodline was sacred. Yet so was her ancient wisdom. Slowly, she began undoing her plait.

"Karl, I agree with you, but this maid is highborn."

He stared at her, "Inge! She wears white thrall-cloth."

She told him the maid did not sit like a thrall. But far more important, thralls had two signs above all else which set them apart: pigs' ears and flat feet.

"Her ears are curved like a well-wrought brooch, and her feet have a high, dainty arch, most pleasing. Karl, come to bed. I am a good Swedish wife, and follow our ways. Let me remove your skin-tight breeches."

She finished her plait. He lay atop the straw tick, and she stood, her toes curling away from the cold floor. She eased his pants down slowly, speaking softly about how fine it would be for him to have his own skald traveling from farmstead to farmstead, reciting lays at the hearth fires, praising her brave father, ship captain Karl-Eirik. Not all chieftains had their own skald.

But what would men think of Karl and Inge, to see a mere thrall reciting lays, wearing thrall-cloth?

Karl folded his arms behind his head. "Scrub her up, Inge. Buy her finespun. We need not adopt her."

She fluffed her hair and dangled it over his sex, as always, grateful for its size.

She told him a thrall could be bought. Her skaldic powers would make her valuable. But a daughter would always be their own. Karl took off his tunic, and she hung it alongside his pants, put the fur cover over him and snuggled down.

"Karl, she is comely. Her hair is as blond as our sons'. If I had birthed a daughter when I lay in the straw, she would look like this maid. She has her father's eyes."

Eyes as far-set, as shrewd, as Karl's. He put his arm about her, and she put her head on his shoulder. It was always easiest to talk to a man in bed.

He said he was concerned: how had this thrall learned swordcraft? She told him it was one more sign the maid had highborn blood, for ay, no thrall touched a weapon.

"Karl, she is a woman. Do you know any woman skilled with the sword? Nay, nor I. But when you are gone, we will walk the fields together taking joy in gathering plants, and she will forget the sword."

He told her that one other thing bothered him. As was the custom in an attack, Lars would have let the women and children escape to the forest, where they would be safe. Yet this thrall did not leave, but hid beneath otter skins.

Mayhap she wanted to be found, Inge said--hoping to be taken to a better farmstead. Surely Karl would agree it was brave. Few thralls tried to improve their station. She was most unusual, and it could only be highborn blood behind it.

"Wife, you have answered many doubts, but nay, we will not adopt the thrall as our daughter. Not now, or ever."

Ah well. The thought had been planted. It was enough for one night. She was not easily discouraged, and he knew it.

She guided his fingers into the softness between her legs, kissing him round and round with sweet fast kisses in the Circle of Love, stopping to lick his lips. Karl's hands closed around her breasts. She put her hand on his belly, and he nudged it lower, and she played with the wiry hair until she felt his sex swell. She opened her mouth, and he licked the inside of her upper lip. The goddess Freya had been wise to keep this excitable part of her body well-hidden.

When he climbed over her, they lay two as one, and she held him fast with her legs, his tongue probing her mouth. Her whole body rose to meet him. She felt the stirring begin deep within, and the flood of sweetness came unbidden. Inside her body her wetness throbbed with a life of its own, twisting beneath him, squeezing every last tremor that swept through her, up through her belly, her chest, even out her fingertips.

Karl moaned, shivering with pleasure. Inge sighed, content.

She could not live without this. They rested, Karl still a part of her.

"Karl," she whispered, "could the maid be sent by the gods to keep us young, able to enjoy sex till we are as shriveled and old as the witch-seer?"

"And why not then, Inge?"

They laughed together and kissed. Ah, she would miss him, for the six months he would be gone a-viking. He was always shouting orders to his crew, the thralls, or the servants, and she knew they thought their master was too strict, asked too much of them. But here in the secrecy of their bed closet this hard captain vented his tender side.

"Ingeborg, my life is so simple when I am on my ship."

"Ay, but when the wide waters are frozen and you cannot sail away, where would you live? With your mother, Halldis?"

He chuckled. Nay, he needed a wife, never more than in the long winters.

"Sleep, my love," she whispered, and he crawled off her body, though he lay close, his hand cupping one breast.

* * *

The next morning when she awoke early, he was already gone, awake even earlier for last minute tasks at the boatshed.

Inge walked around the farm. She was a countrywoman in her bones. Each year she loved Planting more, the tiny seeds bursting their hulls, poking up between clods of dunged soil, yearning toward the sun. Two of the hounds bounded up, barking, and she scratched them behind the ears.

This was the fresh time of day she loved. Beyond the green fields was the wildness that nurtured her: the Sacred Grove where she worshipped. The tree-covered hills, with huge boulders and caves, the healing pine and ash and birch against the pale blue sky. She wished to linger, but thralls and servants worked best when she kept herself visible.

She greeted each by name, stopping to check how fully they packed dried herring into salt barrels for Karl's voyage, how smoothly they ground barley in the quern. And she checked out their ills.

Tofa's pimply skin looked clearer, and she told Inge she washed with burdock water every day, as her Mistress suggested. Odd said his gout was improving with the fennel seed tea she told him to brew and drink. From the way Vaenar walked, Inge guessed the broken knee she had set was healing well.

She sent Skani to scour a barrel, put it in the oak grove, and fill it with heated water. Inge needed a clean maid to present to Karl, but who knew what was hid beneath the dirt? She wanted to be the first to see if the maid was scarred or ill-formed.

This maid with no-name would not be in the byre or the fields or the woods. She would be where Karl's men jested round the grindstone, sharpening the axes and spears and swords for the voyage.

The men standing around did not expect to see her, and so did not. She watched as the maid and Anders feinted at swordplay. This thrall loved the attention. She was using a scramasax, a short sword with a blade one ell long. As good for cutting brush or butchering, as for battle.

Anders used his own sword, sized for him by Gunnar, but still the maid was pushing him back. Inge could not believe the maid's skill. She was quick, but it was only part of it. She had the Norse love of fighting.

Per was the first to see Inge.

"Mistress, we are surprised how good she is at swordcraft. She knows a secret of a Norseman's success, to allow the pommel to slip past the hand rather than lock into the wrist. It gives the sword more play. We are wondering who taught her this. We asked, and she would not tell us."

One more thing she must learn, Inge thought, calling the maid to her and telling the men to put a sharp edge on the weapons, Karl-Eirik's sword and axe most of all. She took the maid by the hand and pulled her away, though she was reluctant to give up the scramasax.

On the way to the oak grove the maid knelt and picked up two yellow flowers, closed her eyes and sniffed. Inge caught her breath. The maid loved plants! No woman could be a healer without the love of green growing things.

The scramasax would soon rust and be useless, while they walked the fields gathering plants, bunching them to hang from the storehouse beam, the maid learning all Inge had to teach.

"See this leaf shape? " Inge said. "It is the plant called Foal's Foot, and it is said the son births the father."

"Nay! It cannot be. A father births the son."

"The plant is so-called for the way it flowers before it leafs out."

The maid giggled and ran ahead, still clutching the stems. Inge felt the happiness in her chest and raised her arms high, sending a silent prayer of thanks to Freya. The maid had begun learning the herbs. The next time they walked Inge would tell her what sickness Foal's Foot healed, and so little by little the precious knowledge would be saved.

In the grove the maid was standing on tiptoe looking into the barrel, the flowers nowhere to be seen. Skani had left old cloths, ragged and spotted, to dry her, and Inge thought the servant would like to dunk the maid in the fjord, to have her come up with ice in her hair.

Inge told the maid to take off her shift and foot coverings, but she did not, and Inge dribbled warm water onto her palm. The maid put her hands on the rim of the barrel, jumped up and drank.

"Nay! It is for bathing," Inge said.

She held out the piece of soapwort, and the maid stuck it in her mouth, then spat it out. Could it be this thrall knew nothing of soap? Inge let it suds in a handful of water, thinking of all the chores to do for Karl--bread to bake, curds to press--and this maid to clean. She picked her up and dunked her in the barrel, shift, shoecloths, and all. When the maid came up sputtering, Inge pulled the shift over her head and scrubbed. She began with the hair and worked down. In truth, she had never seen a dirtier maid, and she had to wash her twice.

But she was fairer than Inge had imagined. Ah, she had seen fourteen winters--her breasts were well-formed. Inge washed and rinsed, washed and rinsed the tangled hair. But what was this? Around the neck she wore a chain of chased silver, the kind made by the finest silversmiths in Sweden. Was it a gift from Lars? Nay, he was not one to waste silver on a thrall.

Inge knew an amulet was beneath the wet hair on the neck and she reached for it, but the maid was too quick, clasping her small hands around her mane.

Inge washed and rinsed and said, "Silver is often made from coins, pounded flat. But gold--ah, gold is a gift of the gods. I will trade you a look at my amulet of Freya to see your own."

Inge turned Freya's face inward and held it out. She could feel the maid's longing. A thrall's body knew nothing of gold, but still she held her fingers over her neck.

Inge lifted the maid out and wrapped her in the cloths, rubbing her nose on her shoulder. Not for many winters had she bathed a child. From now on they would go to the bathhouse together and be happy whisking each other with birch leaf twigs. She held out a clean shift, and as the maid struggled into it, the amulet slid around to her chest.

"Aiyiii!" Inge cried. "It is the amulet of the god Thor--his hammer Mjolnir! How came you this? Do you remember when they clasped Thor's hammer on your neck?"

The maid clutched the amulet to her.

"Nay."

Inge thought fast. This amulet was finely wrought. It was not to be bought in the market town of Birka, not from a charm-seller outside the hazel wood fence at the yearly assembly of The Thing. Inge had never seen any so well-crafted. It could only be a gift, from someone who loved the maid and wanted her safe. Thor's hammer Mjollnir was more than an amulet for luck. It was protection for one of The Chosen.

"Thora, they call you?" Inge asked, and heard her voice shaking.

"Ay."

"Come, let us sit upon the warm rock, and I will dry your hair."

Inge took a deep calming breath. As she toweled the blond hair she knew she must learn all about her, so Karl could not refuse the adoption of so valued a maid.

Thora. Inge loved saying the name to herself. Thora. Good Swedish names had been chosen for their three sons--Waendael and Solwi and Aeirn--but ah, they were not The Chosen. Inge worked slowly, pampering the girl.

"Thora, tell me. How came you to learn swordcraft?"

To Inge's delight the maid answered freely, though she played with her fingers. Inge saw she did it whenever she was uneasy.

"Tyrkir had someone teach me. Sometimes he did it, too."

"And who was Tyrkir?"

"The master of my farmstead, Gotardal."

"Tyrkir? What else do you know about him, Thora?"

"He was kind. And when my Mistress was harsh, he defended me. Though why, I know not. He was not partial to any other thrall. But he said I had a natural bent for swordcraft, better than many of his men."

Inge sifted the silken hair between her fingers, and thought it was more than that.

"Thora, where did you learn to make a lay about Karl-Eirik?"

The maid giggled, and told her that Tyrkir let her stand in the corner, unseen, when skalds came to Gotardal, and she would listen to them and so learned the kennings. She soon found out the skalds made poems only of the times men won in battle--never the times they lost.

"It was the same in the bed-closet, when Tyrkir was a-viking and my Mistress made me sleep with guests--they bragged."

Inge's heart went out to her. The maid had learned that an overnight guest, uncaring of her tender feelings, could be stalled while he talked of his successful forays in battle.

Ah, there were still more questions about this maid. After Karl left, Inge thought she would send a messenger to ask the neighbors in the area around Gotardal. She spread Thora's hair over her shoulders in the unmarried woman's loose way, and draped the towel on a branch.

"Come, Thora. We will go to Karl-Eirik. We have news of some moment to tell him."

* * *

She heard Karl shouting orders before they found him in front of the boatshed. The Seafarer looked fine on its rollers, newly painted and tarred, ready to be pushed into the fjord. Karl had let her name the boat, though she knew the men would have preferred it to be named Dragon's Blood. She called him, and he came with that light step she saw each year when he was ready to go a-viking, never in the fields at Planting or Harvest.

She told Thora to go and look at the boat, and the maid's thrall-ways made her obey a Mistress. Inge knew she must speak with Karl-Eirik alone.

They walked down along the fjord, the cold wind from the water chilling her. Yet from an inland pond she heard a sure sound of spring--garumphing frogs. She spoke softly, holding his hand, and told him how Thora had learned the kennings. She stroked his flesh scarred with cuts and nicks and slashes from sword-fighting, and told him how she had seen Thora's skill with the scramasax for herself. The maid had been well taught by a man named Tyrkir. This impressed him, though he knew him not at all.

She forced herself to breathe slowly. The wind from the fjord stiffened. She felt his eagerness to return to his boat.

"I learned the maid's name, Karl. It will please you."

"Ay?"

When she finished talking, he was no longer as eager to go back. He dropped her hand and pulled her to him, kissing her. He laughed. He kissed her again. He held her out with both arms, and pulled her back, dancing a few steps.

"Thora, a fine name for my skald. She is one of The Chosen? And the gods have chosen us and sent her to Breidal. Inge, I never thought such luck would come our way."

She smiled to see his joy.

"Ay, and you are the most deserving of men." She took his arm and continued walking. "Karl, I would be loath to offend Odin, our All-Father, with less than a full adoption. Not the knee-seating, which could be easily undone."

He looked hard at her, grinning, and told her that as always he admired her for the way she thought ahead. But he said Grynon would not have time to make the adoption boot before The Seafarer left to go a-viking. When they returned in six months...

Nay, she would harry Grynon to finish, she said, though he would not be happy.

"Karl, we must have the ceremony tonight."

"Tonight. Tonight! You are afraid the maid will escape?"

She told him Thora wanted to stay. She spoke again of how valued a skald was to a master, and how she would be prey to a thief. But if she were his daughter, then a thief would think twice about stealing her.

And how could they let his skald talk of him at hearthfires in the shift she wore? On the morrow he would travel to Birka to get ship's roping and such. She and Thora would go along and buy finespun cloth for her. On their return he would go a-viking, and the maid would learn to sew. When he came back at Harvest she would have a row of fine dresses. Inge knew he did not begrudge them a trip to Birka, but he moved apart from her, looking at the fjord.

"Karl, I could cut down my clothes to fit her, but she is a skald, and should not have her clothes shame us when the lays of her brave father will make us proud."

Karl sighed. "It has come so fast, this fathering of a near-grown maid, Ingeborg."

"You are the one leaving soon on your voyage, not I. Everything must be done before you leave."

"Ja. I must go a-viking." Turning back to her, he said, "I have ever loved you, for the way you take problems in hand and solve them." She thanked him and kissed him. The witch-seer's runes foretold a journey, and it would be so.

"Come, let us go back to the boatshed, Karl. On your return from Iceland I will have solved the mysteries about the maid. And she will have many lays to say about her father. Next winter we can take her from farmstead to farmstead with us."

Happiness flowed through her. Nothing could stop her now, but she must harry Grynon, though he would protest. She must have the full ceremony of adoption. The maid would step into the boot, and out. Then Inge, Karl, his crew, one by one her household, the servants and fieldfolk. And when the last bond-maid stepped into and out of the boot the ceremony would be complete, to be undone only by death.

Karl steered The Seafarer out of the fjord and down the Baltic coast to Birka. Standing next to him at the stern, Inge kept a watchful eye on Thora perched on the bow, her arm round the Gripping Beast carved into the high prow-post. Inge had always thought the leering face of the Beast frightening, but Thora sat calmly. One animal was not enough for Karl and his men. The fierce Gripping Beast was part bear, part wolf, with a wild boar's body. A fearful red jeweled eye gleamed in the Beast's head.

Inge asked Karl if the eye of the Beast looked for danger beneath the waves? For rocks or the sea draug...?

"Ay. And if the fen-dwellers in Frisia are frightened by the eye, we like it."

He kept one light hand on the steering-oar tiller and held the other round the waist of her blue overdress. The men rowed past the water weeds lining the shore, and she smelled brine.

She marveled at how Karl steered so easily between the maze of skerries and islands off the coast. Some were covered with birch and pine, some with orange lichen or grass, some barren, cold and gray. Some were as big as a byre, and some big enough for a house, with fish nets drying outside. On the points she saw buckets of oil hanging from slanted branches set in a stone cairn, oil to be lit at night to warn incoming ships of the rocks.

"She takes to the water, our Thora, as befits a captain's daughter, Karl-Eirik."

She knew it pleased him that Thora was not seasick. The wind stiffened, and Ingvar climbed the mast feet first, untangling the flapping sail. He called to Karl-Eirik that the wind today was more changeable than a woman.

"Ay, but there are more steadfast women than steadfast winds," Karl shouted up to him, with a teasing wink to Inge.

Ingvar jumped off the mast with a backward flip and landed at Inge's feet. She giggled, knowing he was showing off for her.

"I trow, Ingvar, you are the most agile man I know."

She remembered how he flipped through the air over and over down one side of their hall and back the other, amusing guests. Ingvar could walk a tight rope--on his hands--without falling off. Not only agile, but so thin he would be blown off the mast if he were not strong enough to hang on with legs and arms when the ship ploughed the seas. The shape of his round eyes were those of a man who knew no fear, and the way his eyebrows angled up to a point and then down revealed he loved attention. And control.

The sail filled, and the men pulled out their oars, the oar covers clacking closed. She watched the crew doing their familiar tasks without being told, for each life rested on another's. At the farmstead she had no time to dwell on how Karl's men looked, but now she saw them as though for the first time. Tall and lean and well-muscled, a few wearing their hair in the bachelor's topknot. She knew Karl chose them not for their looks but for their sailing skills. And the way they balanced each other on a ship crowded with gear.

Gunnar, Karl's smith, reached into the worn leather bag of tools used for repair on their long voyages. He set out his tongs and awl, hammers and saws, shears, chisels, nail-iron--a mold for making filigreed earrings--and his axe. With it he carved all spoons for eating and stirring at Breidal. Gunnar had the large forehead befitting a creative man.

Beside him Olaf sat, checking the spring and points of the tools one by one, and put them back in the bag. Olaf was the oldest of the crew, apple-cheeked and bald. Inge knew Karl relied upon him, always solid, steady, and unruffled.

Finnvid walked about the deck tightening the stays. He had long fine eye-lashes a woman would covet--the same lashes that concealed a temper. Had she ever seen Finnvid smile? Nay, but he was necessary to Karl, second in command, the only dark-haired man.

Sven was born to be a story-teller, with his long thin lips, and he had a pleasing ease with words. In truth, he was always talking, as now to Per, turning the beit-ass, the long spar beneath the sail, to catch the wind. Per felt a change of direction in his bones or perchance his hair, for it was as fine as duckling down and lifted in the slightest breeze.

She heard Anders's step-drag as he moved around coiling the lines. She wondered how this seaman beset with a limp could move faster than any man. He was equally quick with a jest, and always merry.

She watched Hrolf, Karl's berserker, and thought how hard it must be to live within a body too large for other men's chairs and beds. He wore no chainmail in battle, protected only by his booming voice and his size that frightened enemies.

What would the men say if she told them about the time she came upon Hrolf sitting on a stump deep in the forest, stroking, crooning to baby hares, his hard, grizzled cheek upon their fur? She saw he had built a willow cage to keep them as pets. Silently she had backed away, his secret safe with her.

She felt the crew's quiet pride in their ship, how they worked together as one. And Karl's pride at the steering-oar as well.

"Inge, we travel on a fair ship. She knows how to bite the wind when I steer. She would sail if we put one of your shifts up on the mast."

She had not sailed to Birka since Aeirn was ten, and she had forgotten how noisy it was aboard ship: the groaning mast, the creaking of the stays, men running from one end of the ship to the other, tightening and untightening the lines, and always the splash of the wakes at prow and stern.

She looked back at the gable-ends of her storehouses, their carved horseheads sharp against the blue sky, and felt a twinge of lonesomeness. Then they vanished behind the trees, and she turned. A journey for her, the witch-seer had foretold, and how fine it was. The Seafarer sailed on, past small bobbing boats tied to trees. Past farms and grazing cattle, a plume of smoke rising above a great hall, fields with the green haze of the new crops.

Karl sniffed, and said today there would be no fog.

"Our Mistress brings weather luck," Anders said.

Pleased, she touched her amulet of Freya. Seamen were wary of women aboard ship. She saw Karl took no chances on the weather. His eyes roamed from the gray-green sea to the fleecy sky and back, reading the changing clouds and currents.

"In calm seas every ship has a good captain, the saying goes," Finnvid said.

Inge saw they were not afraid to jest with Karl. Away from the cares of the farmstead he looked younger, more like his crew's older brother.

She looked at the swatch of gold the sun made on the water, like a golden neckring, and sat, drowsing. At home, Grynon would have thrown the boot for the adoption ceremony into the shit hole by now. He had not been proud of it, he told her, scraping out the bone. Calfskin did not dry to fine leather in just a few hours. Still, she would have nothing less than the full ceremony. And it had been done.

But when she and Karl told the maid she would be their daughter, and no longer just a thrall, Thora surprised them. She was silent, her eyes cast down. Karl told her she could now call them Modir and Fadir, not Mistress and Master.

"Well now, Thora," Karl had said, "have you aught to say about becoming a chieftain's daughter?"

She sat, playing with her fingers. "Nay, but Gunnar promised to show me how he sizes a weapon for a sword arm…"

"Go then," Inge had said, letting Thora escape.

Inge did not hide her disappointment in the maid's reaction, but she told Karl they must be patient. Thora needed to get used to the idea of being free, of being a chieftain's daughter.

"I hope time is all it takes," he said, and she knew he too had expected a happier response from the maid.

Now Inge woke from her drowsing to Karl's shouts.

"Finnvid, pull her down," he called the length of the boat. "Come here, Thora."

The maid walked toward them, unafraid, not holding onto the gunwales, stepping around the oars and piles of gear. A born sailor, Inge thought proudly.

"Thora, aboard ship you must sit quietly, not climb on the gunwales," Karl said. "We have rules aboard ship."

Inge thought she must not drowse again. Nimble-footed as the maid was, a sudden lurch of the boat would pitch her in the Baltic. Thora was restless. In truth, a small boat was no place for an active young girl. She stretched, moving gracefully among the gear to find a place to sit. Finnvid went to tighten a line, and Thora happened to be in his path.

"Thora, move."

She planted her feet. "Nay, go around me."

"The hel I will. Move."

"You can't order me around. You are only a seaman."

Finnvid squeezed the line. "I do more than take up space. If you won't move, grab the stay and pull."

She folded her arms across her chest.

"My father is the captain, and he gives the orders, not you. You are nothing but a common--!"

"Thora!" Inge snapped in the voice she used to berate thralls. "Sit down. Now."

The maid turned a sullen face to Finnvid and sat down on a sea chest. Nothing could be hid on such a small boat, and Inge knew Karl would be displeased at this show of temper, but he was absorbed in talking with Anders. Olaf went to Finnvid.

"We know by instinct how to get out of each other's way, Finnvid, but the maid has never been aboard. Give her some slack."

"She can have all she wants, as long as..."

Inge remembered how Finnvid oft did not finish a sentence.

"It's a short voyage to Birka, Finnvid," Olaf said. "Before you know it we will be on our way to Iceland, and she will be back at Breidal."

Inge heard Finnvid say it could not be too short for him. She asked Thora to apologize, but she refused. Inge insisted.

The maid sighed, whispered, "I hate him," walked to Finnvid, said "I am sorry," and without waiting for a reply, leaned against the gunwale with her back to him.

It was better than nothing, Inge thought. If Finnvid had asked Thora to move instead of ordering her--but these seamen were rough-hewn and not given to tact.

Still, Thora must behave . She and the maid were like guests on The Seafarer. Thora was a captain's daughter, and must act like one.

Inge sat her down next to her and tied her wind-tossed hair back with a ribband, talking of the finespun they would buy her in Birka, of silks and linens and wool. Thora had no interest, and played with her fingers.

"Fadir, I am wont to see your sword," she called to Karl.

Finnvid stared. Anders gasped. Inge saw the men's faces harden. None of them would dare touch Karl's sword--it was not a toy. Why, then, this daughter, not natural, but adopted?

"It is too heavy for a maid, Thora," Finnvid said.

"Nay! I am strong," she said, glaring at him.

The men argued with Karl: "She is too slight..."and "Karl, she will drop it..." and such.

He looked at his crew. He was the one at the tiller of his boat. He would decide. Now he gave the tiller to Olaf and walked to Thora. With his free hand he undid the peace bands and pulled the sword from its leather scabbard trimmed with gilt tendrils. He placed it in her open arms, and she turned it over and over.

"Oh, Fadir, I have seen no sword so finely-wrought, with jewels and gold. What mean the runes carved on it?"

Inge knew Karl loved talking of his beloved sword. "Thora, it is writ Shield-Thorn. It was my father's father's sword, and his father's before."

"The hilt gleams in the sun."

"When Shield-Thorn is in use," Gunnar said, "the goldwork shines as though lightning flakes from it."

Thora thumbed the blade and found it sharpened to her liking. No one could mistake the maid's admiration for its leather grip and brass pommel.

Sven told her Shield-Thorn was a worthy sword for a worthy chieftain, and always brought them victory-luck.

Per said it was a charmed sword, and slayed every man in its path. It was thought wounds given by it could not be healed.

"Ay?" Thora said. "I have heard men speak of such swords, how viper's blood was mixed with the iron when it was forged. When the sword strikes, the serpent throws its tail."

"Your daughter is as quick with the tongue as the sword," Sven said to Inge.

"Fadir, I am wont to see your spear and axes, hid in the sea chests," Thora said.

"Nay, nay. We have had enough of weapon-talk," Inge said. "The river to Birka is up ahead. We will stop for bread and curds. You can pass the ale."

Thora sighed. She was strong, Inge had to agree, watching her hand the sword to Karl and heft the ale cask. Inge longed for the day she could begin filling Thora's hands with the shuttle and the digging stick, swords and axes forgotten.

As they approached the river the farmsteads were smaller, closer together. Inge kept Thora at her side, and they sat with Karl, eating and drinking. He talked of how the farms looked more serene than they were-- there was much unrest in Sweden. Instead of traveling the countryside, keeping peace among the chieftains, the king kept his ass safe in Uppsala. Many men complained about the high taxes he imposed to build new roads from one end of the country to the other.

It looked peaceful enough to her on shore. The women were doing the spring wash in the creeks, as they would be doing at home. Women lived much the same all over Sweden.

On the river leading to Birka, the wind abated, and each man set his oar and leaned into it. With pride, Inge saw none of the boats they passed were as fine as their own. None had a beit-ass, or a half-deck like The Seafarer to conceal cargo.

She could see the cords standing out on men's arms. Rowing against the current was a killing task. Only sea-talk could make it bearable.

Anders told Inge that in Birka she would see that Karl-Eirik was a man of ready speech when they met with others from Danmork or Skotland. He asked Karl how he knew the words to talk in their tongues. Karl told him to stay out of the ale hall and away from the women and close to his near side, and he could learn.

"When it comes to trade all men understand one another," Karl said. "Mark this: our word 'skinn' is like the Englander's 'skin.' The cloth we call 'ull' they call 'wool'. To the Danes, many words are the same. Our work 'fisk' is 'fisk' to them."

Inge pretended to be astonished, and hoped he did not trade fish for fish with the Danes. He told her fish for fish was not a good trade. All Norse stink with the plenty of it already.

"Karl-Eirik," Finnvid said, blinking sweat from his eyes, "the Danes dig rivers and line them with planks to make quick passage from one part to another. They charge toll. I would fain sit upon the bank and take toll."

"Good," Karl said. "We will leave you in Danmork on our journey," and the men laughed.

Gunnar told Finnvid not to be so glum. Had he forgotten laughter was Odin's favorite sound?

Still Finnvid was sour-faced. Inge talked of how Swedes would build a bridge. She told them about one near her childhood farmstead. The iron caster set bells hanging beneath it so he could hear friend or foe coming. Karl agreed it was the Swedish way to build with iron and not root in the mud, digging yet another river.

Boats began thronging the waterway, boats of all sizes, some with ten men at the oar, some with one, boats in purple or red, or needing paint. Two ships had gold work on the prow, but none as lavish as their own. To her pleasure, other boats moved to the side and let The Seafarer through.

"Who is your master?" one captain called.

"None, we are all equal," Karl called back.

The men smiled at each other, sitting a little taller. Though they were all equals, only one man's hand was on the tiller.

Thora got up on her knees. "Our crewmen are not equals," she yelled. "My father the captain--"

Inge pulled her down with a jolting tug. "Hush!" Karl's mouth was hard-set. The maid was lucky he was too busy steering to take a hand to her.

"Aboard ship no one questions what the captain says, Thora," Anders said. "Whether he is your father or a pig's knuckle."

"A pig's knuckle? Karl-Eirik?" Gunnar said, laughing, and all joined in but Thora.

It was not the first time Anders's jesting took the edge off trouble on The Seafarer , Inge knew. Was Thora making up for all the years she was a docile thrall?

Inge was relieved when they saw the town, set above a cliff. On the landward side a thick rampart of earth and stone higher than a man enclosed it, with guards standing atop, their cloaks pulled back so their swords were plain to see. From here they could look to an escaping thief and sound an alarm. Birka was an island, and all must leave by boat or swim. They saw people clustered around the gates within the firewall. Inge was excited, and squeezed Thora's hand.

Karl told them he would land at the harbor of Salviksgroven. Inge knew he must remember with his mind's eye where the huge, unseen rocks to slow boats down were hid in the harbor. The only map was in his head. He dared not make a mistake--the wealth of furs he brought to trade, the boat, even their lives, were in danger if he struck a rock beneath the surface.

The crew was quiet, and Inge knew they too worried. She fingered her amulet of Freya. Karl turned the tiller with quick movements, now forward, now back, to the right and forward again. The boat bobbed and swerved a path between rocks that could not be seen or felt until it would be too late.

Finally, safe, they sailed inside the breakwater of wooden pilings. The men cheered Karl-Eirik. They pulled slower at the oar, ready to obey him for the docking.

"Hard now, Per. Put by, Finnvid. Hrolf, harder!"

They reached the wooden jetty, and Anders leapt ashore to fasten the lines taut around the tree trunks. Inge kissed Karl and said she had been reminded again that Karl was a fine captain.

"Ay, Fadir is the best," Thora said, and the crew agreed.

Now the sea chests opened, and Karl's men began a flurry of primping with antler-bone combs, changing into fresh tunics in bright reds and blues, except for Finnvid, who always wore dull grays and drab browns. Ingvar appeared in breeches red in front, green in back.

"Wear your bright clothes aboard ship more oft," Karl said. "If I have to see an ugly crew at least I can see fair colors."

"Like Ingvar?" Anders asked. "His pants are two-colored. If we see red he is coming towards us, green he is going away."

Laughing, the men slipped gold rings on their calloused fingers. In Birka they wanted to be seen as the freeborn men they were. Inge combed the snarls out of Thora's hair, and the maid did not protest. From her seapouch Inge pulled her golden diadem, rubbing it against her dress to polish it. She set it around her brow and gave Karl his own. He portioned out the watches, so all would have time in the market town. From under the floorboards Per and Anders brought out the leather pouch of trading furs, the deepest and thickest winter pelts.

Karl and Inge walked along the quay with Thora between them.

He counted out eight eyrir and gave them to a man wearing the trader's shirt and lace hat. Karl said it was money well-spent, protection money. He did not want The Seafarer to catch fire while they were shopping.

This was only one of the changes Inge saw from ten years past. There were more ware-houses, and bigger ones. More traders. Birka was thriving.

Karl said he would sell their furs to Arnibjorn the Moneyer, a Swedish trader who knew quality, and could be trusted to give full measure. Inge thought it one of Karl's faults to trust every Swede.

"He does not ask if I am prime-signed, Ingeborg," Karl said.

"What is prime-signed, Fadir?" Thora asked.

"A kind of half water-sprinkling, half-way between the Christians and those of us who follow the true faith of Odin."

Inge liked Arnibjorn, though she wondered if he was showing off his wealth-
-armrings covered both arms from wrist to elbow. However, his price seemed
fair. She suggested he hold their gold marks until they left Birka, so they would
not fritter them away on trifles.

She trusted the trader, but she picked up a wooden tally stick from the counter and carved Karl's initials and the price. She broke it in half lengthwise and
put one part in her seapouch, and gave the other half to Arnibjorn. He raised his
eyebrows, surprised a woman knew the runes and how to use a tally stick. Karl
told him they would spend the night in town and be back on the morrow.

They heard the yapping dogs long before they approached the town gate. A
snot-nosed thrall beat away dogs from the two pigs hung and drawn for sacrifice.
Birka was crowded and noisy, with one wooden hut after another, the big ones
made of logs, the smaller ones from sticks interwoven with mud. Craftsmen in
leather aprons stood at the doors, guarding side tables with samples of gold and
silver earrings and neckrings, carved wooden bowls and trenchers, and statues
of Thor and Freya and Odin in bronze. Inge slowed before one side table piled
high with rolls of finespun silk, but Karl guided her down the board walk. Later,
he said.

She heard the familiar tapping on an ironmaster's forge. Smells, too, she
knew: sweat and horse shit, leather, smoke from fires.

Here were dark-skinned men with no beards, but moustaches draped over
their cheeks to their chins. Men with folded arms keeping their hands hid in the
long silken shirt sleeves. Who knew what they kept there? Knives?

Swedes in reindeer skin cloaks and bearskin caps passed them, using their
axes as walking sticks.

Thora was trying to see everything at once, till a juggler with four wooden
balls threw them to her one by one. She caught them with ease, tossed them in
the air and threw them back, giggling. Ah, this maid was as skilled with a ball as
a sword, Inge thought.

Thora dragged her feet at a side table with an array of chainmail shirts.

"Fadir, I would have one of those. With a fourfold shirt of mail, no point can
get through, ay?"

"Four-in-one does not protect from a direct thrust, Thora," Karl said, and
Inge thought the Norse loved anything to do with fighting.

They watched a swordsmith use tongs to pull out bars of red-hot iron from a heap of smoldering charcoal, the heat reflecting red on his face. Karl said the surfaces had absorbed enough carbon to become steel, but the cores were still good Swedish iron. The smith would twist and weld the bars together in a different order again and again, each time reforging them. The blade must be strong enough not to bend, for the Norse fought with bold, sweeping strokes.

They watched a pattern begin to form on the blade. Thora said, here was the viper throwing its tail. Inge said, nay, the pattern was a twig, or a flower stalk.

Karl agreed with neither, but told them that when the blade had enough carbon the swordsmith would quench it for the last time, but how he did it was his secret. Even Gunnar did not tell anyone, but worked behind a closed door.

Each trade had its secrets, Inge thought, watching Thora pick up one sword, put it down, pick up another, and begin swinging it. Inge pulled Karl aside.

"Karl. I do not want Thora to have chainmail, or anything else. She must put aside all thought of the sword, and pick up the shuttle."

"Inge, she can use both. Thora is quick, but knows how to be patient and wait. These are the same skills you use at the loom--I have watched you weave.

"With all the unrest in the country, I would be happier to know our daughter has a sword to protect you while I am away a-viking."

Inge stared at him, open-mouthed.

"Karl! A sword of her own? What are you thinking! You have elvist. And I would have elvist to agree."

"Nay, nay, Inge. These are dangerous times we are living in. I have thought at times of teaching you swordplay."

She tried to hide a smile, but could not.

"And I will teach you the shuttle, Karl-Eirik."

The swordsmith stopped poking out the hot iron bars, watching the slight young girl, as skilled with her left hand as her right. His eyes were on Thora. His ears, though, were on the quarreling parents.

Karl reminded Inge they had adopted Thora as their own, vowing their love for her. And Thora was most comely. He feared she might need to protect her honor.

"Honor!" she said. "Your brother Lars traveled with her on his boat, and I think they did not sleep apart."

"Ay. Yet a fine sword could be part of Thora's brides-goods. In one more year she will be ready to marry. One sword seems to have chosen Thora--she likes it best. If I cared little for the maid I would say no, but I am wont to be a good father."

Inge sighed. All Karl said was true, but still...after Karl left she would teach the maid that greening plants and colorful yarns were more joyful than a metal sword, cold to the touch.

"Karl. She must have the peace bands."

"I would not buy a sword without. And the leather strap across her shoulders so it can be concealed beneath her cloak. We want no stranger to lure her into using the sword without cause."

When all was bought, he fastened the scabbard to her, and Inge pulled the cloak to hide it. Thora put her arms around Inge's neck and kissed her cheek. It was such a sweet, tender kiss Inge closed her eyes so no one would see her tears. This daughter was full of surprises. Karl smiled, happily rewarded for the coins he put in the swordsmith's palm.

Thora stroked the concealed sword. "Modir, all my life I have wanted a sword of my own. Never did I think I would get one. It is the best of gifts, and you are the best mother and father."

Though Inge still had misgivings, no one would guess Thora wore a weapon. She looked like any maid skipping down the board walk between her parents.

Karl told Inge to buy more fine-spun than she needed, for herself as well as Thora. Determined to forget the trouble with the sword, Inge chose much more: brocades, silks of many colors, the whitest and sheerest of linens, wadmal soft enough to wear in the bed-closet. Karl pleased her with a gold legring to be worn well above the knee.

"Only I will know it is there," he whispered.

He bought walrus rope for the boat--it did not break when wet--and unwilling to sleep in Birka with the stink of walrus, Inge asked to have it sent to Arnibjorn.

At the ale hall Thora made her mother happy when she said the ale and bread were not as good as at Breidal. In truth, the bread was softer and whiter than at home, with none of the stone grindings from the quern. Karl told her it was from Danmork, and they would take flour home. In their room, Thora fell asleep with her sword at her side, clutching her amulet of Thor. Karl pushed open the shutters and said the bright yellow sky with ragged clouds boded well for sailing home on the morrow. Inge stowed their diadems in her seapouch.

The room was plain, with only a side table and a pitcher of water and a bowl, but the beds had linen sheets over the straw. Karl lay down, and Inge began pulling off his breeches.

"Karl-Eirik, at the next assembly of The Thing I will ask our Lawspeaker to change this custom. Men can begin pulling off the underclothes we women wear beneath our dresses."

Karl laughed, sat up and pulled down her underbreeches, kicked off his own and undressed them both. The gold legring was deliciously cold when he slipped it on. She rolled onto her side and Karl curled around her, seeking her breasts.

"I trow, Inge, I am wont to have six hands. Two to hold both breasts, two to stroke you between your thighs, and two for where they meet."

He undid her plait slowly, running his fingers through her loosened hair and kissing her neck. Ah. In the dark every full-grown woman was a maid, and every man a fair-haired youth. He slipped smoothly into her. No other man had ever loved her better. He knew here to touch her to make her skin come alive. He gripped her inside and out, with his hands, his legs, his sex, holding her fast, caressing her, stroking himself as well.

The sweet tickle began in her crotch and moved up where even Karl could not reach. The tremor shook her body, and the flood of sweetness spread. She gasped. She pressed her mouth into the straw so as not to waken Thora. He buried his open mouth against her back to hold in his moan.

The smell of sweat and sex mingled, and, as often, Inge hungered after more. She moved sensuously, Karl's sex within her, and he licked the salt from her skin. The sweetness pierced her belly, and it burst, sharper. She shuddered with a spasm of pleasure. Karl never denied her, in or out of bed. He sighed.

"Now you are one up on me, Wife. I will not forget. I am thinking of joining the Guild so we can live in Birka and enjoy bedplay every night, instead of only half the year."

How would it be? There would be no half-crazed homecoming, with Karl taking her into their bed-closet day and night, with an urgency that had no end, until it hurt, though she could not stop herself. A better reward than the gold and jewels he brought home was his body hungering for hers.

She reached back and stroked his thighs, her fingers light on the long, jagged battle scar from crotch to knee. We trade when we can, fight when we must, Karl had said. If he was home all year round, there would be no more sword wounds, no more scars.

"Karl, we can sell The Seafarer on the morrow."

She heard a quick breath. She had surprised him.

"Sell my boat? Nay! I cannot sell my boat."

"Then let us have no more fool's talk. Sleep, for on the morrow we sail for Breidal."

Sailing was in his blood, and both knew it. While he was gone the hard task of prying Thora's new sword from her hands must begin. Ah, Inge thought, it would require all of a mother's love and patience. And a hardened heart.

V

The next morning Inge found Karl in the inn yard sharing lively sea-talk with other sailors. He kissed her and moved over to make room for her on the bench. The men became silent, but Karl told them he took counsel with his wife in all things. His words pleased her more than gold. He told her Thora was seeing the sights of Birka with Hrolf and Olaf. Inge need have no fear for Thora's safety, but could enjoy her curds and fine white bread.

An old gray-haired man in brown wadmal walked into the yard, and Inge ran to him, kissing him on both cheeks.

"Einar! I am surprised to meet you here. But happy."

He told her she had not changed since she was a maid growing up, and he was her father's steward on his farmstead. She laughed, and said he too was unchanged. She would know him anywhere. His face was still round and cheery, his beard as scraggly, but he stooped, sparing a stiff back, holding a fear in his body.

It had been many years since they had met, and she had an uneasy feeling he was there for a reason. She shook her forebodings away and moved with him to another table. Karl waved at the old man and turned back to the sea-talk. She ordered an ale bowl and cups, and while Einar drank they exchanged news: he told her the retired herdsman, Gorm, was outlawed a year for stealing four cows. The neighbor, Askell, drowned in the fjord, but whether for love or drink, no one knew. Einar wiped his sleeve across his mouth.

She told him about their adoption of Thora, but not the reasons for it. He swirled the ale in the cup, not looking at her.

"Inge, I can tell you about the maid. Have you heard of a man named Tyrkir?"

She felt a pain in her chest, and knew it for fear. Now she would learn about Thora's beginnings, like it or not. She put her hand on his arm.

"I know the name. Thora told me he taught her swordcraft."

"Inge, the chieftain, Tyrkir Onundr, was Thora's father."

"Ay? I knew it! There were too many signs that Thora is highborn. We must tell Karl."

"Wait, Ingeborg. There is more to the maid's story."

He told her Thora's mother was not Tyrkir's wife, but a thrall on his farmstead. Tyrkir's wife did not want a bastard child growing up to compete with her own son. The chieftain was off a-viking when Thora was born, and the wife had the servants put Thora out to be exposed outside, naked, and so die.

Inge's eyes filled with tears, and Einar put his rough hand over hers, continuing.

"You know the custom, Inge. A child born of a master and a thrall is yet a thrall, unless the master declares it to be his own, and gives it liberty within three nights after the birthing."

Ay, she knew the hateful custom. Her Thora exposed to die, when only a babe! How she hated Tyrkir's wife. Inge poured a cup of ale, and drained it, but the ale did not help her anger.

Thora had always been comely, Einar said, and the servants set her out to be exposed at the side of the path to their fjord, wrapped in wadmal, hoping someone would see her and save her life.

The gods were watching over Thora. Four days after she was born, Tyrkir came home from his journey, and he walked up the path, past the crying babe. Thora's mother was there weeping, and told Tyrkir the babe was his own. He must have been touched, for he picked Thora up and took her to his cloak. She stopped crying, and Tyrkir ordered her life saved.

"Einar! All would be different if he had returned one day earlier."

"Ay, but our customs, like our laws, must be obeyed, for the good of Sweden, and ourselves. Thora remained a thrall, but Tyrkir kept her at his side when he was home, teaching her swordcraft, so she could defend herself, for she was not beloved by other thralls nor servants nor freeborn."

"Pah. Least of all the wife."

"She died, some say of grief, when Tyrkir never came back from a journey. Thora was ten."

And so then she was truly alone. Einar's news made Inge love her more. Ah, it could only have been the father who put Thor's amulet on the maid for protection, and named her Thora.

Karl came and sat with them. The news about Thora would wait until she and Karl were alone. He told Einar he was pleased to see him. He reminded him that Inge's father would have given him to them in Inge's bride's-price, but he could not manage without his steward. She saw the words delighted the old man. He told them he was managing Inge's old farmstead only until their sons returned to take it on. It was a fair place to live, closer to the king than Breidal.

Karl poured ale for them, and raised his cup.

"I have a toast for our king, Einar. To Hel with him. Let him rot on his high seat in Uppsala."

"Karl-Eirik! Lower your voice," Einar said. "The king's men are known to drink in ale yards."

"Ay? Then let me repeat my toast, louder, and they can tell him. To the dark abode of the goddess Hel with the king."

"Karl, do not be a fool," Inge said, glancing around. The others in the yard had stopped talking, staring at Karl. Inge shifted on the bench, and she saw Einar's ale, like her own, was untouched. She knew Karl could drink many cups before his judgment was affected. Why then was he courting trouble?

"Inge," he said loud enough for the whole yard to hear, "this day I learned the king is levying taxes on all goods brought from Danmork or beyond."

"Karl!"

"Ay, Inge. Five for every hundred, though we all have ways to get around this loathsome tax. Let the king go a-viking himself, Einar, and with any luck he will drown. I care not who hears me."

Einar swallowed hard.

"Karl-Eirik, this is a dangerous game you are playing, in a public place. It is said the king has the good of Sweden at heart. Too many Swedish ships are being sunk in western waters. The king levies no taxes on captains who sail east to Kievan Rus. Why not sail east?"

Inge saw Karl drank no more. Einar talked too fast, desperate to convince Karl-Eirik. She could have told him there was no way. Einar was no seaman. He took joy in the greening furrow, and had no feel for the adventure of the open sea that beckoned men with a goddess's power, that beckoned each captain to go where he wanted to go.

"My men and I will sail where we choose, Einar, west to Iceland. Ah, here is our daughter, back with Hrolf and Olaf, all three chewing on honeycombs. Come, Ingeborg, I am wont to buy you a gift before we leave Birka within the hour."

He told Olaf to have the boat and crew ready. Einar stood, and he and Karl clasped arms.

"Farvell, Einar. It was good to see you again."

Karl took a bite from Thora's honeycomb, and the maid protested, giggling.

Einar stood and whispered to Inge. "Karl is too headstrong, Ingeborg. The king has unfriendly thoughts toward him."

Ay, it was not chance that brought Einar to the ale yard that morning. She kissed his cheek.

"Einar, Karl-Eirik is himself a king on his boat. Any freedom-loving man who has Karl's luck would not be liked if he disagreed with the king. But thank you for your caution. Farvell."

Ah, it would be good when Karl was on his way a-viking. A king who kept his ass safe in Uppsala would not be sailing west to harry a captain fool enough to insult that king in public. She looked around, but all the men had returned to their sea-talk. She took a deep breath. She would leave her fear in the aleyard, and not spoil their last hour in Birka.

As they strolled the board walk, Karl told her he knew she was distraught, but all he said about the king was true. She decided the news about Thora could wait a little longer. He led them to a large hut with no side table outside.

Once inside, Inge blinked. The light from blazing torches lit up shelves filled with goblets, vases, bowls, cups--tall, round, square, all so thin she could see through to the far side, in more shades and colors than she knew existed. She yearned to have yarn in this blue, that purple, that red. Inge wagged her head from side to side, and the colors changed. Thora giggled, and did the same.

Inge asked Karl the name of this treasure, and he told her it was called glass, made an old, old way, done long before their father's father's time, but new to them. It was made from sand.

"Nay," Thora said. "We cannot see through sand, Fadir."

At the back a thick-necked man hunched before an open fire, turning a long pole with a blob at the end. He cut it at both ends, set it on a board, and set the blob spinning. Inge thought she had never seen anything so wondrous--a bowl formed before their eyes. It was a hard task, she thought, for his clothes were sweat-stained, the hut so hot it was hard to breathe.

While the craftsman worked, Karl spoke with him in Frankish, and Inge felt a quiet pride in her husband who could speak the language of men from other lands.

"He is a glass-caster from Saxland, Inge, and he says this glass is stronger than the steel in my sword."

"Ay, and mine," Thora said, and Inge hushed her.

There was no need for swordtalk in this place of beauty. Karl told the glass-caster he had never seen colors like these on his travels, and Inge saw the words pleased the glass-caster. Karl lifted one bowl and turned it, then another, and they saw how it held light as a vessel held water.

"Ingeborg, let us choose one piece for ourselves, so you do not forget me in the six months I am away."

Inge kissed him. Karl-Eirik, the gold-giver, generous in all.

He lifted one bowl, not the biggest, but the fairest, and put it in her hands: the most beautiful thing in all of Sweden. She held it aloft, watching the light weave in and out of the blues and greens.

A huge, mangy dog wandered in through the open door and hid behind Inge. Yelling in Frankish, the glass-caster waved his apron at it, and the frightened dog circled her. Giggling, Thora chased it, and Karl shouted at both of them in Swedish. The dog struck Inge's legs and the bowl flew from her hands. She grabbed for it, but it fell with a crash, breaking into slivers.

Inge felt a wave of shock course through her body.

"Karl-Eirik, this glass breaks!"

"Ay, I should have told you. Though stronger than steel, it breaks. We will choose another piece and pay for both at the same time."

"Out of my shop!" the glass-caster shouted, flapping his apron at them.

"You dare to flap your apron at my wife!" Karl shouted, throwing a handful of silver coins atop the broken glass. "This is more than enough silver."

"Nein! Pay me what it is worth--I will hold your wife until you do."

He grappled Inge's arm with his hand, and she pulled, but could not free herself--his strong fingers pinched. Behind them she felt the shop clog with people, silent, watching.

"Take your hand off her!" Karl roared, his own hand on his swordhilt.

Inge heard the slip of a sword out of the scabbard and caught the glint of torchlight on steel.

It was the maid, sword in hand, advancing on the glass-caster. There was no mistaking the gleam in the eyes or her intense young face, her whole body focused on him. Nor any mistaking his fear-filled eyes.

"Thora, nay!" Inge cried, and tried to move toward her but the glass-caster held her fast. Though she tried to shake him off, his fingers dug into her arm like claws.

"Karl--stop her!"

But he only stared at the maid, transfixed. Curse him for his Norse love of fighting, Inge thought.

Thora pricked the leather apron with her sword, and the glass-caster side-stepped. With wild eyes he looked around for an escape, but the room was jammed with people, watching. The maid closed in, touching his arm, his leg with the point, threatening him. Inge reached for Thora's sword arm, but the glass-caster yanked her back.

With a growing horror Inge watched the two, attacker and prey, doing a strange dance: Thora advancing with the sword, nicking his arm, his leg, his neck, torturing him, while he leaned back, trying to avoid the worst of it. If only the glass-caster or Karl would give in, Inge thought, this foolishness would stop.

"Enough, Thora," she cried. "You have taunted him long enough."

She never knew whether her words gave the maid permission, for Thora lunged and slashed his shoulder down the chest with the blade, so blood ran down the leather apron in rivulets over the huge belly. He fell, slow and heavy, staring at Thora.

"Catch him!" Inge shouted, but no one moved.

He landed on his back with a thump.

His claws clung to Inge's arm until the end. Finally free, she fell beside him. She looked up at Thora. The maid's face was flushed and jubilant, as she slipped the sword back in the scabbard.

"Now he has unhanded you, Modir."

Inge worked swiftly, pulling the glass-caster's leather apron over his head, tearing his shirt from the wound. Thora had struck his chest, but thanks be to

Freya, she had missed his heart. Less than a handspan more, and she might have done real harm.

Ay, the maid was quick. The wound was cleanly cut, but the blood was spurting. Inge told Thora the flower Days-eye grew near the ale house. She must bring the leaves quickly. Inge turned his head to the wounded side and pressed the glass-caster's arm nearest the cut tight against his body with her knee. She grasped his neck and with one hand, pushed down on his shoulder. With her other hand she put her fingers on his collarbone and pressed down and back. Through her palm, she felt a strong heartbeat, a good sign.

The blood slowed to a trickle, and someone brought a bowl of water. Inge washed her hands and tenderly dabbed the cut. Thora knelt beside her holding a sheaf of flowers.

"Now you can learn to stanch blood, Thora. Crush the leaves and put them over the wound."

As she did, Inge tore the shirt and bound the wound and though the blood came through, it was slow. She lifted his eyelid and saw he was not hard-pressed. His color was good.

"The wound is clean and he will heal soon, with rest," she told the crowd.

She changed the bandage and put her hand on his heart. The beat was strong. She washed her hands and told Karl she would fain be gone when he awoke.

She took Thora's hand and the three left by a back door, making all haste to Arnibjorn's to exchange the half tally stick for gold marks, and get their walrus rope. There was no time now to stop and buy white flour.

"How went your stay in Birka?" Arnibjorn asked.

"Well enough," Inge said. "Farvell."

He would hear of Thora's swordthrust with the next customer.

On The Seafarer Inge sat Thora close to her. Once underway Karl told the crew what happened, and their need to get away fast. He steered through the wooden pilings and between the hidden rocks, and Inge saw how fast the boat could speed under oar. She watched the shore, but no people pointed to them, no boats were launched. Still Karl took no chance: he steered behind the row of small, tree-thick islands, keeping the boat hid from the men atop the ramparts. Inge held fast to Thora and thought with luck the glass-caster had no kin from Saxland to avenge his honor in Birka. By now he might be boasting about the maid who could not vanquish him for long, though in the telling Thora would change to a woman more a powerful goddess than a maid.

One other thing Inge knew full well: she could not get Thora to woman's work soon enough. Her speed with the sword was frightening. Even now, Inge saw Thora was not contrite, but proud, unheeding of any evil that came of her swordplay.

They passed the last island and could be easily seen on the open water. Still they saw no crowds, no boats coming after them, only smoke lazing above the treetops. Could it be the glass- caster had decided to forget the slight wound?

Karl's face was hard-set, and the men rowed in a fury, glancing at the maid with puzzled looks. There was none of the usual teasing, only the splash of oars cleaving the water, and the grunting as the men strained. When they were far enough away so the rampart was only a hazy line, Karl spoke to Thora.

"You must not draw the sword each time you are angered."

"The glass-caster was hurting Modir," she said, staring back at Birka.

"Ay. It was seemly of you to defend your mother--it is ever the way to protect kin--not that you could not defend yourself, Inge."

"The maid acted from love, Karl," Inge snapped, clenching her amulet. "I cannot fault her for that. But I fault you for buying the sword for her. You wanted her to be able to defend the women of your farmstead, and she did."

"Ay. But the deed is done, and we are lucky it was no worse. Thora, if you had killed the glass-caster, you would be subject to Outlawry. It is the law."

Thora trembled, and Inge hugged her. For the first time Thora seemed to feel the seriousness of her deed. Inge said they were now far enough outriver to wash the blood from the sword. The maid leaned on the gunwale, watching the blood mixing with the water, wiping the weapon before putting it back in the scabbard. Ay, it could be forgotten, Inge thought, as the river widened into the sea, and Karl turned the ship north. With a clatter the men put down oars, and the sail billowed forth.

Ah, the men would be glad when they left all women behind and went a-viking toward Iceland, Inge knew, as she passed rounds of barley bread and the ale cask, though she took no joy in either.

She and Karl talked of tasks before her at home.

Soon it would be shearing time, and she would busy Thora with new fleece to wash and card and spin. Later she would take the maid to the fabod, the summer pasture for the cows up on the mountain. Inge thought, but did not say, they would stay awhile, the sword left behind to rust, forgotten.

"Karl-Eirik," Ingvar called from the mast, "a horseman on shore is beckoning to us."

Karl cursed in a strange language Inge never heard, and kept a firm hand on the tiller.

"It is Einar, Ingeborg. I have enough on my mind without listening to him tell me why I should sail east for my king. Row, you bastards. You can beat a horse!"

Under both sail and oar, The Seafarer skimmed the waves, but Einar urged his mount into the water and kept up. Though the sun was bright, and the sun's neckring a rich gold, and the prow post gleamed, Inge felt dulled by fear.

"Karl-Eirik, the glass-caster is dead," Einar shouted.

"Dead?" she shouted back. "Dead? How came he to die? His wound was not mortal. I tended it myself."

"They held a mirror before his mouth, Inge, and there was no breath," Einar called.

The men paused, holding their oars. Inge heard a mewing at her side, and gathered Thora into her arms.

"Inge, how can this be?" Karl asked.

She forced her voice to be calm and told them that when the body has a great shock, the heart may stop beating. It might have happened in battle, but Karl did not know of it.

"Modir, I did not mean to kill him!" Thora cried, shaking.

"You did not kill him!" Karl shouted.

Ay, Inge thought. Still, if Thora had not struck him?

Einar said the story was on every man's lips in Birka. And one thing more: the king's men had been at the ale yard, and were even now riding to tell him about Thora's swordthrust.

Ah, it was a burden to be married to a headstrong fool, Inge thought. Karl steered close in, shouting that Einar knew he feared no king--he intended to call a special assembly of the Thing and bring the matter forth to be judged by the Lawspeaker, Ragnovald. He would send the summons to all his neighbors to stand with them at the Thing. Meet us back at the farmstead, he told the old steward. Inge's mind raced as she watched Einar gallop away.

Would their neighbors stand with them? Some were jealous of the way Karl built up their holdings with stolen gold. Still, she had never turned down any who needed her help at a birthing, or to give the final draught to a dying man or woman.

It was the longest trip of her life, but finally she saw the carved horseheads of her store houses through the trees, and smelled the brine at the shore. Karl touched her shoulder.

"Fear not, Ingeborg, we will not let the king outlaw Thora. She is not yet a woman. Who would send a maid out of Sweden on a charge of Outlawry?"

Only one, Inge thought, one who knew a maid's father as a threat, and wanted to be rid of him, too.

Not an hour ago Karl told Thora that if she killed the glass-caster she would be subject to Outlawry--it was the Law. "...our laws must be obeyed for the good of Sweden and ourselves," Einar had said.

Inge took heart from the new green of each plant and vine and tree along the fjord. There was one law a loving mother was justified in flouting. She would hide her daughter from the king's soldiers.

She thought about a story her mother's mother told her. One farmstead was attacked by men from another, and the family hid their daughter in an empty well for safe-keeping. After several days of fierce fighting the attackers left, and the father put down the oaken ladder to climb down and bring up the girl. Inge's stomach knotted with terror as she remembered the rest of the story.

The father carried the girl up, lifeless. By some evil trick of Loki, the water had flowed back in, and she had drowned.

VI

Ragnovald the Lawspeaker could recite the law at the assembly of The Thing for half a day with no pause, and now he opened the trial with the Peace Declaration. Granni Gunnarsson sat next to him, listening and learning, so one day when Ragnovald's memory grew faulty, Granni could take the Lawspeaker's place.

"All Swedish men and women of any age are Peace-Holy, in or out of the country," Ragnovald said. "It is their right. And on Swedish soil, all others are also Peace-Holy."

Ay, Inge thought from her place on a low wooden bench. A glass-caster from Saxland had been Peace-Holy. The reciting of the law had always been tiresome, but today she listened carefully. Her daughter, sitting quietly apart on a second bench, was the one on trial. Ragnovald told the crowd that every man and woman has the right to avenge self and kin, and he began the terms of wergild, the legal value of a life.

When Ragnovald got down to wergild for third cousin, four marks, Inge figured the life of a distant kin would be worth 120 and a half cows. Gladly would she cut one of her cows in half and give the best half to the glass-caster's third cousin.

Ragnovald was known for unbiased judgments. His face was wrinkly, and his hair and beard had been gray for many winters, but his eyes missed nothing. He had gone a-viking in his youth. He knew the lust for adventure, and the sacred bond of kin, never to be broken.

How, then, could Ragnovald judge the daughter of a chieftain as less value than a foreigner's? Ay, he could, and they must abide by his ruling. Though the maid had not killed the glass-caster, he lay beneath the mould, dead.

Inge was grateful Ragnovald agreed to try Thora, but it was frightening to think one man could decide her daughter's future. Yet she and Karl had agreed Thora would fare better under Ragnovald, than under the Council of Twelve, chosen by the king.

Still, Inge knew she must not be downcast. The Thing was enclosed by Sanctuary Bonds of hazel wands, the wood given by the gods to insure a fair hearing.

53

She watched a cabbage butterfly flit: a sure sign there would be no more winter. The fine weather mocked her worry.

"One eyrir for singeing, half a mark for narrow wounds..." Ragnovald continued.

At her side Karl squeezed her hand. If he regretted the delay in his journey, he never said, and she loved him for that. Behind him stood the crew, and their freeborn servants and their neighbors who had all come, in answer to Karl's summons.

Ragnovald droned on, and Inge and Thora smiled at each other for comfort as they had done all week, at the quern, at the hearth-fire. When the winter-weakened cows were carried out to pasture from the byre, Thora was there to calm them. When Inge brought the sheep into the fold at even, Thora was there to coax the new lambs inside.

Ah, she would have missed much without a daughter, Inge thought, despite this harrowing trial.

Her three sons had followed after Karl to the boatshed as soon as they could toddle. She remembered their joy--and her terror--at the way they leapt off the storehouse balcony onto the backs of horses thundering below. But this daughter had stayed working quietly at her near side.

Today Thora looked fair in a blue dress and white overgarment. Karl and Inge had decided she would wear no gold, but should be seen as plain. Though her hair in the sunlight was wreath enough, and more.

"Six aurar if a scar causes pain when the hair is combed," Ragnovald continued his list of wound-indemnities. "Payment of the healing fee: two allowances of meal and two of butter."

Inge thought she would not give the tasks to servants, but grind the meal and churn butter herself if Thora could be saved from a harsh punishment.

A hawk wheeled above the red haze of the maples. After this day Thora would be free as the hawk, but more likely, serving a sentence for the wrongful death of the glass-caster.

Ragnovald kept on through Indemnity of Laziness, refusing to help the slain. Six rings payment to the king.

She and Thora both had stanched the bleeding wound. Laziness the maid could not be held for.

Back wounds: double indemnity, Ragnovald said, his voice even.

Nay. Thora had struck him full on.

"All are equal in wound-indemnity, thrall and freeborn," he said, and finally he was through.

He brought forth the altar-ring for the swearing of the oath. Thora was but near-grown, and Karl had offered to take the oath for her, but Thora refused. It was her sword that struck the glass-caster, not his.

Inge was hard-pressed not to cry when her daughter walked up to Ragnovald and put her hand on the oath-ring and swore all she said was true and not base, without flaw. He looked at the maid before him, and Inge saw he wanted to smile, but dare not.

"I am bound to ask you, Thora: are you the night hag, the evening rider who travels on wolves at twilight?"

"Nay, I am not."

Her voice was strong. A good sign. Inge forced herself to breathe slowly and deeply. Ragnovald told the maid to sit.

Two witnesses brought from Birka told what happened at the glass-caster's. Olaf and Gunnar, both men without reproach and fair-spoken, had offered to be co-swearers for the maid. They talked of how she had won their hearts at the farmstead, how obedient she was to her adopted parents. Yet nothing of her skill at swordplay.

Ragnovald thanked them, and they sat. He called for witnesses to speak for the glass-caster. Inge looked about at idlers walking to and fro, flirting with the bondmaidens from her farmstead. None of the men appeared to be from Saxland.

Ragnovald called once again for witnesses. Though a small breeze ruffled the dull grass, Inge felt the sweat down her backbone. The witnesses from Birka had sworn to Karl that the glass-caster had no kin there. Yet in a week kin could come all the way from Saxland.

Inge let herself hope Thora's trial would soon be done. Ragnovald was readying himself to sit apart and think the matter over before he made his judgment.

"If there be no witnesses for the glass-caster -- " he said for the third and last time. "Ay, there is!" a rasping voice cried out.

Inge clutched her amulet against her chest. Who could it be? An enemy of Karl-Eirik's? One of their neighbors, jealous of their holdings? The crowd parted, and the witness came forth. A noise and tumult broke as all talked at once.

Inge's stomach turned queasy: the witness had gold spurs catching the sun, so his feet seemed to travel on streamers of gold. He was girt with gold, this king, and made a fine show.

"I will be the glass-caster's witness," he said.

Ragnovald hid his surprise, bowing. Thora looked curiously at this king. From Karl's tight jaw Inge knew he liked it not at all. She held fast to his hand.

"The glass-caster was a skilled craftsman," the king said, "a guest of Sweden, protected by the Peace Bond on Swedish soil to be Peace-Holy. Yet he was killed. If he were alive he could assess whatsoever gold or silver he felt entitled to for his injury, thereby satisfying the offense."

"Ay," Ragnovald said. "It is so."

"How much would it be?" Inge asked Karl.

"A freeman's price is 120 ounces of silver. Gladly would we pay it."

"To offer money to the glass-caster's kin in Saxland would be a poor way of settling his death," the king said. "It would stain the honor of Sweden. He was a wealthy man himself."

The king raised his voice, triumphantly to Inge's ears. "His kin is entitled to revenge, thereby."

"You speak for the dead man?" Ragnovald asked, and Inge was pleased he was not afraid to stand up to the king.

"Ja. I am his witness. The honor of our country I am sworn to uphold, and I cannot let this deed go unpunished. Else each would take the law into his--or her--own hand."

Inge knew he had touched on one of the deepest fears in the people at the trial. In the back of the neighbors' minds was the worry of revenge for death caused by the sword. They might be judged as Thora would be judged today. Wrongful deaths must be atoned for, one way or another. If not, it could lead to battle, farm against farm. The king leaned toward Ragnovald.

"There are Ordeals," the king said, "Ordeals Odin has given us to settle an account. Little-used, but still..."

"None have said the maid is not guilty of the sword thrust," Ragnovald interrupted.

"Ay," the King said. "Yet who knows what the maid felt? Was it her intent to harm him?"

The crowd drew in its breath as one person, and Inge clenched her teeth together, so she would not cry out. The Ordeals, set forth by Odin, were indeed one way to settle an accounting. The Ordeals were in truth little used, but they were legal, and one of the worst was the Ordeal of boiling water: Thora would put her hands in a cauldron of bubbling water over the fire and bring forth three stones from the bottom. If her hands were not scalded, she would be judged innocent.

Inge cast her mind over Things she had attended since she was a child. If only she had listened more to the Lawspeaker and less to the young men as they stood together, laughing. What did her mother and father talk about on the way home, as she lay in the wagon, half-asleep? Was there not something to help Thora?

Inge would not let herself think of the worst Ordeal--walking on red-hot Ploughshares, and if Thora's feet were unburnt...

The king's smile was greasy. "Yet I could not sleep if I put the maid to an Ordeal. She is not yet full-grown, and we must search for other ways to look for an accounting."

The crowd leaned forward with relief. It seemed to Inge every blade of grass on the hillside was waiting. The king stroked his beard.

"If he--or she--attacks another in his house it is called nithing-slaying or coward-slaying, is this not so?" the king asked. Ragnovald nodded agreement.

Inge felt a pinch of hope. The glass-caster had not been in his house when Thora struck him. He was in his shop.

"It was the only house the glass-caster had in Birka," the king said. "He slept on a bed of straw and cooked over his working fire. All his clothes and goods were within the hut. He was a wealthy man, and some would ask why he lived in the shop."

Ay, he was in his house, Inge thought, her heart hurting. The king paused, and all hung on his words, waiting.

"His craft was so beloved by him, he dared not leave his pieces of glassware."

Like the one that broke, Inge thought. Ah, if Karl had only told her glass breaks. Yet she, too, was guilty: she had agreed to buy Thora a sword.

"There are two causes for Outlawry," the king said.

The crowd buzzed at the word, turning to each other, but Inge sat mute, her body numb.

None could miss the import of the king's words. "The first cause is if the fine cannot be paid, and we have seen no kin of the glass-caster come forth to receive wergild. The second cause..."

He looked up at Karl-Eirik, and Inge held herself from pulling forth Karl's sword and stabbing the king.

"The second cause is secret or unprovoked murder!"

The Thing exploded with noise. Murder! The king had linked Thora's deed with murder, and it would not be easily undone. She looked stricken. Inge did not know she could hate any man so much. The sun glinted from the king's golden visor, blinding her.

Tears stung her eyes, and she blinked them away. Murder must be matched by the worst punishment--Outlawry. An outlaw from Sweden was known as a Wolf in the Sanctuary.

There was a second name she hated more: Forest Man. Denied any contact with human-kind, killed by any, man or beast, with no penalty...

Karl put his arm about her and pulled her to him. She ached to put her arms around Thora, who had recovered and stared straight ahead, unblinking, letting no one guess her thoughts.

The king spoke to Ragnovald. "No one can be outlawed for more than twenty years--is it not so?"

Twenty years! Inge trembled. The maid would be prey to every man. And how could she speak any tongue but Swedish? She would die by the sword, one way or another.

"Ragnovald," the king continued in his oily voice, "this is the law is it not: if wergild cannot be paid for a slaying--and no kin has come forth--the kinsmen of the slayer must send him--or her--out of Sweden for a committed murder."

Inge gasped. She and Karl-Eirik must send their new-found daughter to Outlawry, themselves. Thora was as good as dead, not for murder-- but for a foolish, headstrong deed. Frantically Inge cast her mind back over other Things. Thora played with her fingers, always the sign she felt dread.

"Is there anyone to answer the witness for the glass-caster?" Ragnovald asked.

The crowd was so quiet Inge thought she heard stirrings beneath the spring sod. She looked at her daughter. She loved her as none other. Freya had given Thora to her as a gift, and no king would take her away.

Inge stood. "Ay, there is a witness."

She felt Karl's surprise, and Thora's, and heard the crowd mutter. The maid turned to stare at her. The king's head jerked up, and he too stared. Who would dare to question him?

She would dare.

"Come forth, Ingeborg Andersdottir," Ragnovald said.

The king spat and walked toward his men, grinning, hiding his anger. The jagged scar on his cheek was a red slash.

She walked to Ragnovald. She knew she looked comely in her purple dress and white overgarment and linen headdress. She wore the brooches and neckrings of a woman of substance.

Help me, Freya, she prayed, pressing her knees together to stop their shaking beneath her long dress. She turned her head from the king, from Thora, from Karl-Eirik and his men and all their neighbors, and spoke alone to Ragnovald.

"Our daughter Thora did not kill the glass-caster. I am a leechwoman, skilled in healing herbs, and I have tended many wounds. He was not dead when we left him. Thora and I bound up his wound, and it was slight. He died not from the sword thrust."

She took heart from the calm face of the old Lawspeaker. He had heard many speak in defense. From him she would get a fair hearing.

"Our Thora was quick-tempered, and rash, but she acted out of love, nothing else," Inge said. "Who could fault a maid for defending her mother? Though she has lived but fourteen winters, and been at Breidal but a week, Thora knows the sacred bond of kin. Never to be broken.

"The attack on the glass-caster was not murder by intent. Thereby it falls under the law as a Simple Slaying."

She heard the crowd murmur over this twist in the law she brought forth. The hated king would not speak of it, and Ragnovald could not. The old Lawspeaker looked hard at her.

"We will look at the deed to see if Simple Slaying holds, Ingeborg Andersdottir. Firstly, was the swordthrust done in secret?"

"Nay, the room was crowded with others," she said and the two witnesses from Birka nodded.

"Secondly, Ingeborg, was it done as a plighted skill between the two--Thora and the glass-caster?"

"Nay. He had no sword to parry the blow. It was not done as a plighted skill."

Inge saw the skin crinkle around Ragnovald's eyes. If he was pleased at this turn in the trial, he could not say it.

"Are any wont to answer Ingeborg Andersdottir?" he asked.

Let the king answer, she thought. The people were thinking of the sacred bond of kin, and how it was the mother who brought forth the idea of Simple Slaying. Though they stayed in their seats, Inge felt the crowd turn away from the king. Perchance it was the maid's innocent face, or the king's desire for revenge was too strong--or maybe they balanced each other out.

Inge felt weak and knew she must sit or fall. As she walked to the bench, she thought she had done all she could for her beloved daughter. Who knew if it was enough? Karl-Eirik slid close to her and held her. Thora had stopped twisting her fingers.

"Ingeborg, how knew you of this twist in the law?" Karl asked.

It was an effort for her to speak. She had never been so tired.

"Karl, I knew not what I would say until I stood before Ragnovald."

Freya had smiled upon her once again--it was the only reason she knew. She must drink many health cups to Freya. For Inge could not say how the words came to her. Unless, in truth, one night when she was half-asleep and half-awake in the wagon going home, her mother and father had spoken of a Simple Slaying. Or she had heard a Lawspeaker say it while she was flirting with a boy from another farmstead, and the words had stayed hidden till now.

Ragnovald spoke. "If none talk further for or against Thora Karlsdottir, I will make my decision. The deed will be judged as a Simple Slaying."

He walked to the Law Rock, looking out at the fjord. Inge thought waiting could be the worst of Ordeals. Her father's herdsman, Gorm, had been outlawed for a year for stealing four sheep. How many years would be taken from Thora for a sword thrust that ended in the death of a foreigner?

Karl's men stood close about them. Einar smiled at her, though he knew she was beyond cheer. To live through this waiting, she must be as stone. Thora looked neither right nor left, but straight on. Whence came the maid's strength to bear the trial without tears? From having thrall's blood, yet treated by her father as highborn?

From being one of Thor's Chosen?

Ragnovald turned from the Law Rock and called Thora to him. She walked slowly, her back straight, her head high, though Inge saw her pulse going too fast in her neck. Inge's own heart pounded so hard she thought all must hear. Karl held her tightly.

"Thora Karlsdottir," Ragnovald said, "you are not yet a woman, though you are near-grown. I thereby sentence you not to full Outlawry, but to Lesser Outlawry."

Inge's eyes teared, and she leaned into Karl, too weak to sit upright.

"Thora Karlsdottir, you must leave Sweden," Ragnovald said, "for a time of six months, to return at Harvest. In the eye of the Law you are yet a child, and I outlaw you in the care of your father."

Inge ached to hold her. It could have been worse.

"By law," Ragnovald said, "I can but set forth the length of Outlawry. Wherein you go must be set by our king."

Inge felt a jolt to her stomach when the king walked to face Ragnovald. His face was dark with anger, and the scar on his cheek twitched. His gold helmet no longer gleamed. The judgment of murder he tried to bring forth had failed. His voice was harsh.

"It is not a gladsome task for a king to set forth a place for Lesser Outlawry, but a king cannot choose his duties. The sea lanes are too danger-filled for a young maid to sail west. I will not send her towards England or Skotland. Nay, not to Iceland."

Did he know Karl-Eirik was heart-set on going to Iceland, Inge wondered. Ja, the king knew. Karl was oft a fool when talking at an ale house, where any king's man could be listening. The king spared a half smile for the maid.

"There is a land where a young girl's sword can be of full use. She and her father are to be outlawed to the land called Kievan Rus, our Gardariki. And thence to sail down the rivers to Miklagard, the city the Greeks call Constantinople, below the Varangian Sea."

The crowd murmured, but Inge scarcely heard them. She felt a great weight lift off her chest. Her daughter would live. Exiled in the care of her father to Kievan Rus, not to Iceland where Karl chose to go, but where the king would send him.

But Thora would live.

Ragnovald closed the assembly with the final ceremony and left. The king walked off the hill in the opposite way. Inge saw him wrench his helmet down over his face, so none of the people would bother him, and plead for the maid.

Thora came to Karl and Inge, and both held her in their arms. Inge could not let her go. Did the maid know the Ordeals she had been spared? Or the ordeal of Full Outlawry Ragnovald had chosen not to give her?

Inge sat with Karl, shaking hands with their neighbors and their servants and Einar and Karl's men, everyone talking at once. Granni stood nearby, talking with Finnvid, while Thora listened. Inge hoped Granni had learned compassion, as well as respect for the law, today.

Granni left down the hill without a backward glance for Thora. Inge thought if the two had met otherwise, they might become fond of each other. He was a handsome lad, sturdy, with ears low on his head--the sign of a born lawspeaker, one who weighed everything before making an opinion.

But a maid who served a term for Lesser Outlawry would not be apt company to walk at solarfall with a man who would one day take Ragnovald's place. The breeze brought the sour-sweet smell of freshly-turned loam to Inge, and she breathed in the earth's healing power.

A term of Lesser Outlawry was not death. Thora would live.

VII

Inge looked at the casks and barrels and sacks, the coils of rope, all neatly wedged atop the floorboards. The Seafarer would not be such a bad home for Thora for six months. Karl caressed his beloved mast, the rigging. She thought how peaceful the boat was at night, tied up to the tree trunks ashore, gently rocking. She hung on to the gunwales. We need to be alone to talk, Karl had said.

This would be a different journey, with a maid aboard. Inge told him to show Thora much love. To hide her beneath the half-deck if fighting broke out. To watch for men who would have an eye for a fair young maid. To mix half honey, half vinegar from the casks if she got seasick.

And now she watched him fretting the stays. It was unlike him to fret.

"Karl, if a boat is fair to look upon, if the lines have a pleasing curve, like The Seafarer, is it easier to sail?"

"Ay."

He took her in his arms. "Inge, you women have mysteries men cannot hope to understand. When we were raising our three sons I never thought how a woman's body is somehow changed by the turnings of the moon. But now..."

She thought how Karl knew everything about building and keeping boats sound, how to manage his crewmen, to give the last ounce of strength. But to a man with no sisters, women could well be a mystery. She said she would give Thora some of the moss women use at their moon times and tell her what to do with it.

When she first told him of Thora's early years, they agreed she never had a mother, only the bitch who put her out for exposure. And now, when she had a loving mother, she must leave her behind. Inge sighed, and said they were lucky it was only six months, though she and Thora both grieved over her sentence. He tightened his arms about her.

"Inge, it is not for Thora alone I want you to go with us."

"Go with you? Go with you to Kievan Rus?"

Her body went numb, and she knew it for shock. Go to Kievan Rus? It was a fool's thought. She stepped back, staring at him.

"In truth, Karl, you have elvist. Never in twenty years have you thought to take me a- viking."

He told her he could not when she had three sons to raise, but now she was free. She stood back and faced him.

"Free! Karl, you have never been home in spring and summer. You know naught of how much work there is to do."

She told him she was up at dawn every day, to deal with problems such as the ones that must be settled on the morrow: Hil was again with child, and only the farmstead's Mistress could see that the father paid for the foster-mothering. The thrall Angrim wanted to earn his freehold, working by torchlight after even, and she must choose which land he would plant. She alone could decide which herds-women would go to the summer pastures. As she spoke, her heart ached. Thora would not go with her this year.

He stroked her hair, calming her. "Enough, Inge. No one can take your place, but Einar has agreed to stay on."

She pushed his hands off her.

"Einar? You asked him?"

Karl stroked his beard. "He offered. Einar knows Thora needs a loving moth-er, more than Breidal needs a Mistress to manage it."

It was true all she knew of managing crops and thralls she had learned from Einar, but even if he stayed on, there would be enough work for both of them while Karl was away.

He unrolled his leather sleeping bag, spread it on the dew-wet deck and pat-ted it. She smelled old sweat.

"Sit with me, Inge, and I will tell you what it is like to be out on the sea at even, when there is no land to be seen, not even by Ingvar from the top of the mast."

She sat, but apart, while he talked of how the waters quiet when the sun goes to its home in the sea, casting pinks and purples across the sky in colors found nowhere else. Then there is nothing we want, he said, nothing gold can buy. "We dip your barley bread in the water to soften it and eat slowly, our small boat a part of the great waters that are all one. A wave sets the boat moving to and fro, but who can say where it comes from? At length, the sun sinks to its home in the crack between water and sky, taking the colors with it."

Inge sat, bemused. Was this the same man who gave short, hard commands to both crew and thralls?

"Karl, are you frightened when the dark descends, and you are all alone on the great waters?"

We are never alone, he told her, but part of the whole--part of both earth and sky. He pointed up at the first stars. An Arab they met in Danmork showed them how to make animals out of them--now the crewmen saw dogs, dragons, a Viking with a belt of stars.

He pointed to another part of the sky. Look you, how those three stars turn down. It is the bear's tail. The four stars below, one at each corner, are the bear's ass.

Inge giggled. "A square ass, like a bear."

"Ja. All the star-pictures go home, but the Great Bear forever circles the Guiding Star I use to steer by. And, Inge, most wondrous of all: some nights we see stars fall into the water all around us--they streak across the sky on all sides."

"Nay! Karl, you must put Thora under the floorboards! A star could fall on her!"

"I think not. I would fain you see the nights of falling stars. Our trees at Breidal grow so thick and high, they shut out the sky. Your life is a round of never-ending tasks, and you have no time to spare for star-gazing. But aboard ship you would have long hours to sit and talk with Thora. There are days when the sea is so calm the men play hneftafl, with the board on their knees."

She and Karl had played at hneftafl, when they had long hours of leisure, before they took on the farmstead and began a family. Could she still beat him at the game as when they courted?

"Karl, like all seamen, your crewmen think women bring no luck aboard. Thora you must take, but--"

"To Hel with my men. They are freeborn. I have trained them well, and they could hire on to sail with any captain. But I think they will stay with me. They are eager to see this new land of Gardariki with a golden tree, and golden birds who sing, each in his own voice. You are a weaver, Inge. In Miklagard, I hear, there are many hundreds of colors in silk. I am wont for you to see them."

"Thora can bring some."

"But a few. There is little room for silk on the boat."

He tilted her chin so she had to look into his eyes.

"Ingeborg, all this talk is circling around your real reason for not wanting to go: you fear the fool witch-seer's foretelling."

She looked off at the white birch dappled by moonlight. He had always been able to see into her heart. She was wrong to try to evade him.

Karl had grown up on the coast. His family were all sailors and fishermen. They believed in building lithe ships, in keeping them in good repair, the nets mended. A witch-seer was for sport and gaming.

Yet her mother and her mother's mother followed the old ways, and often invited a hag for foretelling. One who visited her father's hall told Inge she would marry a great man and live in a great hall and wear many gold neckrings, and have four children. She and Karl had always laughed at this, when they had but three sons.

Now their children numbered four. Inge shivered.

She told him she was the one who chose the runes. The first, ur, was the rune of passage, perchance a passage into darkness. Karl reminded her it is never dark forever: light always follows. When she chose the second rune, reidh, it was the rune of a journey, part of which could not be shared. To this Karl had a ready answer.

"You do not share all with me, Ingeborg. You have secrets I will never know. In truth, the third rune, wyrd, the unknowable, is what frightens you, the most. You fear it portends death, ay?"

She stared at him. The witch-seer and I whispered, she said, so I would not frighten the servants. How did he hear?

He asked why she thought the gods gave us two ears, one set apart from the other, if not so captains could listen to two crewmen talk at the same time. At the tiller, he listened to Finnvid with one ear, Anders the other. In their hall he had heard Lars with one ear, Inge and the hag with the other.

She scrunched close to him. For all his hard-set ways, Karl knew how to gentle her.

"Inge, death is always close by. I have looked it in the face in battle. As a leech-woman, you have seen it. We must hold fast to life, and not fear an old woman's foretelling."

She got up and walked to the prow-post, leaning her cheek against the Gripping Beast. Here in the dark it was not frightening, but only another pattern, made in wood, not wool.

He told her he would ask Gunnar to carve a new prow-post with her likeness, and she said her face could scare the land spirits on shore, when he beached the boat. Karl laughed.

"Inge, you are possessed by the greatest of fears--fear of the unknown, ja? I have never met a sailor without this fear, but one they try to hide. You are a sea captain's wife. Has none of my courage entered you with my Come?"

She giggled. Karl had always known the power of charm.

"Ingeborg, on this journey I need you."

She felt the runes carved in the mast: fe, wealth. Tyr, success in battle. How male The Seafarer was! With her finger she traced the rune, bjarkan, the birch goddess, the breasts of the earth mother. In truth, she had no desire to be cramped into this little boat with eight unwashed men and Karl's little horse, Volnir, that always traveled with them. Seamen and Viking horses were used to close quarters, but she was a countrywoman, used to space and freedom. She was not a sailor. Beneath her the deck rose and fell, and she held the mast tighter.

"Karl-Eirik, I walk a hundred times a day, from the hearth-fire to the dairy to the ale house to the Homefield. Where would I walk on the ship, with all your gear?"

If only all my problems could be solved this easily, he told her. Every night we are at sea I will hold your hand, and you can walk atop the gunwales. And when we get to the rivers of Kievan Rus, we can walk at night on shore.

She pondered. Would it be safe in this strange land? Karl knew no more about it than she did. She shook her head, turning away. She looked back at the carved horseheads of her store houses above the trees. She loved managing Breidal, she was good at it, never wanted to do anything else. She was proud their land and cattle had increased fourfold.

But on Karl's boat she would manage nothing. She would be but a passenger, under Karl's complete control. He would still be her lover, her husband, but he would be the captain, and all aboard must obey a captain. He stood behind her, not touching.

"Ingeborg, how think you Thora will learn the healing ways if her mother is not there to teach her? I know not one plant from another. And my crewmen are worse. When we walk on the shore at night we can all look for plants."

"They may not be the same."

"We will not know until we look, ay?"

"I can wait until Thora returns. The plants will not stop growing in Sweden, Karl. Next spring-- "

"Next spring the maid will be fifteen--old enough to marry."

He did not need to say it. A maid so comely would have many suitors, and a bridegroom might take her anywhere.

He wrapped her in his arms, and she felt his strength.

"Ingeborg, I have tried to tell you why I need you on this journey. Yet nothing is certain, and I cannot promise you anything in an unknown land. The choice must be your own."

Inge touched her amulet of Freya. Her fears, her dislike of being cramped on a small boat, even her loathing of being under the command of another--even if it was Karl-- meant naught as much as the bone-truth: nothing in life was certain, on land or sea. Six months on The Seafarer might be the only time she had with Thora, the only chance to train the maid in the healing herbs and charms, to get her to forsake the sword.

She listened to the hiss of the fjord flowing up and back, up and back through the water weed along the shore. A great owl hooted from his perch on the summer oak. She had heard owls all her life. She watched a whitetail bound to the water, bend its long neck and drink. She had seen whitetails since she was a child. They would be here, or others like them, long after she was beneath the mould.

"Husband, I make choices without much brooding. I will go with you to Kievan Rus."

She heard his quick breath and a mumbling, as he thanked Odin. He clasped her around the knees, lifting her for a long kiss. When he spoke his voice was thick. He told her he would not ask why she agreed to go. After they were at sea a few days, then she might tell him.

She sat down on the leather bag and began undoing the brooch of her cloak, damp from the night dew.

"Karl, we have not sailed together in a boat for six months, with eight men and a horse and a maid. If you are quarrelsome I will throw you to the sea draug, and you can do the same with me."

"We have always been lovers, Inge. You come to the fields or the boatshed to bring ale or water, though you could let a serving woman do it. After even we are never apart, in or out of our bed closet."

She looked up at the moon, a gold bracteate climbing the sky, a pendant to wear about the neck on an unseen chain. She asked him if he had ever seen the moonrise from his deck. He told her by the time the moon came up, he was often asleep. Now it was getting late. They should go back.

She yawned and stretched, untying her plait.

"First, Karl, we must learn how to love each other in a leather sleeping bag."

She wriggled out of her cloak, kicked off her boots, pulled her night shift over her head and gave them to him, as she slid into the bag, giggling.

"Ooh. Karl, the leather is cold, but the rough feel is pleasing."

She watched him undo his cloak and lift off his night shift and pull off his boots. A man could undress himself, if he was in a hurry.

"Husband, you look most fair to me in moonlight. I am fain to let us warm each other." He slipped into the bag, and she pressed her breasts against him, stroking his sex until it swelled to the size she liked. Their bodies were so close they could but breathe together. There was no room to turn, no way for Karl to sheathe his sword in her. She squeezed his sex, pulling gently to and fro, and he groaned with pleasure, opening his mouth for her tongue. In their close quarters, he put his hand over hers and with his fingers, stroked her softness as far up as he could reach.

There was no way to turn, but their bodies would not let them be still, and so they rubbed each other faster. His seed sprayed into her hand, and she felt the tickle begin in her belly and spread up and out her fingertips. She twisted, unwilling to end the course of the sweet flowing. The tops of her thighs tingled.

When it stopped, she lifted Karl's fingers to her face, smelling him, tasting the sour-sweet Come, and she thought she never got too much of a man. For the first time she would not have to give this one up for six months.

Not all days aboard The Seafarer would be smooth enough to play hneftafl, or the nights clear enough to watch the stars move in their arcs. Storms happened at sea, as on land. Karl's men would turn fretful, if they were too long at the oar. Thora must sit still for long hours. And the Rus? Would they greet the Swedes with a welcoming cup or drawn swords? Once they left Swedish soil, they would no longer be Peace-Holy, but must abide by the law of others.

Only within the leather bag could they forget the hardships, and the dangers, ahead.

VIII

Inge looked past the line of rowers to the shields notched in place on the shield rack. At her side Karl's hand was light on the tiller of The Seafarer. He and his crew were never meant to be land-locked. They were truly happy only when they trod the ships' boards. As for herself, she would always be a countrywoman. She looked hard at the gable ends framed by the reddening maple flowers and stifled a shiver. Would she see ever them again? She fingered her amulet of Freya.

She must not be downcast before the journey toward the island of Gotland, the Eye of the Baltic, began. The choices she had made since adopting her daughter all had led to this moment, rowing down their fjord to the open sea. Thora was not plagued by fear of what lay ahead, but kept her eyes facing forward, from where she sat at the bow.

Ah, they were as prepared as they could be. She and Thora had crammed every sack and cask with grot and barley rounds and dried fish and pork. The casks of ale and mead and water could not hold another drop. And if the Rus were unfriendly, the sea chests were filled with sharpened swords and battleaxes, with spears and chainmail and helmets.

Inge moved to sit upon the chest with Thora's sword inside. If an enemy appeared, she would shove Thora beneath the floorboards and hide her, no matter what Karl or Thora wanted. The one time the maid used her sword had been a near disaster. There would not be another.

One thing more important than food or weapons lay in Karl's head: a map of their journey. When Karl went to say Farvell for six months to his mother Halldis in Uppland, he found she had invited two men who had traveled to Gardariki in their youth. Karl had questioned them and listened while they drew a map in sand.

He returned and drew it in mud, for his crew and wife and daughter. The route seemed as straightforward as when Lars talked about it--across the Baltic to the island of Gotland, on to the rivers of Kievan Rus, down the Varangian Sea to Miklagard.

Straightforward except for two parts Lars did not tell them. When Anders pointed to a place where the two rivers did not meet, Karl told them here The Seafarer would be portaged, dragged overland to get from one river to another. How could eight men and two women pull a heavily laden boat, Inge asked, and Karl had reassured her. They would find a way. They had faced troublesome times before.

The second part concerned seven wiggling lines Karl drew on the Dnieper River--seven waterfalls, one after the other. These they would ride down. Both boat and crew--though not his wife, he teased--were used to rough waters. The men laughed, but she could not hide her fear.

It all looked so simple in the mud. Sailing is simple, Karl told her, if you follow the Rules of the Sea, and had he not followed them all his life, with benefit to them all? Ay, she agreed. Gunnar asked if they would travel with Lars's Golden-breast, but Karl said Lars had had too big a start. For Lars there had been no trip to Birka, no trial to delay a crew.

Now from her place on the boat she saw the housefolk and fieldfolk on shore, waving Farvell, and she waved back. They liked working at Breidal, Geda had told her--broken tools were always repaired, the food stores lasted through the long winters. And their Mistress never beat them.

Einar called out to have a safe voyage. She could trust him to follow her instructions. Like all people with short noses, he was good at details and routine. He would remember to hang rowan flowers from the rafters of the byre, so the cows did not get milk-sickness. To tie a rope to the wagon on the way up to the summer pasture, so the wolves would not outrun the cows. To make sure everyone ate Midsummer dew at dawn, when the strength was greatest. Ah, she wished she had Midsummer buns made from the dew now. It was a sure cure for worry.

The silver chain hanging from the oval brooch on her green overdress was too light. Dangling from the end were the tools of her trade--a knife, scissors, bone needles in a leather pouch, but not the usual keys to her storehouse. Einar had them now.

* * *

She took heart when she heard a lowing from the mast. Not only Karl's small horse Volnir was tethered to it, but her beloved bell-cow, Brattahlid, though she had not been eager to board. Bratta did not want to leave Breidal until Inge sang the plaintive herding call, "Follow Me" from the ship. Herding calls needed mountains and bogs and meadows, not a wooden ship, but Bratta had cocked an ear to her Mistress's song, put her hooves up on the gunwale, took a mighty leap, and landed on deck.

Inge watched the skittish horse and cow, each no bigger than a sheep. They must get used to being together, as Bratta's mistress must get used to the up-and-down and sidewise motion of the boat, both at the same time. Inge felt her stomach turn queasy, afflicted with the countrywoman's curse, one a sailor never knew. Bratta chewed her cud crosswise fast, and Volnir stamped his mighty hooves, mighty for such a small horse. She moved to stroke Bratta, and the cow's bristly hairs beneath her fingers calmed her thoughts, if not her stomach.

"Mistress, you have a way with beasts," Anders said.

"And men," Finnvid said softly, so Karl would not hear.

Finnvid had wanted to grapple the bellcow aboard, but when Inge protested, furious, Karl let her use the herding call. She had never been on a crowded boat with eight men and a willful child, and she must try to get along with all, Finnvid included.

A gust from the Baltic lifted her headdress, and The Seafarer moved out to sea, this time Karl steering east through the skerries. The lookout, Ingvar, climbed the mast feet first and she smiled, remembering how the agile man flipped through the air up one side of her hall and down the other, amusing guests.

"Mistress, never since I came to Breidal have I seen you sit, doing naught," Anders teased her, pulling on a stay.

She laughed, and agreed. She looked at the men at their tasks and thought that each knew what to do without orders from Karl. Never before had she bothered to think how each was different from the other, though all had hands scarred from battle. Did the most fierce warrior have the most scars? Or the luckiest one? Karl-Eirik's victory-luck was one reason they followed him wheresoever he sailed, that she knew.

She closed her eyes to try and forget her churning stomach. She would know these crewmen in the dark if she felt their beards. Per's, as wispy as his hair. Gunnar's, a luxurious growth that lay upon his chest, so heavy the wind did not lift it. And Finnvid? Scratchy, a dark dirty-blond, while the others were soft, a pleasing shade. Moustaches and beards were necessary to these men, for it was their outward show of virility.

Now they worked hard, lifting and pulling the stays, making the gear as compact as they could. At the farmstead they dallied about their chores, flirting with the bondmaids, until she sent them on the hunt. They could not plow a straight furrow, and always forgot to pour ale in the trench at Planting to please the god Frey, though they were good at drinking it.

But she never saw them waste it, as Finnvid was doing.

"Finnvid, stop! That is my best ale you are pouring into the sea!"

"Mistress, I am only sacrificing to the gods for a safe journey. And I will offer some of your fine dried pork as well."

"You must use my best meat and drink?"

"Ay. The gods would not like tainted meat, or ale that tasted of wood."

Thora turned and yelled, "My mother would never give us tainted meat, or bad ale."

Inge told her to sit back down and hush, though in truth it was pleasing to have a daughter to defend her. On such a small boat everybody's voice could be heard, despite the creakings and groanings of the ship. She heard a new sound from shore--a familiar, long, sad note. It did not help her stomach.

"The bedamned bear-lur," Finnvid said, twisting the swivel closed on the ale cask.

A lonesome call, Inge thought, remembering how sore her cheekbones were from blowing it at the summer pasture to scare the bears away. She felt the dull ache of homesickness. Sven began piping the flute Gunnar carved from the long bone of her sheep. He played a song they all knew, though this was the first time they had left Breidal with women's voices joining in song:

Who can sail without any wind? Who can row without oars? Who can part from their dearest friend Without shedding bitter tears? I can sail without any wind I can row without oars But not part from my dearest friend Without shedding bitter tears.

They all looked back at the birches, now a white blur. The last trace of home. Inge thought these northmen were hard-cast, yet within them was a tender spot that could be moved by a woman. From onshore the bear-lur answered the flute and the two sounds were like them all-- part in Sweden, part on the boat traveling to a new land they knew not at all.

They sailed past the Egg Rock, and the men teased Anders about the time he tried to steal some, and the seabirds pecked his head until he came down, empty-handed. Inge told him she and Einar had taken one of her hen's eggs and made a hole in the bottom of the shell so a ship would not be holed and sunk. Though it was not said, all knew which ship she meant.

Thora sat with her, twisting a strand of hair forward. Since the trial the maid had grown beyond playing with her fingers, but when she was nervous, as now, she played with her hair. Thora needed to talk, and Inge waited.

"Modir, my Outlawry is thine. I know you would rather be at Breidal, waiting for Skulda to birth her piglets."

"Ay, I would, though I like sitting here with you. I will tell you a secret, Thora. Each time I lay in the birthing straw, I asked Freya to send a daughter, and each time she sent a son. And now I have my daughter."

Inge hugged her and talked softly of Thora's guilt, and how both mother and father had a part in it. As a leechwoman she had judged the glass-caster's wound to be well-tended, and it was, but if there was a sign his heart was frail, she had missed it. Perchance if Karl-Eirik had not bought Thora her sword--but they must leave their mistakes behind and enjoy the voyage. Thora seemed soothed. Inge's heart ached for the maid and her burden of guilt.

Inge thought she must take her own advice and enjoy the journey. She sent a deep calming breath to her lurching stomach and watched how the men used the rhythm of work and rest to their advantage. When they opened a water cask, each man took his time drinking, looking off to the horizon for a broad view, away from the small chores that must be done over and over. Each man handed on the cask to the next. A small thing, but pleasing.

The sea was smooth, and Olaf and Anders took out the hneftafl game board and set it on their knees, while everyone stood around jesting. From above, Inge saw Olaf's bald, freckled pate turn red from excitement. When Anders lost to him, Finnvid told him that when he was as old as Olaf and had played as many games, he would be more skilled.

"Skill has little to do with throwing the die," Inge said.

Finnvid's jaw clenched. He told her he believed that skill has everything to do with throwing the die, but would she like to settle this dispute with a game?

Inge had not played for twenty years, but she sat down opposite him. Behind his back he held one piece of bone, one of antler, and she chose the antler. She would throw first.

They lined up their twelve pear-shaped pieces, and as they advanced toward the center of the game board Inge felt his tension. Finnvid needed to win. Or he needed to have her lose. Freya was with her, but her win was close, closer than she would have liked. When she told him they seemed evenly matched, he stalked to the bow.

Sitting down, Thora said, "Modir, I have never been allowed to touch a hneftafl piece. Will you teach me to play?"

Inge explained the game--"too well," she said, after Thora beat her with ease. Anders asked Thora if she was certain she had not played before.

"Nay. But I watched."

Though she did not like losing to someone who never touched a piece, Inge admitted to herself the maid had soaked up much at Gotardal. What a fine leechwoman Thora would make with her quick mind, her memory. Unafraid to chance a daring move. And when Thora gloated that the women played the men and beat them, Inge thought it might not be the last time the two women stood together against these men.

"And I beat you," Thora said. "Finnvid, would you like to play me?"

He did not answer. Working quickly, Sven stowed the game pieces and the board into a leather sack and put it behind the gear. Ay, they beat the men, he told her, but it mattered little who won or lost. Hneftafl was played for fun.

Triumphant, Thora looked at Finnvid. "But it is good to win."

"A fine day for sailing, Mistress," Gunnar said, hammering a chunk of seaweed to the mast. "If the seaweed swells, it will rain soon, but it is dry. You brought us weather luck."

Finnvid walked back from the bow, and said women and priests were known to bring bad luck aboard ship. Once, off Skotland, a priest was wont to travel back to Sweden with them, but Karl said nay. Olaf told him that they were lucky. In Uppsala there were women priests, and how would Finnvid like that?

Inge looked beyond the quarreling men and saw only blue-green water without end--not even a strand of waterweed. Her throat burned with unspent tears, and she thought homesickness did not help a queasy stomach. She pulled her wadmal cloak tighter.

"Mistress, if you look straight at the horizon you will feel better," Sven said. "Before you know it you will be used to the rolling of the ship. It is hard to be sick and homesick, both. I too get homesick."

"For your wife, Mila?"

"And the goats. For a wedding gift you gave us a sack of barley seed. We planted it and sold the grain to Anselm, two farmsteads north of Breidal, and with the profit we bought two goats. Now we have ten."

Ten! What little she knew of these men's lives. Sven prattled on about how the goats ran free, but Mila had learned the goat tongue, and so called them for milking. She was learning to make goat cheese, and he had some in his sea chest. Would she like a taste? The ship hit a spate of rough sea, and Inge's stomach lurched. She said she knew he was trying to help, but please not to talk of food until they got home.

"Ingeborg, come to me," Karl called, and she sighed. Aboard ship a captain must be obeyed, no matter how queasy she felt. She patted Bratta and walked back, hanging on to the gunwales.

Karl pulled her to him, speaking into her ear. He told her he knew she was lonesome for Breidal, and she said ay, but she had agreed to come along. He reminded her he promised to hold her hand and let her walk upon the gunwales when she was restless, but he had something better. She must reach in his sea chest and bring him an earthen jar. She found it beneath the axes and chainmail and his helmet and Thorn-Biter, and brought it to him. Coarse, gray-brown, harsh to the feel, it was small enough to hold in her hand.

"Open it, my Ingeborg," he said, watching the sea and sky.

The stopper came up with a pop, and the sweet-sour smell she knew so well brought forth tears.

"Karl! Earth from Breidal!"

She kissed his face round in the Circle of Love, and told him that if they were home she would take him to their bed-closet and attack him. He laughed and told her to wait until solarfall when they were together in their leather bag in the bow. If she ran out of smell, they might find more dirt beneath the floorboards,

For an hour she held her earthen jar and sniffed, and then stoppered it to save the smell. Her stomach felt quieter.

From her seapouch she took a wad of black fleece and rubbed it on her face, and Thora's, though the maid wrinkled her nose at this smell. The oil would protect their skin from sunburn.

Karl and the others had well-tanned faces and never burned, but Finnvid was fair: he would burn and peel and burn and peel.

"Finnvid," she called, holding out the fleece.

He looked, and turned away. She should have known he would accept nothing from her. She rubbed a strand between thumb and finger, stretching it to test the strength. So was she stretched, between home and an unknown land.

From a niche behind a plump sack she pulled out her hand spindle and affixed the fleece, held the tool in the crook of her left arm, and set the spindle going so it dropped to the deck, twisting the fleece into yarn. Thora could not resist touching the distaff atop the spindle.

Inge told her Karl had carved the pattern of hearts and flowers, entwined, as his betrothal gift. One day a man will carve one for you, Inge teased. Ay, when this dread Outlawry was forgotten.

"Modir, may I try thy hand spindle? At my old farmstead I was not allowed to touch one."

Ay, the bitch would have seen to that, Inge thought, putting the spindle in Thora's arm and setting it going. The first try was lumpy, but she kept on, until she had a tangled mess. Inge told her it was somewhat like twisting grass for a snare, but still Thora could not do it.

"Swedish women no longer have the thighs they had when they rolled fleece on their legs to make yarn," Karl called from the stern, and Inge laughed. Her thighs were still thin, and both knew it. Hard-working Swedish women need not worry about heavy thighs.

She watched Anders push aside ship's gear and set up a three-legged cauldron. She was so curious she forgot her roiling stomach. He put rocks on the iron bottom, and Gunnar gave him kindling. Anders borrowed Karl-Eirik's strike-a-light, and lit a fire. Inge gasped when the flame leapt up. A fire--on a wooden boat in the middle of the Baltic! The two men coaxed the fire to burn, blowing, adding more kindling, shielding it from the wind with their bodies. Gunnar filled a small iron kettle with water and set it atop the flames.

"Now, Mistress, the water is boiling. You have mint among your healing herbs, ay?" Anders asked. "I need enough for a cup of tea for you."

She found the mint quickly. With a stick he lifted out the little kettle, and she dropped the leaves in, watching them swell.

"Anders, how can I thank you? Just the smell of mint makes my stomach feel better. Mint tea is always calming, but I knew no way of making it on board ship."

He grinned. "Gunnar made the three-legged cauldron small enough for Karl to agree to bring it, and we are wont for you to calm your belly with tea. We will make more as needed."

She kissed him, kissed Gunnar, kissed Bratta, blew a kiss to Karl, and told Anders she would drink the tea with pleasure. Each sip helped her stomach. Even her homesickness abated.

Holding onto the gunwales she walked back to Karl, and told him he was the best of husbands. Now that she felt better, she looked forward to Gardariki. What else did the men who had been there in their youth tell him?

Karl told her she would like the sheep. In Kievan Rus sheep were born black, but turn gray. And the ewes were highly sexual--they return to the rams four weeks after lambing. She wished she could have met the men at Halldis's hall. A leechwoman could tell whether men told the truth, or not.

"Inge, some parts of Gardariki have no snow. The men said in some places it is always summer."

She smiled up at him, letting him know she enjoyed his joke. No snow? There had never been a winter without snow. She watched Thora struggling, biting her lip. Inge was hard put not to remove the spindle.

She told Karl this sea was not like their farm. A field of oats was the same piece of ground from one summer to the next, but the sea was ever moving. Nay, the sea was as fixed as land, he said. She giggled and told him she loved him, though he had elvist. She pointed to the waves moving against the rocks, and he told her to look at the seabirds floating atop the water. So their boat floated, as a chip of wood, each drop ending where it began.

Talking to Karl eased her.

"The farmstead will be there when we return, Ingeborg. You are weary from too much work and not enough sleep. I should have asked the king to help you prepare our foodstuff."

Steer to Uppsala, and they would get him, she said, though he would be a poor seaman, weighed down by so much gold. Karl said he would do anything for her but sully his boat with the stink of the king. And as always, he sensed what troubled her.

"Inge, you fear the king's men will take it into their heads to rob our farmstead while we are away."

He smiled at her, though his eyes never stopped roaming from sea to sky and back. He told her their neighbors set a watch on their forest trail, the only way from Uppsala, except the sea.

"And, Ingeborg, I tell you one thing not known. Our king gets seasick, and never travels by sea."

The crew and Inge laughed. Breidal was safe, and she felt a great lightening.

"Now, Ingeborg, our farmstead is safe, but you do not quite trust me to sail to Estland, ay?"

She told him she trusted him, but he had never sailed east. He said that all the earth's waters were one, though at times they narrowed to rivers. The only change in sailing east is that the wind blows from a greater distance.

From the beitass Per said that clear weather was more important on the open sea than wind. Ah, why should she be fearful, Inge thought, when Karl had no fear in him? He had been born on the coast, and storms were his lullabies. Halldis had told her Karl was ever into mischief on land, but on water, he quieted.

A captain knew how to manage his crew, as she knew how to manage thralls. He called to Finnvid, sulking up at the bow. Karl told him to check their speed and he obeyed, heaving the long knotted rope over the side.

"Eight knots," Finnvid said, pulling it up.

Karl nodded, and Inge thought Karl did not care how fast they traveled, but he wanted to get Finnvid moving.

Per pushed the beitass so their sail caught the wind, and they skimmed across the Baltic. One of the hard parts of the journey for her would be the cramped space. But she could move around by standing and reaching behind the gear, so she did until she found her seapouch of herbs, and put the mint back. Just to touch them soothed her, each in a twist of wadmal, each tied with a birch withe in a different knot.

Anders hunkered down beside her, and for the first time she saw he had the heavy eyelids of a man of compassion. And the curved chin that went with a kind heart. "Mistress, we have had naught of your leechcraft when we went a-viking. How know you one healing herb from another?"

He surprised her. She knew no man who would ask.

"By their smell," she said, holding a packet to his nose. "This is willow bark, for fever, pain, and aching joints."

"Mistress, why are healers like you called leechwomen?"

"Do you know leeches?"

"Ay, they are worms, slimy and black. I like them not."

She laughed, glad Thora was close enough to hear. "I love them. As a leechwoman there is nothing better to make a sick man or woman bleed. The leech suctions itself to the skin with one end and bites into the body with the other."

She held out packs of herbs for him to sniff. "Anders, you wonder why I wish to make a sick man bleed, ay? Many, many times it helps to draw off the blood when the body is in danger--the heart or the lungs, the eyes, the teeth, a sore throat..."

"A sore throat, Mistress? How does the leech get to it?"

"On a stick, tied tightly so it does not slip. Or get swallowed."

"Swallowed! Ycch!" Thora said, sticking out her tongue.

Anders shuddered. "Mistress, promise me if I get a sore throat on this voyage you will use herbs, and not stick a wriggling leech in my mouth."

"I promise, Anders. I am glad you warned me. I have no leeches with me but after we dock in Kievan Rus I hope to buy some. And maggots too. Would you like to know how I use maggots?"

"Maggots? Nay, nay, Mistress, just the herbs."

"I think herbs are boring," Thora said, putting down the spindle. "They are so dead."

"Boring? Dead?" Inge asked. "Nay. They only look dead. They are alive with power. As alive as leeches and maggots."

Finnvid joined them. "And what do you like, Thora?"

Inge took a deep breath. He knew full well what she liked. Finnvid was getting back at both herself and Thora for his losses at hneftafl. The maid jumped up, facing them all. Inge looked at Karl, and both smiled. Thora was a born skald.

"Weapon oaths like this one are what I like:

"May that sword pierce thee which thou dost draw! May it sing only round thine own head."

"A sword pledge is a good thing for a man--or woman--to make. If a man breaks his word, the sword will turn against him in battle," Olaf said.

"Ay. The anger of the gods will be brought upon him," Gunnar said. "And if he does not accept the challenge to battle, his own sword will play him false."

"Thora, what other sword oaths do you know?" Anders asked, and Inge thought his interest in herbs was less than in the sword.

Before she could answer, the breeze freshened, and the men scattered to tend the rigging. Inge touched her amulet, thanking Freya for the diversion. Ah, if only she had an herb to tame a wildling daughter more skilled with the sword than the spindle, Inge thought, stowing the herbs. The two gray stones in the seapouch, used to crush dried roots and leaves into poultices and draughts, were more Thora's nature, than the feathery herbs.

As if to prove it, the maid yanked the fleece loose from the spindle, drew her sword from the sea chest and pulled it out of the scabbard. Carefully, she pushed the piece of fleece to the bottom, with the strands toward the hilt, and put the sword back in.

"Thora, why did you do that?" Inge asked.

"It is what Tyrkir taught me. The oil in the fleece protects the sword from rust."

She put back her sword, and now all the men asked Inge for a piece of fleece, but she refused. She would not again let her fleece be used with a weapon. Fleece was meant to be spun and woven. Every Swedish girl could spin, every one but her own.

She told Thora to put the spindle behind the gear. Ah, the maid's eyes were dull when she tried to spin, but how they had gleamed when she handled her sword. Weaning the maid from the weapon would be hard, but it must be done.

Bratta began stomping, ready to milk on land or sea. Inge asked Thora to milk, and the maid enjoyed it, giggling when Bratta lolled her big tongue back to lick her hand. Thora passed the bucket so all could drink, and Inge gave out rounds of barley bread and fish and ale, though she ate naught but a few swallows of milk. The others ate silently, their eyes on the vastness of the sea, the clouds as wispy as Thora's hair.

"Our first day has been fine. A good omen. I like this journey eastward, without the sun in our eyes, as when we sailed west," Per said.

* * *

At even, Inge sat down next to Thora. She must try to reach her daughter halfway. "Thora, tell me about swordplay. Why you love it."

The maid looked off to sea. "Nay. You can never understand."

"Try me. Tyrkir, the man who taught you, was he good?"

"Better than anyone here."

Finnvid scowled. Karl's men took pride in their swordcraft.

Inge ignored them. "Thora, tell me how it was, learning. Was it hard holding a heavy sword the right way? To know when to thrust, and when to parry?"

The gleam came into Thora's eyes.

"Nay, nay. At first Tyrkir had me sit on a stump and watch him with his men."

"And you asked to hold the sword?"

"Ay, and the men laughed. I was but a thrall and could not touch one, but Tyrkir had the smith cut down a sword sized for me, and it was all mine, and, Modir, the first time I held it I knew how to use it, and I never forgot--Tyrkir said I was born to the sword--and soon he had me use it with all the men, for none fights the same. But best I liked swordplay with him. He would lift me onto his black horse, and we would ride into a woods far from Gotardal and then we would practice together."

Inge felt a sudden, stupid jealousy for this Tyrkir. She chided herself. He was dead beneath the mould. Thora had learned love and sword craft at the same time, and if the maid had not learned love...Did Thora know Tyrkir was her father? Inge thought it best to wait till Thora told her, ay or nay.

"Modir, I liked Tyrkir. His wife, our mistress at Gotardal, made me sleep with the guests, but when Tyrkir was home I could sleep in the loft with the women. And she took my sword away."

How Thora hated the bitch, Inge thought, but said aloud, "Thora, none of our servants or thralls are asked to sleep with guests at Breidal."

"Ay. I know."

Inge looked at her nose turned down at the tip ever so slightly, like Karl's. The sign of shrewd minds. When Thora first arrived at Breidal, she would have asked the thralls what was expected of her.

She began a restless drumming on the gunwale, in time to the splash of the bow's wake. Inge was pleased by the way Thora kept rhythm. A skald needed music to make good poetry. Per picked up the beat and thumped the beitass. From up on the mast Ingvar tapped in time. Inge laughed, and picked up a cask and drummed.

Karl-Eirik struck the steering oar in rhythm. The desire to join in passed through the crew, each man taking part. Hrolf stamped the boards. Gunnar reached into his smith's chest and pulled out a saw. He bent it just so, gliding his fingers up and down, and the music was strange, but music.

"Ah, Gunnar," Inge said, "I would never have learned you can make music with your smith's tool if I did not travel with you aboard The Seafarer."

Lighthearted, they all drummed until the sun slid into the sea, and the wind dropped and dark gathered round the boat, and the moon rose like a shield. Ingvar tied the sail, and Finnvid threw over the kinnick anchors. The stars studded the sky, and Inge was reassured by finding the square-assed Bear. Karl lashed the tiller and carried the leather bag to the bow where husband and wife would sleep apart from the others, though with Thora, soon asleep, nearby.

Inge mixed a Cup of Roots for herself. Carrying the cup she walked forward, where Finnvid worked alone, tying down gear. The deck was so crowded she could not get past him. "I need to get to the bow, Finnvid."

"Ay, Mistress. You know about sheep. When I was young, before I went to sea, I had sheep myself. I learned if a ewe dies, and the lamb is put to suck at another mother, that lamb is never like the rest. It is always a little different, and the new mother feels it too. Have you seen this?"

Finnvid, you are a bastard, she thought, but did not say.

Instead she tightened her fingers around the cup and said, "Finnvid, it has been a long day for all of us, but I will not let you insult Thora or myself. She is not a sheep."

"Mistress! I did not say she was."

Inge stepped closer, but still he did not move. Hands could not hide what the heart felt, she knew, and she saw his fingers harden on the lines. It was but a step to pour the cup over his head.

Before she could tip it, Freya came to her aid. A wave slapped the boat, and it heeled. Inge caught a line to steady herself, but Finnvid tried to stand upright without holding on, and his boots slid into animal dung. Karl came up to them, laughing.

"Finnvid, you have found a surprise. Now you know what it is, you can clean it up."

Inge saw the men watching. A vein knotted in Finnvid's brow as he struggled with his anger.

"The cow is not mine, Karl-Eirik."

"Ay, but the shit on your boots is. You can get rid of the rest of it."

He and Inge crawled into the leather bag, and she said she hoped Finnvid did not walk in his sleep. She told Karl she felt safe in the middle of the Baltic--and she was getting used to the rocking boat, the sweet music of Bratta's rangle bell ringing as it did at home. On Midsummer Eve she would put the bell beneath Thora's pillow to make the maid's wish come true.

"Ingeborg, do not wait. Put it there now, so I do not hear the everlasting clang."

She looked up and saw the waxing moon over their mast. Kneading his tense shoulders, she told him this moon phase was a reassuring sign: now was the time for Karl to begin a new venture. Karl cared naught about moon signs. "Inge, did I ever tell you of the time we met a man with yellow skin in Danmork?"

Yellow skin? Why would he dye his face with onionskins? Unless he used dandelion or goldenrod--if she saw him she would know by the shade.

"Inge, this yellowskin called the meeting of men and women in bedplay Clouds and Rain. The clouds form in you, and the rain comes from me."

Karl knew much of the world, yet he never spoke this way to her at their farmstead. Being aboard ship freed his tongue. From far off she heard thunder, but she must not fear. Thora wore the amulet of Thor's hammer, Mjollnir, and he was the god of thunder, even now traveling across the sky. She saw lightning split the dark--but only heat lightning. They were safe.

Karl undid her plait and said, "The Yellowskin told us a man's rain can be made more plentiful by a woman."

"Ja? How?"

"The longer they stay lovesome without the rain falling, the more of a woman's mist from the clouds he will absorb. And Inge, the man must bring the woman to her sweet Come, for the mist of her clouds is strongest then."

Karl had never talked this way within their bed-closet. Was this the man she knew? She groped for his cock and put it high up between her damp thighs. He kissed her face round in the Circle of Love.

"Inge, the lips of your misting clouds are like the lips I kiss," he said, moving one hand to her breast. "And your breasts are like your ass, two honeyed mounds, together."

The husband she knew had been left behind in Sweden. She liked this new Karl. She wiggled as much as she could within the tight bag, aroused by his hardened sex, by the cold leather, by his words.

She felt his body holding back, and then he breathed once, hard, and shuddered: his rain was meeting her clouds. He had not been able to stay lovesome long without the rain falling.

Karl was never this way at home: always he was able to wait until both were roused.

"Inge", he murmured, and she put her finger on his lip.

"Shhh. It is all right. Sleep now, Husband."

She must be patient, and glad Karl had the relief of a quick Come, even if her belly was heavy with her unspent clouds. And though she was restless, she kissed his cheek. Once they were across the Baltic they would sleep ashore, aside the rivers, and he would not be so exhausted. Then she would make up for this one night. She looked at his careworn, sleeping face in the moonlight.

She had never loved him more.

Finnvid looked down at his breeches. One leg was splattered with cow pee.

"The bitch cow did it on purpose. Shit shit shit."

"Nay, Finnvid. She has not shat upon you, but only peed as you passed her," Per said from his place at the beitass. "You should learn the difference."

"Owww!" Finnvid howled, gripping his leg at the knee.

"Though no one would mistake the kick she gave you just now," Anders said. "Does it hurt?"

"Shut up, the lot of you," Finnvid yelled, moving out of range of the cow's leg to lean upon the gunwales.

"Finnvid, squeeze your pants, and put your leg up," Sven said. "Baltic winds are far-famed for drying cow pee. Is it not so?" he asked Olaf, as they worked together rearranging gear.

Inge and Thora bent together giggling from where they sat upon the sea chest. Inge sniffed the calming earth in the jar.

"Women and their secrets," Finnvid said, spitting over the side.

"Finnvid, it is no secret my bell cow has a good memory for finding her way to the summer pasture. She remembers well how you shook the grappling irons in her face yesterday."

"If we must travel with a cow, she should learn the tool seamen use to board ships."

She reminded him that Karl had let her use the herding call "Follow Me" and that Bratta had leapt aboard. She saw the sharp way Karl looked from sea to sky and back, trying to hold in his anger at the argument. Though Finnvid was Karl's second in command, Inge marked the men were not fearful of standing up to him. She must not be fearful either. She took a deep sniff of Breidal's earth.

"We never had trouble on The Seafarer before," he muttered.

"Before you had cows and women aboard?"

"I did not say that."

"You were thinking it."

"Do not tell me what I am thinking, Mistress."

Thora twisted her strand of golden hair forward, watching the quarrel. Inge pondered. Finnvid was right. She did not know what he was thinking, though she could guess from the way he glowered at her. She glowered back. His brows almost met above the bridge of his nose. He was most angry.

"Finnvid, you have insulted my innocent Brattahlid who keeps us in sweet milk, and even curds, forming in the bucket as it rolls with the ship."

He looked at the bell cow calmly chewing her cud crosswise. "In truth, she takes up space we could put to better use. Tonight I will butcher her, and we will have a feast of fresh beef, not dried pork."

"Aiyiii! Never!" Inge said, jumping up to put her arms about the bellcow's neck. "You will have to butcher me first."

Finnvid shrugged. "As you say, Mistress."

Inge forgot her resolution to get along with him. "Go ahead and try, Finnvid. Go ahead and try. Bratta, no one will butcher either of us."

Karl-Eirik called them both to the stern, and Inge led the way. He stood them in front of him, and, as always when he was really angry, she saw how wide his cheeks were. Always a sign of leadership that expected to be obeyed. Finnvid's lashes had never looked more delicate--a sign of a quick and deadly temper.

Karl told them he faulted them both. On such a small ship they must get along. Finnvid could not ride up to the mountain, and Inge could not walk to her storehouse to vent their anger. Finnvid must give the bell cow a wide berth. He snorted, and said he would try, but Bratta was wide-assed and took up so much room... Inge protested. Her bell cow was not wide-assed.

"Enough!" Karl shouted. "Enough of this wrangling."

Inge pressed her lips together and looked off at the sea, so empty, so different from the commotion of her beloved Breidal. She ached for the peace of her Sacred Grove. Until they landed in Kievan Rus, thinking of it would be her only escape.

"Karl, you will not let him butcher Bratta, ay?"

"That I can promise you, Inge. Finnvid, that is an order."

Finnvid said he never meant it, and Inge asked why then he said it, and Karl said this was what he meant by getting along. They must stop taking to heart what each other said.

It was an uneasy truce, but one they honored by turning their backs on each other. The weather helped. One fair day followed another on the Baltic, a steady north wind driving the standard flying aloft from the mast. Anders said he for one had never seen such weather-luck as their mistress brought, though Inge thought sailors and countrywomen knew the same weather signs. A northern air always brought weather fair. Each day at even, the sun set red in the western sky, and one night they saw the Green Flash at the horizon.

"Glimpse you ever the Green Ray and count the morrow a fine day," she said, and noticed Karl alone did not take fine weather for granted, but his eyes roamed from sea to sky and back, looking for change.

The journey to Gotland was tedious for the men only when the fitful wind slumped the sail, and Karl kept them at the oar. Their strong, barrel chests gave them power, and they could row for hours without tiring. But if they wearied, Inge and Thora peeled garlic and put it atop barley bread for energy. They sang all the songs they knew, and Thora taught them new ones. Their strong voices rang out across the water, the rhythm helping them row together. To Inge's joy, her stomach was at peace, her queasiness past.

They had no shelter from the sun, and Inge wondered if this sea had any healing secrets to soothe burnt skin. On a hunch she asked Anders to pole seaweed from the water. She rinsed out the salt and put it on his raw, red shoulders. His relieved smile was her reward, and she asked him to bring it up by the pailful for the others.

Thora wandered from bow to stern, bored, in the crew's way. And to Inge's distress, often sullen. Milking Bratta twice a day and passing the pail was not enough to keep her busy. Inge worried, fingering her amulet of Freya. A small, cramped boat was not a good place for a maid--she needed to jump and run.

One day when Thora could not sit still, Gunnar asked her to hold the rune stock while he carved, recording each day's passing on the wooden stave. He knew the custom was to carve two bad days each month, but there were none so far.

He asked Thora if she had ever carved, and she said nay, in a small voice. Thralls did not touch a carving blade. Gunnar dug into his tool box, and found a small knife and a chunk of wood. An animal lurked in it he told her, and she could carve him free. She giggled, but sat where she had a good view of Brattahlid, and to no one's surprise she was skilled with the knife. A rough carcass slowly appeared.

From then on Thora was captivated by carving, and sat by the hour, trying to make a wooden copy of Bratta. Gunnar began freeing a horse from another chunk.

"We will arrive at Kievan Rus with four animals, not two," Thora said, and all thought her winsome, now that she was no longer in the seamen's way.

Carving did more than keep the maid quiet. It freed her tongue, and Inge was grateful the maid sat still, talking.

"Gunnar, know you this riddle?" Thora asked. " 'I am possessed by the rich man, and clothed in red. Once I was a hard, high field, the place of brilliant plants. Now I am the survivor of fire, confined and adorned. Sometimes the bearer of gold weeps because of my touch, when I must destroy.' "

Gunnar smiled at Inge. "Your daughter has an ear for words, ay, Mistress? It sounds like the riddling men do at night over their ale cups. If your mother gives me leave, I will answer."

Inge laughed. "Speak. I am not your captain."

"Gunnar, do you know, or shall I tell you?" Thora cried out.

"I know," he said. "Red is jewels, or perchance blood. The hard, high field is the iron in the earth. The plants are sparks we smiths make by beating metal with hammer and anvil. It is a sword riddle, ay?"

"Ay! Here is another."

"One is enough today," Inge said. "I have a better story."

"A sword story, Modir?"

"Nay, nay. A better one, about magic plants and trees."

Thora groaned. Yet she did not move away. Inge took a deep breath. This story must be a good one. She must reach her daughter's heart.

"Thora, do you know that Gunguir, Odin's spear, is ash?"

Thora squinted at Bratta. Ah. Inge must touch Thora another way. Did the maid know the god Balder, Odin's beloved son, the one killed by a dart of mistletoe? Ay, she did. But did anyone know what the white berries stood for? No one did.

"They are droplets of semen, and as the berries fall, they must be caught in a white cloth held by virgins. If the berries touch the ground, they lose their power."

The men gathered closer, thinking. Where in Sweden would they find enough virgins to hold the cloth?

She talked of how mistletoe grows on oaks, and none dare cut one bearing it. One such was cut, hewn not far from her childhood farmstead, and the woodcutter broke his hip. The men working with him suffered bad luck too--injured beyond a leechwoman's healing.

"When any oak is cut, there is a wrenching cry," Karl said. "I like not to hear it, but no tree is better for shipbuilding. On that Hervor the Shipwright and I agree."

"Ay, Karl-Eirik, there are Rules of the Forest, as there are Rules of the Sea. Hervor knows he must fell an oak only during a waxing moon, and tell it what he means to do, and plant an acorn next to the stump, so the Tree Spirit will have a new home."

Though Thora did not put down her knife, Inge saw she stopped carving. Good, she was listening.

Anders asked why mistletoe only grew on oaks, and Inge answered she knew not, but the oak was a sacred tree, and perchance the mistletoe learned it many years past. Did he knew the twigs were good for calming overwrought hearts? Or of a healing potion called Swallow's Water made with mistletoe, elderberry and twenty-four live baby swallows?

"Ycch!" Thora said. "I would not drink it."

"Nor would I make it. But it is good for sore throats. Thora, you like riddles. Know you this one? 'The willow will buy the horse before the oak will buy the saddle.' "

Thora shook her head, but Gunnar said he knew wood, and willow was a fast grower, but oak, ah, oak was slow.

Karl said they had talked enough and set them to their tasks, all except Thora and Inge. Though the maid had no questions about oaks or mistletoe, Inge thought she had made a start in weaning the maid from the sword. They sat side by side, and Inge told her that for her, each day on the Baltic was a time of ease. All her life, from the time she was a child, she had had a spindle at her elbow:

round the hearth fire, when she walked back and forth to the byre or the store-houses, sitting with guests. Now she stowed her spindle away. She walked to Olaf, who was tightening stays.

"Olaf, what call you that wooden piece on the rigging?"

"It is called a virgin, Mistress."

A virgin--a name most apt, though not for holding a cloth to catch semen. In the wooden piece she made out two arms, two legs, and the rigging through the crotch.

"Olaf, why is it there?"

"To hold the rigging in place, Mistress."

Ah. There was much to learn. She stood with Karl, and told him he was the best of captains and the best of husbands. She loved journeying with him. She was glad the winds were fair, and now that he was well-rested at night, their bedplay had never been more joyful. She leaned against the gunwale and smiled at him.

"Karl. I am wont to learn to sail."

Finnvid dropped a chain and cursed, though not at the chain. Per and Anders looked at each other, eyebrows raised. Ingvar slid down the mast. Gunnar and Sven stared at her. Olaf walked to the bow, muttering. Hrolf alone did not stop coiling rope. Thora looked at her with pride. Karl's face was grim.

"Inge, you know your loom was too large to bring, and you are bored, ay?"

"Nay, I am not bored. I want to learn to sail."

Finnvid glared at her, and spoke to the men.

"Tell me, have you ever seen a woman working with the rigging or aught else aboard ship? I have not, in all my years of journeying with Karl-Eirik, or before."

"Nay", "Not I", and such, the men agreed.

"Women do not learn to sail, Inge," Karl said. "You agree our lives are bound by the rules in the Havamal, set forth by Odin, ja? There is nothing in it about women doing men's work aboard ship."

Inge was grateful her mother taught her the Havamal so well. She saw Karl grip the tiller, controlling his anger. She told him there was nothing in the Havamal about women learning to sail or not learning to sail.

"Inge, I am the most forbearing of captains, but if I saw a woman at the tiller I would give it wide berth, for I would have no trust in that ship."

The wind abated, and there was no time for talk. The men put the oars through the oar holes, cursing and frowning. Only Thora came to her, giving her a hug. They were allies, Inge thought. Perchance there would be other times the two had to stand together against the men.

Ingvar bunched the sail. Inge stood and reached to help.

"Drop it, Inge," Karl shouted, and she pulled back her hand.

The boat heeled, one corner of the sail dipping into the water. The men swore. Though there were no other ships to see, a corner of sail in the water was shameful, a sign of a careless captain. A mistake Karl avoided. He spoke sharply to Ingvar.

Inge sat. She would not spend her days spinning. For the first time she was glad The Seafarer was so small. She would see and hear everything--the crew's mistakes, bad judgments, what they did to make the boat sail well. She would learn without Karl teaching her.

Though she had argued with certainty, she could not say why she must learn to sail, but this she knew: a leechwoman trusted her own instincts.

From then on Inge kept her eyes on the men. She saw how Karl steered, when the wind changed. First in one direction, then another, then back to the first as crooked as a snake's path.

When Karl saw her watching, he told her she was not born to be a sailor. It was not in her blood. His father took him aboard his boat when he was a babe, only a week old. But she had not grown up within sound of the sea. She had deep ties to soil and crops and trees and the healing herbs. She had a skill at dying wool, and weaving it into things like their beauteous sail.

"Ay, Husband, I love my weaving, but I leave the plain weave to Geda and the others. I am always trying new patterns, learning new ways. This sailing is another thing I am wont to learn."

To this, Karl had no answer. And so she listened when Olaf called to Anders to tighten the forestay, and learned the name of that line. She found out how Finnvid knew when to slide the sail-stick out, how Anders pulled on the reef ropes to bunch the sail and made it smaller for smaller winds. So Karl and all sailors must have done at one time, she thought.

And she watched and learned how the men worked together, saving their energy, each man's strength added to the others. If Karl yelled at a seaman for a mistake, five minutes later it was forgotten, and they were laughing. There was no room for grudges aboard The Seafarer.

Each night the stars were close and twinkling. When they lay within the leather bag, Inge told Karl she was beginning to love the sea. The same endless rocking that turned a pail of Bratta's milk to curds rocked her as well. She pointed to the Guiding Star, and said she had heard Anders call it The Nail. Did it nail the sky together? Karl got up on one elbow to look at her.

"You are most interested in the Guiding Star, Ingeborg. You have not given up your fool's thought of learning to sail?"

"Husband, forget I asked. Let us not spoil this beauteous night. In truth these nights aboard ship are like the first days you return from going a-viking."

Karl lay back down, looking up at the stars.

"Like the first days after our betrothal, when we met in the forest and lay together in the grass until we married, and had a bed."

She snuggled down, remembering. Inge asked Karl what the Yellowskins called the body parts of women and men. In one more year Thora would be of marriageable age, and Inge wanted to tell her.

Karl said there was an end to a man's Rain, but no end to a woman's Clouds, as Inge knew. And so the Yellowskins had fewer names for men's parts, than women's.

"Ingeborg, the part of me that brings you your pleasure is called Swelling Mushroom."

When she laughed, he said another name was Jade Stalk, though his sex was not green jade. There was another kind, white.

The woman's path of pleasure had many names: Flower Petals, Vase, The Golden Cleft. The entrance to her Cleft was called Cinnabar Gate, after a beautiful cinnabar red. She told him she had seen different shades at birthings, but all were red.

Ah. No man or woman would need a potion of Freya's Grass, with such talk.

"Inge, one story the Yellowskin claimed as truth. Do you Swedish leech-women know how to make the Jade Stalk bigger, or the Golden Cleft shrink for a better fit?"

"Nay! Tell me."

She scrunched down to where she could fondle his sex, and he talked. First she must gather some herb or other and mix it with sweet grass, and then with parts of a white dog's liver, killed during the first moon in that month. Then put the potion on the cock three times, and wash with early morning well water.

By how much would it be bigger, she asked.

"It is said, by three barleycorns, Inge."

"The length of one thumb? Not so much." They laughed.

Ah, she was a lucky woman, and needed no potion using a white dog's liver. And where would she would find a white dog in Sweden? Among their own hounds, she had only seen gray or brown.

She giggled, and told him she would not use the potion on a Golden Cleft. What if she used too much?

That night, Karl was most loving. All the next day they looked at each other and often broke into laughter, so the men and Thora were puzzled at this foolishness.

Thora began carving four legs, and the cow looked more real. Sven asked her if she knew any lays of chieftains who had no victory luck, and she told him she knew none told around the hearth fire. But at Gotardal she had heard ones told by the serving folk, one to another, in the byre or the drying rack, though she could not remember any.

How well-spoken her daughter was, Inge thought. Ah, if—nay, when--this bent was turned to learning herbal healings…

"If I could make a lay, I would sing of the time Karl-Eirik was hit on the head by a priest who struck him with a gold crozier," Sven said, and Inge heard the yearning in his voice.

Karl told him to spare the maid his lies that belonged in the shit hole, and the crew laughed.

"Ingeborg, on the morrow we will land on the island of Gotland."

She went to him and kissed him, her eyes smarting with tears. They could spread their leather bag beneath the trees. She could pick up a clump of earth, and smell fresh loam.

"I see naught of Gotland," Thora cried out.

"Nor do we, but we are sailing straight for it, Thora," Olaf said. "We can trust our captain. When he says we will land on Gotland on the morrow, we will. Karl sees what we cannot."

Thora asked him how he did it, but he said if he told all his secrets, the men would be at the tiller, and he would be at the oar. Inge saw he never took his eyes from the direction of the swell, the height of the waves. Perchance the changing color of the water had a message for him.

"Wife, before we reach landfall, we must talk."

The crew moved toward the bow, and Gunnar steered Thora to follow, though she would fain linger. The men sensed Karl had something important to say to Inge alone. She felt his intensity.

"Ingeborg, we know not how the Rus will greet us. It is likely we will have to defend ourselves during the six months."

She leaned on the gunwales and looked at the gold streamer of sun, and took a deep, calming breath. She knew what Karl wanted. Gotland would have an armorer, and she must take a stand against the elvist of buying Thora chainmail. Now, before they reached land.

"Karl-Eirik, Thora's sword has already provoked trouble."

"Ja. But I would like to see she is as well protected as my men."

She knew some selfish chieftains only bought chainmail for themselves. Karl had talked of how glad he was that she wanted to adopt Thora. It was unlike fathering sons. But they knew not what lay ahead. She felt her stomach knot, and pulled her cloak tighter.

"Inge, swordcraft is in her blood. If she has no protection..."

"I will protect her. I will keep her from jumping into the fray by hiding her beneath the floorboards."

"I do not want to frighten you, Inge, but not all battles are fought on land. If an enemy should board..."

She shuddered. It was so, but if she and Thora hid quietly enough...still, she knew it for a fool's thought.

Quietly Karl talked of how they had always been successful in battle, with the Franks and the Frisians, the Englanders and the Irish, and he expected they would be in Kievan Rus, but--

She pounded the gunwale and told him Thora was too young, too slight to fight grown men.

Karl looked up at the bland sky and said that because Thora was so slight, an enemy would strike her down first. She stifled a cry. He put his hand on her shoulder.

"Inge, I would be a poor father if I did not try to protect my daughter, and my wife. We have seen how Thora fought to save you from a glass-caster who only held your arm. How would she fight to save you from an enemy? There would be no holding back her fierceness."

"Why is she so deft with a sword and knife, and so inept with a spindle? Tell me that, Karl."

He said he knew not, but perchance the bitch struck her with a spindle? Whatsoever, Thora had learned to handle a sword from a loving father--the only way he could protect her.

"Inge, I want to do as well."

Inge looked at his face. He seemed to have aged since Birka. Ah, what a burden it must be to have the care of two women in an unknown land. The idea of outfitting Thora was not a sudden fancy of Karl's, but well thought out, while he stood at the tiller.

Inge sighed. "Karl, I am getting no closer to teaching Thora the sacred knowledge of healing."

"When we get to Gardariki, you both can walk alongside the boat, gathering plants. But we must keep Thora safe and not let her be a victim. Inge, you agree then to the chainmail?"

What else could she do? Protest, and if by chance Thora was harmed? Inge's heart ached. She clenched the gunwale.

"Ay, Karl-Eirik. I agree."

"And a helmet."

"Nay! I did not agree to that."

"An enemy would see her without a helmet and strike her first, Inge, cleaving her head like a…"

"Enough, Karl! Buy her a helmet."

"And a shield. Then we will have done all we can, as good parents."

Inge leaned into the gunwale for support. How had she got herself into this fix?

"Buy her what she needs Karl, but mind, get a good fit."

"Aiyii!" Thora cried, and Inge thought there were few secrets aboard The Seafarer. The men gathered around the maid, all talking at once. Whether kite-shaped or round shields were better. How heavy a handhold should be, how far down her small face a nose guard should come. Whether safety made up for heaviness.

Inge watched Thora's shining eyes. As a loving mother, was she making a mistake? Was she giving the maid help to survive or encouraging her to fight? She knew not.

* * *

She still felt broody the next day when Ingvar called from atop the mast.

"Karl-Eirik, I see a smudge on the horizon. What can it be but Gotland?"

The men cheered, and Inge thought how strained and taut they were from cramped days at the oar. They needed to be at an ale house, bragging of this journey or another. For herself, if she did not soon get away from the salt-spray she would be pickled by it.

Finnvid asked if Karl wanted him to remove the prow-post, and Karl said nay, this was not the Faroes where the land spirits were frightened by a dragon ship prow. This was Gotland where all men were rich from trading with travelers back and forth to Miklagard. Rich men had little to fear from land spirits.

Anders said there was so much silver men walked upon it, and Karl said it was plentiful, but they did not walk on it. They buried it to keep it safe. Anders said he would borrow a spade from a farmer and dig up silver, and be rich himself.

"Anders, we know you," Karl said. "Once you get to the ale house, there you stay until you find a woman. If you are so eager to use a spade, use Gunnar's and get the shit off the deck."

Anders was not one to complain. As he worked, he told Brattahlid and Volnir they would soon be shitting in sweet grass. As Gotland loomed large, the gulls swooped out to greet them.

Inge made out trees by their bark, maple and birch, the summer oak and willow. She heard the welcome bleat of sheep and saw cows and plumes of smoke, and near a grove of pines she saw pine dust, sun-lit, and a rill of silver. She felt dizzy with joy.

She expected to see more ships in the harbor, but Karl said it was early in the season. She thought, but did not say, that most of the northmen were sailing west. From the mast Ingvar spied hidden rocks, but not as large as Birka's, and Karl worked with the current so they would not land in a trough.

The animals stomped the deck, smelling land, and Per untied them as the keel grazed the bottom. Volnir leapt, and the men followed. Bratta lingered.

"That cow will send us all to Hel's home," Finnvid said.

"Nay," Inge said and softly sang the "Follow Me" herding song while she slid over the side. Bratta's nostrils flared with fear, but she obeyed Inge and leapt, making a great splash, soaking Finnvid head to toe. He cursed this stupid cow and all others.

The bellcow's legs crumpled beneath her, and so did Inge's. They walked, unsteady, leaning on each other while Thora scampered around the gravely beach.

"Women and cows have no sea legs," Finnvid said.

"Shut up and push," Karl said. "Here we will beach the boat."

The men tried but The Seafarer moved not a bit, though the slope was slight. Karl took the lead, and still it did not budge.

Inge motioned to Thora to help, and the two set their shoulders to the hull. They saw the men frown. They did not like to be helped by women. Karl looked around.

"Inge, beaching a boat is work for seamen, not women."

She and Thora backed off, and the boat stuck fast, no matter how hard the men pushed. When Karl's back was once again turned, Inge and Thora helped. Slowly the boat slid up from the water, though Finnvid's jaw was tight.

Inge knew some tasks needed only a few hands more. She was a countrywoman, strong from the everlasting lifting, dipping, carrying, pulling, hauling. She had often pulled stubborn beasts by the tether or sleds piled high from the storehouse in winter. Pushing a boat up a gravel beach was not so different.

Now there was the flurry of combing and brushing, as at every port. Inge held the hand mirror for Anders, as he trimmed his beard with her scissors.

"Inge, you are not primping for the men of Gotland?" Karl asked. "After I outfit Thora we will go to the ale hall, where I hope to hear news of Lars and learn more of Gardariki."

She told him she would meet him there after she gathered green seaweed. The sun would burn on the rivers as it did on the Baltic. He should choose the best chainmail and helmet and shield from the armorer, and not let any man steal their comely daughter. Men would not care that Thora was serving a sentence for Lesser Outlawry.

Karl was loath to leave Inge behind, but he gave Per and Olaf the first watch, and she could ask them for help if she needed it. Though she was strong, he teased her. If need be, she could wrestle a man to the ground.

Olaf made a fire, knotted a cloth on a branch, and Per poured the curds through it into a bucket to make whey butter. The men dipped their fingers in the sweet whey.

"Karl, go. Take the men and Thora, or they will eat it all before I can make butter. Go before the men mess their pretty hair."

Karl and Thora left hand in hand, the men following behind. She watched Karl take coins from his pouch and pay a man in the trader's shirt. On Gotland, as elsewhere, captains paid protection money to keep their boats whole while in port.

Olaf wanted to gather seaweed with her, but she told him to stay and guard the boat as Karl asked, and gather enough wood to keep the fire going, or the whey butter would curdle.

She set off with an empty seapouch, and saw the gravely beach had all sizes of boats pulled up on it--some covered with hide, many worn with chipped paint. The Goldenbreast was not among them. Good. Lars was far ahead. Perchance they would not even see him. Life would be simpler if they did not.

Men called to her, but she did not answer and kept her eyes from making contact. They might know things about Gardariki she needed to know, but they might have been too long without a woman, and would act more and talk less.

She walked to the curve of shore where The Seafarer could not be seen. For too long she had smelled brine and a tarred boat and unwashed men. She might not be free to be alone again. In a strange land they must all stick together. She shook off a lump of fear in her chest, fear of the unknown, and climbed a small hill until she found a tree-lined path hiding her from the beach. She sang as she walked, bypassing the outskirts of town. She passed ship graves, stones set around the dead in the outline of a ship. Some stones glinted in the sun, and some few were as pink as the sky at even. Runes were writ on the stone at the ship's bow, but she did not stop to read.

She giggled out loud. Who needed silver-covered streets to be happy? She passed fishermen's huts, with oinking pigs rooting in piles of rotting fish. She was lonesome for her sow, Skulda. How many piglets had she birthed? Were they all live and squealing? Ah, a countrywoman had a love of earth and its animals a sailor like Karl could never feel. She took a deep breath and thought it wondrous to be away from the sour smell of old sweat from an unwashed crew. Yet they were far from her bathhouse at Breidal, and she could not urge them to bathe in the frigid Baltic.

She heard soughing pines and followed the path where it led uphill. Per and Olaf would never have let her come here alone. There was little to fear in a strange place if a woman was strong, strong enough to wrestle a man to the ground, as Karl said.

She heard the beloved sound, fairer than a flute, and ran towards it.

X

Inge raised her arms in delight. A silver waterfall plunged without end over rocks to a pool below. Here was the silver rill she had seen from the boat. She ran down the slope.

She lay on the sun-warmed rock and felt the water. It was cold, but she was used to bathing in the cold water of her fjord. She sipped, and ah, here was no brine of the Baltic or stale taste of the cask, but fresh. Later she would tell Karl, and he would bring the men to bathe and refill their casks.

Inge looked around, and saw no one. She took off every piece of clothing, unplaited her hair and turned her body to the sun and felt Sol's blessing.

She stepped into the pool and her foolish teeth chattered, but she sat, wetting her hair. She could not stay long, or icicles would hang from her nipples. She stood, sun-warmed and frozen at the same time. She dug out a sliver of soapwort in her seapouch and sudsed her hair so the froth ran down her body. It was astonishing how such a small thing as soaping her itchy head could be so pleasing. There was no way to keep the salt off on the Baltic. Though they did not drink it, nor wash with it, the very winds were salt-filled.

Rivulets of suds got into her eyes and stung, and she swore, bent and splashed water into her eyes over and over, but still she was blinded.

"I trow, Ingeborg, this is not where I thought to find you," a man's voice said from the rock.

Inge sank into the water. From the direction of the voice he was close at hand. She sank deeper, splashing her eyes again and again. Still she could not see.

"Inge, do you know there is talk of some kings putting a statue of an unclothed woman on their ships' prows? I would put one of you on my boat, with your great breasts."

Inge was cold and blinded, but not helpless. She scraped wave after wave of cold water toward the voice.

She was most pleased when he screamed, "You are a bitch from Hel!"

"Ja, I am. I would know your voice anywhere, Lars."

She listened to his footsteps as he scrambled up, and stood too far for her to splash him.

"Ingeborg, your clothes are now in my hands. Would you like them dropped into the water to wash, like your headdress, now floating and wet? I would fain see you walk to meet Karl-Eirik in sodden clothes, so all men could see your breasts and your sweet ass. Or perchance you would walk unclothed."

Inge stood and hugged her arms, trying to cover her breasts, but she knew she could not. She could no longer bear the cold water. Her eyes still stung, but she opened them a crack and saw Lars dangling her clothes and shoes close to the water. She grabbed for her wet headdress and put it on her chest.

"Lars, if you so choose to shame me, Karl will beat you senseless, though you are his brother."

He laughed. "Ay, he would, but I would beat him back, and you do not want to have your beloved Karl harmed. Inge, come and lie with me, as you are, and I will give you back your clothes."

She shivered and walked out of the water. She blinked her eyes open, though they stung. Lars looked no different from the first time she saw him, drinking her betrothal ale so many years ago. The cares of a large and growing farmstead and a family that had worn Karl's face were not so writ on his brother's. He had the soft, unformed face of a babe--smooth cheeks, plump skin.

"Come, Ingeborg, we are family. Do I get a kiss? Are you not glad to see your husband's brother?"

"Ja." She reached up to pull him into the water, but he was too quick for her and jumped back. "I am wont for you to be wet, Lars, so your swollen manhood between your legs will show to all, men and women both."

"Inge, we are family. We have nothing to hide from each other. Come up and let me warm you, and I will give you your clothes."

"Ay?"

"You can trust me, as Karl trusts you. Husband and wife have no secrets from each other, have you?" He laughed. "Poor Karl. While he is sweating at the armorer, trying this helmet and that on Thora, you are here bathing, most joyful. He knew you would be here, ay? There was no reason not to tell him, though you said you would be gathering seaweed."

Inge shivered. Even Sol's rays could not warm her.

"Lars, you have seen your brother?"

"Ja, he greeted me more warmly than you, though I asked him not for a kiss. Come, we will rest, and then go together and tell him why you walk about in wet clothes, or perchance naked, showing every man what Karl sees in the bed-closet."

He unfastened his sword and spread his cloak for them to lie upon.

She sighed. "I will freeze to death if I have no clothes. I will grit my teeth and close my eyes tight, and force myself to lie with you. I will be as stone. As rock."

"Nay, nay. Families must be lovesome. You would not have a daughter, unless I brought her to you. And now we will all go down the rivers of Kievan Rus together to Miklagard. You in your boat, and me in mine, The Goldenbreast."

Ah, it would be a long, long voyage. What gossips men were! At ale houses all over Sweden men were telling Thora's story, as they would tell one of herself and Lars at the waterfall, if he had his way. She eased herself up on the rock, and Lars sat by her, idly stroking her shoulders. She slapped him, and he lay back.

"Lars, I will scream if you do not give me my clothes, and leave."

"Who will hear? You chose a waterfall far from town so you could bathe naked. Looking at you, I see why it is hard for a woman with a ripened body to be chaste when her husband is away for six months every year."

She swatted his chest. How much did Lars know?

"Inge, last year while Karl was off a-viking, an arrow-maker came to your farmstead for yew wood, ay? They say he tripped in a hole and hurt his ankle, so he could not leave your farmstead for a few days. Some say he was looking for a quiver for his arrow, and some say he found it."

"Lars, go to Hel."

"Fear not, Ingeborg. Karl will not hear the truth about his loving wife--we are family, you and I."

Inge remembered the arrow-maker and his soft ways, how she had cared for his ankle with her herbs and the healing charms. How her hungry body had betrayed her.

Now she looked at Lars's grinning face and lay on her back, fondling her breasts until she saw the center of his eyes widen. She stretched, and knew she looked good with her nipples enlarged by the cold.

"Lars, there is a custom all Swedish men love in bedplay. Your brother taught it to me: wives pull the men's breeches off, and I do this for Karl each time we lie together. It is a custom that enlarges the manhood."

"Ay? I have not heard of it."

He swallowed hard, and she saw he could not keep his eyes from her breasts. She lifted one and licked the nipple: ah, it made him restless.

"Do it, Inge, pull off my breeches. Teach me for the night I marry."

He lay back, and she saw the lust writ on his face. Men like Lars did not marry. She undid his belt, and pulled his breeches.

"I am hard put to pull past your sex, Lars. You are as big as your brother, I trow."

"Ay, bigger! Do not slacken. Can you not work faster?"

"It must be done slowly."

"Ay, but no slower than need be. Hurry, Ingeborg."

"Close your eyes and enjoy it Lars. Karl-Eirik says it is best that way."

Lars eyes flickered closed, and his mouth opened. She pulled his pants to his ankles, and Lars began writhing.

You could wrestle a man to the ground, Karl had said. Lars began panting. Ah, the better to swallow, she thought, twisting his body.

With a huge splash Lars fell face down in the pool of water. He came up, spluttering, but fell again, his legs bound by the wet pants at his ankles.

"Bitch!" he screamed.

"Ja, I am. But we are family, Lars. No one will hear you call for help. We are far from town."

She laughed and grabbed her clothes and seapouch, and ran, unclothed, while he stood up and walked toward her, and fell again.

Ah, it would be easier for him to pull up his breeches now that his sex had returned to its natural size.

XI

She ran fast and found the path. It would not take Lars long to pull up his breeches and chase her. He was quick and strong, and his anger would give him extra strength. No man, not even a berserker, was more frenzied than one who had been laughed at by a woman.

She did not stop to dress, but slipped her shift and overgarment over her head as she ran, holding fast to her underbreeches, shoes and headdress. She heard thrashing in the woods below. The brush and brambles would help her by snagging his wet clothes.

"Bitch!" he yelled, over and over again, but she need not stop to agree now. She pounded the packed dirt, upslope and down, leaping over fallen logs, tripping on roots, caught herself and ran on. She was most grateful to be a countrywoman. She had always loved walking barefoot, and her feet were toughened.

Then she heard the one sound that made her stop, shivering-- silence, from the woods below. Pain stabbed her right side, and she ran harder. A running woman was most in danger from an enemy she could neither see nor hear. Had Lars given up the chase?

Nay, a wrathful man was not easily stopped. He might have found a trail up to her own, and would be waiting round the next turn of the path. Wildly she looked for a way to take her towards town. Now she regretted choosing a waterfall farthest from the safety of people.

She must run harder, praying to Freya, but she knew she could not keep up the swift pace forever. Her chest hurt with every breath.

The forest opened out onto a grass-covered hill, with no trees to shield her, and now she was truly at risk. The chase would favor Lars. Yet still she ran, panting now, hunting for the biggest plume of smoke in the sky, from the biggest ale hall. It would be what Karl would pick, with the most sailors who could tell him about Gardariki.

Her eyes smarted from tears when she saw all smoke from the ale houses blurred into one. She ran downhill, sliding on patches of mud, stubbing her toes on hidden rocks, and still she ran, but no longer fast. Her chest was on fire.

If she guessed the wrong ale house, Lars would soon grab her, and she would scream for Karl, but who would befriend her? Lars was family. And all men listened when men like Lars talked.

Her legs ached, but she would not let herself think of pain. Now she could see men sitting at benches and tables in an ale yard, beneath a birch bark roof. She saw Hrolf's huge bulk.

A warm current of relief flooded her body. She was safe enough to slow to a walk. She tried to control her heaving breath, and dropped her underbreeches in the grass. It would not do to come to Karl-Eirik with them in her hand, and she was loathe to put them on in full view of men at an ale server's.

Karl ran to her, and she fell into his arms, still panting, her legs so weak he had to hold her upright. The crew joined them, looking at her unplaited hair and unshod, muddy feet and damp clothes, but they were silent.

Karl led her to a bench, and wiped the sweat from her face with her soggy headdress.

"Ingeborg, your headdress is soaked, your feet are scratched and muddy, and your clothes dampened. You look as though you were chased by a bear. Olaf, bring the ale bowl."

While she drank, she looked for Lars. He was not to be seen. Karl asked if in truth, she was chased by a bear, and she was saved an answer by her daughter. Thora came up to her, and Inge could not but laugh. The maid's small, pretty face was almost covered by an iron helmet.

"Does the noseguard tickle, Thora?" Inge asked, and the maid giggled.

"She will not take it off, Inge," Karl said. "The chainmail and shield are being remade to fit. We will go back for them on the morrow before we leave for Gardariki. Two Swedes from Roslagen have an armory here. I trow, Thora, we must get some protection for your mother. She was chased by a bear."

With great care, Inge spread her headdress to dry on the bench. Sven asked if it was a brown bear. Finnvid said surely it was a white one, and she shook her head, her eyes intent on pulling her headdress taut.

Karl lifted her wet hair from her neck. "You stopped to unplait your hair, when you were chased by a bear?"

How much should she tell him? The brothers had always been close. Now they would be traveling together, side by side down the rivers for weeks on end. She dare not cause a rift between them.

She heard the squishing of wet boots, and Lars appeared before them, his bachelor's topknot limp. She thought the colors in his yellow tunic and purple breeches brighter when wet.

"Lars, what happened to you?" Karl asked. "Like Inge's headdress, your clothes are soaked."

"It is nothing, Karl-Eirik. I slipped and fell in a pond, that is all."

Karl's men were glad to see him and moved over on the bench, and he sat across from her. Anders pushed the ale bowl to him, looking from Inge to Lars and back, one to another, saying naught. She began plaiting her wet hair.

"I trow, Karl-Eirik, travel has made your wife younger," Lars said. "She has removed her wifely headdress and unplaited her hair, as maidens do."

"Both were salt-filled, and I washed my hair and headdress at a waterfall," she said.

"Lars, Inge has been chased by a bear," Karl said.

"Ja?" Lars said. "On Gotland? What kind of bear?"

Inge took a drink and fingered her amulet of Freya. "I know not, Lars. I heard it thrashing around in the forest below my path."

"Perchance it was not a bear," Lars said.

Inge smoothed her headdress, making sure it had not a wrinkle. Again she was in luck. The burly ale hall owner appeared, his huge fists anchored on his hips. He accused Lars of getting water all over his bench.

"It will clean off some of the filth," Lars said.

"Filth! You Norse talk of filth--"

Lars gave the ample belly a pat. "Nay, nay, we Norsemen like to tease. Your bench is clean enough for my brother's wife to spread her headdress to dry." He took a deep draught. "Your ale warms my blood. I taste no wood in your fine brew. Can you outfit me with seven casks of it for our voyage? My ship leaves on the morrow."

Inge felt the chill on her arms. She must be careful. During the long jour-ney, if she and Lars became at odds he would tell Karl about the silver-tongued arrow-maker. Lars was unlike her servants and thralls who pretended it never happened. Curse all men's love of gossip. She turned her headdress over.

The ale hall owner looked at Lars and grunted. "Be here after day meal. You should sit next the fire and dry, Northman."

"Do not take off your clothes, Lars, or you will get every wench on Gotland with child," Finnvid said to him.

"Nay, Finnvid. Not every woman is worthy of my manhood."

He looked over the rim of his cup at Inge, and she thought tonight when she and Karl were in the leather bag she would tell him what happened. If Lars did not blurt it out first.

Lars did not, but he had a surprise. He reached in his tunic and brought forth her underbreeches, holding them out for all to see. Vainly, she was glad the lace trim was delicately made.

"These are yours, Ingeborg?" Lars asked.

She was distressed. If she admitted the underbreeches were hers, all in the alehouse would suspect how Lars got them.

"They are your size, Ingeborg."

Sighing she said, "Ja, they are mine."

She grabbed her underbreeches and stuffed them in her seapouch. She wished her headdress, the sign of a well-married woman, was dry enough to wear. She turned to Karl.

"Husband, I have had no chance to tell you the whole story. Women must take down their underbreeches when they piss in the woods, ay? The thrashing bear frightened me so I could but run, and leave them behind."

Lars threw back his head and roared. "I drink to your safe return from being chased."

She hated the way he lingered on the last word. Ah, she had been chaste when she was with Lars, that she would tell Karl. The owner brought them a full ale bowl.

"Put away your coin. This bowl is on the house. You are the first Norse I have seen this year on your way to Miklagard. Rus, you are called here in Kievan Rus, and you are known as shrewd traders."

All happily refilled their cups.

Lars said that in truth they were shrewd traders. One time in France they took a town by force, and stayed on after the peace treaty was signed. They opened a market, and sold back to the people what they took by pillage.

The owner laughed, and Inge wondered if he believed Lars.

"Drink up," Karl ordered his men, putting a handful of silver coins on the table. "Lars, we must talk."

And alone, Inge thought, away from listening ears. Had Karl-Eirik finally learned there were men not to be trusted in these aleyards? She hoped so. She sensed some dispute to be settled between the brothers.

Karl led the way back to the harbor, talking quietly to Lars. The crew bunched up in a circle, with Inge and Thora holding hands in their midst. Groups of Gotlanders, ankle-deep in cutting thatch in the fen, stared at them. They wore billowy breeches. She wondered how they found pleasure in having their women pull off the pants if they were not skin-tight. Lars winked at her.

She ignored him, and held her headdress out to finish drying it. Ah, it would be a long journey downriver. She must be most careful to be with Karl whenever she could.

She looked about and saw much scat of deer and boar, but no bear. The animals were up and moving after the cold vise of winter. The harbor was a natural V, an enclosure sacred to the gods. Karl had chosen a better harbor than he knew.

Per had spread green seaweed to dry on the gravely beach, and was stirring whey-butter over the fire. She saw little foam, and thought he had been skimming it off. Men and women believed the foam strengthened men's sex. True or not, what people believed had great value.

Sniffing, Thora said she smelled mutton cooking, and Olaf brought all of them a chunk roasted on a stick. Inge thought it the best meat she ever eaten. Men, and women too, grew testy without fresh meat. Gotland would have one less sheep to shear.

The brothers sat alone on a rise, and all could see they were arguing, eating little. Inge felt fear tighten her chest, and knew she must do something to protect them all.

She told Thora to help her make a step-pattern. At home she would use meal, she told her daughter, but a quern to grind it was too heavy to bring along, and they must use sand.

Inge chose a simple pattern of a line circling back upon itself in swirls. She blocked off a two-fold square, twice as long as it was high, and big enough for the gods to see. She walked the pattern of two straight lines and a dot in each corner, with up-and-down edging. Peering through the eyeholes of her helmet, Thora stretched her legs, and followed the pattern of footsteps.

When it was done, Inge felt better. She had protected them as best she could.

Bratta lowed, and Inge stroked her bell cow, and called to Ingvar to bring her a pail from the boat. Milking had always soothed her.

"Ingeborg, let Thora milk, and sit with us," Karl called.

There would be nothing soothing in the men's dispute. She climbed the rise and sat next to Karl. She should be glad he took counsel with her. Most Norse men did not. Karl said he was happy Lars had waited to go downriver with them. He and Lars were the best of friends as well as brothers, and it would be more joyful for both captains to have each other.

Lars said he welcomed the chance to sail with his older brother, who had always been his hero. But he did not want to impose on their family. Did she have any objection to The Goldenbreast sailing along with them?

Inge shook her head. Any objection she had could not be voiced. She would just manage not to be alone with Lars. Karl kissed her, and said he was pleased. He and Lars rarely had a chance to sail together. And they would all be safer.

Now, the only problem was choosing the route to Miklagard. Did she remember the map he drew in the mud before they left home? Ay, she did. Karl said he had talked with the armorer, Gest by name, a man who could be trusted, for he came from Roslagen, and knew Halldis.

Ah, Inge thought, it was a fault of Karl's to trust every Swede. She listened with care. Gest had said that Prince Helgi the Wise, called Oleg by his people, ruled all of Kievan Rus and watched over river traffic from a great city on the Dnieper River called Kiev, though the Norse knew it as Konugard. It was second only to Miklagard for wealth and beauty. The prince had a fine stone palace, and each of his subjects paid tribute to him of one marten skin a year.

"And, Ingeborg, this prince has Swedish blood, and welcomes all Swedes as his guests. He is said to be descended from Rurik, a worthy fighter. Fal Christiantius they called him--The Gall of Christendom, much feared in England and Danmork, Skotland and Ireland."

She asked why this Helgi who ruled all of Kievan Rus, and had Swedish blood, was called prince and not king? Karl knew not, but they were certain to meet, and she could ask him.

Lars said he was concerned for her safety, and Thora's, above all. He had been on Gotland a week, spending hours in ale halls on her behalf, asking about routes to Miklagard. She knew he expected her to be grateful, but she said naught.

He told them the seven waterfalls on the Dnieper were aptly named: Sleep Not was one, for no man could sleep next to the thundering water. Another was called Ferocious, a third, Never Navigable. And the land with the waterfalls was owned by a warlike tribe called Pechenegs-- nomads, born on a horse, their only pillow their saddle. They were fierce fighters, and hated Swedes. They call us invaders, Lars added.

Inge forced herself not to shiver. She hugged her arms over her chest. Karl said Gest told him that Helgi made a pact with the Pechenegs to let convoys through their land.

"We have two boats. That is a convoy, Kinsman."

"Ingeborg," Lars said, "we need not sail down the Dnieper and chance our lives with the Pechenegs. There is another route."

She saw how serious Lars had become. In truth, he might have heard more about the Dnieper than he was telling. He talked about a river called Volga, another river flowing south. A river so beloved, the people called it Mother Volga.

Karl told him Gest had spoken of this, but it was half again as long as the Dnieper, and at the end they must portage the boats over sand to reach Miklagard.

Looking idly at the boats in the Gotland V, Lars argued that on the Dnieper they would portage through forest, though he agreed it was shorter. The Volga had no waterfalls, but was so easy-flowing men built houses on log rafts with flowers.

"Karl, around the Dnieper are runestones of men who died there. On the Volga there are none."

And how did Lars know if everything he heard about the Volga was true? Karl asked, chewing a grass stem. Lars had seen neither river. This was so, Lars admitted. They need not decide which route to follow until they arrived at Gardariki, Karl said, but he wanted Inge to think about their choice. Ay, she would think.

She went back to the fire. Each man, except the two captains, dipped barley bread in the whey butter, praising Bratta. When the ale cask went round, all drank without measure, except the two captains. They sat together, talking.

Inge took Thora with her to sit upon a flat rock and look at the solarfall--without the helmet. Thora took it off, but kept it at her side, her hip touching the metal. Inge told her she could not imagine how hard this journey would be without a daughter to share it. Pleased, the maid worked at her carving, and said she was glad the days were lengthening, because she had more light to use her knife.

In truth, Inge thought, a wooden cow was emerging.

How pleasant it was to sit, enjoying the day at even. Tonight it seemed possible she could wean Thora away from the sword to the healing joy in the natural world of cows and plants. They watched a band of pale pink at the horizon with dark clouds above, and it broke apart, forming a giant fish-bird. It had wings and scales, a fish tail and feathers. Inge saw an eye, an open mouth. They watched till it sailed off to Miklagard.

Thora said she decided the fish-bird would be her next carving, for it was unlike any ever seen in Sweden. Inge hugged her daughter, and told her about Prince Helgi the Wise and the dispute over which river to choose. Thora wondered whether the fish-bird chose the Dnieper, or Mother Volga, to follow south.

Inge thought about the armorer, Gest, who had spoken forcefully for going down the Dnieper. Why? Was he truly concerned about the safety of a fellow-Swede from Roslagen? Or did he have a stake in Karl's choice? Ah, perhaps she was too untrusting. On the morrow she would go with Karl when he went to get Thora's shield and chainmail. She would study Gest's face, his movements. A leechwoman saw what others did not.

Both rivers were dangerous with hazards the Swedish captains could not imagine. The witch-seer had read the runes and foretold 'a passage, perchance into darkness, a journey, part of which could not be shared...'

The runes never lied. For the two small boats, there was no safe passage. Inge pulled her daughter close and kept her arm about her shoulders, to keep herself from running up the rise and crying out.

The night brought her a fitful rest, and she woke the next morning to the grinding of casks rolling on gravel, and the curses of men pushing them up a plank. Lars had sailed The Goldenbreast into the Sacred V. Karl and Thora were already at the armorers, while she had overslept. She was angry with herself.

When she saw Anders sitting alone on a spar, he still wore a fine gold-trimmed shirt men wore to impress women at ale halls, but his hand dangled, useless. She could not leave him and go to the armorers. As she feared, Anders's wrist was broken, and he was hurting. She quickly mixed a double draught of willow bark. Waiting for it to dull the pain, he told her what had happened. He had left the ale hall with a wench, and in the moonlight they took a ride in her father's cart, but got lost and started down a dark, narrow road—one supposed to be haunted. At one time a ship came up on the beach there, and the Gotlanders killed the crew.

The horses must have seen the ghosts, for they reared and bolted, and pitched him into the road. He heard the wrist bone crack when he landed. The wench took the cart and left him to walk back to the ship. Anders declared he was through with women.

"You will not be able to pay for any more," Finnvid said. "She took your pouch of coins as well as your rowing arm."

Inge sent Finnvid back to work. She asked Hrolf to hold Anders down, and Per to cradle his head for comfort.

"I will work fast, Anders," she said. "Better a wrist than a leg."

She was glad the bones were not poking through the skin. She put her ear to it and heard no grating. Ah, a clean break. She sent Hrolf for a bucket of sea water and put the wrist in it to hold down the swelling. Gunnar brought a branch of beech wood that had broken and healed straight. From it he axed a splint. As Hrolf held him fast, Inge gritted her teeth and set the board splint beneath the arm and began easing the ends of bones toward each other. Gently, she pushed the bones into place and squeezed the wrist. Anders's yells were fearful. She was glad Hrolf was strong enough to hold him down.

"The worst is over," she told him, wrapping cloths around the splinted wrist. "The healing is beginning."

She began the cure, as all leechwomen did, by telling him the pain would soon lessen, and it would, for his eyes were dim from the double draught of willow bark. She said the healing charm to Eir in her mind, over and over, till the goddess fain would hear. Hrolf lifted Anders over the gunwales, and put him atop a leather bag in the bow. Inge wrapped a cloak about him and put woolen rags on his head, to hold in his warmth. The gulls screamed "kyew, kyew" all around them, and the men tramped the deck, piling the gear so Anders would have space.

His tongue was thick when he spoke. "Mistress, Karl will expect me to row."

"You cannot. Now rest."

Karl was most angry with him, Finnvid told her. The cart had overturned, and one wheel was set awry. Though it was a small thing, Karl thought the Gotlanders might take offense, using it against them. There were more of them than the Norse. And it was their island.

Ay, they must leave quickly, she thought. Karl and Thora appeared, the maid bedecked in chainmail, though she staggered beneath its weight. She carried a round shield in both hands. Inge sat and fitted an oar into the lock, as Karl jumped aboard.

"Inge, what in Hel's name are you doing?"

The men stopped working to look. Anders lifted his head, groaned and lay back down. Inge looked at Karl unlashing the tiller. A pity all rowers had to face their captain in the stern.

"Anders has broken his wrist and cannot row. I am taking his place."

The men looked away, getting the beasts up the planks, stuffing dried seaweed into a pouch. Hrolf brought the heavy bucket of whey butter aboard.

"Inge, put down the oar," Karl roared. "Women do not row!"

She held fast to the wooden handle, looking straight ahead. He would have to pull it from her, and she was a countrywoman with strong hands.

"Ingeborg! Do you hear me?" Karl shouted.

"Ja, Karl. They can hear you all the way to Sweden."

She wet a finger and held it up.

"The wind is friendly, Karl. We can soon be free of the harbor and under sail before an angry farmer catches us, perchance bringing the Gotlanders to break Anders's other arm."

Karl's face was hard-set. The men took their places at the oar, and Thora sat beside Inge. They waited, idle. Inge touched her amulet, Thora, her Thor's hammer. The maid giggled and moved closer. Once again the two were together against the men. Olaf stood in the water, his hand on the bow, ready to shove off. From the corner of her eye Inge saw Lars on his boat, grinning.

Karl stalked back to the steering oar. "Row!" he bellowed.

They began pulling together, and Olaf jumped aboard.

Inge matched her stroke to Thora's. Rowing was not so hard. It was a pleasure to be working with her body again, and not running from a fearsome bear. The mind was free when a rower pulled the blade back, lifted it, leaned forward, and pulled once more. Across from her Gunnar and Olaf rowed as a pair.

She knew Karl would like Anders to be up and rowing with his one good arm. But she could not let this happen. No leechwoman could.

Lars shouted across the water. "Karl-Eirik, you are shy an oarsman? I will loan you one."

"Nay," Karl shouted back.

Inge knew Karl would take nothing from his younger brother. She glanced at Lars and saw his red cloak was fastened with outsized fibulas. She hoped their weight would pull his shoulders down.

She watched the men snatch an instant of rest between the ever-lasting push-pull, and she showed Thora how to do the same. They rowed against the stiff current in pairs, except for Hrolf, who rowed alone. Inge looked at Gotland and saw its three parts: the beach, the hills, and the ridge where she had run from Lars. The new leaves of the birch turned in the light breeze, a shifty wind, and she hoped it strengthened when they got away from shore. She saw a flash of silver, and then it disappeared. Did Lars too see the waterfall? Nay, he was busy pouring ale and dropping meat overboard for sacrifice. Finnvid did the same for The Seafarer, and the two men jested across the water, though Karl did not.

Inge turned and looked back at Anders curled up asleep in the bow, with the splint atop his chest. She said the healing charms to Eir once again. For Anders, and herself, she hoped the wrist would heal aright. In battle, the northmen often fought with a weapon in each arm. If a storm came up, she would be hard put to keep Anders from tossing and turning on a pitching deck, and the bone would not set straight. She would be forced to break his wrist herself, and start again. Only once before had she done it. Once was enough.

The clump of seaweed nailed to the mast was no fuller or leaner. Fair weather would hold. The sea was scaly, with little ripples and no foam. A sailor's wind, not a storm wind, Gunnar told her. Yet she knew that at sea the weather changed in an eyeblink. The drumming of a woodpecker carried over the water, and she felt homesickness settle about her. She must not give way. She breathed deeply to calm herself, and the scent of pine came across the briny water. Ah, the healing plants were everywhere to help a troubled woman.

She felt the pull in her legs: rowing was hard labor. She looked at Gotland and saw a large gravefield, with many runestones. Some might be to honor men who had not returned from Miklagard. She pulled her cloak tighter.

Bratta lowed, and Inge asked Thora to milk. When the bucket was passed, Thora stood before her, rocking with the boat, the heavy chainmail giving her ballast. A born sailor, Inge thought.

Back rowing, Thora began singing a song. "It is one I made up, 'My Mother at the Oar'. " Inge told her to hush. Karl would not like it.

She told Gunnar that rowing was much like turning the quern. The body found its own rhythm. He told her he thought of everything but rowing when he was at the oar. All of them could row and sleep at the same time.

She felt the pull between her shoulder blades. She looked at Gotland and saw a thatched roof fold in the lee of a hill, where sheep would be protected. Never again would she complain about losing sleep during lambing time. Soft, wet fleece between her fingers was more pleasing than a wooden oar.

At last they rounded the tip of Gotland, and they saw the stone labyrinth made for raising the wind. The sail went up, and with relief the men put by the oars, glad for rest. She stretched, turned her face to the west and felt the freshening breeze, teasing the edges of her headdress when she tied it.

The north end of Gotland was rock-strewn: a land of slabs and rubble stone and gravel beaches, fishing nets weighted down to keep them from flying away. A herd of wild horses came out of the trees, and Volnir whinnied. Karl quieted him with a word, steering out, away from a tall rock pillar shaped like the headless body of a man. The sea rushed to and fro between the legs.

"A troll, turned to stone, much-weathered," Finnvid said.

"Nay," Inge said. "It is no troll, but a sacred pillar, rife with power."

Behind her, she felt his smirk. They all stared at the last of Sweden--the beacon on the last spit of land, and Inge and the maid rowed one-armed, hugging each other. They watched until the pole was a line angled against the sky, and then not even that.

Inge pulled her cloak about her, knowing not even a cloak of the finest woolen wadmal would warm the lonesomeness mixed up with fear that she felt deep in her bones. She held her amulet tight.

There was no turning back, whatsoever lay ahead.

The men were seasoned sailors and turned toward Kievan Rus, and Sven took out the flute. Not the sad song, "Who Can Sail?" but "The Laughing Dance." Thora began carving.

Karl's hand was light on the tiller, and Inge felt how carefree he was to be sailing again. In the bow she put her fingers on Anders neck and felt the pounding blood: ah, the healing was begun. For the others she gave them barley bread with dried beef and whey butter and curds. In truth, these men never complained, even if they had no whey-butter.

Karl asked her to pass around the ale, and she touched his fingers, but he drew back. She had done the one thing he could not forgive, and she knew it. She had gone against a captain's orders.

Though she would do it again if need be.

She sat on a sea chest and dozed. When she woke the waves were lengthening, and they were sailing through a purple sea. No one spoke for the beauty of it. The men and the sail and Karl at the tiller seemed sharper than ever, and then blurred. Shadows crept up from the bottom of the boat and spread, thickening. Karl announced he and Lars would sail through the night.

"A spring wind is often more blustery by night than day."

A trick of sailing she must remember, Inge thought.

"Mistress, know you Gotland was an enchanted island that sank every day and rose every night?" Sven asked.

"Naught but an old sailor's tale you picked up in the ale hall," Finnvid said, scoffing.

Sven swore it was true. Only when a man named Tjelvar came and brought fire, did Gotland stop sinking and rising.

True or not, they all listened as Sven told the tale.

With sun-warmed water from the cask she mixed a draught for Anders. He asked about the herbs. She told him one was yarrow, the great healer; another, fennel, to help him sleep; and knitbone, to speed the bones growing together. Inge spoke loud enough for the maid to hear, but Thora ignored her, standing alongside Gunnar, both talking softly.

"Mistress," Sven said, "Thora has asked me to tell her a sword story. I know one with chickens. May I tell her?"

"Chickens, like my hens at Breidal?"

"Ay, Mistress."

She took a deep calming breath. She must not let homesickness overwhelm her. There were stories behind the herbs, but Thora would want a sword story, if she bore broken arms and hands and legs and feet and head from battle. Ah, when they got off this accursed boat and could walk upon the earth, then Thora would learn to love the beauty of growing plants.

Though truth to tell, dried herbs were not fair to look upon. And a skald could not hear too many stories. For one who brought forth lays, a story could be the gist. She told Sven to tell the story, and his voice was pleasant in the dark.

"There was a smith named Velent who made a sword for his king, and the king liked it, but Velent said it must be better. In his smithy he filed the sword down to dust, mixed the filings with meal, fed it to his chickens. He took the droppings to his forge and used them on the soft iron and made a second sword. The king was pleased, but Velent said he must make it better. And again he fed the chickens with the filings and made a fine sword, for Velent was a good smith. Now the king truly wanted it, but Velent said he must make a sword belt first, and took it away."

"And this one pleased the king?" Thora asked.

Sven laughed. "Ay, but Velent quickly made an inferior sword and gave that one to the king. Mistress, know you how the chicken droppings strengthened the iron?"

Inge pondered. "I know fowl like to peck at glittering stones. There must be something in the droppings that smiths use."

"It is a mystery," Olaf said in the dark, "but I hear that in Kievan Rus they cut their swords into small pieces, mix them with meal and feed their ducks and geese. Know you this story, Sven? A swordsman was at odds with his father the king, and so he put a huge bundle of charcoal on his shoulders and walked to Danmork. When they asked him why he carried such a strange load, he said he would sharpen the dull wits of his father to a point with charcoal."

The men laughed, and Inge thought they liked tales that made fun of kings and queens.

"Both your stories were good," she said, "but Thora is yawning. It is time to sleep."

Around her Thora and the men bedded down where they could. She sat by Anders, watching Lars lash their boats close together so they would not drift apart in the dark.

She picked her way among the sleeping men to the stern and told Karl she was surprised how happy she was to be back aboard The Seafarer. She had missed the openness, and the water. She talked of how well their boat compared with others in the Gotland V, and how every ship had walrus hide rope, and she was glad Karl bought it.

"I am wont for you to have the best, Karl-Eirik."

He looked out at the moonshine on the water. "Then do not tell me how to run my boat."

"Karl! I would not! I know naught of sailing."

"Ay, but enough to take Anders's place at the oar."

She spoke softly to blunt his anger, telling him she was the luckiest of women. Never did she have the chance to face him, watching him steer, as when she rowed. He looked at the swell and not at her.

"Watching and learning, ay, Ingeborg?"

She thought that on land or sea people were often at odds. If they were home, Karl would rant, and then go down to the boatshed and work out his anger. They would become friends and soon lovers, but here, he could not go to the boatshed.

She turned her face to the streamer of gilt the moon cast upon the water. She knew Karl was remembering: he was the one who asked her to come along. Did he regret it?

"Get some rest, Inge."

"Nay, I have slept enough at our farmstead. I want to be with you."

She looked at Lars, steering close by, listening. Men unweighed by marriage loved to hear a couple wrangle. He whistled a tune, and the brothers laughed.

"Karl, what is that song?" she asked.

"An old sailor's song about how women are steadfast when men are with them."

She had made a great mistake. She should have drowned Lars when he was helpless with his breeches down. He called across the water, and she thought there was no way to shut out his voice.

"Ingeborg is like a marten, Karl. When he tracks his prey he never puts by the chase, but stays until he can pounce on it. Your wife is the same. The only difference is that she has not far to track you on The Seafarer. Inge, everything I know I learned from Karl. But he will never teach you to sail."

She looked at Lars's bland face in the moonlight.

"Inge, come and travel with me on The Goldenbreast , and I will teach you. Karl is fearful you will learn the big secret about sailing."

"Go to Hel," Karl said.

"What is the secret?" Inge asked.

It was strange to have Lars on her side against Karl-Eirik.

Lars laughed. "The secret, Ingeborg, is that there is no secret. There is no mystery to sailing."

Once Karl had told her sailing was simple if you follow the Rules of the Sea. But she did not know them. She gasped when Lars leapt over the water between their two boats. He leaned against the gunwale, as at ease aboard The Seafarer as The Goldenbreast. She could but admire his blue shirt and green pants. Even aboard ship Lars dressed like a king.

"Lars! You might have fallen into the Baltic."

"It would have been worth it, for you would have fished me out."

Nay, she would let him flounder. She peered at his boat and saw a slight young boy at the tiller.

"Lars, who did you leave to steer?"

"A young man called Halfdan, half a Dane. He has the makings of a good seaman. Now, Ingeborg, you cannot learn all in one night, but ask me a question about sailing, and I will answer."

Inge knew she must jump in and ask. Now she was glad she had not drowned Lars, though Karl's frowning face made her wonder if he might pitch his brother overboard himself. She asked Lars how night wind was different from day wind.

For one thing, a night wind can be trusted, he said, though only until a few hours before dawn, no more, no less. The night wind was good for running, as they were doing now, but not good for going into shore.

He said much of sailing could be felt through the hands and feet. He told her to listen to the squeak of the ships' boards. If she listened well it would tell her how fast The Seafarer sailed. As Lars talked on, she thought this must have been the way he listened when Karl taught him.

She made cups of mint tea from lukewarm water in the cask and gave one to Lars. In Karl's cup she put a pinch of Freya's Grass, for love.

"You leechwomen have your secrets, Inge," Lars said. "It is time for you to share."

No man, except Anders, had ever asked her. Ay, she would share, and gladly.

"Lars, do you know the eight winds go round the earth like a snake biting its tail, and each wind has a part in our lives?"

She turned to the west and breathed deeply. Lars grinned.

"And what message does this west wind bring, Ingeborg? To choose the Volga?"

She listened to the water splashing aside the prow. She heard the stays rubbing. She looked up at the stars, at the Square-Assed Bear. On such a night Einar would have the thralls in the fields, planting due north-south, for on such a night the moon releases the power in the seed.

She would fain be with them. She ached to kiss Karl-Eirik, but she could read the set of his shoulders. He spurned her, now when she needed him.

"Lars, the message the west wind brings is the same message the spakona's runes brought, back at Breidal."

She turned away from both men, but Lars put his hand on her shoulder.

"Inge! Why do you let these fool runes frighten you? They were chosen in a different time, a different place. And it was only sport and gaming."

Nay, it was not sport and gaming. A passage into darkness... a journey that could not be shared...

Yet she could not control everything. She had nothing to do with breaking Anders's arm, but she could not have left him to go to Gest and learn why Karl wanted the Dnieper for them.

"Lars, thank you for the sailing lesson."

Bowing, he said, "The first of many. We will be many weeks going downriver."

Though neither brother said which one, the Dnieper or the Volga. Lars leapt across the water and landed easily on the deck of The Goldenbreast. He blew her a kiss. Ah, she must take on some of Lars's carefree ways. His lower lip was twice as thick as his upper, the sign of someone with a natural gift for persuasion, and in truth he was glib. His lips were smooth in texture, so they looked fuller than normal. In a word, kissable.

She turned back to Karl-Eirik, who was not carefree, but detached, bowed down. He had always had victory-luck when he went a-viking, and part of his luck was in making the right choices. Now he must weigh the two rivers on his bronze trader's scale. And so choose the fate of his beloved brother and the crew of The Goldenbreast, his own men, and Thora and herself.

She ached for Karl. He knew a loneliness the men at the oar would never know. No man or woman could share this pain.

Anders groaned in his sleep and she walked to stroke his forehead, warm to the touch. She wished she could so soothe Karl-Eirik. It was the worst part of loving a man, when she had no comfort in her pouch of healing herbs, her charms, no help in the practical magic, the ancient wisdom her mother had taught her.

She had naught to give tonight, not even the warmth of her body, for Karl chose to sail on through dark hours, alone.

XIII

Inge woke to the scent of mint. Karl-Eirik sat on his heels next to her holding a cup of mint tea. His kindness surprised her. Gratefully she sipped, her hands over his, as much to warm his cold fingers, as the tea. She looked at the weary set of his shoulders. Karl had slept not at all.

"Tonight, Inge, we will sleep together. It is not good to spend the night alone."

She agreed and nodded toward the three-legged cauldron that heated her tea water, and said she would cook grot for day meal. Karl said nay, the winds favored until dawn, but soon the men must be at the oar, and the cauldron would be in the way.

He told her he knew it was a sorrow to her that Thora showed interest only in the sword and carving knife. They talked of the night she recited her lay about Karl, and Inge thought the maid would learn the healing charms with ease. How Thora had picked the flower, Foal's Foot, and Inge thought she had a love of plants. She told him she was rash to adopt Thora without knowing of her beginnings, but she wanted the full ceremony of adoption, not the knee-seating, which could easily be undone. He shrugged.

"Inge, I am not sorry we adopted her."

"Nor I. But, ah, Karl, she has changed our lives. If not for Thora, you would be on your way to Iceland, and I would be home watching Skulda's piglets wallow in mud."

"We would not be sharing the leather bag aboard The Seafarer, ay? By tonight we will be in sight of landfall."

She could not hold back a joyful whoop. They would sleep on the solid earth, not this ever-rocking ship. She rubbed his taut shoulders with one hand. His night had been long, standing alone at the tiller, thinking.

"Inge, once we land, the men must practice swordcraft nightly, by firelight."

She held his fingers tightly on the cup. "And you want Thora to practice, too. Karl, she is so slight."

"Ay. Our Thora has a gift for the sword, but she has much to learn. I trow she would be overmatched among any of my men, but Lars's crewman, Halfdan, is as slight as she is, and the two would work well together in practice. Do you agree?"

She looked at The Goldenbreast and saw Lars jesting with the young man, Halfdan. Karl was right. He was the only one Thora's size on either ship.

"Come, Inge, do you agree? We are in luck this boy Halfdan is sailing with Lars."

She knew Karl needed to keep both swords and swordsmen sharpened. But step by step Thora was getting further from Inge's thoughts and dreams. Ah, the gods often played cruel tricks.

She sighed. "Ay, Karl. I have no choice. I agree."

He kissed her and went back to his tiller. Around her men were stretching, yawning, rolling up their leather bags. As she dressed, she felt the ache between her shoulder blades from the rowing yesterday.

The water was rippling with whitecaps, the sky thick with high fish-tail clouds. She shielded her eyes from the sun, an orange disc on the horizon. A good day for Anders's wrist to heal. She saw he was up, and slipping an oar into place with one hand. How strong these northmen were!

She gave him a draught for pain, and looped a length of wadmal beneath his arm, tying the ends round his neck, to hold the arm close to his chest. The swelling was down--a good sign. Gunnar smiled at her and took his place next to Anders, doing his share and half that of the injured man. Karl's men worked in tandem, she thought, one's strength helping another's weakness. The men jested, and called Anders, "One Wing."

She milked Bratta and told her bell cow that soon she would toss her head, and the bell would ring, and every beast in Kievan Rus would follow them down the rivers. To each man Inge gave a handful of grot to chew and a drink of milk and barley bread with whey-butter. Thora slept on, through the racket.

Lars's boat came alongside and he called, "Are your men tired already, Karl-Eirik?"

"Nay, they are not wasting their strength."

"Ay? Farvell--we will see you in Miklagard."

The Goldenbreast pulled ahead and Lars laughed, and Hrolf bellowed his fearful roar, and Lars laughed again.

"Nay!" Finnvid shouted, and Karl's men began rowing as though possessed with elvist, leaning into the oar. Inge knew they could not help but race--it was in their blood. The skin tightened over their cheekbones, and now there was no jesting until The Seafarer shot ahead, an arrow from an unseen bow. Karl's men laughed and taunted the other crew, and now they rowed side by side, sharing tales of other journeys, listening to each other's lies.

While their captains steered around chunks of floating ice, the men talked of times they had been trapped between floes, their boats jammed solid. How they had chopped through five, six--nay ten--ells of ice to free their hulls. How they had escaped from one floe to another, jumping over twenty, thirty feet of open water. They bragged of dangerous voyages to the Faroes and Orkneys.

One of Lars's crewmen teased Anders about the girls waiting for him to return this year, and Anders said when next they saw him, he would be wearing golden breeches.

So the long, sunlit day passed. The weather held, and Inge learned when the men tightened some lines and loosened others. She saw how Karl handled the tiller when the sail filled, and when it luffed. Carving the rune stock, Gunnar told her the Baltic was known as a sharp sea, stealing fishermen's nets in sudden storms. But the women brought the two crews weather-luck. Finnvid snorted, and Inge ignored him.

Karl called her and asked her to face him. He fingered her amulet of Freya and slipped his hand inside her undershift, squeezing her breasts, each in turn. She tried to pull away.

"Nay, Karl! Not in front of the crew."

"Your back is to them. They can see naught. How can I look at you all day and not desire you? I have always loved making your body respond to my fingers. Now, my Ingeborg, I must talk with Finnvid."

She sighed. "Talk to Finnvid and play with me at the same time."

He laughed, and told her a captain's burdens kept him from much he wished to do, and put both hands back on the tiller.

Her crotch was wet, though Karl had not touched her there. She walked back to the gunwale and stood beside Thora, grateful the swell was long and gentle to keep the boat calm enough to help Anders's wrist heal. The maid was so taken with carving a cow she did not ask Gunnar for a sword story, and Inge dozed, content.

At even, dark red water clouds hung low in the sky, and Per checked the seaweed on the mast and said they would have no rain for a day or more, unless the wind blew from northeast to south. Inge thought if she kept her eyes and ears open she could not help but learn the Rules of the Sea.

Karl wanted to begin the journey in Gardariki in daylight, so Finnvid dropped the killick anchors at bow and stern, and Karl lashed the tiller. He told Lars to tie his boat close by, for he had a message for them all.

When the two boats were close enough to walk from one to the other, both crews waited, some sitting, some leaning. Thora and Inge huddled close together on a sea chest, and Inge breathed deeply, trying to calm her thumping heart. This message was important. Karl waited till all were watching him. Inge felt he looked at her alone, and she knew each man felt the same. It was a knack he had.

"We will be going on the Lower Road to Miklagard," he said. "Down the Dnieper. Not the Upper Road, the Volga."

Inge felt a slap of water against the hull. The Dnieper, with its portage through the forest, the waterfalls, the Pechenegs, the Swedish Prince Karl hoped would protect their pitifully small convoy. She looked out to sea, the water red at the tops of the waves, black in the troughs.

"Karl, why did you choose the Dnieper?" Finnvid asked, speaking for all of them.

The armorer, Gest, had no route to speak for, Karl said, but as they knew, he was from Roslagen. Karl trusted him. Gest had told him the land along the Volga was owned by men called Khazars. Not followers of the White Christ, or the true faith of Odin, but they were called Jews and worshipped a god named Yahweh. This Yahweh brought them much luck. When some Swedes went down the Volga a few years back, the Khazars had defeated them after three days of fierce fighting.

Karl leaned against the mast and said if their countrymen had defeated the Khazars, the Swedes would then have control of the Volga, but now all captains must ask if they can sail down it. He was loath to ask any man if he could use his river. Ten per cent of every ship's cargo must be paid as tax to the Khazars.

But there was more. No man dared approach their leader without lying down in the dust at his feet.

Striking the mast, Karl said, "I for one will not rub my face in the dust for any man!"

The men cheered, and both crews shouted "Not I!" and "Never!" and "They can rot in Hel!" and such. Karl let them vent their anger till each was done.

"Are there any who wish to kiss the dirt before a king?" Karl asked, and the men tromped their feet and banged the oars against the boat while Inge marveled how simply Karl swung them to his view, though he merely spoke his own mind.

"I like this man Helgi, the Overlord of Konugard on the Dnieper," Karl said. "Until the city came into his hands, each household had to give a sword to the Khazars as tribute."

Old rusty swords beyond use, Inge thought, the kind the Swedes gave for sacrifice every nine years. Still, they were swords. The dark was gathering in the boat, and Sven lit a torch and held it high to light the flickering shadows on his captain's face.

"Now Helgi has said throughout Kievan Rus, 'pay no tribute to the Khazars,' and they do not," Karl said. "They pay tribute to Helgi. If any man holds for the Khazarian Way, let him speak."

The men chanted "nay" and "not me", until Finnvid leapt upon a sea chest. The men muttered: Finnvid was keeping them from their rightful ale.

"These Khazars are fierce warriors," Finnvid said, "but since when are we ones to shirk a fight when there is a prize waiting to be plucked! In the ale hall at Gotland I heard that a Khazar princess travels in a tent made of the finest silk, with gold doors and floors covered with marten fur. The Khazars walk on fur!"

Inge knew Karl would listen to Finnvid's grievance now, rather than let it fester. Karl said it was true the Khazars had much gold, but attacking them would not be as easy as a lone church in an island off Skotland. The Emperor of Miklagard had built the Khazars a chain of stone forts, many miles long.

"But, Finnvid, no man is bound to me but by choice. You are a freeman, and if you wish to go down the Volga you can find passage. Though you will see a strange custom among these Khazars."

Karl paused. "All who are born have the foreskin of their manhood cut at eight days."

"What is that to me?" Finnvid asked.

"The Khazars do it for all who join them. Gest said it is simply done. The skin is lifted, and a blade cuts round in a circle to remove it. Either an iron knife, or flint."

Gunnar groaned. "It is not for me. Why do they do it?"

"It is part of their faith. They do it for cleanliness, and Gest said they think they father more children this way."

"That has never been a problem for us," Anders said, and both crews laughed.

Inge shivered. Ah, it was a curious world beyond her fjord.

"A friend of the father's holds the babe upon a cushion for the cutting," Karl said, "but for a grown man, I know not who would hold you, Finnvid. But I do not think we will hear that you cried out, ay?"

Finnvid's brow was damp with sweat, though the night was chill. He looked out to sea and pulled on his beard. Inge knew a man in tumult could not be still. He turned back to Karl.

"Karl-Eirik, you have had good luck on our voyages. Who knows what kind of luck the Khazars have? I will stay."

The men cheered and stomped, and Karl put his arm around Finnvid and gave him the first cup of ale.

All drank to Karl and the Dnieper and the full moon lighting their path to Gardariki. They drank to the Guiding Star and the Square-assed Bear. Inge and Karl stood, arms about each other, and all drank to Bifrost, overhead. They drank to One Wing, first to fall asleep.

Inge was happy to crawl into their leather bag with Karl. One night alone had been enough. Bedplay was one place she could steer Karl's body into pleasure, one part of their lives they could control. On this journey they were at the mercy of the fickle winds, but in the leather bag each man was a king, each woman a queen.

She talked with her fingertips, searching for softness in this hard man who had made a hard decision. Her fingers found soft skin on his earlobes, behind his ears, inside his collar bones, and as she stroked, she felt his manhood grow. She licked his lips and as always, it excited her to excite him. She put his Jade Stalk into her Golden Cleft, and as always it seemed to belong.

She whispered that as a leechwoman delivering babes, she had seen no two women with the same color Cinnabar Gate. Some were as dark as the dewberry, some pale as the mallow, and she asked him about her own color. Karl offered to get her handmirror, and they laughed, thinking how dark it was within the bag.

Some men pumped their sex into a woman as a fencepost was pounded into a fence hole, but not Karl-Eirik--she would not let him. It ever astonished her that stroking a part of the body hid from all could have an effect on thoughts. She could see his manhood as clearly as with her eyes. She giggled.

"Ingeborg, do not giggle. I will slip out of you."

"Ja, I will try. It is the ale giggling."

Karl's fingers turned round and round the small button of flesh on her Cinnabar Gate. The familiar trickle began the flutter in her stomach.

She moved so he could play with her breasts. All men and women had the need in them of a babe to suck and be sucked. Though the longer they spent in bedplay, the longer the sweet Come lasted, her body would not wait, but moved to and fro on its own. He pushed his sex higher, and her Golden Cleft opened and closed, opened and closed around him, squeezing him the way her mouth squeezed his tongue, greedy for the way he filled her. Up inside, the sweetness came unbidden as always, and she felt the flow of it, out from her center, up her spine, down through her legs to her toes.

Each time the sweetness came it was different, and she wiggled, riding the second wave, and it seemed this wave lifted the boat higher and higher, and then crashed down. Karl moaned, and she felt his Come spray within her, their juices mingling. The sweet-sour smell of his musk rose around them. She felt cleansed. How had she ever lived without Karl-Eirik for six months every year?

Had he made the right choice of river? He had seemed so certain in front of the crews, but she knew no captain could decide something so important without worry and doubt.

There was only one way to know. If they survived, Karl's choice was right. And if not...a journey into darkness...part of which could not be shared...

Her chest hurt, and she knew it for fear. She pulled Karl to her. She must put aside the seer's foretelling, and like the crew, put all trust in her captain.

XIV

The next morning the gulls flew out to meet them, and Inge saw that these birds in Gardariki were much like the Swedish ones. The handsomest, with the whitest tail feathers, would be the goddess Freya, who could assume bird form. Freya landed on the gunwale next to her, and then flew off toward the new land. Inge felt warmed and welcomed. Whatsoever happened, the goddess would be with her.

The number of boats increased, and many were new to both crews. While they combed and brushed and put on their brightest tunics and as many rings as they had, all marveled at a boat made of sealskin, with a reindeer hide sail, its mast a tree trunk. It was from the far north, Karl said, and he steered close by so all could see the fine fittings of whalebone.

They saw deep-hulled ships of burden, and Inge knew the men were figuring how much plunder they would carry. But they turned stiffly, Gunnar said, and were no good for running onto beaches or shallow rivers. Their own ships were best.

Karl and Lars sailed in to the harbor to show off their well-crafted boats, so the oar men were free to gawk. The town had timber houses, roofs newly-thatched and a few of mud-and-wattle, with older, blackened thatch. Karl steered to the higher west bank of a river, choosing a quay with no broken staves. Per threw over the line, and it was caught by a man in a trader's shirt with gold thread trimming the cuffs. He tied it to a trunk, and the two captains leapt ashore.

"Välkommen to Daugmalé, where you connect with the Dvinna River," the trader said. "I am Tosti."

Inge saw the lace of his hat was finely-wrought, but his eyes were hard and tense from counting silver. When he spoke she heard the singsong Swedish she loved. Both Lars and Karl took coins from their pouches and paid protection money.

Each captain left two men on watch, and the crews walked to town, past horse-drawn sledges and high-laden loads with men guarding them, their swords out of the scabbard for all to see. The quay was lively, with women selling loaves of black bread and ale. They could not keep from watching the swaggering northmen, and flirted from demure eyes. Karl bought cooked lamb on sticks and bread and drink for the crews. Inge saw the women wore overgarments with aprons of three squares tied at the waist by a leather throng. All of them were dimply, with good teeth. Anders flirted with them in Swedish, until Olaf led him away by his one good arm.

"Anders, I know you have not had a woman since Gotland, but we know not what these women's bodies are like beneath their long skirts." He chuckled. "What you seek may be crosswise."

The crews laughed. Inge saw some of these dark-haired women wore a head-dress and beneath it, one plait like her own.

"I trow, Karl," Lars said, "I thought you had the only married woman who plaits her hair in a single braid."

"My Inge has ever been a woman of her own mind, Kinsman."

The men on the quay wore tunics and breeches, much like the Swedes, but with cone- shaped fur hats. Every man was bearded, a few pointed, like Finnvid's, but most bushy and long. Everywhere men thought long hair gave them prowess in bedplay, Inge thought.

Tosti the trader walked with them, telling the captains he liked the way they chose manageable sizes for their ships, and they seemed not over-crowded. Karl answered that every ell was in use. Tosti asked if they spoke Greek, the tongue of all who lived in Miklagard.

"Nay, but we will find a countryman to interpret," Karl said.

Tosti said Swedish interpreters were few there, but because they were all Swedes he knew a Greek for hire here in Daugmalé, one who could also help interpret the tongue spoken in Kievan Rus. He offered to pay them to take the man.

Inge stopped walking. "Why?"

Tosti said he felt sorry for the Greek. At first he was amusing with good stories, but now he could scarcely talk. His teeth were loosening, his gums bleeding. Soon he would starve to death. Inge asked if a leechwoman had looked at him, but he said he had no coin to spend on a healer. She looked at his silken shirt with gold on the cuff, gold scrollwork on his shoes.

"I am a leechwoman. Take me to him."

"Ingeborg!" Karl said. "What if he has a dread sickness? What if you catch it and give it to my men? Or Thora?"

"Nay, nay," she said. "Eir, the goddess of healing, protects all leechwomen. I have treated hundreds of sicknesses and never gotten sick. You and Lars stay on the quay."

Karl cursed, and said he would not let her go into a hut in a strange land alone.

The Greek sat hunched on a bare dirt floor in a draft, leather thongs binding him to a pole. Slowly he forced his body upright by sliding the thongs. His face was sallow, and covered with red sores, oozing pus. Pig-bristles stood up from his scalp.

"Phew, he stinks," Lars said, and both men and Thora put their sleeves to their noses. Inge thought she had never seen so wretched a man, and she asked Tosti his name.

"Zeno," the man said through a bleeding mouth, and slid down.

Ah, this Greek understood Swedish. She told Tosti he had the sickness called The Sores and there was no sickness easier to treat: wild onion, poultices and draughts from the pine, cow's milk, fresh air and sun, and he would be well.

The trader snorted, and said he had no time to make a poultice.

"Ay, run him through with a sword and throw him in the river," Lars said. "Then you can breathe in here."

Out on the board walk Inge asked Tosti to tell them the wretch's story.

He had been a linen-weaver in Miklagard, Tosti said, much in favor with the Prefect who oversaw all work for the Emperor. The wretch worked from dawn to even, but he wove too much, and the excess had to be sold in the market place. The Emperor, Basil I, was a soldier, and he ran Miklagard like an army camp with many rules and strict punishments for any who disobeyed. A weaver must take to the market only as much linen as he could carry on his back, but the wretch had so much he hired three asses to help. This was against the law, and the Prefect had Zeno flogged, shorn, and sent out of the city as an outlaw.

Ah, Inge thought, a word they knew full well.

"And now his hair grows out bristly," she said. "Karl, if he worked for the Emperor, he would know the law and customs and could teach us much, on the way down the Dnieper."

Karl reminded her he had two ears full of men talking all the time. He needed no more.

"Speak you Greek?" Inge asked Tosti, breaking off a sprig of pine.

"Some few words, Mistress. Anthros, the word for "man". Dendron, for "tree." " "Ah. For "boat" and "tiller"? For "gold" and "emperor"? "

"Only a man who lived in Miklagard would know those."

Lars asked how the Greek got to Daugmalé, and Tosti said the wretch had wandered the countryside looking for work, but the tribes grew sheep, not flax, and he knew nothing about weaving wool. He found passage upriver to Konugard, where Prince Helgi befriended him, and Zeno learned Swedish. Helgi offered to let him collect the yearly tribute from the tribes for a living. But nobody would trust him with their marten skins, and so he wandered to Daugmalé.

The trader spread his hands. "Helgi is Swedish, and hospitable to all strangers. It is one of our faults, is it not? But it is in our blood."

Inge looked at his finery, and said naught but that she needed to talk with Karl and Lars alone. Tosti wanted to say more, but left them.

She answered the men's objections. When Karl said the wretch would stink up his boat, she told him there was enough water in the Dvinna to wash him. They could drag him on a rope till he was clean. When Lars said the wretch would eat up her good food, she said he could fish for all of them, and get more. With feet bound, he could do little else.

She slipped her arm into Karl's. He was a shrewd trader who prided himself on a sharp deal.

"Husband, Miklagard is not Birka, where all men speak Swedish. How do we know we are getting full measure for anything unless we know Greek? Tosti says interpreters are few. What care we if we have our own with us? The wretch is a bargain at little cost."

Lars suspected he was a spy for the Emperor, and she answered if so, he had been well- trained and could be doubly useful. On a small boat it would be easy to watch this Zeno closely. She clasped the brothers' arms.

"I will make a pact with you. If the wretch gets troublesome, we will drop him over the side of the boat."

But not before he teaches us the Greek tongue, she thought. And much, much else about Miklagard. Once healed, his long-simmering anger would abate.

"Over the side to drown," Lars said. "I will drink to that."

Karl agreed, and they set off for the ale hall, Inge holding fast to Thora's hand.

* * *

They began passage down the Dvinna River, with Finnvid offering sacrifice to the gods. Inge faced into the north wind, the wind of change, and said the summoning charm three times. No man or woman could control the magic in the restless air, but still she was bound to invoke the favoring wind. The sail hung lifeless, and the men were hard-pressed, rowing against the current, for they had learned a quick, hard lesson. The Dvinna flowed towards the Baltic, against them.

"You are calling the winds?" Zeno asked from his place in the bow, bound hand and foot. "Better you pray to God."

"Perchance it is the same," Inge said.

She walked to Karl in the stern, touching the seaweed on the mast. It was shriveled and damp--wet weather was on its way. But the waves of a river would not be as high as the Baltic, and Anders would not be pitched about.

They sailed past wooden houses no bigger than her bathhouse. At the river edge women knelt at flat stones doing the familiar tasks of the spring wash: plunging and wringing and spreading the clothes out to dry. Inge felt a pang of homesickness.

She kissed Karl, and thought she must not be downcast. She had survived the Baltic and its pitching waves, and now they would be going down placid rivers. She asked if he was easier in his mind to be steering downriver than the ever-changing Baltic--he could not lose his way. He told her he could see in every direction for friend or foe on the sea, but going downriver he knew not what awaited them around the next bend.

The Goldenbreast sailed behind them, and the two boats passed the last house, the river winding between pines, as far as she could see.

"Karl, look out!" Ingvar called from atop the mast. "Steer to shore!"

He did, and quickly, and a flotilla of enormous trees surged past them. The men marveled, and all said they had never seen bigger trees, as wide and deep as a boat.

"That is what Helgi will use them for," Zeno said. "Many men come to Kievan Rus, and their boats are too big for the twisting rivers. But your crafts are small enough."

Was he belittling their boats? Inge wondered. She must not let the Greek spoil their journey. And so she looked at Karl. Like their boat axed from trees, her husband was solid as an oak, rooted in his beloved ship. Zeno, on the other hand, was proving less than a joy, and there was no way to escape his grousing.

"I am no better off than when I was in the hut," he said. "Your wooden boat is no softer than dirt to sit upon."

"Ay, you are a pain in the arse to all of us," Anders said, rowing with his one good arm.

Inge began preparing a poultice for him.

She told Zeno his hands and feet were tied with the knots of Eir, the goddess of healing. He was out in the sun and fresh air. At even he would have fresh milk, and healing medicines from the pine. In a week he would be well, if not before. Already his mouth was healed enough to talk, after one draught of yarrow and rose hips. She suspected he would have spoken more with Tosti.

The sheep's wool clouds were beginning to gather, but not fast enough, Finnvid said. Rain to wash the stinking Greek was not likely today. Finnvid wanted to pitch him overboard. Per said to put an oar between his hands, and he would have something to whine about

Inge told them any man kept in a hut would have a stench, and he was afflicted with The Sores. Once he was healed, he would take his place at the oar. His bones were weakened through no fault of his own.

Only Bratta and Volnir seemed unaffected by the wretch's stink. After their romp in town, they settled in on the swift-flowing river, their rumps to the stranger.

Finnvid said if the wretch was bigger they could sell him as a slave, but he was too puny, even for battle.

"I am a linen-weaver to the Emperor," Zeno said. "I am a Roman, not a Greek."

"But you speak Greek," Gunnar said.

"Yes, but the Emperor's city that you call Miklagard is known among civilized people as New Rome, and I am a Roman."

Karl told Zeno to shut up--he was not in New Rome now. Inge fingered her neckring of firestones which Tosti had given them to take Zeno. Karl had not made a bad trade. He had refused to stink up his boat with the wretch unless he was paid with a bag of fine furs and a neckring of firestones for his wife.

Inge loved the amber neckring. She told Tosti the gods made them from sunlight dancing on the water, but he said they were made from pine resin long hid in the earth, and washed ashore on beaches at Amberland.

She and Thora had laughed together. How could firestones come from water if they were buried in the earth? Tosti told them he had seen firestones with insects locked inside. One time a fly, and two times a spider. That proved her mother was right, Thora said. Spiders and flies lived above the earth, not within.

Now Zeno was complaining about boats he had seen in New Rome, bigger than their own, with more gilding on the prow post, higher masts, a bigger hold below the deck, not as cluttered. The men pulled against the current, and looked their hatred at him.

"The red of your sail is not as bright as the red in sails at New Rome, where we feed madder plants to the sheep. If you did this, your sail would not be as drab."

Inge remembered how her back ached digging the prickly madder, stirring the dye pot, working side by side with Hervor, Karl's shipwright, pushing the woven stuff over and under in 168 a basket-weave strong enough to resist harsh winds, to make a strong and fair sail for Karl-Eirik. She had done it all for love.

Inge stood before Zeno and picked up a line. She snapped it against the gunwale, and read fear in the way his shoulders hunched.

"Zeno, you have insulted my sail."

She snapped the line again. The men cheered.

"He deserves a flogging, Mistress," Finnvid said.

"I dyed and wove the sail myself," Inge said to Zeno, "and you have insulted it.'

Struggling, he sat up as straight as he could.

"In New Rome our healers do not make sails! We have a carder's guild, a spinner's guild, a weaver's guild, a sail-maker's guild...I myself am a linen weaver to the Emperor and..."

Inge snapped the line closer to him.

"The rope is for lowering you overboard to wash your stinking body."

"No, no! Flog me, but do not throw me into the water--there is still ice floating in it. I will freeze!"

When Hrolf lowered him over the side, the Greek flailed and bobbed and splashed and whimpered each time Hrolf lifted him and lowered him again. A shard of ice struck him and he screamed. Lars steered close by.

"Inge, say the word, and I will cut the rope."

"Let the Greek dangle. Zeno, we will haul you aboard if you promise to talk of Miklagard only to answer our questions."

Hrolf lowered him as far as his mouth.

"For God's sake, let me up, or I will freeze to death!" Zeno said. "I will do anything you ask."

"Is there no cold water in Miklagard?' she asked. "Lift him up," she told Hrolf.

The wretch banged his body against the hull, and Inge was unsure if Hrolf slammed him into the boat or not. She wrapped the shivering man in a piece of wadmal. In truth he smelled better after his warm bath.

Though the water was clear all the way to the bottom, this Dvinna was rock-strewn, and she saw Karl had to steer with care. She leaned back to see the tips of the trees, silvered with melting snow. She heard air bubbles popping beneath the cracking ice. Though the trees were bigger than in Sweden she knew their names: the spruce, the pair-needled pine, the true and false firs, all with healing power for The Sores. The wretch was lucky.

They sailed past fish weirs set in the water, and Inge thought the dark pilings crudely set, remembering the fine, meshed patterns of fish weirs on Swedish rivers. She moved to the bow.

"It is true fish have bad eyesight, and they care not at all for a well-set pattern if they are caught in a weir, but what manner of man set these?" she asked Zeno.

"The Finns," he said. "They keep to themselves and are fearful of being captured by you and sold as slaves in New Rome. They are very shy. I will tell you how shy. They sit in front of their houses waiting to be invited to a funeral."

Zeno laughed, but he was the only one. This Greek was a blabber, but she preferred that to a sulker.

She took out an old overdress and began cutting the skirt down the middle below the waist, stitch by stitch, front and back. She remembered weaving the cloth one night, waiting for Karl to finish tarring the boat, and when he came they lay together on the floor, two as one, the smell of meadowsweet rushes mingling with the smells of sex and sweat.

She never dreamed she would be traveling on the boat through an unknown land, cutting the cloth she wove stitch by stitch. She found it pleasing to spin yarn, and thread a bone needle, and sew half of each front to half a back. She would do the same with a dress of Thora's. No northman would wear these breeches, but she was not a man. Zeno looked curious, but dared not ask what she sewed.

That first day Inge never tired of looking at shades of green trees, each different. The shore was never the same for long. Often she saw bog land and lakes. She untied Zeno and gave him a fishing line, and in truth he had the knack of calling the fish. He soon had a full bucket for their meal ashore.

Zeno got the same measure of Bratta's milk as the crew. Per passed around several loaves of the black bread from Daugmalé, and each bit off a chunk, except Zeno, who broke his share delicately with thumb and forefinger. The men were too tired to tease him. When dusk started to fill the river, Karl steered to shore, and Inge untied Zeno.

"Karl-Eirik looks for a level part sheltered by a stone bank, so we will not get washed out by a sudden flood," Gunnar told Inge, and she thanked him, knowing docking for the night was part of sailing.

Gladly they leapt ashore, men and beasts, except Zeno who lowered himself, his feet banging the hull until he could no longer hang on and dropped into the water. The men foraged for firewood and cleaned fish, while Karl lit their need-fire with his strike-a-light.

"Fire has ever been your father's favorite weapon," Anders joked with Thora.

The men cooked the fish on hot stones while Inge tended to healing the Greek. She said a quiet thank you to the Goddess Eir for healing power aplenty. Gunnar axed off the outer pine bark for her, peeling the inner bark in shreds to boil with spruce blossoms, both pink and yellow. He scraped resin, and Inge made Zeno chew it. She gave him twigs, and had him spread the oozing pitch on his sores. With the greenest, newest needles she made a tea for him to drink. Some she spread on the hot stones and had him breathe it in, a piece of wadmal wrapped round his head. He coughed and spat, and she was pleased. He was coughing up his sickness. The Goddess Eir was helping.

When he complained he had a headache, and that Inge was making him sicker, she crushed pine needles and steamed them and bound them in a band to his forehead, and the headache left. She used the Tree of Life to the full. She wanted to get the wretch healthy. Not alone to row, but to teach them the Greek tongue, and much else about Miklagard.

Lars noted her eagerness.

"Ingeborg, healing with the Tree of Life increases sexual desire, does it not? With so much pine used on him, the wretch will attack us all, men and women both."

She tossed Lars a twig of the pair-needled pine.

"It is true, Lars, pine strengthens the manhood, along with the rest of the body."

When Zeno needed to piss, she sent Hrolf along to guard him. When she and Thora went into the woods to lift their skirts, Thora took the peace bands off her sword, though there was no sign of the Finns. A daughter protecting her was new. Inge decided she liked it. She saw much scat of wolves and deer, two animals often found in the same place, but not at the same time.

After they ate the fish, the men piled the fire high to keep off the encircling dark. They spoke of the journey, and Inge saw there was no fear in them of this new land. It was but one more adventure. They drank ale, telling stories to pass the time.

Zeno said he heard the north was a strange country with a wall dividing it into two parts, and Finnvid told him he was full of shit. There was no wall.

Zeno said he heard one side was healthy with fine crops of grain growing, and fat cattle. The other was filled with pestilence and poisonous snakes, and no man dared live there.

Finnvid kicked a log, and said the Greek had learned foolish tales about the northmen.

"Yes? Here is another. Fishermen leave their women's beds when they hear a mysterious call to go out and gather the dead floating on the water. They must row the dead through the mists to their final resting place."

"Shut up!" Karl said. "We will have no talk of bodies floating on the water. We bury our dead, and they stay buried. Ingeborg, you are healing him too quickly."

In truth, the talk had frightened her, and she heard rustlings beyond the fire circle. She looked back and saw gleaming red eyes lit by firelight, and cried out. Karl threw a firebrand at the beast and it slunk away, crashing through the bushes.

"Greek, we have had enough talk. You came with nothing, and we do not begrudge your passage, but I will not have you frightening Inge." He threw Zeno a piece of wadmal. "Sleep in this."

The men curled up in their leather bags and were soon asleep. Sailors could sleep anywhere, she thought, but a countrywoman liked a bed-closet with four walls and a turf roof overhead. All day she had heard the taiga's gentle dripping snowmelt, but now she heard great booms, the muffled thunder of the ice cracking up north, sheets of it splitting, shifting, breaking, as they struck each other. The river brought the sound down to them, and she found it fearful.

She had much to ask Karl about river sailing, but he yawned, and said he wondered if Thora would ever spout another lay. Inge rubbed his hard shoulders and told him they must be patient. It was not easy for a maid to be a thrall one day and a chieftain's daughter the next. Thora was a skald, and could not be forced. She would speak in her own time. Inge nestled her nose into him and listened for Bratta's soft lowing. All were soon asleep.

Toward morning Inge awoke and heard Thora singing a poem from what seemed a great distance:

"The silver river flows as a sword, a tongue in a green scabbard, a serpent twisting down the blade, a serpent throwing its tail, held fast by venom-thong. Drawing blood each time it is loosed, making wounds never healed."

Inge shivered. A strange lay, unlike any she had heard, Inge thought, and squeezed close to Karl-Eirik. The river as a sword...drawing blood each time it is loosed...and most frightening of all--making wounds never healed.

In the leather bag she rolled away from Karl, and cried silent tears with an open mouth. Only one with a warrior's heart could make such a poem. And what was a warrior's lot, but a short life, death close at hand in the next battle, or the next, or the next? If warriors did not die early, they knew loss and maiming, blood and pain.

Of these the maid knew naught. Learning swordcraft had been a way to be close to Tyrkir, but now Tyrkir was dead, and still she loved it.

The tears stopped, and dread filled Inge's throat, threatening to choke her. She rolled back, pressing her neck against Karl's back. She reached her arm around his chest. She loved him for wanting to protect Thora, for arranging sword practice with Halfdan for her. Karl did it out of love, and if perchance he was competing with the memory of Tyrkir, the maid had father-luck.

Inge felt the battle scars on Karl's chest with her fingertips. We trade when we can, fight when we must, he had said. A maid who was only a fighter would soon have scars of her own.

A log fell in the fire casting a shower of sparks. Fire is Karl's favorite weapon, the men had teased, and she knew they meant a raging fire in battle. What healer could understand the love and awe for a wild fire or a harsh sword?

A healer's weapons were a woman's: the charms sent by the goddess Eir, healing plants, alive and breathing, with power far greater than iron or fire. With the greatest power of all, for a leechwoman brought the gifts of life, not death, to kings and thralls alike. Inge hugged Karl tighter. She would not abandon her daughter to the sword. Not now, not ever.

XV

Inge was the first one up, gathering wood, stoking the banked coals into flame, heating the water for mint tea and draughts for her two patients.

Brattahlid had found patches of scrub grass to munch at the edge of the pines, and her milk had a fresh sweet-sour smell. As Inge cupped her fingers around the teats and milked, she took comfort, as always, from resting her head against the warm, stolid bell cow.

Comfort on mornings like this, when the fog was thick as a wall, cutting them off from the forest and from the river. Though she heard cawing and twittering from the pines, she saw no birds. Tree tops melted into the gray mist, and other pines had tops, but no trunk. It was not the fog that dismayed her. Last night Thora had loved fighting so much she talked of the quiet river as a sword. Karl's men knew the price of battle, but the maid did not.

Inge sipped her tea, and pondered. If she knew that adopting Thora would lead to this moment of fear on the fog-choked river, would she still have arranged the adoption ceremony?

Ay, she would. Love finds us, she thought, and we are bound by its power.

Now, when she alone was awake, was the time to invoke that power. She walked to the sand spit, scratched a circle around her body and sent forth her fear, letting the silver-gray fog absorb it. She shivered and stepped forth three steps, and repeated the ritual.

At home she had often used fog-magic to send forth her fear for Karl-Eirik's safety, and had had faith returned, but Kievan Rus was not Sweden. Still, Freya had followed her. She touched her amulet. She cared not at all that her damp headdress clung about her hair, or her wet cloak soaked her shoulders. She stepped forth three more steps, made the third circle and sent out her fear. It was her last chance.

When the warmth came, touching her face, spreading over her breasts and down her body like a woolen overgarment, she chided herself. Freya had always protected her. Thora herself was one of Thor's Chosen. Why else would she wear Thor's hammer Mjollnir as an amulet?

145

Inge basked in the warmth of faith, holding it to her with crossed arms. When it left, she looked up and saw a pearly light in the fog overhead. A good sign.

Thora awoke, and Inge set her to cooking grot, to give both crews hot food. The men roused, yawning, stretching, jesting. Sailors were ever cheerful, she thought, whether awakening in fog or teeming rain.

Not so Zeno, who grumbled and whined and scooted closer to the fire, complaining because he came from a warm country with bronze braziers, little metal boxes filled with hot charcoal to warm the bones. Inge gave him a draught, and pointed out that his sores no longer oozed pus.

By the time they finished day meal, the fog began splintering into wisps and shards. As soon as Karl could see the far side of the river, he was eager to be gone. Men and beasts clambered aboard the boats, Zeno slipping on the fog-wet wood. Inge thought this river was a lure to the northmen--it was in their blood to follow wherever it led. Some of them had grown up looking out over the sea, watching boats leave, chafing to leave themselves.

The days passed much as the first, and if it rained, day or night the men raised the tent for shelter, and were content.

One night Inge asked Karl to dock early. She put Olaf and Zeno to cook, and took Thora firmly by the hand--to explore the taiga, she told her daughter. Karl told Thora to wear her sword and helmet. She might need to protect her mother from a Finn. Or a bear, Lars said, grinning.

In the forest Inge jumped from one dry hummock to another, Thora dragging behind. It was boggy, but with no bog plants. In truth no plants at all, only spongy grass and moss.

"I want to go back. It smells like piss," Thora said.

"Only a dead animal. Still, it is pleasing to be alone. The boat is so small. Come, sit on a fallen tree trunk with me."

She sat, but Thora remained standing, her hand on her sword.

"Tell me, Thora, is swordplay with Halfdan fun?"

"Ay. I like him. He is not broody like Finnvid, but jests a lot. He is a good swordsman, Modir, and I am learning from him."

Inge pulled out a packet from her seapouch, and put it in Thora's hand. Anders had asked for a herb to stanch bleeding if he was cut a little during practice.

Inge had a packet of yarrow for him, and one for Thora and Halfdan. The maid set it on the log.

Inge looked at the bag, hiding her disappointment. "You are so skilled you will never be cut? Or Halfdan?"

"We are careful, Modir. He is a man, and I am wont to be as tough as he is."

A boy. He was a boy, yet Thora wanted to be like him.

Ayiiii! Inge felt a chill on her neck. There was more than one reason Thora wanted nothing to do with herbs. Inge looked at her comely daughter, her long blond hair concealed by her helmet. Still, no one would take her for a male.

"Thora, you wish you were a boy, ay? Rather than a girl?'

Thora turned away and said, "I want to go back and practice."

Inge touched her arm, but the maid pulled away. "Answer me, Thora."

"Modir, men have all the fun."

Inge talked softly. No, not all the fun. Sex for a woman was the sweetness that came unbidden through a woman's body again and again, and lingered, so her soft flesh where a man entered was alive, even after he finished. Sex for a woman was suckling a babe, feeding it from her own body. Was it not wondrous?

Yet Inge was unsure if Thora listened.

When they returned to the fire, Halfdan came to meet them, and Inge saw how happy Thora was to begin practicing. Ah, the lad might yet prove useful. Anders was grateful when she gave him both packets of yarrow. The men thought no less of him if he seemed to have a bent for healing, along with a love for the sword. Then why not Thora? The maid admired men and wanted to be like them. If only she could model herself on Anders.

That night in the leather bag Inge whispered to Karl-Eirik that Thora wished she could be a boy. Karl was not surprised. He stroked her hair, soothing her, and said she must not fret. Thora was enjoying her freedom, even being a rebel, after so many years under the bitch's control at Gotardal. When they got home, he promised, he would start inviting suitors for the maid. Once she was wedded and bedded, she would be glad to be a woman.

Inge ached to tell him about Thora's poem likening the river to a sword. Yet how could a warrior understand? Curse all Norse love of fighting. Karl reminded her they had adopted the maid out of love, but more--Inge thought she would be useful. She answered that Thora was one of The Chosen, more apt than just any maid. Inge slept poorly, one hand on her amulet of Freya.

The goddess came to help two days later, though Sven suffered for it. At practice, Per cut Sven's forearm to the bone, deeper than he meant, he told Inge. Anders was at her side, watching, as she put on a potion of yarrow and rue, and wrapped the wound tightly. She said the charms of Eir silently, and mixed a sleeping draught. The men agreed that Sven would not have full use of his sword arm for weeks.

She asked him if he saw any swamp oaks in the taiga. He was in deep pain, and cared not what he saw. But she did. Where there were oaks, there would be hollow oak stumps. She told him his wound might not take long to heal. Anders questioned her, but she would say no more.

When next she changed his bandage aboard ship, she did not drop the bloody cloth into the Dvinna, but told Anders to save it. "We will make magic with it," she told him, and he laughed, but wrapped it in wadmal. Thora stopped carving her cow long enough to look up. Inge pondered. Perchance magic was a word needed to excite the maid's mind toward healing.

That night Inge saw a hollow oak stump at the edge of a clearing, and asked Karl to dock early. She put Sven's old bloody dressing into the hole, repeating Eir's healing charms. The men gathered around, puzzled. She told them that Sven's wound would be healed on the morrow. And though they did not scoff at their mistress, she knew they doubted her powers. Some would believe she had succumbed to elvist on the long journey. Ah, let them think what they chose. The Greek said he could not see why anyone would hide a bloody bandage in a tree stump.

"You will see," she said, ignoring his doubt. "You can trust a Swedish leech-woman. Your body is almost healed, ay?"

Though none dared laugh, she alone kept faith, and she forebade them to touch the stump. In truth, even to look at it.

In the leather bag she and Karl talked of everything but the bandage, and she knew he too doubted her wisdom. Just before she dozed off she stifled a twinge of fear. Would the healing power of Eir be strong enough? The old ways had never failed her. She must trust them now. Even so, she slept with her hand on Freya's amulet.

The next morning the men and Thora were up early, standing around the fire, and she teased them. Were they waiting for their grot? Nay, nay, they told her. What then? she asked, and they shrugged, looking at Sven, pacing the clearing, too nervous to sit. When she asked the men if any had touched the hollow stump, or even looked at it, they told her nay.

"Good. I am wont to change your bandage for the last time," she told Sven.

"The last time, Mistress?" Anders said. "Last night the wound was open and bleeding. Such a deep cut...to the bone..."

"You think such a deep cut might need weeks to heal, Anders, but we leech-women know magic. With Eir's help."

She asked Sven if he trusted the power of an oak to heal him, and he shrugged. He said nothing as she untied the wadmal sling. The men crowded close, Thora among them, not carving, not practicing with her sword, but watching, as unbelieving as any of them. Slowly, slowly Inge unwrapped the bandage, telling Sven that this time it would not hurt. The men gathered closer, jostling each other. None wanted to miss what their mistress was doing.

A last wrapping of cloth remained. Inge stopped, saying a silent prayer to Eir, and one to Freya, and another to Eir. She took a deep calming breath. Slowly, slowly she removed the last of the bandage.

"Aiyiii!" Anders cried, and all the men talked at once.

Sven and the others could not stop looking at his arm. The flesh was whole, as though he never had a wound. With gentle fingertips, Olaf touched where the wound had been. The men looked at her, and she saw their puzzled amazement.

Anders raced to the stump and pulled out the bloody bandage.

"It has not changed!"

"In truth, our mistress works magic," Sven said, and the men agreed, their voices thick with wonder.

"Nay, I cannot take credit," Inge said. "It was the goddess Eir, goddess of healing. And the magic of the oak."

Karl knelt, and said he was most proud of her. Was he married to a goddess? Inge laughed. Karl whispered that he did not hear her deny it.

"Then I will deny it, Husband. I am not a goddess," she whispered. "I am only a countrywoman, trained in healing."

Hrolf brought Sven's sword, and he hefted it with his newly-healed arm. To Inge's pleasure he used it as skillfully as ever. Olaf told Sven to save the bloody bandage. He might get hurt again. Or someone else, Anders said. Inge told them to leave it. Per told Karl they must uproot the stump and take it along, but Karl said nay--they had not an ell to spare.

While Inge snapped pine needles to make a potion for Zeno, Thora came to her and said her mother had surprised them all. What other secrets did she hide from them? Inge smiled and said she had many secrets she would gladly share, if Thora wanted to learn the healing herbs...

The maid turned away, and Inge sighed. Only a dramatic kind of healing would interest Thora. Yet most cures were slow, and gradual, and sometimes none worked. Few made a man's arm whole overnight. Still, Thora had shown a spark of interest, and Inge was cheered.

Zeno healed rapidly. As soon as his gums were no longer spongy, and his teeth set, Inge had him teach them Greek, word by word. Both crews found that repeating the words helped them pull as one at the oar.

She asked him to begin with words they would need as merchant-traders--furs and gold and such. One day she told him he was now strong enough to help at the oar. He could row and teach them at the same time.

"Neh," he said.

"Do not nay me. You will row."

Zeno laughed. "The Greek word neh is the word for yes, do you not remember? I will be glad to row."

He was not at all inept. He was, he told them, a linen weaver to the Emperor, and knew how to lift heavy rolls of cloth, how to push a weighted comb and beat a strand of linen into place, all while saving his strength. Inge put him next to Hrolf to row. The pig-bristles on Zeno's head were growing, but she could still see the tops of his ears sticking out while the middles lay flat against his head. The sign of a good talker.

But one humid day he talked too much, saying Volnir was so small. Did the Swedes breed their horses with dogs? Finnvid patted Volnir's thick white mane and stroked the chestnut brown coat, and told Zeno they liked small horses. They were easy to saddle. Zeno replied it was easy to see Volnir's sire was not an Arabian stallion. So why should he waste his time talking with barbarians? Inge asked him to tell them what "barbarian" meant.

"Unrefined," Zeno said. "Primitive. Inferior."

Gunnar shook his carving knife at him and roared, "A smith knows that word. It means of poor quality."

The men all talked at once. "Poor quality, are we? Nay! Gunnar is a smith who works in gold and silver as well as iron...what is your linen-weaving to that?... Finnvid is the best bowman in Sweden...Karl has never gone off course in twenty years..."

"Enough!" Karl shouted from the stern, and called Zeno back to warn him against riling the men. Accidents could happen to anyone.

Lars steered close by and told Inge to forget the Greek's insults. Did she know a captain sees weather changes by the way the bow noses into the current? Or that the rigging sings a different song if dirty weather is coming?

She thanked him, but wished Karl would be her teacher. She tried, but could see no change in the weather by watching the bow nor hear a song in the rigging. She knew much of weather by the sound her turning quern made at the farmstead, by the swath of wind through the barley, but this boat did not speak a countrywoman's tongue. Here in Gardariki she did hear the everlasting drip of melting snow. Where the shore was ridged, water collected in hollows. The river was high with snowmelt, and some trees stood up to their knees along the bank.

As the days wore on she spent long, joyful hours sitting with Thora, teaching each other songs. The maid finished carving a passable cow, and moved on to the fish-bird she saw on Gotland. The Greek words came easily to her. Thora said she had not known life could be so sweet. She cared not if she ever saw Sweden again.

Karl alone sensed Inge's lonesomeness, cheering her with a touch or a glance, though she did not tell him she ached to see Breidal. A hundred times a day she walked up the path from the fjord, a hundred times a day she sat at her loom, looking out at her Homefield. She missed every tip of barley breaking through the sod, every lamb jumping straight up in its excitement in being alive. She often closed her eyes, sniffing the earthen jar.

She was most lonesome at night, when the need-fire cooled to embers, and the dark forest with its strange noises of snuffling animals was all about them.

Then she could not get close enough to Karl in the leather bag, could not kiss him deeply enough. When the sweetness came, she seemed to rise to him, her blood dancing. Karl filled her, and she felt his shudder in her own body. Then the peace between them was like no other, flowing about them like the river.

Most nights, when they steered to shore, two of the men set out with bow and arrow and brought back a deer or other game. Inge put One Wing and Zeno to help her skin it and cook the meat, while Karl kept the men and Thora at swordplay.

Halfdan, the slight youth from Lars's boat, chosen by Karl to practice with Thora, was a fierce fighter. Thora often shouted at him, because he was so much quicker than she was, but Halfdan gave her no quarter.

"He is so small he is but half a Dane," Karl whispered to Inge, "yet he is a good teacher for our daughter."

One night Finnvid hunched down before Zeno.

"Greek, do you know how to use a sword? A spear? An axe?"

"A Roman linen-weaver to the Emperor does not waste his energy fighting," Zeno said. "He has a whole army to protect him. I am named after an ancestor who wrote a manual on how to fight."

"Ja?" Thora said. "Are the Greeks better than ourselves?"

"Better? Yes, they are better. They fight with finesse. You fight as you do everything else--with the strength of brutes."

Finnvid cursed, lifted Zeno by his hair, and stood him against a tree.

"Greek, you will see how we can fight with finesse."

He picked up his bow, and set a pebble atop Zeno's head.

"Do not move, Greek, and you will be safe."

'Finnvid!' Inge cried out. "You are using a barbed arrow."

"I am an excellent marksman, Mistress. I will not harm this Greek bastard, as long as he stands still."

Zeno's eyes swelled with terror. Sweat ran down his cheeks into his collar.

"The arrow will not go through stone," he said, his voice shaking.

"Ay. It will go between the stone and your bristly head, if you hold still enough."

Finnvid nocked his arrow, drew back his arm, and relaxed it. All the men and Thora gathered to watch. Though Finnvid was a good marksman, was he good enough? A barbed arrow made a savage cut.

"Karl, stop him!" Inge shouted, but he held her, so she could not leap up and grab Finnvid's bow.

"The stone is too small," Zeno said, trembling.

"Nay. It is the right size," Finnvid said, drawing the bow back. "If you can stop shaking."

Inge watched him sight along the arrow's length. The Greek's eyes were closed but his lips moved, and Inge knew he was praying to his White Christ. His body was rigid with fear.

"Greek, mark my finesse," Finnvid said, and the arrow left the bow, flew straight ahead, and passed with a swish between the stone and Zeno's head.

The men cheered and praised Finnvid, while the Greek slid to the ground, eyes closed, shaking from head to foot.

"Thank Christ," he said aloud, and Inge saw his pants were wet at the crotch.

That night Finnvid gave him the first and tastiest haunch of roe deer.

"Here, Greek. You are almost as brave as a Swede."

Zeno had not forgotten how to whine.

"I am tired of your food--the cereal and cow-curds and meat and stale bread. In Miklagard we soak the bread in wine, not river water. In Miklagard even the poor eat pome-granate sauce, with figs and apricots."

"Then swim to Miklagard and get them," Halfdan said, surprising them all by speaking what they were thinking.

One day after day meal when a breeze came up Gunnar put by the oar and sat with Inge, making two knots, one at each end in a length of line. He left to tighten the afterstay, and she picked up the line. She undid it and made the same knots. It was not hard. She used both the bowline and a hitch in her weaving and twining. She made the two knots over and over. Lars steered his boat close enough to talk.

"A good sailor can be told by his clove hitches, Inge. Any captain would hire you on the spot when he saw one of yours, ay, Karl?"

But Karl-Eirik was intent on talking with Zeno, so softly no one else could hear. Was the Greek telling Karl of dangers to come? Inge knew the crew put all faith in their captain. He was skilled at dealing with men, in sifting half-truth from truth.

And so Inge looked at her daughter. Thora and Halfdan had quarreled last night as they were practicing swordplay, but now they were smiling at each other across the water. He saluted the maid with his oar, and almost dropped it in the river. Both crews laughed, and he did too.

Everyone liked Halfdan. Inge looked closely at the large, deep circles within his ears, signs of warmth and a readiness to love. Even his tapering face spoke of yearning. Ah, there was a reason why Thora smiled at him.

The breeze brought an unsavory smell, and she knew the dried pork was beginning to stink. She told Anders to throw it overboard.

"Do not throw out the pork," Zeno called from the stern. "You will need it to grease the wheels when they smoke."

"What wheels?" Anders asked, holding his nose.

"The wheels we will need to haul the boats overland at the portage."

Inge thought back to the picture Karl had scrawled in the mud next to their fjord, the portage that would take them from the Dvinna to the Dnieper. Karl asked Zeno to tell them about it.

"The portage is a dreadful labor. Many have died there."

"No one will die," Finnvid said, "unless we cut off your head and put it atop our mast. You are one to talk freely of dying. I think you fear it."

Zeno leaned against the mast, facing them. "All men fear death."

"Ha! We northmen know how to cheat it."

That night around the need-fire Karl asked the Greek to tell them what they needed for the portage. Zeno said they must have two things: oxen for dragging the boats, and dragöl for themselves, a special dragging ale, strong and bitter and flat, and tasting of smoke.

Lars sent a man with a cup to a cask aboard The Goldenbreast.

"We bought this in Daugmalé. Drink it, Greek. Is it dragöl?"

Zeno sipped, and made a wry face. It was dragöl, but did not taste like the fine wines of the Empire. He told Lars to save it, and not let any man drink it until they were well into the portage.

One morning as they sailed downriver under a fitful breeze, they saw the shore had less scat, more charred wood where fires had been made, more broken twigs used for kindling. Zeno said they were coming to the town of Polotsk. It seemed a small, raw town with no wharves or warehouses, and huts with no windows. Some did not even have a smoke vent. Karl steered out and said he would keep to the river. In a poor, unseemly town, a thief might jump an alesot seaman.

The sound of bells on a horse's hame came to them, and Volnir stomped the deck, straining at his tether, neighing. Inge and Karl smiled at each other. At home Volnir had a hame with tinkling golden bells he wore on fest days. Volnir, too, got lonesome for Sweden.

Eventually the river became so low the men got out and pulled the boats from a line ashore, while Karl and Lars poled. Hand in hand, Inge and Thora walked a messy path, stumbling over parts of runners and planks and half-buried wheels.

Zeno told them the portage was near, and he would see about hiring oxen. At a small rise he took two cups of ale and a cask and called two words they had never heard, over and over. To the amazement of the Swedes, two men walked out of the woods. They were barely taller than Halfdan, rounder, dark of face and hair, wearing leather breeches and sheepskin over their shoulders. Zeno gave each a cup of ale, and Inge saw they were unused to it. Their black eyes glittered, and their cheeks reddened.

She wished she had asked the Greek to teach them some words used in Kievan Rus. She would feel more at ease if she could bargain. While Zeno talked with Karl she studied the two men. The skimpy beard on one of them could not hide his broad chin. Good. Men with broad chins could endure much hardship. When he laughed she saw two large front teeth. He was stubborn, more stubborn than his oxen, she hoped. At home, when an ox planted his feet naught could move him, not even the switch.

The other short man, beardless, had a pointed chin, but a large jaw. He too could outlast much suffering. She sent a prayer of thanks to Freya. The gods had sent the Swedes oxen-drover luck for their long trek.

Zeno told Karl the men were Ulb and Frudi, and would loan their oxen for a pound of silver apiece. Too much Karl said, and sent him back. Zeno muttered that the Norse haggled like Arabs.

Back, Zeno said, "It is not more silver they want, but your wife's firestone necklace."

Inge covered her neckring with trembling fingers. She loved the feel of it. She had worn it day and night, and it had warmed her when she was most lonesome for Breidal. She tightened her hand.

"Greek, tell the bastards to go to Hel," Karl said. "We will get other oxen."

Zeno frowned. "All of them live together as one family: husband, wife, children, uncles, aunts, grandfathers. If you say no to these two, no one will have oxen for you. We cannot get through the portage without them. We may not do it with them."

Finnvid spat.

Inge looked at Ulb and Frudi. Women everywhere loved fine jewels, and the men who gave them.

"Karl, let us promise them they can have my neckring at the end of the portage. By then I may tire of the weight of it."

"You can buy another in Miklagard," Zeno said. "There, firestones can be found as big as whorls on a hand spindle."

Karl-Eirik ignored Zeno and fingered the neckring. He told her it was beauteous with her eyes, and when he took it from Tosti he had not thought to barter it for stupid beasts.

Karl was never one to fret over choices.

"Greek, tell them we will give half a pound of silver for each. Half of that now, and the rest and the neckring at the end of the portage. Food and dragöl to be shared in equal measure."

Karl took out his copper trader's scale and measured the silver, and Ulb and Frudi agreed to be back in three days with oxen for each boat.

The dread labor of the portage began when the crews axed the first of many trees to make runners and rollers and wheels. Volnir was harnessed to a rough sled to bring wood out to a clearing. Karl and Lars worked side by side with the men, all day, and half the night by torchlight. Zeno whittled wooden treenails. Thora hammered them in place, using the tool as skillfully as a sword. One Wing sorted gear to lighten the boats, pitching anything worn or useless into the woods, and Inge cooked great cauldrons of grot and tea from the Tree of Life to sustain the men, all of them working hard as thralls.

By the time Ulb and Frudi came out of the woods with twelve oxen, the wheels were on the boats. Though Lars and Karl were bone-tired, they did not forget the sacrifice to the gods before starting the journey.

Like Bratta, the oxen chewed their cud crosswise, and like Bratta, they had hooves where stones would lodge, and long tails to switch away flies. The way they stood, unmoving, was like the bell cow. But when Zeno told Inge the drovers wanted to hitch Bratta to help pull, she defied him.

"My bell cow will give us fresh milk. She is a milk cow, not built to pull men's burdens. I will yoke myself to the boat, before my Bratta."

Zeno fumed. Then keep the milk cow at the end of the line, he told her. The oxen-drivers were unwilling to walk in any more cow shit than necessary.

Karl put a leather band across Volnir's chest and attached a rope to the boat. The little horse reared up when the oxen were harnessed behind him, but Karl talked to him until he calmed. It took most of the morning to get the beasts in place, and everyone strained to get the two boats moving. Later it would not take as long, Karl said. The brothers kept the prow posts on, unafraid of offending the land spirits.

As the portage began, Inge smelled the dead-animal smell Thora thought was piss. The only light in the dim forest came from two leering dragon's eyes on the prows. In truth, fear of the unknown was the strongest of fears, and they were chancing their lives, trusting three strangers and twelve oxen to lead them safely through an unknown wilderness.

XVI

As the days wore on Inge often thought it was wrong for a boat, always a proud sight skimming the waves, to be dragged overland. The sail was furled, and stored on the boards beneath the mast, the singing rigging wound sunwise and mute.

Two of the men cut their path, and the rest guided the boats, pushing and pulling The Seafarer in the lead, The Goldenbreast behind, bumping over sinewy roots. Branches tore at the sides, leaving long scrapes. The hulls ground over rocks. After day meal Sol pulled her chariot across the sky, and the mud softened, caking around the wheels so thick they had to hold sticks and strip it off, as the boats bounced on. Yet there was no complaining. Inge sang to her bell cow, and Karl's hand often rested on the side of his beloved Seafarer.

It was a swampy land, with hummocks and ridges, but a bog was fed by springs, and the men could drink and splash water on hands and face, and run back to the boats, for nothing stopped the oxen until night came on. These were men of the sea, Inge thought, and their element was water. They were uneasy if they were too far from it. Even at Breidal the fjord was rarely out of sight.

For her part she was happy to be back walking the earth, though her shoes never dried. How quickly the plants take over, she thought, stepping over roots--they were like wild grasses hidden beneath the soil that came forth when the ground was ploughed for barley and rye.

The trail stretched ahead endlessly, and none knew when it would end. The oxen plodded on, and seemed not to tire, but one slipped in the mud and his heavy foot came down on Finnvid's.

"Stupid oaf! Dumb splay-foot!" Finnvid shouted, and the oxen kept on plodding. He broke off a stick to switch the beast, but Zeno held his arm.

"Do you think the ox understands Swedish?"

Inge longed for a change in the flat land until they came to the first hill, and The Seafarer, in the lead, stuck fast. She felt fear as a pain in her chest. Perchance they would never get the boats uphill, and the ships would rot here, going back to boards, and boards to splinters, and splinters to soil.

But Karl would never let his beloved boat die in Gardariki. Both crews pushed together, and Gunnar and Olaf put rollers beneath the hull, and Thora and Inge spread branches beneath the prow, and inch by inch the boat climbed. At the top the drovers lashed thick branches behind the wheels to slow the boat, but still it jounced downhill with the beasts bellowing, as though a howling wolf was after them.

And then they started over with The Goldenbreast.

When they stopped, exhausted, at even, Inge made a potion from flaxseed for Finnvid's foot.

"Flax is a magic healer," she told him, "a gift from Freya." He was too tired to do more than gulp it down. While Thora cooked grot, young Halfdan scrunched down next to the cauldron and gave her a stone he found in the woods. She fingered the stone circle divided into many parts, and blushed. She had not been given many gifts, Inge thought.

"It is a snakestone, Thora," Halfdan said, "from Thor."

"From Thor and Halfdan." She touched her amulet.

Inge smiled at Karl, but he did not smile back. She went to him where he sat, resting. Husband, it is only a snakestone, she said, such as people build into walls to protect the family within. It can do no harm. He told her it was not the snakestone, but the short young man giving it, and he should stick to swordplay.

Though Karl knew as well as any of them the men had no energy for the sword at the end of the day. He got up and went to help Gunnar check the planking, as the smith pounded each one to see if it was sound after the day's jouncing. From the blows she knew Karl used the hammer harder than need be.

She must not ask much of him until they were back on the water. No captain would take pride in his boat--mud-caked, paint-flaked, with long scratches.

She told Zeno they would feel happier if they had some dragöl, but he said he had asked Karl to withhold it tonight.

"Tomorrow the dragging will be worse. We will need it more."

In truth, the trek never got easier. Inge was glad Zeno told her to keep the stinking pork. She hated the smell, but she and Thora were ever on hand to rub the axles when the smoking started.

It seemed to her they were fighting the forest. Often fallen Trees of Life barred their way, and all had to heave together to pull them off the path. Now

Karl had no complaint about using her strength to push and pull, as he had done on Gotland.

All of them had aching backs and sore legs. The men's shirts were glued to their backs by sweat, and dried and glued again. Inge's dress was caked with sweat and mud, her plait plastered to her neck. The weather, all-important on the Baltic, meant nothing now. If it rained they wore the wadmal with the water-shedding hairy nap, and walked till dark, and stopped too tired to talk.

Ulb and Frudi knew how to get the most out of the beasts, using soft words or the stick or a kick, when needed. One day the trail was so rugged Karl had all the men put sheepskins over their shoulders with ropes on top attached to the boats, so all could pull, yoked like slaves to help the oxen. Inge saw how long hours of rowing had toughened them. In other lands the sun set earlier, but in the north, men sailed as long as the light held in summer.

And now she saw why the brothers were captains. Each man in the crews was a hard worker, but when they tired, Lars and Karl did not. The brothers were quick with a jest or praise, or an arm about the shoulder. They were everywhere at once, and missed no hint of impending anger, mixing the crews to allay trouble. Anders was apt to slip, but the men never let him fall. Lars teased the Greek about becoming tough as a northman, and Inge wondered if Zeno was a spy. If so, it mattered not. They were all in the portage together, plodding on like oxen.

One day Finnvid asked him if the drovers know where they were going. Were they leading the crews into a trap?

The Greek glared at him. "They are forest dwellers and want no part of your muddy boats. They want silver and firestones. You Norse can find your way across the sea. Trust these two. They can find their way through the forest."

"There is somewhat of a path," Inge said.

"You have eyes to see," Zeno said. "The others are blind."

Sven lifted his arm to strike the Greek, but Karl told them both to shut up and save their strength.

Later the forest became more sparse, the path fainter. The drovers called to the oxen to stop, and Volnir jerked back in his harness. Inge leaned against the boat and wondered if it was worth using her energy to scrape the mire from her shoes.

"Greek, what is it?" Karl asked.

Zeno shrugged. "The drovers think we missed the path. We must go back."

The men shouted and cursed, and the light in their eyes was murderous.

"Karl, the bastards brought us here to be ambushed," Finnvid said, "but I will take seven before they kill me."

"Put by your sword," Inge said. "Ulb and Frudi are like their oxen. They plod on and on until the way is unmarked, but a countrywoman sees unlike men or beasts. Karl, let the men rest."

She walked beyond them to where five pines stood alone. She leaned against the biggest, feeling the strength of the tree flow into her, waiting until the path revealed itself. Her eyes saw another clump of five trees. Beyond it a mound, a spring, a standing stone.

It was the Sacred Pathway, as clear as though Karl drew it in the mud--the pathway that lay beneath the forest floor, linked to the energy ond. The air above it was different--lighter.

"This way," she beckoned the men, taking the lead.

"Inge, you are certain?" Karl asked.

"I am."

She found it pleasing to be in the lead, and away from the steaming oxen dung in the rear. She kept her hand firmly on Volnir. Soon enough, the forest once again thickened, and they found the portage.

"As clearly marked as the Divine Mese, where the Emperor walks," Zeno said.

She dropped back to be with Brattahlid, and the Greek told her they were lucky to have her. She told him any countrywoman would have done the same. Countrywomen knew where to find the Sacred Pathways.

The days became a pattern of mud and great weariness. Karl began giving full measures of dragöl at night, but no jesting followed. Inge could not remember waking to take joy in the day. Her tired muscles burned day and night, and she heard how easily the men grew angry with the drovers, the oxen, each other. She kept Zeno back with her. The Greek was unsafe with short-tempered swordsmen who walked with one hand on the hilt.

Thora and Halfdan alone had the energy of the young to spare, and their jesting was most annoying to the men, to Karl above all. There were times when the giggling of the two youths made even Inge wonder. How could they laugh?

One day she pondered if she could lift a mud-covered shoe one more time. It came to her--what was she doing on this portage, with the everlasting muck and mire? She belonged on her farmstead, watching the newborn lambs lower themselves on their knees to suck. Her fingers ached to dig into the spongy damp wool. She walked away and sat on a log, and let the tears fall. A leechwoman knew the value of tears.

Karl-Eirik stood before her, but she did not look up. He sat and held her fast, and she sobbed until her tears were spent.

"Karl, you should not have let me come with you. I am unworthy of this dread portage. You could travel faster without me."

"But not as happily, Inge. I would have to share my leather bag with the Greek."

She smiled, picturing Karl and Zeno asleep, backs to each other. Even weary beyond belief, Karl knew how to cheer her.

"Wife, we are all mud-daubed. We will feel better when we can wash ourselves and the boats in the river, but we cannot stop now. Come back with me."

He held out his hand, and they stumbled back, Karl to the head of the waiting men, herself next to Bratta at the rear. She kept her hand on her bell cow, and she saw Karl did the same with his filthy boat. Ay, they must let nothing stop them. They had come too far.

The lines in Karl's face had deepened since the portage began. Like the boats their bright tunics and breeches were dull with layers of slimy mud. They had no protection from scratching branches that tore and ripped their clothes and skin. They all had lines of dried red blood on their cheeks and foreheads. They never left behind the dead animal smell. The songs they had sung so cheerfully on the boat would torture their throats. Only Zeno had enough energy to carp and complain, but he did his share of lifting and pulling and pushing. One day his temper snapped.

"There is no end to this portage," he whined.

"You are not bound to a pole in a stinking hut," Thora told him. "Go."

The Greek's broody silence started Thora chattering.

"Gunnar, Halfdan and I need you to settle an argument. He says the first sword was forged by a dwarf. Is it so?"

Inge clamped her teeth in a dry mouth. She was not wont to hear stories of the sword, but only a story could free their minds, and take them away from the muck, and their weariness.

Gunnar smiled at the maid. He, too, knew the value of a story.

"It is said," Gunnar began, "that the Finns made the first sword. They had a giant among smiths called Ilmarinen, who gathered bog ore from swamps and marshes and heated it using his bellows and anvil, until it was soft as bread dough. This he shaped into spears and axes and tools. But he needed stronger metal for swords."

Inge saw the men straighten and walk with less slump in their shoulders, listening to a story about their beloved weapons.

"And so Ilmarinen made a sword, and quenched it in ashes and lye water," Gunnar went on. "But it did not please him, so he called a bee to bring honey. Instead, a hornet snuck in a poison of snakes and toads, and the iron was poisoned in the quench. And this, Mistress, explains how evil swords were brought into the world."

Too tired to laugh, Inge could only say, "Ay, in battle swords are of more moment than my shuttle or spindle to men."

"And a maid," Finnvid whispered, and Inge thought only she heard.

Perchance Thora heard too, for before Inge gave a cutting answer the maid said, "Gunnar, tell us about quenching."

"Nay, it is one of the mysteries a smith keeps to himself."

"Tell us. We are alone here--your secret is safe. Ulb and Frudi and the oxen don't know Swedish. If we guess it, will you tell us if we are right?"

"Nay, Thora. Then you would be a smith, and I would have to milk Bratta and cook grot, and practice swordcraft with Halfdan."

"Gunnar, of all my men you are the one I could not replace at the next port," Karl said. "Keep your secrets. Though I hear you use only the waters of the Dal."

"I hear he uses goat's urine," Per said.

"Hair from a red-haired boy," Ingvar said, pulling a hair from Halfdan, who pulled quickly away. "Here is one."

"I hear you use the juice of radishes mixed with cutup earthworms," Finnvid said, and Thora said "Yecch."

"I have a sword story," Inge said, and saw surprise on their faces. They did not expect a sword story from her. She had caught their attention, even Thora's.

"The old leechwomen used a trick called a leek-wound. When a victim was cut down in battle and on his deathbed, the old healers gave him cooked leeks to eat. If they changed the bandage and smelled onions at the cut, the healing power in the leeks was at work."

"And the dying man lived?" Anders asked.

"Most likely. A true story, and one that has the sword and healing both."

Thora said nothing, but the men talked of the wild leeks growing at Breidal, and how they must take some with them when next they went a-viking.

It was the last time they felt like story-telling. The next day the forest ended. An open, endless plain stretched before them as far as they could see, on all sides. Inge looked around and despaired. The underground path, ond, was somewhere beneath this sea of grass, but where? There were no trees or stones to guide them, not even a beaten path an animal used. The sun hid beneath the leaden sky, and though Gunnar took out his piece of feldspar to point a direction, it was useless without sun. Zeno said the drovers did not know which way to go. Karl looked at Inge with questioning eyes, and she shook her head. She could not find the ond, and it was bitter to admit it. Karl told everyone to stop for day meal and rest.

Inge was too fearful to eat, and sat by herself. The heat baked the mud on her hair, and she cared not at all. Had they come this far only to die a long, painful death in an empty, sweltering plain? Thora joined her, twirling a plant by its stem, but Inge took no joy in it. What did her dream for Thora matter now?

"Modir, when Tyrkir took me out learning swordcraft near Gotardal, he showed me this plant. It soothes pain from swordcuts."

Inge looked, and saw it was not one she knew. Idly, she asked for the name but Thora knew not. Now, when it was too late, the maid showed some interest in a plant. Ah, the trickster Loki played cruel tricks.

"Modir, Tyrkir told me to look for it when I was lost."

"Lost?" Inge stared at her.

"Ay. I have not seen this plant since Gotardal, and it may not work the same here."

Inge licked her dry lips. She touched the prickly leaves.

"Thora, how did it work in Sweden?"

"Its leaves twist edgewise to the north and south at midday. Tyrkir said if I could find north and south, I could always find my way back home."

And if these northmen lost in Gardariki knew south, they could find the way to the Dnieper. Inge peered at the plant. Its leaves did not move. Perchance it was not yet midday. She looked up at the blank sky with no hint of sun. She felt a despairing thought as a blow to her stomach. Perchance midday was past. Yet she must not give up hope.

"Thora, we will try it. Help me yank out this tough grass, and make space to stick the stem in the ground."

When they were done, Inge sat back, exhausted, her hands dry and cracked. The only thing to do was wait in the scorching sun, and hope they had not missed midday. She watched Thora feed a few leaves to Volnir, who chewed with joy and nuzzled Thora, asking for more. The maid giggled.

"Modir, it is the same plant," she called. "Horses love it." She came back and sat close to Inge. "Now all we do is wait."

Wait, and hope midday is yet to come, and the leaves turn before their water gave out in this searing heat, Inge thought. She watched the men shaking their waterskins for the last few drops. Karl drank not at all. Zeno alone had a full one, and stood guzzling. Finnvid pulled it away from the Greek's mouth, and passed it among the men. Zeno had no energy to protest.

Karl came to Inge, and asked why she sat looking at a plant. She told him of Thora's idea, and said she was wont to trust her daughter. They watched the oxen lying down in their yokes, their tongues hanging out. She knew the men dared not share their precious supply. Inge watched Finnvid whispering through parched lips to each man where he lay, too exhausted to move. Head down, he came to his captain.

"Here comes trouble," Karl said softly to Inge.

"Karl-Eirik," Finnvid said, "we have decided to go back into the forest and seek another path before we rot."

Karl's jaw hardened. "Who is we?"

"All of us. We are willing to take our chances."

"Nay. I have decided we will stay. By nightfall there will be dew on the grass to drink."

"By nightfall we might be dead. Or the oxen. Zeno says they are dying. And Volnir and Bratta are close to it. Anders tried to milk, and the teat was dry. Now I will say no more. We are leaving. The men have agreed to it."

"Not Halfdan," Thora said, her eyes on the plant.

"He is the only one of us who will not leave. Ulb and Frudi and the oxen, we have not invited."

"Finnvid," Karl said, his voice taut with unspent anger. "I forbid anyone to go back."

"Karl, how can you stop us? We are freemen."

In truth, Inge thought, Karl could not stop them. She stifled a shudder. The survival of the men and beasts, her daughter and herself, depended on her trust in an unknown plant. Would the leaves never turn?

"Finnvid, do you see this plant?" Inge asked. "Its leaves follow the sun. Soon they will begin turning, and we will see which way is south."

"Pah. I trust myself more. It is only a plant."

He pulled his sword free of the scabbard and took a step toward cutting it down, but Thora was too fast and jumped up, grabbing his arm. Inge thanked Freya for her daughter's quick lunge.

"Finnvid!" Thora cried. "Do not touch this plant. It is sacred."

"Sacred? Pah."

"Ja. All plants are sacred. See, the leaves are beginning to move."

Was it the sudden warmth of their movements that began the leaves turning, slowly, slowly? The way they stirred the air around the plant? Or in truth, was it midday? It mattered not, Inge thought, for Finnvid could not naysay what his eyes saw. Inge pointed off to the right.

"That way is south, Karl, and that way leads to the Dnieper."

The word spread that Thora had saved them with leaves of a plant that followed the sun. Once again the caravan moved, both men and beasts plodding on, lifting one foot at a time, but they moved. The maid and Halfdan walked together, holding mud-dry hands. Finnvid remained at the rear, turning to look at the leaves until they were too small to see.

"Thora, you saved us, and we are grateful," Inge said.

"It was the plant that saved us, Modir."

Before long the plain merged with the forest, and men and beasts fell into a small stream, wallowing in it, yet careful not to suck up too much too fast. Immersing his waterskin, Finnvid grinned at Zeno. "I told you we northmen know how to cheat death."

Zeno listened not, slurping from cupped hands.

That night in the leather bag, Inge whispered to Karl that she and Thora would talk again of healing plants. The maid had said in her own words that this plant was sacred. Ay, Karl said, one plant. He warned her she had gotten hopeful about one plant before, but Inge would not let him spoil her joy.

* * *

The next day Karl gave them a half-day rest. As they sat around the fire eating grot, Zeno said they could finish the last of the dragöl that night. Lars told him nay. The Greek had said they would never get through the portage without it.

"Tomorrow will be our last day," Zeno said. "By nightfall we will be on the Dnieper."

Finnvid slapped the Greek's shoulder, and he winced, though he was pleased.

"Greek, you bring us news we are wont to hear. The morrow will be our last day of dragging?"

All took heart from the promise of an end to the trek. The men whooped and yelled with hoarse voices.

"We will pitch the wheels in the river, and watch them sink!" Anders said.

"And the runners!" Per said.

"And the rollers!" Ingvar shouted.

"And the drovers and their fucking oxen!" Finnvid said.

"Nay," Karl said. "We will bury them all for our return journey, except the drovers and their oxen."

The men groaned.

"But we will leave the mud," Lars said. "Though the boats that come after us will have a drier time. Greek, will you wait at the side of the trail for them?"

"No. My Emperor awaits me in Miklagard," Zeno said. "I will go with you."

That night the men filled their ale cups to drain the cask. Ulb and Frudi got silly, whirling around till they dropped, and the northmen cast them out of the fire circle to sleep it off.

"We could not have done it without you," Inge told Zeno. Unlike the others, he did not drink freely, but sat watching.

"It was little enough. I would be dead by now if you had not cured me."

"Leechwomen heal when they can."

He asked if she remembered the first day on the boat she dropped him overboard in ice water. She remembered. To cleanse him, and begin his healing.

"I talked of your red sail, and I told you the reds in the Empire are brighter. I hated you then, and I did not say it, I will tell you now: the Scythian rue they use to make the dye beautiful drives weavers mad. Stay away from it."

Inge thanked him, and thought how strange and often fearful the world was, beyond her fjord. She and Karl drank cup after cup of ale. She knelt behind him and kneaded his stiff shoulders, her cheek on his hair.

"Karl, we have survived the portage, though there were times I thought I would die on the path. I am wont to spread our leather bag apart from the others and share our good fortune. We have had no energy for bedplay."

She watched as Per played the flute, and the men danced with each other, both partners clumsy and laughing. Anders too danced, one arm held against his chest by the dirty wadmal.

"Karl, I am overjoyed to see the men dancing," Inge said. "Life has returned to them with an end to this wretched portage."

He was silent, looking at Thora and Halfdan standing close together at the edge of the clearing, holding hands, whispering.

"I am going to stop them," he said.

"Nay, Husband. Let them be alone this night. They worked as hard as the men. How could we have managed without them? And both were always cheerful. On the morrow they will once again be traveling on separate boats."

He stood and set their leather bag close by the others, not apart as she wished. The merriment touched him not at all. After they climbed in she fondled him, but his body did not respond, and she turned away.

Halfdan and Thora crawled into a separate leather bags, but close enough to touch fingertips while they slept. Inge knew it was not their pleasure Karl resented. Thora had seen fourteen winters and was approaching an age when it would be seemly to be betrothed.

But when Karl saw them walking hand-in-hand, laughing together, he thought of his own graying hair. He begrudged Halfdan the carefree days with energy to spill that were only given once to a man, and that Karl would never see again. Halfdan did not bear a captain's ever-lasting burdens. If Karl could, would he exchange the power of command for youth? She knew not. But though it was elvist, she knew he was beset with an envy he would not admit, even to himself.

XVII

Volnir and the oxen smelled the river before it could be seen. The small horse pawed the ground, whinnying, his nostrils flaring. Karl-Eirik held him back from racing too fast for the oxen, who ran in their clumsy splay-footed way. Ulb and Frudi tried to hold them, switching and cursing, but the beasts only lumbered faster, mad to get to the river.

Inge watched Karl struggling to control Volnir, and thought some Swedish horses were as headstrong as some Swedish men. Unlike her docile bell cow, who took her time before daintily stepping into the water.

The Swedes stood on shore, looking up and down the blue shimmer of the Dnieper opening before them. Then fully-clothed, both crews fell into the cold water with whoops and yells, alive with joy. Sven spoke for them all when he said he had never been so happy. There were times he had been pitted by mud and pain and exhaustion.

Inge removed her beloved firestone neckring and gave it to Karl-Eirik without looking at him. He sifted the stones between his fingers, and told Zeno he would make the final payment of silver when the boats were dragged for the last time, into the Dnieper.

Inge and Thora walked upriver to bathe off the caked mud. Inge touched her barren neck. She felt unclothed. But she must not be downcast. They had survived the portage, and perchance the promise of her neckring was more of a lure than anyone would admit. She watched Ulb and Frudi lead their plodding oxen back into the forest, and thought Zeno spoke truth. The Norse would never have dragged the two boats without the beasts.

The women floated lazily, dragging their clothes to wash out the mud and grime, while the suds formed on the soapwort. Thora had changed since meeting Halfdan, Inge said, sudsing her daughter's golden hair. Ah, happiness was the best medicine for the body.

"Modir, I am not sick."

Not sick, Inge told her. Love-sick. The maid tilted her head back for the rinsing. "Modir, we thought to hide our feelings for each other. Halfdan thinks Fadir likes him not a whit. But Halfdan is brave. He will speak to him soon about our betrothal."

"Thora, not now. Your father has the weight of all our lives depending on him and much hardship ahead. When the time is right, Halfdan can speak."

And perchance by then Karl would take more to the youth. Inge looked at her daughter's lissome body. There was an hour, a day, when every bud turned into a flower, a flower that soon bore fruit. It would not be long before Thora must watch the changes of the moon and drink the Cup of Roots.

Young lovers were too passion-filled to be able to thresh inside, and winnow outside.

Thora babbled on, and Inge marked what pleasure the maid took in saying his name. Halfdan had taught her more about swordcraft than any man, she said. He learned from her too, but not about swords. Inge thought how natural it was for these two to fall in love--it would be elvist if they did not. Karl had only himself to blame, for it was Karl who thought of putting the two together to practice swordcraft.

Inge gave the maid the pants she sewed out of their dresses, and both put them on. Karl and the crews were so busy no one saw they wore billowy pants, and not overdresses. They spread their clothes on the gunwale to dry, and found the cauldron.

The men were eager to be underway and worked with renewed energy, scrubbing the mud off the boats with scouring rush, setting up the mast, stretching the rigging in place. Both boats were scratched and paint-chipped, but Gunnar pounded each plank and pronounced the hulls whole, and the seventh strake was still strong. The men praised Hervor, the shipwright. He had built a boat that was landworthy as well as seaworthy. To give the men strength, Thora and Inge cooked huge cauldrons of grot, and soaked barley bread, and passed around ale. Joyful tasks, they agreed. With rest, Bratta's milk returned.

* * *

On the third day Karl said they would leave as soon as the runners, wheels and rollers were buried for the return trip, and the men dug deep, in a frenzy to get them out of sight. Finnvid said he was wont to use them for firewood, but Karl reminded him they would be gladsome to have them on the return trip.

Bratta and Volnir willingly leapt aboard, and Karl steered out. The river was broad as a lake, and the breeze was brisk. As the men rowed, Anders said he never thought he would be happy to be back at the oar. Inge warned him to use one arm only, and let the other finish healing.

When they turned downriver they cheered. Inge thought the crackling, filling sail was the fairest sound she ever heard. They no longer needed to fight the current of the Dvinna flowing against them. This Dnieper would carry them down to the Varangian Sea, and Miklagard.

Gunnar took out his rune stock and carved in the days. Thora put the final flourish on her cow's wooden tail, and began carving her fish-bird. Sven and Olaf set the hneftafl board on their knees, and this time Inge stayed in the bow and did not compete. The men talked of Ulb and Frudi, and the wretched portage. Another tale for the ale hall was in the brewing.

Inge sat facing the changing forest. Among the pine and fir and spruce she saw ash and birch, maple and beech, and the Way Tree in blossom. There would be no holding back spring now. The maple wings were ripening. Geda would be gathering them for pickling. Spring was the busiest time on a farmstead. Yet here she was, sitting with her hands in her lap.

She felt Karl's eyes upon her. He asked her to come and sit with him and look at the new river together, but she said nay, she would see the dangling oak flowers first by sitting at the bow. He told her there were but a few ells difference between the view from the bow and stern, but she told him it was enough.

She watched Lars steer close by. Karl's brother could sense when husband and wife were at odds, and like the worst of gossips, he could not forbear to miss their quarreling. She heard Karl call to Finnvid to take the tiller, and then Karl was behind her, lifting her, holding his arms about her beneath her breasts.

He too, felt the urgency of spring. He was making amends for his coldness last night. He told her he had always loved her blue dress that made her eyes bluer than the fairest sea. He turned her away from the men, kissing her hair, his hands moving down the front of her dress, stroking her until she felt him harden against her and dampness begin in her Cleft. Stroking her lower, and yet lower.

Karl stopped, jerking his hands away.

"Inge! What in Hel's name have you done to your dress?" He whirled her around to look at the skirt she had cut stitch by stitch into four parts, and sewn, stitch by stitch into pants. She heard Lars laugh, and she looked Karl full in the eye.

She told him she had done men's work on this journey, and so she had made pants for Thora and herself. With all the climbing and bending, a skirt was not right for a boat.

"Karl, she could have sewn pants as tight as the ones we wear," Lars said, steering still closer. "Hard to pull off."

"Shut up," Karl said to his brother. "Inge, take the pants off, now. Put your dress back on."

She held up her damp dress. "If I wear it, I will sicken."

"Then as soon as it dries, put it on. No wife of mine will wear pants."

"Karl-Eirik, do you think the Norse came forth from the womb, women in skirts and men in breeches?" Lars asked.

"Shut up!" Karl shouted.

Though she knew he had yelled at Lars, Inge shouted back, "Nay. I am not your thrall." Tears filled her eyes. Karl stood a moment, uncertain, then stalked back to his tiller, his mouth hard set. Unspent tears clogged her throat. When she had cried on the portage, exhausted, Karl had held her until her tears dried. Now he backed off from her.

She knew he was their captain, and aboard ship all must obey him, even herself. Five times she had angered him: one time when the corner of the sail fell into the water, and he forbade her to catch it. Again when she helped push the boat ashore on the gravel beach at Gotland. A third time when she took over the oar from Anders, a fourth when she made light of Thora and Halfdan, and now when she sewed her skirts into pants.

Small wonder Karl would not teach her to sail. Ah, there were problems on a boat she never had on her beloved earth. Despite the pain and exhaustion and mud, she had been at home on the wretched trail as she never would be on The Seafarer. She swallowed hard, willing the tears in her throat to dissolve.

Hard, muscled arms encircled her shoulders, and in front of her eyes Inge saw a handful of dripping reeds.

"Modir, Zeno said there is nothing like weaving to help a sore heart. I held these in the river to soak them and make them pliant, so you can weave a sleeping mat. We will work together." Thora giggled. "My fish-bird is asleep, and does not want my carving."

Happily, Inge took the reeds, bending and sorting them, playing with them until the design came to her. In truth, weaving helped a sore heart.

Each day she and Thora sat together talking in low voices, while the maid bundled reeds and lowered them overboard to soak. She was full of questions about her three brothers, about Breidal, about what Inge's life was like when she was her age. Just naming the beasts, talking about the summer pasture, or her three sons, helped Inge's homesickness.

Watching her gather reeds after they steered ashore at night, Inge wondered if Thora's handling of the brown stalks would lead to a love of healing plants? Nay. No one could miss the joy with which Thora and Halfdan wielded their swords in practice.

Still, each day mother and daughter formed a stronger bond, one in which Karl and the men had no part. Inge thanked Freya every day for this daughter who made the journey bearable. Downriver to Konugard, there was a wall none could see, but a wall between Karl and Inge, as real as the wall around the Home-field at Breidal, and none dare broach it. With her fingers Inge wove, but with her eyes, she followed the crew's moves, learning a step at a time how to sail.

Yet she missed being close to Karl, the chatter they had shared. The farther south they traveled, the more she saw the opening, renewing life on shore. She heard the spring peepers in the ponds, and it was all she could do not to call out to Karl to listen to the much-loved chirping. Another day she heard the clucking sound of chickens, and knew it was the tree frogs.

The hardest thing was the way he turned his back to her within the leather bag. She missed sleeping with her head on his shoulder, her Cinnabar Gate resting on his thigh.

One day after a shower she saw a sight so beauteous she turned and called his name, but he was deep into jesting with Finnvid. She turned back, her eyes caught by a bead of water on a branch, flickering blue, then yellow, green, red and then clear. Sunlight had been held, and changed color as the boat passed.

It was a sight she wanted to share with only Karl-Eirik.

Zeno alone ignored the wall and moved freely between bow and stern, sitting now with Karl, now with Inge.

"Are those nettles I see growing?" he asked her one day. "I hear you Swedes weave with nettles. How do you gather them, when they sting so much?"

She looked at the new shoots, and remembered picking them.

"If you move your hand up the stalk, the stingers lie flat, and are not troublesome. Nettle- cloth is wondrous soft, longer-lasting than linen. At our farmstead I have sheets..."

She stopped, overcome by memories of Karl stroking her in their bed-closet on nettlecloth sheets. She took a deep breath, and told Zeno that it was strong enough for ships' sails.

Anders told Zeno that if he was stung by nettles he would never have The Ache in his bones, when he got old.

Finnvid said that nettles grew from the bodies of dead men.

"Nay," Inge said. 'Know you, Finnvid, if a man is whisked with bunches of nettles below the navel he will remain ever virile?"

Finnvid spat over the side. "Another old woman's tale."

One you will be glad to remember one day, Olaf told him.

Inge looked into the woods, and saw a snake sunning itself, two squirrels chasing each other. She heard the sound of rilling water, tumbling to join the river, as all living things rushed together. All except Karl and herself.

One day Zeno joined Inge, weaving his own reed mat, and she asked him to tell them about Konugard. Lars steered close by, and both crews listened. In Kievan Rus they called it Kiev, Zeno said, and it had everything a town needs to grow. A hill for Prince Helgi's palace, surrounded by a rampart for defense. A rich hinterland--a forest for hunting, farmland for crops, and pasture for sheep and cattle. Helgi was a skillful hunter. And a fine swordsman, with the largest collection of swords in Kievan Rus, perhaps in the world.

"I am wont to see them," Thora said, and smiled across the water to Halfdan. Inge saw the boy chose to sit at the gunwale of his boat, closest to Thora.

"A collection of swords does not make a good swordsman," Inge said, as she lovingly twisted the rushes.

Zeno agreed, but Helgi was strong. Once a stag attacked him with its antlers, and Helgi wrestled it to the ground. A bear ripped part of his saddle one night while Helgi was asleep, and he was so angry he fought off the bear. Inge listened to the awe in Zeno's voice. In truth, the Greek could be a spy for Helgi, if not for the Emperor.

Did any of them know about the time Helgi attacked Miklagard? Zeno asked. Now the northmen on both ships listened. The Greek enjoyed an audience. He told them Helgi affixed wheels to his boats, much as Gunnar had done for their portage. Helgi went overland, then removed the wheels and sailed across the Golden Horn. The Emperor was away, and all the people felt doomed when they saw Helgi's fleet. Zeno himself was in his shop and saw hundreds of ships.

Gunnar said Helgi must have many smiths to make wheels for so many boats, and Zeno shrugged. Helgi was a powerful overlord, the most powerful man in Kievan Rus. Yes, he had many smiths.

In Miklagard we had no defense save God, Zeno went on. When Helgi and his hundreds of boats gathered for the attack, the people ran to their churches to pray.

Finnvid snorted. "You would have done better to grab axes and bows, and fight."

Zeno told them they needed none, because God helped them. The Church leader, the Patriarch, went to the Palace where the Holy Relics were kept, among them the Girdle of the Virgin Mary, the Mother of Jesus, the patron saint of Miklagard. The Patriarch lowered the Girdle over the seawall on a plumb line, but it did not stop Helgi.

"A girdle? Why would it?' Finnvid asked.

Ignoring him, Zeno said, "We all came to watch, and it was God's miracle. Though the air remained calm, and there was no wind, none at all, the water rose from the bottom of the Golden Horn in great spurts. Ships were thrown about, masts cracked, sails tore, boats sank, rudders were twisted--it was a miracle. Some of the men tried to swim ashore, but they drowned. As we watched, Helgi left with the few boats remaining in his fleet, and a great cheer went up from the people. The Holy Mother had saved us."

"Greek, you take too much pleasure in telling this," Karl said. "I thought your White Christ talked of love for all men.'

"That is so," Zeno said. "We had many services of thanks to the Virgin, where we prayed for the souls of drowned sailors. When their bodies washed ashore, we did not let them rot, but buried them outside the town walls."

Finnvid said it made a good story.

"It is the truth. Ask Helgi," Zeno said, insulted.

"I trow Helgi would not tell us," Karl said. "Men talk only of their success in battle. Let us ponder where the wind beneath the water came from, though the air stayed calm."

Gunnar remembered one time off Frisia, when the water arose from the sea, though the air was quiet and still. Olaf talked of another time off Danmork, two years past. Perchance Ran and her daughters were quarreling in the waters off Miklagard, Per said. Anders felt Helgi ran out of weather-luck. Yet they all looked forward to meeting him.

Sitting in the bow, Inge was the first to see Konugard. The Dnieper veered east before the town, so she had a good view. It was huge! The town went up and up without end. She gasped and reached for Thora's hand, aching to see this fine city for the first time with Karl. More buildings than she knew existed--more than in Birka--whole groups of wooden halls and byres and stables, separated from each other by palings. The upper part of the city perched atop a hill, well protected by the rampart. Inge saw a large stone palace. Here a Grand Prince would live. A river flowed below the heights, and the hill was criss-crossed by small roads.

"Praise God, there is a wooden church," Zeno cried out. "I can see the cross. I will be able to worship."

"Or at the Norse temple I see, with dragon heads," Lars said. "There are statues of wooden idols next to our temple. I know not these gods."

"Perun is one, Volos, another," Zeno said. "Kiev is a market town, and more. It is the center of Kievan Rus. Men from all countries find a welcome--Jews, Armenians, Greeks, Turks, Danes, Swedes. Your tongue will lead you to Kiev, it is said. Every man is greeted warmly, and Helgi finds a purpose for all."

"Ay, we are welcome," Ingvar called from atop the mast. "Karl, there are no rocks in the harbor to steer around."

Inge saw Karl was relieved to be hazard-free in a strange port. Even so, as the men lined up the shields in the shield rack, they buckled on their swords.

Gunnar said he had never seen so many ships in one port, nor as many deep-hulled. At a ship yard to the side of the harbor, the air was thick with the sound of hammers and axes on wood. Men knelt with nails between their teeth, pounding the enormous logs they had seen in Daugmalé. Thora pointed out a ship with an eye painted on the side, and Zeno said if they met it in battle that eye would follow every move.

"The breeze is fair, and we will sail in," Karl-Eirik told Lars. Inge knew they wanted to show the Norse ships at their best, with sails filled, the shields in place, their standards with the two-headed ravens flying. Though the boats were paint-chipped and scratched and scraped from the portage, the captains took pride in their handsome lines. And in their steering skills, able to dock without oars. Like their ships, the crews wanted to be seen at their best, and they primped and combed and put on their brightest tunics. Inge found clean pants for Thora and herself.

The quay was filled with clumps of old men sitting together, mending nets. Other men rolled casks, some carried bales on their heads, others on their backs. People dodged horses pulling carts piled high with goods. And as at every port, Inge smelled meat cooking, and saw piles of fat bread.

She was taken with one man sitting on the seawall, surrounded by others, and she asked Zeno if he was the trader who would ask Karl and Lars for protection money.

"No. At Kiev no one will ask for protection money. Helgi encourages river traffic. That man is Overlord Helgi the Wise, Helgi the Far-seeing, Grand Prince of the United Novgorod and Kievan Rus States. Ruler of more land than any man in history."

He and Inge saw each other at the same instant, and she felt a shock as though the air between them chopped open. She swallowed hard. She could not forbear looking at him, and clutched Thora with one hand, her amulet of Freya with the other. He lifted out a hidden amulet from his neckline, stroked it with his thumb and put it back. A private signal meant for her alone. Once she had given him a whalebone amulet of a woman like herself, with a single plait, and then it disappeared. How had he found it again?

The crews and captains were staring at the quay, and no one looked at her but Thora. "Modir, you have turned white. What is wrong? Do you know this Helgi?"

Inge pinched her cheeks for color. "This is my first time in Konugard. How would I know a Grand Prince, Ruler of Kievan Rus?"

In truth how would she know an Overlord? But, ah, the man himself she knew well from past lives they had shared, and snatches of memory returned.

She had known him as the dirt-poor farmer Malmfrid when she was his thrifty wife Sfanda, and the year was so wet they threshed in the barn, and there were so many bees they lived on mead and kisses. Another time she knew him as the trader Hallvard. He brought her a two- handled silver cup with a naked babe incised on one side, and they talked of making such a babe until he sailed off, and his ship sank. She knew him as Sigfrier, the warrior, when she was his lover Hultal and he called her Hultalstierna--Bright Star--and she hid in the woods while he fought off an invader, and then she remembered naught except a ravaging fire and putting stones in the outline of a ship at his grave and crying, crying.

She shivered with the strangeness of it. They were linked down through the ages when he had been a farmer, a trader, a warrior. In this life he was a Grand Prince, and she was but a countrywoman. Yet once again their destinies were entwined. He too was thinking the same thoughts. She read his mind as she read no one else's, not even Karl-Eirik's.

"Helgi is here to greet arriving seamen?" Per asked Zeno.

"Helgi is here to greet Karl-Eirik."

Open-mouthed, the crew looked at each other. Though he was their own much-loved captain, they did not know Karl would be known by this Grand Prince. Karl steered close in and threw the lines onto the quay. Before any of his crew could leap ashore and tie up, Helgi caught them and slipped them over the tree trunks. Inge laughed. Though an Overlord, he did not think such a task beneath him. She saw he was not as gold-laden as the Swedish king, but still he wore gold brocade.

"He wears a dress," Thora whispered.

"That is his ceremonial robe," Zeno said. "The Emperor and all his court wear them in Miklagard, but of course Helgi is a Prince, not the Emperor, and does not wear the Imperial purple. Though he wears the ruler's lock on the right side of his head, the jewels in his ear are modest. Only two pearls and a ruby."

"Välkommen," Helgi called, and Karl and Lars leapt ashore, clasping arms with the Prince in the Swedish way. Inge saw that in this life as in the others Helgi had a full, open face with thick straight eyebrows, the sign of a powerful thinker. Though his face was no older then when he left her the last time, now he wore a blond moustache curving to his chin.

She tucked a stray tendril of hair into her headdress and smoothed her billowy pants. Helgi might be a Grand Prince in this life, and she but a countrywoman, but in Sweden she was known as a woman of substance. She had a birch bark treasure chest of neckrings and armrings and fingerings, gold buried where none knew but Karl-Eirik. Her farmstead had increased in value four-fold, and she was four times as wealthy in land and cattle as when she married Karl twenty years past.

Helgi was never among the strangers visiting Breidal, though she never gave up hoping he would appear. No wonder. All the time he was here in Gardariki. He came to her only in dreams as Malmfrid or Hallvard or Sigfrier. Dreams she never shared with Karl-Eirik.

The crews swung over. Helgi lifted her from the bow, and set her on the quay. She giggled with the pleasure of returning to the arms she knew so well, through so many lifetimes. She felt her breasts swell. Ah, she was happy.

The tides of history were too big for one person, or any two people to control, and they were subject to the whims of fate. Yet the separate strands of their lives were bound together in a spiral--and neither she nor Helgi had a choice to do aught but follow. She had him back. For how long, she knew not, but they had always belonged to each other.

And though she was well-married, and he a Grand Prince, she must connive to be alone with him.

XVIII

"Karl-Eirik, your journey has been lightened by fair company," Helgi said, "but I did not know you had two daughters. Where is your wife?"

Thora laughed. Karl put his hand to his sword, and Inge quickly stepped between the two men.

"I am Ingeborg Andersdottir, wife to Karl-Eirik."

"No! I don't believe it," Helgi said, his words a message for her alone. "You have had a hard voyage, and yet you look so young. We will pamper you. And you wear the latest fashion. Women in Konugard find pants like yours to their liking."

Karl's face darkened. She marked Helgi did not miss Karl's displeasure. A man approached bearing a silver tray holding a silver dish of salt and a loaf of bread. Though he did a thrall's work he did not approach his ruler with downcast eyes, but looked curiously at the Swedes.

"Bread and salt. Our welcoming custom," Helgi said.

Zeno broke off a little piece, dipped it in salt and popped it in his mouth. Inge did the same, and the crews crowded around to follow her, though Karl did not partake. Helgi pulled Zeno aside and talked quietly with him in Greek.

As the fluffy white bread melted in her mouth, Inge thought she could not stop the ond that flowed between herself and Helgi--nor did she want to--it was pleasure to them both. But neither did she want Karl or Lars or any of the crews to recognize it. She and Helgi must conceal any feeling. Looking at him offhand, she saw that his eyes had tight lower lids. He was not quite as relaxed as he seemed. Olaf brought Bratta and Volnir. "This is my bell cow, Brattahlid, and Karl's horse, Volnir," she told him. "They have been most helpful on our journey."

"The small Swedish horses and cows. I remember."

How could he forget? He had ridden such a small horse often enough, she thought. He called to one of the men on the quay. In his voice Inge heard the sing-song Swedish she loved.

"Ingeborg, this is a Khop tribesman, an excellent herdsman. When his tribe surrendered to us last month, some of them chose to come to us with their stock.

He will care for your animals. But come, let us go to the palace. We have room for both your crews in the loft."

The overlord walked with the two captains, and said their arrival filled him with joy. He had been waiting. Karl asked how he knew they were coming.

"Word travels as people do, through the forest as well as by water. I know, too, of your daughter's harsh sentence. We have much help for you on the rest of your journey."

Anders pointed to bread piled on carts, and told Inge it would be big enough to pillow his head. She marked Helgi heard everything, like Karl. The Overlord took a coin from his pouch and flipped it over his shoulder to Anders. She knew Karl did not like Helgi to think his men too poorly paid to buy bread. Yet all Anders's money was buying finespun for a girl on Gotland.

Inge held fast to Thora's hand, with Halfdan on the maid's other side. They walked through a stone gate and into the marketplace, where men sat on stools in the sun outside their huts, working with leather, metal, stone or antler bone. Helgi stopped to talk with one craftsman painting a scene of the harbor on birch bark with a squirrel tail brush that had but four strands. Inge thought it delicate.

Helgi told them the craftsmen owned their own shops. It was the Swedish way, was it not? Few men worked harder than those who worked for themselves.

The Overlord had a purpose for everyone, Zeno had said, and Inge wondered what his purpose was for them, though she had one for herself. She was most impressed with Konugard. The cobbled road was swept clean, and the buildings seemed in good repair. They walked uphill past men boiling salt in huge kettles, past a gate Helgi said was The Smith's Gate, home of nailers and iron-workers. Gunnar would fain stop, but they kept on.

Inge heard Karl telling Helgi the news of Sweden. She saw chestnut trees, and longed to rest beneath their shade, but they kept ever upwards on the cobbled road. She heard splashing.

"Is it the washhouse?" she asked Helgi.

"No, no--our public bath. I believe sickness cannot take hold if the body is clean inside and out. Do you agree, as a leechwoman?"

He came back and walked with her, his face carefully bland. They must talk as strangers, though she knew him better than any man alive or dead.

"Ay, and water is most healing," she said. "It rests mind and body, both. On our farmstead we bathe in the fjord. Do you practice dew-walking?"

"I think not. What is it?"

"You walk on the dew in your bare feet, early in the morning. The dew is filled with ond, with energy. It is living water."

"Perhaps you will teach me to dew-walk."

Helgi was paying much attention to her, and she felt Karl's anger, though he was holding it in as a courteous guest.

"Perchance," she said to Helgi.

And perchance we could meet alone early, she thought as the hill steepened, and she stubbed her toe. Helgi caught her before she fell, with a hand beneath her elbow. In the familiar touch she felt a tingle from his calloused fingers through her linen sleeve. He told her he was sorry they must walk so far, but there was no other way to get to the palace. She said she enjoyed walking on her beloved earth. There was an ease between them. And why not? They had been complete with each other before. Many times.

They passed a wooden church with a cross. Ah, close enough for an Overlord to keep an eye on it. She looked at his nose, and saw the tip was small. This man at her side had not changed. He was not money-hungry, but he loved control. As Karl loved control.

They entered the palace grounds, armed guards standing beneath the raised roof. The building was made of stone, and they entered a huge hall. Behind her Inge heard the crews exclaim over the size, and in truth it was two times the breadth of Breidal. The hearth was not in the center of the floor as at home, but she counted six fires burning within large holes in the walls. Stone fat-burning lamps gave a soft glow. The floor was covered not with rushes but a thick wad-mal, soft underfoot. Thora whispered she was wont to take off her shoes and wiggle her toes in it, but Inge said nay. There were no high seats, but many chairs clumped together. The woodenware on shelves was finely carved.

She looked about her and thought Helgi's fortunes had improved since their last life together. Though the crews were awed, their hands rested lightly on their sword hilts.

"My friends, keep your swords, though you will not need them," Helgi said.

" 'A man shall not on the ground go one step forward without his weapons,' " Thora said.

" 'For it is hard to know...if a man may need his sword...' I too know the Havamal, Thora. Rurik taught it to me. Keep your swords."

Inge marked Karl was torn between his duty as a guest and his desire to protect his men. He told the crews to keep their swords, but in the sleeping loft. Unspoken was the message: where they are handy. Inge marked Helgi caught it, too.

"Now, my friends," the Overlord said, "in Konugard we have a custom strong as law. 'At noon, everyone to bed', the proverb says. Rest now. Later we will feast together."

Inge thought he must know she and Karl had not spoken to each other for some few days, or shared anything else, but the Overlord put them in the same bed-closet.

The woman who showed them to it wore a simple linen shift, her black hair wound in a plait about her head. The small room was plain, but the straw mattress most pleasing after so many weeks sleeping on pine duff. Inge sank onto the straw and rolled. Even a countrywoman loved luxury, and being pampered.

Karl rolled over, away from her. Let him be, she thought. The man she was wont to bed was somewhere in this great palace. Would a Grand Prince dare to come to her and take her to his bed-closet? Nay. Could she find him if she searched? She spoke no Slav, the servants' tongue, and how could she tell one she met that she was starved for their master? She too rolled over and saw the amber spinning whorl on the side table--one she had seen when she was Jokulsa. She sighed. Patience had never been one of her virtues, but she must hold herself calm, all the while keeping her ears and eyes open for a chance to meet Helgi alone.

✻ ✻ ✻

She woke to church bells. By the faded sunlight on the wall she knew it was late. Karl was gone. Thora came in, whispering that Helgi had given her a bed-closet of her own, but it was too big for one. Inge told her to enjoy it. Much hardship lay ahead on their journey.

The woman with wound plaits brought them a silver bowl of warm water, a piece of soap, smooth to the touch, and a soft linen towel. Inge washed, and could not remember the last time she felt anything but the cold Dnieper on her cheeks. Karl might have enjoyed warm water too, and his mood would lighten.

She and Thora walked to the hall, and Helgi greeted them. This time his ceremonial robe was blue with gold stitching and fur at the sleeves and hem. He gave them ale in cups carved with fern fronds. Among them Inge read the runes kyss mik, and wished she dared kiss him. She felt the tingle when their fingers touched. Ah, naught had changed. How many times had she looked into his gold-flecked brown eyes--a hundred, a thousand?

Karl came to her accompanied by a short, dark-haired woman in a light red dress and a gold band circling her waist. Gold bells sewn on straps hung at her temples, and were most musical when she turned her head. Like herself, Inge marked, the woman wore a single plait down her back, but with gold rings among the strands. Inge felt a blaze of jealousy and took a large swallow. She must be careful.

Helgi introduced her to Inge and Thora as Ilana, though not as his wife. Inge noted Ilana's round Slavic face and eyes. She loved easily, this woman. Her chin was broad: sex was important. Pah! Helgi's chin had always been broad.

He seated Thora and Inge on each side of him at a long table, covered by a fine linen cloth, lace-trimmed. The crews and Helgi's men were well-mixed. Halfdan was put next to Thora, with Lars and Karl-Eirik on either side of Ilana, across the table, and Zeno next to Lars. Inge remembered now, how important it was for Helgi to control even the smallest things. Beneath the table he pressed his knee against hers, and she returned the pressure.

He had gifts set before him, and to Karl and Lars he gave knives in leather sheaths. The brothers thumbed the knife edges, well-pleased.

A gift always looks for a return, the Havamal taught them. From beneath the table Gunnar pulled a long wooden box he gave to Karl, who handed it to Helgi. Inge felt Karl's pride, for inside was one of the smith's finest Damascened swords with a bejeweled leather pommel. Helgi bowed toward Gunnar when he lifted the lid.

"I will treasure it." To Thora Helgi gave an embossed leather belt and pouch for all the gold she would get in Miklagard, and the maid thanked him. Step by step, Thora was becoming less thrall-like, Inge thought with pride. Helgi gave Inge a bag of finespun. Pulling the strings open she gasped. Here was a beauteous neckring of firestones, larger than the ones on the neckring Karl gave to Ulb and Frudi at the end of the portage. She felt Karl's body tighten.

"Let me clasp it for you," Helgi said, putting it about her neck, and Inge knew no way to stop him. "Firestones from Amberland, Ingeborg. They bring out the color of your eyes."

She thanked him and touched the stones. Did Helgi know her neckring had been traded for stupid oxen--this ruler who knew everything? Ay, he knew. As he knew these firestones were larger than the ones on the neckring Karl had given her.

Servants brought course after course of food, each served on silver plates. The spoons for the cabbage soup were silver, the knives for the calf with mushrooms were silver, and they buttered black bread with more silver. They drank ale from golden goblets. Inge thought she could get used to living here. She ached to know more about Helgi's life, but she must be wary. She told him she had seen everyone in Konugard was his friend, and he said he kept his enemies beyond the town.

"I heard some call you Oleg," she said.

He told her it was the Slavic way of saying Helgi. In Konugard they called him Helgi the Wise, or Oleg the Wise. The word Helgi meant wise in Norwegian. To them he was Helgi the Helgi. Thora and Inge laughed, but Karl did not. Helgi pressed his leg against hers, and she pressed back. Ah, it was pleasing.

A child came up to Helgi, and the overlord lifted the boy into his arms. Inge stifled a twinge of pain. She was not a child, and must wait until she and Helgi were alone to be so close. In the boy she saw his high cheekbones. They were kin. This boy, as did Helgi, came from the House of Rurik, though the face was Slavic round. He introduced him as Igor, and she felt his pride.

"One day Igor will rule all of Kievan Rus. Already he sits with me at council with the boyars, but he would rather be playing. I want Igor to meet all the Swedes who come through Konugard."

For future trade, Inge thought. He asked Igor to show Inge his piece of birch bark with the boy's attempts at writing, and she saw the words were fancier than runes.

Once, many lifetimes ago, she sat with Helgi on a river bank. He had learned the runes from a Celtic trader, and scratched them in mud, teaching them to her. Ah, she felt Helgi, too, remembered. She had learned so well that when her mother taught them to her years later she caught on quickly. In truth, she had known them already.

She listened to Igor speaking Swedish and took a liking to this serious young boy, much less noisy than her sons at his age.

"Igor, tomorrow we will go on a hunt with our guests from Sweden," Helgi said. "Do you want to go along?"

"Oh, yes. I want to see the animals."

He left happily, dragging his birch bark by the hemp rope.

Zeno was overjoyed when apricots in pomegranate sauce were served, though Inge thought them tasteless. The mead was brought, and she tasted rowan berry in it. Helgi served strong drink, as befit any Swede. The toasts began. Helgi lifted his golden goblet and toasted his honored guests who had brought great joy to his palace, and Karl toasted Helgi, who had made them feel at home.

"To a successful hunt tomorrow," Helgi said. "My falconer has been training a new bird, and we will see how he is on the attack." Smiling at Inge he said in a low voice, "We will hunt after we dew-walk."

"Thank you,' Karl said," but we cannot join you on the hunt. We leave early on the morrow."

Inge bit her lip so she did not cry out. How could Karl be such an ungrateful guest? To leave Helgi would be unbearable.

"Karl-Eirik," he said, "you have just arrived. Miklagard has been a city for thousands of years--it will wait for you. The weather there is blistering hot, but here we enjoy long cool evenings in spring."

Inge felt her stomach clench. Did Helgi know Karl was headstrong? Ay, he did. She wanted to beg Karl to stay in Konugard, but it would be unseemly for a chieftain's wife.

Helgi continued to smile, but his tone changed.

"Karl-Eirik, The Seafarer and The Goldenbreast are the first of the season. Nine others will be here within the week, and I will send you all together in a convoy. Two boats are dangerous. You will need to portage around seven deadly waterfalls--"

"We know how to portage."

"Between the Dvinna and the Dnieper, yes, but you have not met the Pechenegs. They live on the steppes around the waterfalls, and while you walk, portaging, they will attack by the hundreds."

"We are skilled swordsmen," Lars said. "Perchance you do not know this in Konugard, but in Sweden we fight best when we have great odds against us."

Helgi smiled. "And you sail best with the wind against you."

Lars could not hide his surprise. Helgi knew too much.

"Let me tell you how fierce the Pechenegs are," Helgi said. "Your women..."

Karl looked at her, and Inge thought he had not seen her for a long time.

"My women I will defend to the death," he said, and Inge felt tears start in her eyes. She blinked hard.

Helgi pounded the table. "Your women will be raped while you watch. And then the Pechenegs will kill you. Very, very slowly, while you beg to die."

Zeno shrugged. "Then the Norse will go to Valhalla. The fools will die happy."

"Fools they are," Helgi said, and Inge saw pain in his eyes.

Karl stood. "You have been kind to us, but we cannot stay.'

Helgi stood. "Then I will hold you here until the nine boats arrive, when you will be free to join them."

Inge felt a spurt of joy. She and Helgi would be in the same city until the nine ships arrived. Ay, they would meet...

Guards in white armor marched through the doors and lined up along both sides of the table. Helgi sat. Karl sat.

Inge's shoulders ached, but she dare not shrug and relax them. Helgi had given no sign to the guards she could see. Yet they had appeared.

"Now, Karl-Eirik," Helgi said, "you are known as a skilled trader, and you know how these things are arranged. The Pechenegs are supplied with goods by the Empire, and they fight for the Empire, to destroy any boats that come through their land. From the Emperor the tribes receive cloth, pepper, and leather."

He sipped his mead, and Inge saw it calmed him.

"But we too give them goods," he said, "and better. From us they get gold brocade, jewels--" he touched his ear. "And so we have a treaty with them. Ten, twenty ships at a time are allowed to portage safely, but never one or two. It is their land."

Lars sneered. "You buy them off."

Inge shivered inside. In truth, these northmen were fearless with this overlord.

"Let us say we keep them friendly," Helgi said. "As you know, I am of the House of Rurik. Before he died, I pledged I would shed no Swedish blood. I cannot let you go without my protection."

Ah, if only Helgi did not say "my" protection, Inge thought. She watched Karl turn the knife over and over.

"The leather handle is beautiful, is it not?" Helgi asked. "When you leave I will give you many furs to trade in Miklagard, though the two finest we will keep to make cloaks for your wife and daughter. You can get them on your return."

"We can get pelts of our own," Lars said. "We need no furs from Kievan Rus."

Helgi turned his goblet by the stem. Ignoring Lars, he frowned at a drop of mead spotting the fine linen cloth.

"More important than fur is wax, Karl-Eirik, and I will give you wax to take to Miklagard, where they use hundreds of candles to light the tile pictures in their churches. Candlelight makes them shimmer, and the people think the White Christ and the Virgin are alive."

"Keep your furs. Keep your wax," Karl said.

"We need not decide tonight. Now come, I have a collection of swords Thora will enjoy."

Ilana walked around the table to him, and they left. Inge knew they had no choice but to follow, between two lines of white-armored guards. The brothers walked slowly, whispering. Not for the first time Inge wished Lars was in Skotland or Frisia--or Hel's home.

Tonight when she had Karl alone, she would be most lovesome and convince him they must stay and travel with the nine boats. Karl had always taken counsel with her, asked her advice and listened to it. She felt a rush of longing for the farmstead, where they had lain together in each other's arms night after night, talking over problems that seemed so simple now.

They had chosen to adopt Thora, and the maid's whole life lay ahead of her. As parents, they had no right to cut it short.

* * *

Helgi's sword room was almost as large as his hall, with the same fires in the wall, but the floor was covered not with thick wadmal, but with wood in a familiar pattern. Helgi looked at her, and grinned. It was a pattern she had woven in linen when they lived long ago at the edge of the pond where the flax thrived, and they had lain amidst the soft blue-flowered stalks.

Dozens of swords, unsheathed, hung on the walls. Inge wondered if the Overlord was showing them so they would realize his strength. A servant passed among them with cups of mead, and they all drank and looked. Thora ran from one sword to another, pointing out this short blade, that jeweled hilt to Halfdan.

"Your daughter is charming," Helgi told Inge. "I would never guess she had been a thrall."

Helgi had always been silver-tongued, Inge remembered, and free with compliments. She ached to kiss his face round in the Circle of Love. She felt his yearning. It was unfair to them both to pretend to be strangers, but there was no help for it. She forced herself to move away to look at a sword with a pommel gilded with the Gripping Beast.

Ilana asked her to translate some runes writ on the hilts.

" 'Quarrelsome,' reads one," Inge said, "and ay, a sword is not used in the peace of the weaving room. This one I like better—'Augumund owns me.' "

She listened to the crews trading lies with one of Helgi's Swedish-speaking guards. He had heard of swords that could lay spells. Was there any truth to it? Ay. A Norse fighter skilled in casting spells could blunt a sword with a breath, Gunnar said. Or a glance, Anders added. Were there swords that never failed? Ay, the Norse knew of one that cleft an anvil.

Lars whispered over Inge's shoulder. "There is the kind of sword a man keeps unsheathed between himself and a woman who will not enter into bedplay with him."

"Hush, Lars. It is only a seaman's story."

"Perchance I have not been lucky enough to have the ear of a beauteous woman, as did a certain arrow-maker at Breidal."

She walked away, and Helgi came to her.

"Ingeborg, do you know of the Great Sword of Miklagard? It is magical, and when broken, would mend itself and become whole. It fell into the hands of one of the Emperor's bodyguards, and he put it beneath his pillow every night, but every morning it would be found some distance away. The Emperor Basil bought it for three times its value in gold, it is said, and keeps it over his bed."

"From what I hear of the Empress, he may need it," Zeno said, and both men laughed.

Helgi lifted a sword off the wall, and called to Thora. He pointed it down to the floor and up again, and everyone gasped. A snake seemed to run up and down the blade.

"This is the far-famed Twigs of Venom?' Gunnar asked.

"Pah. Acid was used to etch the blade," Lars said. "That is all."

Ever the good host, Helgi smiled, put it back, and lifted another. He bent the point to the hilt and let it spring back.

"Life's Sleep-Bringer, it is called, Lars."

He touched his swords with pleasure, Inge thought. Norse blood ran strong in him.

She said Zeno had spoken truth when he told them Helgi had a fine collection of swords, the largest in the world.

"He has been useful to you? I was hoping he would help."

Inge looked from one man to another.

"Ah. Did you put him in the hut where he would get The Sores?"

"No, no, though I am glad you healed him. He is indebted to us both now, is he not?"

She watched how lightly Helgi handled the heavy swords. He led her to a wooden bench and called for mead. How often they had sat together in the past on plain wooden benches, on tree trunks, on fallen logs.

"Ingeborg, the Empress is of Swedish stock on her father's side. Her name is Eudocia Ingerine, something like your own name."

"Somewhat."

"Eudocia was the lover of the former emperor--Michael III, known as The Drunkard."

"You are right," Zeno said. "He liked his wine."

Helgi sipped his mead. "More than a little--he was a drunk. But Michael is dead, and the Emperor Basil rules. An intriguing man. He was a poor country lad, and part of his boyhood was spent in prison. He came to Miklagard and took part in wrestling matches--he is strong. Michael's uncle, Caesar Vardhus, took a liking to Basil, and put wood chips on the mud where he wrestled, but none where his opponent stood. He slipped and fell, and Basil won, gaining Michael's favor. And then Basil killed Caesar Vardhus."

"Nay!" Inge cried out, shuddering.

"Yes. Caesar was Chamberlain, second only to the Emperor, and after the uncle's death, Basil became Chamberlain, with a room next to Michael's bed-chamber. One night while Michael was away drinking with Eudocia, Basil twisted the key with his bare hands so this door could not be locked, and when Michael went to bed, he entered and killed him."

"Nay!" Inge whispered, her stomach churning. She must watch Thora closely in Miklagard, and protect her. This Emperor, with the help of his Swedish Empress, killed when he chose. "Is there no Thing-Assembly in Miklagard to judge these crimes? No Lawspeaker, no Council of Twelve?"

"The Emperor is above all of these," Zeno said. "But to his credit Basil has become a fine Emperor, a protector of the poor, and a good general. The people love him."

"Some believe Basil would have been killed by Caesar," Helgi said. "Or by Michael, and rather than be killed..."

"I believe none of it,' Inge said. "This Basil is a murderer."

"Many of us would agree."

She felt Karl stand close enough to touch her, though he did not.

"Karl-Eirik, have you enjoyed my swords?" Helgi asked.

"As much as any prisoner."

"Karl, I want us to be friends. I want you to trust me."

"When all of Kievan Rus is a network of your spies? Why should I trust you?"

To her horror, Karl had no fear of this overlord at all.

"Because I trust you, Karl-Eirik," Helgi said. "There is a Slavic proverb 'What you do not hear with your ears, you will feel at the base of your neck.'"

He stood, and Inge marked he was no longer drinking.

"It is true I have a few men spying for me, but an overlord never has too many. What I want is this: my first attack on Miklagard was a disaster--you heard this from Zeno, I am certain. It is the wealthiest city in the world, and I wish to hang my shield on the city gate. Not to show I have conquered it, but that I am ready for peace, an old Swedish custom I learned from Rurik."

"Two small boats will not help you conquer the wealthiest city in the world, well- defended, I trow," Lars said.

"Karl-Eirik, the Norse are known everywhere as the best sailors in the world. Hundreds of northmen work for the Emperor in his navy."

"Then they need no more. We work for ourselves."

"Your lust for freedom is one of the many things I like about you Swedes. I ask only that you keep your ears open for anything that might help in a second attack on the city. That is all."

"You have been hospitable, and I do not like refusing you, but I must."

Inge wanted to scream that Helgi must know that Karl was headstrong, that he had insulted the king at Birka. "Anything about the Greek ships, Karl-Eirik, the habits of their captains, anything a seamen might pick up in a wine hall... Tell me, have you heard of wet-fire? It is a kind of fire that burns on water--water does not put it out--most useful in a sea battle. If you had the secret of wet-fire, you Norse could rule the world as the Empire does now."

Karl's voice hardened. "Find someone else to learn the secret. The trappings of state entrap men. Kings and princes serve more than they rule. I will keep my freedom on The Seafarer."

"And I on The Goldenbreast," Lars said.

Inge wanted to strangle them both. She latched her hands together.

"You Swedes are known as blunt men, and I like that," Helgi said. "However, when you return to get your fur cloaks for your wife and daughter you may have picked up some news. Who knows what you will learn. No man can read the future."

"Ah, but we can read the past," Lars said. "Tell me, Helgi, which sword did you use to kill Askold and Dir when you took over Konugard? This one with a steel crossguard? Or this with a five-lobe pommel?"

Inge felt the guards surround Lars, and she wanted to tell them to take him to prison and leave him, but Helgi only threw back his head and laughed.

"There are many stories about an overlord, Lars. I learned long ago to believe half of what I hear."

"Ay? If only half is true, then you and Basil are much the same."

Inge felt a stab of fear. Lars often went too far.

"No, Lars. We are different. He has too many enemies to move freely among the people. You saw how I walked in Konugard, unguarded. You saw the people greet me. Were they fearful? Did they bow before me?"

Lars had no answer, and Inge stood up. "Thank you for a fine evening," she told Helgi, and he lingered over his kiss on her outstretched hand. He squeezed her hand so slightly no one else would notice. She hated withdrawing her fingers.

"Farvell," she said, leading the way. She must separate Lars and Karl and the Overlord. Much as she longed to be close to Helgi, a sword room was too dangerous for three men who would fain try them on each other for any paltry excuse.

<h1 style="text-align:center">XIX</h1>

Inge sat on the edge of the bed, removing the firestone neckring. She put it in her seapouch, well-hidden for the night. Karl stood at the window, looking out. Comfort was of no moment to him, and never would be.

"Karl-Eirik, what do you see out of the glass panes? When we get back, we might get some for our farmstead. I like it."

He continued to stare into the dark. "Did you like him?"

She yawned. "Like who? Come to bed."

"Who? Helgi. He is one shit of a sailor. He should stay where he belongs, on a horse's ass."

"He is a good dinner companion, and he admires you. Husband, come to bed. We have been sleeping within the leather bag for weeks. Here we can romp and move about. I need you to unplait my hair."

"Ask Helgi."

"Nay, he is unplaiting his Ilana's hair. Tomorrow we will go on the hunt and be with others all day. I am wont to enjoy each other alone."

Karl turned to look at her, and she saw no softening in the set lines of his face.

"We are not going on the hunt, Inge."

"As good guests, we can do nothing else, Karl. Helgi is only keeping us here until the other boats arrive, to go safely downriver."

But if Karl did not go on the hunt, she would go without him. In her billowing pants she could ride as any man might. She had always loved the hunt. And she could be alone with Helgi...

Now she took off her clothes and undid her plait. She stood face-to-face with Karl, wearing only her hair. She wrapped it about them both, spread it over his shoulders and down his back, stroking his ass, trying to melt his hard body with her fingertips. She kissed his eyes, his forehead, his shaven cheeks, his neck, all the time pulling off his shirt and breeches, hungry to get to his growing manhood. She felt the dampness start within her, and put his Jade Stalk between her thighs, turning to and fro.

"Ahhh. Karl, I am wont to cry out, 'here is the biggest in Konugard', and I care not who hears it."

"Nay. The biggest in Kievan Rus."

She giggled and tied her hair around his back and pulled him onto the bed on top of her, knowing she could not pull him if he did not want her to. She rubbed her knuckles on his beard and kissed the soft skin inside his upper lip, and her mouth opened of its own will, as he tasted her.

"Karl, I am starved for you," she whispered, grasping his shoulders, pushing him down on her. "Lick me. Lick me until I come."

He pushed her thighs apart, and his tongue entered her, and her body twisted.

"Higher," she whispered, "higher."

He thrust his tongue up her Golden Cleft, and she felt the glad sweetness start, and her Clouds came forth to meet him. His tongue tight within her, she pushed her thighs together, the blessed spasms clenching and opening deep within.

Karl came up for air, nosing her wet loins, tasting her.

"Now I will do you," she said, kissing him all the way down, sucking his manhood into her mouth, giving him his Come.

She fell into an exhausted sleep. Ah, loving was the best of medicines for a quarrelsome man. And a fretful woman playing the whore to convince Karl to wait for the nine boats. Relaxed now, she realized the white-armored guards would not let Karl get away. Helgi would want her safe.

It seemed she barely closed her eyes before she felt Karl's hand shake her shoulder. He was dressed.

"Karl, why are you up? It is too early for the hunt."

"We are not going on the hunt. We are leaving Konugard. Get dressed, Inge." He gave her the clothes, and she pitched them onto the floor.

"Karl! The long trip has driven you mad with elvist. We will never escape from the palace. And if perchance we do, we will be killed by the Pechenegs. You heard Helgi. We must wait for the other boats."

He picked up her clothes, and gave them to her once again. She threw them at his chest.

"Inge, we are not waiting for any one."

She got up on her knees. "You will kill us, one way or another!"

"Nay. We have sailed through hard waters before. If we do not go now, we may never get away. Helgi would like to keep us here."

"Karl, that is a fool's thought. The gossip about Sweden would soon stale, and we would be a burden. Helgi will want us to be gone when the nine boats arrive. I will not throw my life away on this whim of yours."

"It is not a whim. It is a plan, well thought out."

She sat. "Thora and I will not go. We adopted her. She is our daughter, and we are charged with her upbringing."

"Thora goes where Halfdan goes. Look out the window."

Out the glass pane she saw two shadows moving in the dim light. She saw two bodies lean together, kiss, separate, move on, stop and kiss.

"The boy is good for something after all, Inge."

"Karl, we cannot chance this. Your beloved boat--"

"My boat is seaworthy. A few rapids, a few tribesmen will not stop us."

Inge felt fear stab her chest. A few hundred tribesmen, more like, but she knew Karl was set on going, and nothing would keep him. If he was stopped outside, he would draw his sword, and there would be a fight between the handful of Swedes and Helgi's guards. Karl's men and Lars's men would die. Thora, too.

Quickly she put on her clothes. Perchance Karl would listen on the boat. She could do nothing here. He opened the door and looked.

"I am glad Helgi is a heavy drinker, and is sleeping it off."

Inge pictured the guards in the raised part of the palace beneath the roof-- even in the dark the escaping northmen would be seen. If they were captured and held, she could talk to Helgi and ask him to let them go as soon as the nine boats came. They were many to feed...many to hold, jailed...many to guard...they were Swedes, and Helgi loved all Swedes...Rurik, ah, but Rurik was dead...in truth, how much did Helgi love Swedes? Or her?

Karl held her hand and led her out. If only the palace doors had been locked, but Helgi trusted Karl. Or so the overlord said.

Karl pulled her after him on the dew-wet grass, downhill to the slick cobblestone road. If she stumbled and fell and broke her leg, Karl would have to stop, but nay, he held her fast, and she could not fall. The road was free of loose stones that might dislodge and make noise. She cursed Helgi for having his roads in good repair. Her thoughts tumbled. Ahead of them lay a passage into darkness...a journey that could not be shared. The witch seer's words would come true.

Freya, she prayed.

She listened for running footsteps, but the night was still. Did Helgi want Karl to escape and be killed by the Pechenegs? Any fool could sense the overlord and Lars and Karl bore no love for one another. If only Karl were not so head-strong. Was every guardsman in Konugard sleeping off drink?

Or had the crews overpowered unsuspecting guards, and had blood already been shed? She shivered. They ran through the gate onto the quay. Was it only today she had walked uphill in the warm sun?

Both crews were readying the ships, and she felt their excitement, how glad they would be to shove off. In a few more minutes they would all be gone. What if she screamed? Would Helgi's guards come running? Or Helgi himself?

The quay was deserted, save for one lone figure in a red tunic and leather beeches sitting on the seawall. He rose.

"You did not need to run, my friends," Helgi said. "We had time to load the furs and wax."

Karl cursed.

"Karl-Eirik, did you think I would try to stop you? No, if you want to kill yourself I will not keep you. But I offer my palace to your wife until you return--if by chance you outwit the Pechenegs. Inge will be safe with us. Women weave in Konugard as they do in Sweden, and I will look after her."

"Modir--" Thora said, throwing herself against Inge. "I can but go with Half-dan, do you understand?"

Inge nodded, stroking Thora's hair. Her daughter was a love-sick young girl, but she was not. She saw Bratta and Volnir aboard, already settled in. There was little time to ponder. She must choose now, choose between Karl-Eirik, or a life of safety, of comfort, of pleasure with Helgi.

She looked at the battered Seafarer. Her eyes followed one long scratch from bow to stern. She looked at Karl, his beard greying. Only an hour before, they had enjoyed each other. After all they had shared on this fateful journey, after the merciless portage, it would end in senseless death.

She looked at the sunrise lighting the tops of the buildings in this fair city, second only to Miklagard in wealth and beauty. She thought of the lace trim on a linen tablecloth and golden goblets and the luxury of warm water and straw beds, its ruler who was making a New Sweden. She could help. She could be happy here, living with Helgi, whose body she knew so well. Did he still have the birthmark on his shoulder blade? Ay, she knew he did.

"Ingeborg," Helgi said, putting his hand on her shoulder, "do not throw your life away. Do not waste it. The Pechenegs--"

Ay, the Pechenegs, and a certain death.

"Ingeborg, stay where you are safe with me," Helgi whispered, stroking her back with the light touch she loved. "For the first time I can offer you riches, the comfort we never had together. You will want for nothing. We will be happier than ever before."

She looked at the overlord. Either choice led to suffering. If she chose to stay, she would never see Karl again, or her daughter. She would carry guilt to her grave. Yet if she left with Karl she, too, would be killed, and all her healing lost.

She looked at him, his hand on the tiller, ready, waiting for her.

She would see Helgi again, in another life, but not Karl.

She embraced the overlord and kissed him gently, gently. "Do not forget me, my Helgi. We will meet again. Naught can keep us apart."

She let Hrolf lift her aboard.

Inge stood in the bow and watched Konugard fade as the boats under oar pulled away from shore. She was glad it was too dark for anyone to see her tears. She had chosen. All she could do was enjoy Karl until the Pechenegs attacked. How long? Five days--a week? There was no denying the power of the runes. She had chosen them herself.

Zeno came to stand with her. "I regret I did not have time for church. Do you hear a bell with a wooden clapper? It is from the catacombs where the priests called The Sleepless Ones live. Someone is always awake, praying. No one is asleep on Lars's boat. What a racket."

The quiet night was rent with shouts and shuffling feet and a sound of wood beating flesh, Helgi's curses and then a splash. A shadowy figure swung onto the deck of The Seafarer.

"Välkommen," Karl said. "Finnvid, put the oar down. On our boat we do not greet a guest with a rap on the fingers. Whether he is invited or not."

Inge was too overjoyed to speak. Helgi was going with them?

"Thank you, Karl-Eirik," he said. "Your brother is not as friendly. I thought Swedes were known for hospitality, but not all."

Inge saw he was not panting with exertion, though he swam to them faster than a boatful of men could row. Nor was he shivering. She gave him a piece of wadmal to dry himself. He emptied the river water out of his boot, and she noticed a knife hidden in the side.

"If you are leaving Konugard, you have chosen a seaworthy boat," she said.

He grinned. "I know. I helped stow the furs and wax for Miklagard, and the brocade and jewelry for the Pechenegs beneath the floorboards. Your boat is well-crafted, Karl-Eirik."

Karl was silent, and Inge wondered how long the hospitality would last.

"You are going with us to Miklagard?" Thora asked.

"No, no. Only far enough to talk to Karl-Eirik."

Inge clenched her teeth so she would not cry out "Stay, stay. I need you." She forced herself to look at the first streaks of light poking through the watery fens on the east side of the river.

Karl pushed the tiller, and the sail filled as the boat swung downriver. Ingvar climbed the mast, and both crews except for Finnvid stowed their oars and slept. Like children they had faith in their captains, and left all worries to them. Lars steered close by with The Goldenbreast.

Helgi leaned against the gunwales. "Karl-Eirik, my shipyard is yours to help you tar and repair your boat. Turn back, and we can have you ready in a day."

"A day? More like a week. Nay, we do our own tar and repair."

"A day, a week, what does it matter. By then the spring floods will have reached the rapids, and it will be easy to sail through."

"We have sailed hard waters before. Our ships are no strangers to rapids."

"Well, then. Let me tell you about the seven waterfalls. One is called Never-Sleep. Another--"

"I heard about them in Gotland. Do not frighten Ingeborg."

Karl's concern was like honey.

"Safety is not the only reason, Karl," Helgi said. "If your Seafarer is harmed, nine crews of the other boats will be there to help."

He watched Finnvid drop ale and barley bread off the stern. "What are you doing?" Helgi asked.

"Making sacrifice to the gods for a safe journey," Finnvid said.

"Rurik did not tell me of this. Perhaps if we made a sacrifice before my ill-fated journey to attack Miklagard...from now on we will do it. Now, Karl, you will be safe at the first three waterfalls. But at the fourth, the Pechenegs will appear. They are the fiercest tribe in all of Kievan Rus, and you may wish to hide your women beneath the floorboards. You will see many, many runestones on the bank--Swedes who have been killed by the Pechenegs. Killed or taken captive, which is worse than death."

Inge listened with growing horror. The sky lightened as Sol began pulling her wagon across the sky. Inge took out her reed mat and began working it. At the fourth waterfall she would burn it. No Pecheneg would sleep upon a mat she wove with her own fingers. She felt Helgi's eyes watching her, as he argued with Karl.

"The Pechenegs live on the Steppes, Karl-Eirik. Let me tell you about the Steppes: they roll on forever. The space is vast and boundless with no end. The grass is tall enough to hide a man on horseback, and the horses thrive--no man can outrun them. There are no trees for hiding except a few in the valleys. You and your women will be prey."

The current carried them smoothly, and Karl's hand stayed light on the tiller.

"Helgi, at every port except yours, someone must be paid protection money or my boat will burn, my cargo disappear. What is your protection price? On Gotland they say you ask a third of all geld and gold brought from Miklagard."

Lars whistled, and Inge was astonished. A third!

"Karl-Eirik, I would not ask a third from you," Helgi said.

"Ay? Why not, when you ask it of every captain, be he Greek or Arab, Khazar or Slav?"

In the dawn Inge saw Helgi shrug.

"The blood in my veins is not Greek or Arab, Khazar or Slav, Karl. It is Swedish."

Did this Helgi know Karl trusted Swedes above all, Inge wondered--this overlord who knew everything?

Helgi sighed, and Inge heard a sadness when he spoke.

"Karl, the Steppes are like the sea. They cannot be controlled or blockaded. There are no ports. It is a no man's land of prairie, with the best archers in the world. The Pechenegs never miss. If they fail to hit a target, they are banished from the tribe."

Karl said nothing. Inge was paralyzed with fear. She stopped working.

"Karl, you are one stubborn Swede," Helgi said. "Yet if Rurik had stayed in the northland, we would be countrymen. I will help you and your women. There is a tribe called Magyar, many thousand strong, now out of favor with the Bey, the Khazar's leader in war. He is driving all Magyars westward, and with luck they will be close enough to the Pechenegs that the two will be busy fighting, and leave your two small boats alone."

"Which side gets your help?" Lars asked. "The Magyars or the Pechenegs?"

"Both, of course, Lars," Helgi said.

The sun burnt off the fog so that Inge saw Thora and Halfdan, gazing at each other from their separate boats. Did the two have any idea of what lay ahead? Nay, they were absorbed in each other.

"Karl-Eirik," Helgi said, "there is another tribe, of women, skilled with the sword. They too live on horseback, in the land of the Magyars. They meet with the Slavs from time to time to get salt, or clothes for their children--they are said to fight with their children on their backs."

"I have heard stories of them in Miklagard," Zeno said. "But they are real?"

"Ilana knows them. She has spoken with their leader."

"No!" Zeno said. 'And all my life I thought they were only tales told around the fire."

"I, too, have heard of them," Lars said. "They cut off one breast so they can draw a bow better."

Inge shuddered. The world beyond her fjord was often dreadful.

"That part is a lie, Lars," Helgi said. "But when they learn of Thora they may agree to help you."

"They hate men?" Lars asked.

"No, no, though they bed with men only once a year, and only after battle, I have been told."

If the women warriors appeared to save them from the Pechenegs, Inge knew she must keep close watch on Thora. She must not let her go with them. Once again she was grateful for Halfdan. He would hold fast to the maid.

Helgi put on his boots and stood. "Karl, do not steer to shore. I will swim from here."

"You are wondrous strong," Inge said, knowing Karl would not do aught for Helgi. "You outswam the rowers."

Helgi grinned, and she saw how boyish he looked, with his wet hair. How his ears stuck out, like Karl's. The sign of men who thought for themselves.

"We have swimming contests in the Dnieper, and an overlord must compete, and set a good example."

When Lars asked if he won, Helgi said the Slavs were not the best of swimmers. Against the Swedes he would have trouble winning. He had heard Karl could swim for miles in full chainmail. Was it true?

"Eight miles off Frisia, two years past," Finnvid said.

Inge heard the pride in his voice. She would never have known Karl was far-famed if she had not taken this voyage. She asked Helgi how he would get back to his palace.

He told her he would dew-walk in his bare feet, though not as happily without her at his side. And then he would find a horse. Helgi smiled at her, and she ached to kiss him. His lips had always been full, with tipped-up corners. Ever the sign of a sensuous man.

"Karl-Eirik, you shall have my help whether you want it or not," Helgi said. "There is a Slavic proverb: 'Do not spit in a well if you mean to drink from it later.' Ingeborg, fear not. Only beware of these stubborn Swedes. And keep watch for the women warriors. You will see them, I promise. You will be safe at the seventh waterfall."

He touched his amulet, and she did the selfsame with Freya, and she thought it a pity the simple gestures were all they had. This time. He jumped to the gunwale, dove off and clove the water with little splashing. Helgi would not lie to her. Full sure he would send help to survive this dread journey. She felt a twinge of hope.

"What think you, Lars?" Karl asked his brother. "Helgi is no better than the cheapest trader at Birka who demands protection money."

Only on a larger scale, Lars answered, steering close by. This treaty he made with the Pechenegs to let ten, twenty boats go through but not two--if this treaty was broken by two skillful captains who sailed through, Helgi would look like a shit.

A ruler who cannot enforce a treaty he made would be known as a fool by every captain up and down the rivers, Karl said. Helgi would be laughed at in every ale hall on both sides of the Baltic.

"Karl, we have more experience with hard waters than Helgi. Do you remember the Pentland Firth off Skotland?"

The brothers began swapping stories. Do not take Helgi for a fool, she wanted to tell them. Helgi had amassed golden goblets, and silver plates. She would like to have his fine linen table cloth to sew finespun pants for herself and Thora. But far more would she like to have nine boats with them. She looked up at the sky, and closed her eyes, shivering.

The moon was waning, always the sign of cutting down, leveling. Separation.

* * *

After a fitful rest she awoke to the sound of metal axes and swords scraping against the schist grindstone. Gunnar and Thora were at work. She roused herself to milk Bratta for the day meal, and marked the pail was fuller. One day of Konugard's good grass had pleased the bell cow. She found a pouch of the high black bread Anders thought of using for a pillow. Helgi had been most generous. She passed around bread and the milk bucket to the men.

She heard a woodpecker tap-tap-tapping a dead tree on shore, and when she looked for it she saw a beacon, unlit. Downriver, another and another. In truth, Karl was right. Helgi had a network of spies up and down the river, a network of beacons to warn him of trouble. Would the beacons be lit one day for them? The overlord had promised his help. Yet she had chosen Karl- Eirik, and left Helgi behind.

She shuddered and pulled her cloak tighter. Would their closeness through other lifetimes be enough to save them? She doubted not that Helgi wanted to help, but often the best plans became snagged. Would he be able to pit the Magyars against the Pechenegs? Would Ilana have luck in reaching the Warrior Women? She clutched her amulet, praying to Freya. She must trust the goddess, and put fearful runes out of mind.

XX

Karl called her, and this time she went to sit with him at the tiller. She had chosen him, whatsoever the future held. She sat and wove her reed mat, an ease between them, ill-will between husband and wife as though it had never been. Talk flowed as the river, at times fast-moving, at times slackened. She noted Karl had no fear. A man who had always been successful in battle would not believe other men could vanquish him.

Zeno told them a story about the Pechenegs. One time they had one of Helgi's towns under siege, and he could not help because his troops were elsewhere.

"That sounds like Helgi, to abandon his people," Karl said.

"Do not belabor Helgi, Karl-Eirik. He is a just ruler, much beloved. But this is not a story about him. The Slavs under siege had little grain or kvass left, but they put it in vats in the ground well-surrounded with dirt, so the vats were concealed.

"The Slavs called the Pechenegs to them and said, 'You cannot overcome us if you besiege us for ten years. We get our grain and kvass from the earth itself.'"

"What the Pechenegs see is what they believe, and so the siege was raised. They are an unlettered people. They do not even have your runes. My own people are not as simple-minded. We have books. And readers who stand on the street and read from them, and so we learn."

Finnvid snorted, and said he had heard of books. At Birka they told him of a Christian papa who sailed with forty of them. His ship was attacked and sunk, and the books now lay at the bottom of the sea, and no one could read them.

"In Sweden we tell children stories, and they tell their children, and on and on, and nothing is lost or at the bottom of the sea, but kept alive."

"Finnvid, I did not know you could talk so long. Still, you Swedes cannot dream of the joy of holding a book in the hand and wondering what secrets lie within."

"Ja, we cannot read Greek," Inge said, "but we will need to speak it in Miklagard."

She set Zeno to teaching them once again, though partly to keep her own mind from thinking about leaving Helgi once again. Her joy had been short-lived. Ahead of her was a future no one could control.

* * *

One day passed as another, and at night on shore Karl set their leather bag well apart from the others, so they could love each other beneath the wheeling stars. She loved so hard, toward the end she cried out with pleasure.

Karl gave command of the nightly sword practice to Finnvid, while he went searching for wild onion with her, and never left her near side.

During the long day's sail they shared secrets. One day the Steppe Eagle soared above them, and he told her he had always wanted to sail across the wide waters, but in truth he wanted to fly like a bird. When Inge giggled, he, too, laughed, and said he tried to think how it would be to spread his arms and leave the tiller behind, soaring, floating on air as he floated on water when he swam.

Inge told him she thought sailing would be open and free. When she had seen Karl off a-viking every spring, the sea was so big, the waters endless. But nay, her world had shrunk to the width of the ship. Karl told her everyone who went to sea thought it would be an escape, but they must learn to live closer together than anywhere else.

Lars kept The Goldenbreast four ells behind The Seafarer, and Inge was glad he did not want to intrude. Karl's men, too, busied themselves away from the stern.

As they journeyed southward Inge marked how everything was meet: the waves meeting the shore, Karl's hand meeting her hair. Their wooden boat seemed to become meet with the water, so they sailed on no hard, unyielding boards but a flowing river. Inge thought their breathing slowed to the pace of the water.

She had never been so happy, and when she told Karl, he said he, too, did not know such joy would be his lot. Time had been a thing she never had enough of, with everlasting tasks that were never done, but here, time, like the river, took her where it willed. She gave not a second to a fearsome witch-seer's foretelling. When Helgi came into her mind she could not keep him out, but she reminded

herself she had made her choice. She told Karl it was fine to be alive and traveling. He kissed her and shouted,

"Ay. Moving forward is our natural state."

The river frothed around their bow, sparkling like gleaming firestones. Who
needed a neckring from an overlord when she had the gleam of the sun? She was
tempted to drop the gift overboard, but she kept it in the bottom of her seapouch,
well-hid.

The river had little coves leading off it, and she wondered where they led to.
Some few places were shallow, so they had to pole the boats across. Often in the
middle they saw islands formed of trees and shrubs.

They all marveled at the Steppes. Beyond the reeds and scrub willows at the
riverbank, feather-plumed grass swayed, glistening in the sunlight, in shades of
green Inge never tired of seeing. In truth, these Steppes were without beginning
or end, owned by nothing but the wind, tall enough to hide a man on horseback,
though they saw none. Or even a sign of horse dung. Zeno told them there were
grasses here found nowhere else on earth, and they saw flowers, too, they had
not seen before.

"The tall red-and-yellow-and-white ones grow in Miklagard. They are called
tulips, from a word that means turban, a kind of hat they wear in Miklagard that
looks like the flower. Tulips grow from a bulb hid underground."

Finnvid was all for stopping to dig them up.

"You surprise me, Finnvid. I did not know you were a flower-lover."

"I care not for flowers, but I could sell the bulbs for gold to the king of every
country for his garden."

Zeno said that soon enough the colors, like the feather-grasses, would be
bleached by the hot sun. But not even when Finnvid said the northern sun was
never that hot, would Karl stop and let him dig.

Once they heard a piercing cry from a small animal standing on its hind legs,
and Zeno said it was a mormat, found only here. Another day they saw a small
animal fall flat on the ground, and Zeno told them it was a souslik, protecting its
young with its body.

"There are farms, deep into the Steppes, and the farmers hate the sousliks, for
they steal carrots and grain and oats for their winter burrows."

Inge saw larks and plovers, and to her surprise they no longer made her homesick. Her life was here with Karl, nowhere else.

On this journey it seemed to her she saw how sex underlay everything. The seed and its quickening was beneath all life. Most wondrous of all, one day while she sat with Karl she felt the sweet Come begin in her Golden Cleft, and spread through her body. She gasped with surprise. Karl guessed what was happening and laughed. He was not a dutiful husband, he said, and they must go to bed earlier and linger in their leather bag longer, so they had more time for bedplay.

And so they did, staying in bed while Thora and Halfdan cooked the grot for day meal. Still, Inge was stabbed by the delicious, piercing sweetness, one day four times while she sat with Karl. He teased her that she was making up for all the times he had been off a-viking, leaving her alone, but in truth neither knew what brought it forth.

They would be talking about their early years on the farmstead, and of a sudden the sweetness would take over Inge's body, and she was hostage to it. She could but yield.

"Inge mine, worry not," Karl said, one hand on the tiller and the other on her shoulder. "It is a gift of the river, this pleasure. The journey is so unlike your pattern of work and more work, on the farmstead. Your body is making up for it."

They never talked of the seven waterfalls, though she knew everyone aboard both ships was listening for the sound of rushing water.

Each night the men practiced swordcraft, and Inge saw they were becoming swifter. How well-suited Halfdan and Thora were. Lars asked his brother if he wanted to exchange Halfdan with one of Karl's crew so Halfdan and Thora could row together, but Karl turned away and answered not.

Ah, it was fated for them to fall in love, Inge thought. What did Karl have against the youth? she asked. He said he had enough to worry about without two young lovers together on his boat.

And then Freya, ever the goddess of love, came to help Thora and Halfdan in an unexpected way. One afternoon they sailed past a cluster of thatched huts enclosed on three sides by a stockade, moat, and rampart, the fourth side open to the river. Dark-haired Slavs were feeding chickens, making charcoal, pegging skins. Children, dogs, pigs ran everywhere. Inge breathed in the familiar smells.

"Steer far out, Karl," Zeno said, and Inge saw a sight that chilled her so she could not be warmed, though she pulled her cloak about her. At the edge of the grave barrows just beyond the settlement was a bleached-white figure of bone, tall as a woman, but fleshless, breastless, with a fanged mouth and glaring eye sockets that followed them.

"The White Death," Zeno whispered.

Ay, the White Death, Inge thought, within an unfenced circle, open, linked to the present, ready to draw in anything that passed. The skin on her neck prickled, and she leaned into Karl, tracing the healing spiral of the goddess Eir on her arm. None of them were ready to accept the White Death's invitation.

Death would come soon enough.

"Parents use the bone figure to frighten their children," Zeno said.

Inge looked toward Thora pointing to it, and jesting with Halfdan. Inge took a deep breath. She wanted Thora's happiness.

"Karl-Eirik, let us drink the Betrothal Ale of Thora and Halfdan tonight."

"Inge! That is elvist. The two can wait till we return to Sweden, with our neighbors and Halldis and--"

"Tonight, Karl. I want to drink it tonight.'

"Inge, once we get home and the two meet others, they may well laugh at how they thought they were in love in Gardariki."

Karl did not see how Thora's eyes softened when she looked at the boy, nor how he glowed when she was near.

"Inge, wait until after the seventh waterfall. We will be past the Pechenegs and can celebrate in safety."

She reminded him how often he had trusted her judgment--for six months every year for twenty years. How they had prospered, how the farmstead had increased fourfold under her care. Then her voice broke, and she could say no more.

Karl touched her shoulder. "Wife, if you are so certain, how can I doubt you?"

He told Per to take out the flute and practice the Betrothal Song for tonight. The men cheered, and Thora reddened. Lars steered close by, and Halfdan jumped onto The Seafarer's deck. Ah, whatever befell them, they would have this night, Inge thought as she watched them together.

Karl steered to shore early, and fear stayed at bay while Inge picked flowers from the Way Tree, sacred to Thor, and violets for love. Lacking birch leaves to signify a new beginning, she plucked Steppes grass and twisted all into a Betrothal Wreath.

For the cake she ground grot between two rocks and mixed it with honey and dried sloes she had saved, added Bratta's milk to make a dough, and baked the mound on a flat stone at the fire.

"In Miklagard bakers make bread and cake for all the households," Zeno said.

"Then when we get there we will have a second Betrothal Cake," Halfdan said, "and our marriage will be twice as sound."

Inge liked this young man, and his joke. She set the wreath on her daughter's golden hair, and Zeno promised her a bolt of silk when they got to Miklagard.

All drank a cup of Betrothal Ale and ate every crumb of cake, and Thora and Halfdan danced to Per's flute playing the Betrothal Song, and the men leapt over the fire to bring good fortune to the couple. Finnvid grabbed Zeno's hand, and they jumped together, and everyone cheered the Greek.

Within their leather bag Inge and Karl lay entwined. She hoped Karl would warm to the boy in the time left to them.

"Ingeborg, I do not want to talk of Halfdan, but of you. Tell me, in truth, are you ever sorry you came to Gardariki?"

She kissed his face round in the Circle of Love, and thought how she knew his body better than her own. Karl had ever made her feel more sleek and beauteous in bedplay than she was.

"Nay, Karl. What I would have missed. We have become so close these last few days I think we have been truly married for the first time."

His hands held her breasts as though he would hold fast to life. They loved and slept, and woke and loved again, wordless. Fear, even of the White Death, washed away in Clouds and Rain.

* * *

When they heard the waterfall, the men yelled, banging their oars, their eyes lit with excitement. Mist rose around them. Within her cloak, Inge shivered. Sensing her fear, Thora hugged her and sat down. They would face this dread time together.

"The first waterfall is called Never-Sleep," Karl said, "and well named."

"Yet no wider than the Thing-Plain at home," Finnvid said.

Inge thought the rushing water of Kievan Rus was wilder than in Sweden. This river raced to fall and then raced on again, and fell and roared on again. Seven times, for seven waterfalls. Both crews looked at the two rocks in the middle, big as islands. Inge thought it fearful to see the water strike with great force and crash down the other side.

"Karl, do we sail between?" Anders asked.

"Nay," Karl said, and all knew only he could decide. "We will pole close to the bank, and the women will walk."

Inge was happy to be back on land, where a countrywoman belonged. The thicket was not yet overgrown, and it was easy going, even for Volnir and Bratta. The hardest part was keeping Thora from stopping to watch Halfdan pole The Goldenbreast.

The second waterfall was not as easy. One island split the water, and a single tree grew atop. Inge looked at the thick gray roots clawing the granite, seeking succor, and shivered. The waterfall was bordered with high cliffs, and Karl said here they would portage.

The ravine was narrow, and the trees met overhead. It would be like walking at even, though it was mid-day. Zeno grumbled he wished he had a candle to light his way. Inge told him a waterfall was a place of great power. It freed the energy in the water, and he should breathe deeply of the ond.

"Karl-Eirik," Halfdan cried out, "there is a second river here. A ditch, dug next to the Dnieper, and the spring floods have filled it."

Thora smiled at him. Inge felt the joy of the men. A ditch would ease their portage more than anything else.

"Helgi told us of no ditch at the second waterfall," Lars said from his post at the tiller.

"He would not," Karl said. "He had reasons of his own to make us wait for a convoy of nine extra boats."

They floated the boats with ease into the ditch, and jested about how the water was helping them get to Miklagard. Ah, in truth there were no better sailors than the Norse, Anders said.

Helgi had told them they would find many, many runestones, but they saw only two. Zeno asked Inge what the runes meant, but she hurried him by. The runes told her two bodies lay beneath the mould.

"A river with strong currents must have a certain number of bodies each year, as tribute, so others may pass freely," she whispered. "The men know this, but they do not talk of it."

"I have never heard this."

"Ja, not everything is in your books."

She told him about the urist found at bigger Swedish waterfalls. Half goat, half man, he followed boats to protect their passage in dangerous waters.

Zeno looked around. He said he saw a frothing river, but no urist, and asked if she had ever seen him.

"Nay, but I am hoping he followed us to Gardariki."

The third waterfall was rock strewn, but the banks were low, and the men poled through. They saw a broken mast and bits of colored wool hooked onto a tree at the base of the fall. Some crew had not heard the noise. Or were they swept into it?

The men gestured to each other, for they could not hear shoutings above the roar of falling water. Once they were past, Karl told them it was named The Shouter, and all agreed it was apt. Anders asked for the name of the fourth, and Karl said it was Ever-Fierce.

It was the most fearful so far, with jagged rocks and clouds of spray. They heard a moan, and Zeno jumped, but Inge told him it was nothing but a whirlpool.

"The current is too violent to sail through," Karl said, "though not as fast as before. We will portage."

He divided the crews into those sliding the boats through the mud and those on watch, for the Pechenegs would appear at the fourth waterfall, Helgi had said. Inge saw nothing but scrub willow and the empty Steppes, and a ferment of water churning from one shore to the other.

This portage was steep, but shorter, and all hands were needed to hold back the boats from getting beyond their grasp. For the hundredth time Inge thought these northmen wondrous strong. She saw Karl's lips moving, and knew he was asking Odin to spare them from the tribesmen until they were through the falls.

By even they were ready to bed down. Karl told the men it was untrue that priests and women aboard were unlucky, for they were safe. Anders asked if his mistress would go on all their journeys from now on, or would Karl rather have a Christian papa, and all laughed, though more from relief than the joke.

Karl and Lars agreed they would not invite the Pechenegs with a fire, and so the men ate a handful of grot and Bratta's milk and the last of Helgi's black bread. There was no energy to do more than fall into sleep, while the crews took turns standing watch. Inge curled up next to Karl. They had survived the fourth waterfall. Not yet would she burn her reed mat.

The next day they found the fifth waterfall burbling like a Swedish brook, and Karl and Lars let everyone stay in the boats while they sailed through. Though she was soaked, Inge felt hopeful. She saw no hoof prints, smelled no horse's dung. Perchance a battle between the Pechenegs and Magyars had begun.

"Seething is the name of the sixth waterfall," Zeno told them and in truth, it simmered like a need-fire.

"Laughter is the name they told me in Gotland," Karl said, "but we have little laughter here."

This part of the river was so wide they could not see the far shore. Every ell was foaming, and Karl said it had a bottom covered with rocks. Ingvar stayed atop the mast, ready to call out. Karl sailed with the current, his hands quick on the tiller. The men sat with oar in hand to push them off the rocks.

Two overturned boats would be prey for the Pechenegs, but two boats afloat might escape, and all knew it. Zeno promised his God he would weave a fine altar-cloth if he got back to Miklagard safely. Finnvid told him to keep his oar ready.

Inge thought how Karl and his men were most alive when danger threatened. Each wore his sword, and could drop the oar in an instant to pull it out of the scabbard, or grab an axe. With much twisting and turning of the tiller, and many jabs of the oar, they finally sailed into calmer waters. Everyone cheered, and none cared if they were water-soaked and cold.

The size of the seventh waterfall surprised them all--small--though the river was wide.

"What Helgi calls a waterfall, we call rapids," Finnvid said. "He has never sailed these waters, I trow. When he attacked Miklagard, he went through on horseback."

Still, Karl and Lars were hard put to keep their boats from turning and smashing against the rocks. They fought an under-current, and tried to keep to the middle. Zeno looked up at the high banks and whispered to Inge that horsemen would find them an easy target, and Inge remembered the Pechenegs were the best archers in the world. Karl told Zeno to shut up, and Inge thought how no talk could be kept from Karl's sharp ears.

She thought there was one thing to be grateful for--this river did not twist and curve--they always knew what lay ahead. Finally, they got through the seventh and last waterfall, and Inge felt a great lightening.

They were alive.

The men were prone to boast, and Karl did not stop them:

"Helgi may have Swedish blood, but not enough of it."

"He did his best to keep us in Konugard, but why?"

"To get a share of the gold we will bring from Miklagard."

"Ja. We will keep that share."

"Perchance we misjudged Helgi. He may have set the Magyars and Pechenegs to fighting, and they do not bother with two small boats."

"Not so small. And well-laden."

"Still, I would not turn my back on Helgi. He might sharpen his sword on my backbone."

Inge prayed her thanks to Freya, and thought if anyone had power with the Pechenegs it would be the Overlord. Who else had such enticing bribes?

Karl steered to shore early, and said they would feast if Sven and Finnvid could bring down enough of the small game. The crews agreed to be ever watchful, though Helgi said they would be safe below the seventh waterfall.

Lars brought a cask ashore, and Inge started grinding barley between two rocks for another cake. Thora milked Bratta, the cow as always licking the maid's arm.

Inge stood, and put her arms about Karl from behind, nestling her head against him.

"Karl, I have never been so happy. Tonight--"

She had no chance to finish. She heard the thong of a bowstring and the soft whish of an arrow, and Karl crumpled in her arms.

Protruding from his throat was a single arrow.

XXI

Karl pulled his sword from its scabbard and lunged forward, both hands clutching the hilt, blood gushing from his mouth. Inge dared not ease him to the ground. The enemy was death, and he would fight it to the end. A terrible gurgling cry came from his throat. He took one more step and his wobbling knees buckled. He fell to the side, still facing the enemy.

A good death. A hero's death.

Inge fell atop him, and the men ran to them. Slowly Karl's eyes opened and did not close.

"Fadir is alive!" Thora cried. "His eyes are open."

"Nay, it is the death stare," Lars said, his voice breaking.

"He is too young to die!" Zeno said. "There--he moans. Listen. He is alive."

The sound was an animal howl.

"It is but the sound of air escaping from his lungs the last time," Inge whispered.

She cradled Karl's head in her arms while Lars pressed his brother's throat and withdrew the arrow between two fingers. He stared at it, and snapped it in twain.

Blood gushed forth from the wound and Inge tore off her headdress to stanch it. Though she pressed hard he bled and bled until the red torrent covered her hands and arms and pants, Karl's blood bathing her.

Only then did she admit to herself he was gone.

Lars looked toward the line of trees. "The arrow came from there."

Sven and Finnvid ran into the clearing, crying out when they saw Karl. Kneeling next to him Sven said, "We saw no one on the Steppes. The archer may still be close at hand."

The men looked on both sides of the river but saw nothing.

"The bastard's aim was true," Finnvid said.

"When we meet," Lars said, "I will repay him."

Anders's eyes overflowed with tears. "I do not want to live without Karl-Eirik. He was our leader. I will stay with his body."

"We are all leaving," Lars said. "If a Pecheneg finds you here he will gut you and hang you from a branch. You cannot stay alone."

"Not alone," Inge whispered, and her throat burned. "I would not leave Karl in life. I will not leave him now."

"None of us will leave Karl," Lars said. "If we buried him here the Pechenegs would dig him up and defile him. We will take Karl with us and give him a funeral fit for a great chieftain, beyond the range of the Pechenegs. Take him," Lars ordered Hrolf.

Though the Berserker's eyes were teary, he picked Karl up and carried him tenderly.

"Lay him in the bow," Lars said, "and then come back and carry Inge. She is most distraught."

Inge stood. "I will walk to sit with Karl."

She thought she would never be able to put one foot before the other, but when Hrolf came back for her, she spurned him. She must walk by herself. She waded into the water, the blood from her clothes reddening the river. Hrolf lifted her into the bow.

She looked at Karl where Hrolf laid him on the floorboards, and she saw he was already stiffening, his skin white as ivory. Lars put her cloak about her shoulders, but she pushed it off to cover Karl.

Behind her she heard the slip of swords being unsheathed, the men sending a message to any waiting Pechenegs: they were well-armed and would gladly die to protect their leader's body.

The boat rocked and they headed downriver, the only sound the muted splashing of the oars. Inge cared not who was at The Seafarer's tiller. A leech-woman knew what death brought to the living, how numb a body could be in shock.

From behind she heard Anders whisper. "We should have a pyre for Karl. He was a great man."

"Ay, and invite the Pechenegs," Finnvid whispered back.

"The right way would be to put Karl on The Seafarer and set it afire," Anders said, his voice thick. "It is the old way, and old ways are best."

"A flaming boat would be better than a pyre to draw the Pechenegs. Anders, you are an ass. We have no boat to spare."

"When I see Helgi my sword will be well-sharpened," Gunnar said. "He told us we would be safe at the seventh waterfall."

Even an overlord could make a mistake, Inge thought, touching Karl. His blood was dry and crusted on her hands and clothes. Lars steered so his stern was opposite her. She saw Thora in Halfdan's arms, both of them weeping.

"Inge, rest," Lars said, pain dulling his voice.

"I hear a faint sound of music--fair, like a flute--but deep like a lur."

"Inge, your grief is troubling you, and you hear what cannot be. I am listening not for music but the sound of hoofbeats and arrows whizzing through the air."

Lars was right. Leechwomen knew ears played tricks on a grieving wife.

"Inge, it should comfort you to know that Karl will go to Valhalla."

She did not answer. Was the sound of music from the Valkyries? No one had ever seen them in Sweden. Why then would she hear them or see them in this strange land? She put her hand on Karl's beard, the hair stiff with blood and death. Only an hour ago he was alive and moving. How quickly death took over.

"We will see word gets to your three sons, Inge, and to Halldis, on the first boat north," Lars said. "Halldis will take it hard. Karl was much beloved by her."

Lars was trying to lure her back to life. Not yet, not yet, she wanted to scream but could not even speak. Lars held his sword out in front of him.

"I swear to avenge Karl's death. Helgi will hear from me."

"And me," the men answered, the simple words stumbling from their mouths. Inge wished she had strength to defend Helgi, but she could not even lift her hand from Karl. Her thoughts twisted around and around. The overlord had sworn not to spill any Swedish blood. Yet Karl lay dead. Helgi loved all things Swedish, including her. Was his vow to help against the Pechenegs only talk? Was he powerless against this fierce tribe?

Lars pointed ahead where two islands loomed. "Inge, men stop there to give thanks to the gods for surviving the waterfalls, but I thought not to stop."

She nodded. Ay, they had survived, all but one. Her own body felt as stiff as stone and as empty of movement as Karl-Eirik's.

The two boats followed the river until Lars decided they could stop in safety and bury Karl, and none disagreed. Like the boats the men, too, drifted. Like herself, they had lost heart, and turned to Lars for direction.

He found a rise, well-protected by trees, and the boats were beached. The men kept their swords unsheathed and ready, breaking ground for the grave with their axes. All agreed with Finnvid they would rather dull their axes on Helgi's head.

Inge knelt and scooped the black soil with her bloodied hands. At her side, Thora and Zeno too, dug. Volnir stood with them, his head drooping. When they had a deep hole, Hrolf laid Karl in it, and all were loath to cover him. Inge once again heard the fair sounds.

"There. Do you hear music?" she asked, but Lars said the only sound was wind sighing through the Steppes.

"The Valkyries must be close at hand, Mistress," Anders said. "They will have no trouble finding Karl, though I wish we could bury him in Swedish soil."

She asked Anders to bring the clay jar of Swedish loam Karl gave her to assuage her loneliness. Kneeling, she drifted it over his body and put the empty jar next to his hand.

"A bit of Sweden will be with him," Lars said, his voice cracking. "Forever," he whispered.

One by one the men spoke of Karl, unwilling to let him go. Heart-sore, they talked, telling the stories that would be told later, from ale hall to ale hall, so part of Karl would never die, but live on in the memories of men.

Anders began in a tear-filled voice. He talked of one time when arrows and spears flew so thickly the sun could not be seen, and they fought an enemy for five days, resting each night to begin again. The enemy leader, Fridthjof, asked to meet with Karl, and said his men needed a day to remake spear handles and repair their shields.

"A less honorable man would not have agreed, but Karl gave them the day."

"Ay, and it gave us a day of rest," Finnvid said. "We conquered them anyway."

Per remembered a time they sailed up a French river to find Danish Vikings living on an island in the middle. The French lord promised Karl a reward of silver if he would drive the Danes out. Karl went to the Danes and promised them their freedom if they paid him silver. They left peacefully, and so Karl was paid by both French and Danes.

"Ah, Karl was the shrewdest of men," Gunnar said.

Olaf remembered one time in Frisia when they were attacking a town and losing, and had to flee. Somehow Karl had the lock to the city gate in his pocket, and locked the townspeople in.

Each man said what Karl had done for him, how he had changed his life. They drank the Burial Ale, and sang the Mourning Song, and still no one was ready to leave him. They laid his weapons, his beloved sword and his axe and his bow, next to him in the grave. Lars handed Inge the knife Helgi gave to Karl, and she hid it between her breasts. Unsaid was that she might need it to defend herself. Still they could not bear to leave Karl by himself in this foreign land.

Thora alone knew how to help them. Holding Halfdan's hand she spoke a lay most apt:

> "He was our helm tree
>   steering his sail-steed
> past the elk's gallows
>   between the bones of the sea,
> unscathed through rains of spears.
>
> Not downed in a fight fair fought
>   with battle-snakes in hand,
> Nor sun-board held
>   to a stream of feathered twigs
> but a single, four-winged swift flyer.
>
> Though earth drinks his blood
>   Karl-Eirik will not die
> but live whereon men and women
>   rattle the weapon-wind
> and spill the surf of the wound."

She spoke so well she gave them peace. Karl's whole life was summed up, and now they could bear to leave him. Mother and daughter held each other, and healing tears flowed from Thora. Later, Inge knew she, too, would cry and keen.

They all knelt around the grave, working as one to cover the great chieftain. Finally they finished, and Finnvid walked Volnir over and over it, so animals would not smell the body and dig it up. It was not a flaming boat, Gunnar said, but it is all we can do, so far from home.

One by one the men said their farvell to Karl and walked away, leaving Inge alone to say her own farvell. They stood close by, swords unsheathed, but well apart.

Though the river fog was dense about them it seemed to her she could see every whorl of bark, the veins in every leaf, and she knew she was deep into shock. Her chest was hard with unspent tears. Ahead of her were months and years to grieve.

Beyond the trees dark was coming to the Steppes and she saw mist forming into shapes, tall as a woman of bone, tall as a man.

The hair on her arms prickled, and she screamed as men with drawn bows burst through the trees.

XXII

Quickly Lars formed the men into the defensive wedge behind him--a row of three, then five, each row wider, backs to the river, facing the archers. He ordered Inge and Zeno behind the last line.

She tasted copper, and knew she was afraid. Any minute the arrows would be sent forth from these Pechenegs, the best archers in the world. The Swedes had their swords, but they needed protection--chainmail, helmets, shields. Shields above all. What would Karl have done?

Volnir was still standing, head drooping, and Lars gave him a swat on the rump. The little horse whinnied and neighed and galloped between the archers and the northmen. He reared and pounded down and reared again and again, drawing the archers' eyes.

"The shields," Inge whispered to Zeno and they raced to the ships, bringing back armloads of shields to pass from the back row up to the front of the wedge.

Zeno said the archers were bemused to see such a small, but fierce, horse. Let them laugh till they choke, Inge answered.

Such a small horse to do so much to help them. Had Volnir done it before, she wondered? Gone was the drooping head. Now his big eyes flashed, his hooves flew as he raced up and down the archers' line. Each time they raised their bows to shoot him, he reared almost on top of them, and they fell back.

But their astonishment passed, and they notched their arrows as one. Sweat covered the horse's hide, foam flecked his mouth as he gnashed his teeth, his neighing more frantic. The northmen's fingers tightened around their shields. Inge wished she had time to get chainmail and helmets, but already Volnir's jumping was not as fierce. He was tiring.

Lars threw the battle spear, and the fighting began.

She whistled Karl's two-note whistle, and Volnir bounded to her. It was cruel because the horse would think Karl whistled, but she must get him beyond range of the Pechenegs. One slap sent him back to the safety of the boat.

A leechwoman could not kill, but she needed to be close at hand when there were wounds to stanch. Inge watched Thora lift her shield in her first taste of battle. Practicing with Halfdan was one thing, but now she must fight for her life. Was her daughter skilled enough? Freya, Inge prayed, protect this maid.

The Pechenegs had yellow skin, high cheekbones, slanted eyes and black moustaches curving over their cheeks down to their chin. And evil grins. Inge felt a flash of anger. These Pechenegs would know the two crews were weary with grief and pain at the loss of Karl-Eirik.

But not so weary they could not hold up their shields to fend off the first volley of arrows. The archers did not shoot at once but varied their shots to fly singly, and the Norse knew not where the next arrow would come from. The crew held their shields to their mouths to make their howling louder, and Inge saw they took heart. They were being attacked over the grave of their fallen leader, who had been killed by this enemy.

The Pechenegs needed space to draw back an arm, space a Norse sword did not need, and the archers had no protective shields. But an archer did not need to be at arm's length to maim or kill.

Ell by ell the northmen gained ground, using their swords to slash, strike, stab, cut, club--knowing by instinct which hacking stroke to use, aiming always for the weapon arm or the leg.

Inge admired their speed. They knew their swordcraft. Thora and Halfdan moved together, twisting, dodging arrows. Inge sent forth a second prayer, this time to Thor, who had seen that his namesake had a well-practiced sword of her own.

Hrolf fought like a man possessed. One archer stepped forward and while he was nocking, Hrolf wrenched the arm. From the scream Inge knew the arm was broken.

"What was that?" Sven shouted.

"The breaking of the enemy's line," Finnvid shouted back.

The northmen crossed back and forth over Karl's grave, each singling out one archer in the one-to-one fighting where they excelled. They parried with the flat of the blade and broke wooden bows. Finnvid wound a bowstring around the neck of an archer and pushed him into the dirt.

The din was horrendous--men yelling, screams of pain, of victory. Though Karl had talked to her of battle, Inge thought it was not the same as watching it.

One Pecheneg lost his bow and threw his arrows in panic, one after the other. Finnvid caught one and threw it back, where it lodged in the Pecheneg's chest, and he fell. Anders picked up a bow from one fallen archer, the quiver from another, and used them. Inge thanked the goddess Eir for healing him well.

Gunnar had only one sword but he could switch hands, and so confused the enemy. Lars was everywhere at once, using his shield to knock the bow from an archer's hand. He reached behind one archer, pulled an arrow from the quiver and drove it into his back.

Which Pecheneg killed Karl-Eirik? Each man's opponent might be the one.

Never again would Inge think dark thoughts about Finnvid. He had trained them well. All over the clearing the crews were smiting men with the sword and when the enemy was dazed, they quickly slashed the chest open.

Inge heard a crack on a Pecheneg head and turned to see Zeno with a branch in his hand, grinning.

She looked for Thora in the melee, and screamed. The maid was swinging her sword above her head, ready to strike, but an archer was aiming for her. Lars saw, and pushed Thora down, but two attacked him from behind. The Pecheneg began dragging Thora by her long hair, and she fought and screamed and struck at him, but he stayed beyond her flailing arms and legs.

Inge pulled the knife from between her breasts, yanked it free of the sheath and ran into the fray. She cut through the rope at the archer's waist, and his breeches dropped. He fell to his knees, entangled, and unhanded Thora. Olaf kicked him over and drove his sword into his back.

Lars grinned. "The same trick works twice, Inge?"

She went back to Zeno, and he said she surprised him. She sheathed the knife and put it back in place. She told him any woman would battle for her child.

If the northmen fought with just their arms and hands they might not tire, she knew, but they had to fight with their whole bodies. Lacking chainmail and helmets, they often had to sidestep an archer.

To Inge the frenzy seemed to lessen. Hrolf moved slower. An arrow grazed Halfdan's arm when he did not lift his shield in time. One Pecheneg paused to drink, and Anders leapt upon him, slashing the goatskin from his hands and stabbing his neck.

Inge remembered the Swedes had had neither food nor drink since the shock of Karl's death, save the burial ale. Anders must be maddened to see a man drink. A cask of water would be of use, and she went to The Seafarer.

When she looked back, her heart ached. There was no end of Pechenegs coming forth from the Steppes in a never-ending horde. There would be no rest for the northmen, but ah, the Pechenegs could rest while others took their place. They could gain space to shoot. The best archers in the world, Helgi had said.

Helgi! Why did he not help them? He had promised to set the Magyars against the Pechnegs, to send word to the Warrior Women.

The cries of the crewmen were fainter now, and Inge saw they were moving back, still fighting hard but overcome by numbers. For the first time she realized the Swedes might die.

But not yet. Karl had told her that in battle the advantage ran to one side, then the other, back and forth.

As she splashed through the water to the boat she once again heard fair music. She was overwrought, Lars had said, and ay, grief had her in its iron grip. She wished she could tell Karl how beauteous this music was--so unlike the din in the clearing.

She knelt to pull out a water cask, and felt a jolt all through her body. A rough hand jerked her up by her hair. She turned and screamed. A short, dark man, in beggar's rags, held her plait.

With a sharp twist she leaned and fell into the shallow water on the side away from the fighting. He jumped in, pushing her down, and she went under. She spluttered to the surface and fighting to stand upright she felt a new danger. With one hand he held her hands behind her back and with another he held a knife to her throat, muttering something in angry Slavic.

Her body was her only weapon. She twisted, rolled from side to side, and the beggar pointed the knife into her neck. She felt pain, but still she rolled, harder, hating his close, fetid breath. She flailed one arm free, unsheathing her knife as she drew it out and slashed, not caring where she struck.

He yelped. He let her go and half-swam, half-ran. The water was red with blood, some of it hers, for she felt it oozing from her neck. She watched him run upriver along the shore, and washed her knife. She climbed aboard The Seafarer and found wadmal to stanch the blood on her neck.

Who was this beggar and where did he come from? She cared not, except that he was gone.

She looked to the fighting and saw the crewmen were upright, mud-covered, but still more outnumbered and moving closer to the river. She stood in the bow, and the fair music was louder. She heard hoofbeats now, from across the river.

The Swedes needed more than a water cask. Soon they would be caught between Pechenegs on both sides and there would be no escape, but the Norse would never drown themselves in the river. Nay, they would stay on their feet, cutting and stabbing until the end.

She too would stay on her feet, meeting the enemy as Karl had done. Perchance she would go to Valhalla, and they would meet, both whole. She faced the opposite shore and the music was louder, the hoofbeats clearer. Many, many were coming. The music was deafening, and she thought it wrong for fighters to sing such fair music, but ah, the world was most unjust.

Horses burst through the trees, rank upon rank, splashing through the water. The riders twirled curved swords above their heads, aiming straight for the northmen, not howling a battle cry, but singing the fair music she had heard.

They wore spiked helmets and were well-protected by chainmail, and never stopped twirling their swords. The black and brown horses were the biggest she had ever seen, and they carried their riders proudly. The gold work on their bridles was fine with wrought flowers and leaves on the hames. She put her hand on Volnir and felt his trembling. She watched as they rode, still spinning their curved swords and attacked.

Yet, what was this? The swords were being wielded not against the Norse, but the Pechenegs! She watched the riders slashing right and left into the archers' midst before they could recover. Standing, they had not a chance against the huge horses. Inge put her arms about Volnir and hugged him. The northmen might yet be saved.

She saw them get a moment of rest, staring at the huge horses pushing back the line of archers. Against the onslaught the Pechenegs retreated, and bolted for the Steppes. A rider slashed an archer, and he fell. The rider reached out of the saddle and stabbed him.

"I like these curved swords," Finnvid shouted. "The rider does not need to lean far out of the saddle to cut a man lying on the ground."

"The swords are well-sharpened," Gunnar yelled, "but they use them for surface cuts only."

In truth, Inge thought, walking to the crewmen, the stabbed Pechnegs were not killed, but escaping to the Steppes.

Inge looked at her daughter, mud-splattered, but happy. Thora had survived her first battle. Inge looked closer. A woman did not wield a sword as a man. A woman held her shoulders a set way.

One rider fell from a glancing arrow, and another lifted the body and brought the fallen one to Inge. Blood seeped through the chainmail on the wrist and she pushed it away from the wound, marveling at how the rider knew she was a leechwoman. As she worked Inge thought how a surprise attack could be most successful. Not an hour ago, the Swedes were desperate. Now they were cheerful, though bone-weary. Anders had enough strength to bring herbs from the boat and help her make potions.

They were lucky to escape with only a few wounds, but more than if they had been protected by helmets and chainmail. Inge tended the cuts tenderly, repeating the healing charms of Eir.

The riders gathered around the fallen victim. As they removed their spiked helmets, their black hair fell to their shoulders.

"Mistress, it is the Warrior Women!" Anders said.

She had known from the first time she saw them. Helgi had sent them to help. Ah, he would never let her die unless he too died again.

They led their horses to the river to drink. Inge was pleased to see they tended their mounts before themselves. After the horses had their fill, the women tethered them at the edge of the Steppes so they could feast on the long grass. Inge whistled to Volnir, and he leapt off the boat to join them. The small horse was most deserving. Among them, he looked like a colt.

Zeno brought two casks of water, and the women and the northmen drank as though they could never quench their thirst. He held cups of water to the wounded and brought the rush mats, so they had a small measure of comfort.

An old woman knelt and ground herbs for the fallen girl, and Inge smelled one herb she knew not. It is salep, Zeno told her, to restore a stricken body.

One woman at a time sat with the fallen girl, and Inge thought their boots beauteous. They were laced with goats' hair plaited in a pattern and scrolled with bronze buttons. But she dare not linger on fancy shoes. There was news she must glean.

"Zeno, ask if Helgi sent them."

The talk went slowly, and Zeno's words did not sound like the women's Slavic tongue, but he told Inge that Ilana had sent an envoy from Helgi's court to meet with one of the Warrior Women.

"There is a signal Ilana uses when most needed, though not even Helgi knows it. The women raced to your side. They only wish they had come in time to save Karl-Eirik."

"Tell them we are happy they came at all, or we would all be beneath the mould with Karl."

Thora sat with Halfdan, singing softly. So much had happened to her so fast, Inge thought, watching her holding the draught of yarrow and rose hips for Halfdan's pain.

"Mistress, you can be proud of Thora," Finnvid said. "Karl asked me to give her no quarter in practice. He knew your daughter could be molded into a fierce fighter. She has a love for the sword. Without it she would be no more than passing fair. With it, there is no stopping her."

Inge breathed deeply, bending low over Per's cut. Much as she might have hoped the first battle would turn Thora against fighting, the maid had reveled in it. A maid who loved the quick flash of a sword would find the pace of growing plants slow. Too slow. Halfdan's eyes closed in sleep, and Thora walked over to watch the women cleaning their curved swords.

"They take in any woman who wants to share their life, I have been told," Zeno told Inge.

Ay, but not her daughter, Inge thought, calling to Thora to milk Bratta and pass the sweetmilk to the wounded first. Tending Ingvar's wound, Inge sent a prayer to Freya for giving Halfdan to her. If she had told Karl what happened at the waterfall, and he had not asked Lars to sail with them, there would be no Halfdan, and her daughter might leave to ride off with the Warrior Women.

After Thora passed the bucket she sat with them, turning each one's weapons over, admiring the glint of metal, thumbing the edges. She touched the curved point and laughed.

"The points of their swords are dull," she said to Gunnar. Perchance women on horseback cannot carry a grindstone."

"Or they are unwilling to strike hard enough to make men prisoners." Finnvid said. "They are not wont to be encumbered."

What would Karl have thought of the Women Warriors, Inge wondered, Karl with his love of freedom, his joy in traveling to new places. Ah, he would be sitting with Thora, learning about curved swords.

She finished with the wounded and sat against a willow. Now she could rest and think of Karl. She missed him, though in truth he had been headstrong, and it was their undoing. If only they had waited for the nine boats...at least Helgi did not betray them. Her thoughts were jumbled, and she knew grief had a hold.

She let the strength of the tree flow into her. She needed time to begin the healing that started with tears. She looked up through the green leaves. In a storm a willow did not break, but bent low to the ground, and lived. Every tree had its lesson. She must be like this willow.

She watched the men clearing the area: piling broken bows and arrows for a fire, scraping dirt over the blood spattered on the ground, using their axes to split firewood, rather than skulls. There was an acrid smell of spilt blood. Anders stood before her. In truth, there was no rest for her.

"Mistress," Anders said, "Helgi said the Warrior Women bed with men once a year after a battle. I would be willing."

Inge sighed, and told Zeno to talk to the women. They listened, chattering and laughing.

"Anders," Zeno said, "they have a saying: 'A man's foot is the same size as his manhood,' and they wonder if this is true of the Swedes."

"Ay! Tell them I will be most happy to prove it."

Once more Zeno talked to the women.

"Anders, they are willing, but they cannot. The men waiting for them at home are much shorter than northmen, with smaller feet. The women do not want to compare--perhaps they would never be satisfied again. Try to understand, Anders. The men stay home and weave goat's hair tents, and cook, while the women ride and hunt and fight. The women are most unready to upset this way of life."

"Pah. I should have learned Slavic, instead of Greek, so I could convince them myself."

"Forget the women, and find us flat stones to cook fish, Anders," Lars said, and Inge marked how the men followed Lars's orders, as they had followed Karl's. She watched Lars choose a spot for a fire circle as far as he could from Karl's grave. She closed her eyes. Not yet did she have to leave him. He was so close she could almost feel him.

The touch on her arm made her jump. She opened her eyes and cried out, but it was Lars squatting next to her. Already he had the furrowed forehead of a leader, with a leader's worries. He held out an iron piece with an iron horseman atop, and she recoiled.

She could not touch Karl's strike-a-light to make the need-fire. It held his soul. His fingers had struck the last spark.

"Lars, I cannot. Ask one of his men."

The old woman whispered to Zeno, and he said to Inge, "The old one says grieving starts in the belly. Hot food will help."

Inge knew it was true. The women were pulling onions and greens from their packs. A pile of fish waited, gutted and cleaned. All was ready for her to use Karl's strike-a-light for the first time.

Lars put it in her palm and closed her hand over it, and she smelled sweat mixed with iron, Karl's sweat. She had never been so tired. How could she walk the few feet to the tinder bark in the center of the fire circle? Nay. She could not even crawl.

Thora knelt before her, holding a cup to her lips and Inge took one sip, tasting borage, the woman's herb. One swallow took all her strength. She pushed it away. Someone brought Thora a cooking spoon, and she began feeding Inge a little at a time.

"Anders made it for you, Modir. After you drink we will help each other and use Fadir's strike-a-light together."

Inge sipped a few more times, and Thora set it down, half-lifting her, one arm tight around her waist, holding her upright. The trees blurred before Inge's eyes, and then formed into separate trunks.

"Modir, you are a chieftain's wife, still."

Ay, though the chieftain was gone. Why had they not killed her too? Somehow she must walk four, five steps to the fire circle and summon the strength to use Karl's tool. Leaning on Thora, she staggered, half-falling. At last she was close enough to kneel. Thora knelt next to her, her fingers closing on Inge's, both of them holding the iron horseman atop the strike-a-light.

Inge tried to breathe deeply, and it was a jagged sob.

Thora held out a piece of flint. Inge's fingers trembled beneath Thora's, but together they struck the iron against the flint again and again, over and over before they had one spark. Then another, and the next time Thora had the tinder ready, and it caught. She set it on the ground, put her chin on the earth and blew the tiny flame until it grew. Lars piled twigs atop, one by one, and the flame leapt up. The strike-a-light fell from Inge's fingers. She fell over, too exhausted to sit.

She had freed the soul of Karl-Eirik.

XXIII

Lars picked her up and held her fast. He put the strike-a-light in her seapouch.

"Next time it will be easier for you, Inge. The first time is always the hardest."

She thought it would never get easy, but she was too spent to answer. Gunnar piled wood on the fire, and it flared up, but it gave her no warmth, no cheer. Her heart ached to be close to another fire, the one in her weaving room at Breidal. Even now it would be blazing, casting shadows on her woven hangings. She closed her eyes and saw a weaving of her childhood home with its turf roof, one of birches in morning light, another of a field of ripe barley and the split rail fence. She had woven the hangings out of love and she needed them, needed their peace, not this racking pain that tore through her body.

The smell of cooking onions and fish drew her back, but when they gave her a trencher, she pushed it away, queasy. Anders brought a bucket of curds and a spoon.

"Inge, you must eat," Lars said, feeding her.

She let one spoonful melt on her tongue and pushed him away. The old woman and Zeno were talking, and he translated.

"She says we will be safe from the Pechenegs now, but the women will ride on both sides of the river until we reach the Varangian Sea."

Let them, she thought. I care not at all.

"I have no strength to go on. Karl is here beneath the mould, and here I will stay."

Lars stirred the curds. "Inge, you cannot. You will die."

Do you think I care, she wanted to scream, but she had no fight in her. The men muttered to each other. Finnvid glowered, and kicked the need-fire.

"Mistress, is there not some potion I could fix to help you?" Anders asked, and she shook her head. If he made it, she would not drink it. He had a bent for healing and knew people could die of a broken heart. But he was a warrior first, with a passion for the sword, and like the rest, Anders shared their lust for adventure. He would want to go on to Miklagard.

Zeno said the old woman wanted to know if Inge owned the boat now. In their land the women owned everything--goats, tents, sheep, rugs.

Answering was a great labor. "Tell her I own The Seafarer, but we have no captain and our boat is battered. We are going home."

A boat can be fixed, Zeno translated. In their tribe if a horse is hurt, they do not go back home. Inge sighed. Did the old woman not know she needed to be at Breidal to grieve? Ah, these women knew not of the strong pull of one place they called home. They moved their goat's hair tents from one part of the Steppes to another. Already they were set up for tonight.

Did they not see she was heart sore, and needed to heal? She looked at the puny willow leaves and thought of the sacred oak at her summer pasture, so big six men could not encircle it, the oldest tree in Sweden. The sacred oak had withstood winter ice, storms, snow, hail, lightning. She longed to lean against it, to take strength from it, and hunt for healing runes in its bark. An oak so stolid, so different from these jabbering women.

Zeno stood before her. "They say it is your boat, and you should take Karl's place." Inge shook her head and he went on. "They wonder if you learned nothing of sailing since leaving home."

"Not enough."

"Ingeborg," Lars said, "from my boat I saw you watching the crews and Karl at work, learning from Gunnar's sea talk."

Like Karl, Lars missed nothing. She turned from him, too tired to answer, and closed her eyes. Could he not see she was too heartsick to travel on? Nay, he could not. What did Lars know of love? If she had more ond, she would tell him.

She and Karl had never been apart, even when he was off a-viking for six months. Through their thoughts they were always together. Though they were separated by hundreds of miles, she knew if the weather was fair or foul, when he was at the tiller. When he beached the boat she smelled the same smoke and cooking meat. When he walked into an abandoned church in Skotland, she was there to tell him which stone to lift and find the buried gold.

She felt a vast emptiness. Karl would never speak to her again through his thoughts. She was more alone than they knew, too weak to do more than sit against the willow, until she withered and died. She looked up and saw the pain in Lars's eyes.

"Forgive me, Lars," she said, touching his arm, "for judging my sorrow as more worthy than yours. Go to Miklagard without me. Karl's men will follow your orders."

She heard a torrent of weeping. It was Thora, in Halfdan's arms. He brought her, and Inge took her on her lap. In truth, there was no rest yet for a grieving woman.

"Modir, I was but a thrall until the adoption ceremony, but Fadir was a chieftain. And you a chieftain's wife."

Ay, she was one still, though the chieftain was no more. Inge rocked her as though she were a babe.

Through broken sobs, Thora cried out "Modir, I killed Fadir! I did not mean to kill him!"

"Nay, nay. A Pecheneg killed Karl-Eirik."

Inge wiped Thora's tears with her sleeve.

"Modir, if only I had not killed the glass caster so the king sent us to Gardariki..."

Inge kissed her blotched and swollen face. Ay, if she had not adopted Thora, or they had not gone to Birka for finespun, or if Karl had not insulted the king in the ale yard ...or if...

"Thora, do not berate yourself for the past. We are the only family we have in this strange land, and we must help each other."

Thora hugged her. "Ja, I will help, Modir."

Though Inge thought that, in truth, no one could help. Lars held a cup of ale to Inge's lips, and she sipped, then pushed it away. Bitter, too bitter. Karl's crewmen gathered around her in a half circle. They were her crewmen now, and she must listen, though her heart burned with pain. Lars was the first to speak.

"Inge, you think you are the same woman who left Sweden, but you are not. A journey changes everyone. You think you long to sit in your weaving room. But after a long winter, when your women are sharp-tongued, and the men talk of far places, you will envy them and regret going home before seeing Miklagard."

She cared naught of birds of gold singing their own songs.

"I watched the deft way you weave," Zeno said, "the quick way you decide to do something, and stick with it. A captain must do the same."

"A captain with runic lore would see more than another," Ingvar said. "You captained us already, when we were lost on the portage, and you alone saw the Sacred Pathway."

She covered her ears. They all hungered to go to Miklagard, and she wanted nothing but to go home.

"Karl was the one who steered us through the hard waters of the waterfalls," she reminded them.

It was Karl's boat, Finnvid told her, yet any of us could have done the same. We can all do everything, including steer. She cared not. Why could they not leave her alone?

"It takes much strength to hold the tiller, and I am weary."

"Nay, Mistress," Anders said. "Karl made the boat so a pliant willow branch holds the steering oar, and it is easy to turn."

At another time she would have been intrigued, but not now. Did these men not see she needed to heal? And she would not, sailing on a crowded boat to a strange land through unknown waters, with herself as captain. No one knew better than a leechwoman that nothing could hasten the pattern of grieving or loosen its fierce grip, but time.

"There is an oak at home," she began, and stopped, too drained to go on.

"Each oak is one with every other oak, is it not so?" Lars said. "The Seafarer is oaken. Karl chose the wood himself, and part of him went into the boat. He is in every thwart and crossbeam, the keel and kerling."

The weight in her chest grew heavier. She ached to be alone.

"Inge, Karl worried that the runes you drew from the witch-seer's pouch kept you fearful."

Ah, if she had more ond she would get angry, and defend the runes to a man who thought them but sport and gaming. She whispered to him that all came true. She had known they would, when she chose them. She knew when she agreed to come with Karl, knew when she refused to stay safely in Konugard. Ah, Lars felt nothing of the power in the runes. Anders spoke with Zeno about runes, and the Greek translated for the women.

"The runes came true," Inge said. "The passage into darkness, a journey that cannot be shared..."

Again Zeno talked to the women, and they talked back.

"The old one asks," he said, "if the second rune is 'a journey that cannot be shared,' the meaning is that the journey goes on, yes?"

She was too tired to speak, but she must. "A journey back to Sweden, Zeno, though I feel the men's sorrow not to see Miklagard. But The Seafarer is now my boat, and only I can decide where to sail."

Thora kissed her cheek. "Modir, you and Fadir sat talking quietly together for hours and hours since we left Konugard. But I remember one thing he said out loud. Then you went back to whispering and laughing."

Ah, nothing could be hid on such a small boat. Inge's tears came unbidden, the healing tears, and she covered her face, sobbing, leaning into Lars's arms. She could hear Karl's strong voice, as Thora said his words.

"Fadir said, 'Moving forward is our natural state.' "

"Forward," Lars whispered. "Not backward, Ingeborg, to the comfort of a weaving room or the safety of Konugard, but forward."

Forward to an unknown land, she wanted to shout, where nothing was known and comforting and safe, all of them burdened by sorrow. She looked at The Seafarer, its bow pointing downriver. How easy it would be to turn it around and sail home.

How easy, and how hard. She looked at the crewmen she had come to know and love, at Thora and Halfdan, at Zeno who had been most helpful on this journey. Their lives were now in her hands, not Karl's, for Karl was beneath the mould. The choice was hers alone.

"We sail on the morrow. Forward it will be."

* * *

Next morning the problems did not wait until they were underway. Ingvar called to them from The Seafarer before they were fully awake. He held their sail in shreds.

"Our sail has been slashed!"

Finnvid cursed. "One of the Pechenegs stole behind us, and cut it. I hope he rots in Hel's home."

Inge remembered the ragged man who attacked her. Did he use one of her own knives to cut the sail? They could never go downriver with it shredded and torn. What would Karl do?

"We will buy a new sail at the first town, but for now..." She reached in her sea chest and pulled out a shift. "Though it is wrinkled, we will put the crossbeam through the sleeves and the beitass through the hem."

They looked at her as though her mind was unhinged.

"Mistress, you will need your shift," Ingvar said.

"The Seafarer needs it more."

Anders groaned. "Mistress, we will be laughed at by the Warrior Women."

"I think not. They know everything about horses, but nothing about boats. Or care."

What had Karl said on the way to Birka? "The Seafarer is a fair ship. Inge. She would sail if we put one of your shifts up on the mast."

She gave it to Olaf to set in place and went back to the need-fire where Thora was cooking grot. She listened to the men while she sipped the tea Anders brought her. The men jested about the mast up the middle, and she thought beneath their jests lay the seaman's saying: women and priests bring bad luck aboard.

Nay, it was not herself who would not wait for the nine ships at Konugard. It was Karl. And now she was captain, heading for Miklagard, though she would fain sail home. She had made her first stand with the shift. The men would expect her to lead. She felt the burden on her shoulders. She must make a second stand.

She asked Sven to bring the gold brocade and jewelry that Helgi gave them to buy off the Pechenegs, and she handed them to the old woman to divide among the Warrior Women.

"You have saved our lives, and we are grateful," Inge told Zeno to translate.

She mixed the healing draughts for the wounded with Anders's help--and one for herself for a sore heart, and then walked to Karl's grave to say farvell. Between husband and wife was a connection only they knew. She longed to crawl into the leatherbag and lie next to the grave, to sleep until death took her.

But Hrolf was already hoisting her bag on one shoulder, his own on another, carrying them to the boat. She traced Karl's name and date in runic letters that Gunnar carved in a stave and stuck in the grave. An apt marker, better than a runestone. Karl had loved wood, the way it warmed to the sun, responded when stroked. Wood spoke to him.

The crews were waiting for her, Per holding the prow to shove off, the women holding back their raring horses.

She was so loath to leave Karl she seemed to walk in a dream, wading out to the boat, climbing aboard, walking to the stern, to the captain's post. Out of the corner of her eye she saw movement and turned to see Karl--but it was Finnvid, making sacrifice.

Per pushed off, and she clutched the tiller. They gave her no time to think, and for a moment she hated them, and then her mind cleared. Grief left a woman unsteady, and she must force herself to watch the river, and its currents and bendings. She could do nothing for Karl, but much for herself.

She turned the boat downriver and looked up at the sky, feathered with clouds, long veils hanging.

"A fine day to start, Mistress," Finnvid said. "If the wind holds."

The shift filled and served, though it looked strange. Another time she would have laughed. The Warrior Women said nothing, but Lars's crewmen jested about the places it billowed out: now full in the buttocks, now in the belly, now as two large breasts. Lars told them to shut up.

Her crew took turns standing with her, and Lars steered close by. The Warrior Women rode next to them on both sides of the river, while larks soared and dipped. Gunnar carved the days on their runestock, and his eyes teared when he made Karl's name.

"Together we will try to be as good a sailor as Karl-Eirik, Mistress. He was the best."

It was the quietest passage she had known. The men took out hneftafl, but did not play. They spoke about Karl in low tones, keeping his memory with them. Without a sound, Thora milked Bratta and passed the bucket. Per made music on the flute until Finnvid asked him if the only songs he knew were sad ones, and Per put it away. The men petted Volnir each time they passed the horse, standing and looking back, head drooping and tail limp.

Ah, there were many forms of grieving, apt for each, she thought. Hanging onto the tiller gave her strength to stand. She gave commands, and by noon she realized she knew more than she thought about sailing, and could tell Hrolf when to turn the beitass.

A single seabird landed near the stern, and Anders cried out it must be from Sweden--they had seen none other with yellow feet. The two, bird and woman, looked at each other and Inge knew it for Freya in bird form. The gull lifted its wings, first one, then the other--it was speaking. It flew off with a kyow, kyow and she felt bereft, but thankful Freya had brought the message: helpful runes are in rivers in Gardariki as well as Swedish oaks. Runes were everywhere.

She looked at the foam off the bow and back at the wake. Here was the rune lögr for protection, made stronger by the lucky rune, thurs. She even found the same runes in her daughter's blowing hair. Thora sat with her, and though they did not talk, the maid's presence helped fill the terrible void.

Inge's composure did not last long. Over and over, those first days, she would be holding the tiller watching the river and the sky, when she was overcome by sobbing, wracked by tears that would not stop, and she collapsed in a crying heap as though she had no bones to hold her upright. After the first outburst, Thora and a crewman stood with her in the stern, Thora to catch her and hold her when she fell, and a seaman to grab the tiller. The weeping stopped only when her strength to cry gave out.

Thora never left her near side. When Inge asked if she had given up her woodcarving, Thora said ja, for the nonce. If the boat lurched, she might harm Inge with an open blade. Later she would sit with Halfdan, not now. The old woman had said in these first days the daughter must mother her mother.

Lars sailed close by. When Inge's grieving overpowered her he leapt between the boats, and talked softly. He told her the men knew she could not throw her grief overboard. It would travel with them and come forth when it chose. There was nothing she could do but give way. It would pass.

She wanted to believe him, and then once again she would fall, swept by grief. She would rest against Thora's strength, and then stand and captain the ship. She soon learned Finnvid spoke the truth: each man knew how to hold the tiller and steer as well as the next, and it mattered not at all who grasped it when she fell, overcome with grief and loneliness for Karl and her farmstead, and all things loved and familiar.

Of one thing she was certain. Though they said little to each other, Thora's presence was more than comforting. It was the one thing a grieving woman could not live without.

One day at even Lars told her she was doing better every day. She thought he lied, but in some strange way helping her helped him with his own sorrow. She often saw tears fill his eyes. He had to make an effort to stand straight.

When her grieving did abate for a while, she ate curds, and Anders set up the three-legged cauldron and heated water for borage tea to help her aching heart. She thanked him, and asked him how he learned to make tea that helped so much.

"I watched you, Mistress. I saw you put a little red in every potion, and today I put in red clover, the way you would do. You cannot steer our ship and make tea at the same time."

Ay. She could not. Sometimes she could not even steer the ship. She thought how many things were different beyond her fjord. Here in Kievan Rus women, like herself, wore pants. Women captained a ship. And men made tea, practicing leechcraft.

Each night she kept them sailing until the sun dappled the upper trunks of the trees, and then steered to shore, exhausted. Zeno would set a reed mat beneath a willow, and she would sit and lean against it, unable to move. Each night the men brought down fresh meat, but she could not eat.

And each night Lars lit the need-fire with a burning coal from last night's fire that he kept in a jar. Once was enough for her to use Karl's strike-alight, he said, squatting down with a cup of ale for her. The two sat together separate from the men, as he and Karl had done, talking of the day's sail. He would tell her she was a born captain, and that they were one day closer to the Varangian Sea and Miklagard, and she thought herself: one day closer to the trip back home and her beloved Breidal.

In her lonely leather bag she slept fitfully, waking often, her body aching for Karl. While the men slept and the small beasts of the Steppes roamed, she lay awake wondering if she would have strength to live through the next day. Or wanted to.

And then came one day the two captains were at odds. The river meandered, their way separated by islands, the course as twisted as the plait down her back. Zeno told them this part of the Dnieper was called The Braided River. Lars said they should hold to the center, or they would go astray and cover more ground than need be.

Inge told her crewmen to put by their oars while she let the boat drift, and sought the Sacred Pathway. She closed her eyes and let the river speak to her.

"The river flows to the right," she said, and turned her tiller.

She heard Lars curse, but he followed, and she called back.

"The river beneath the Dnieper is the river I seek, Lars. There is a stream of energy, the ond that leads to the open sea. Like the Sacred Pathway I found for us on the portage."

That night he told her the men all thought they would go aground on the right branch, but they did not. As always, he praised her helming and told her they were not too far from the Varangian Sea.

Zeno came to her, and said the old woman told him the will to life is strong in women. Inge smiled at her, and thought women had ever lost men in fighting between tribes. That night she slept poorly, but dreamed of Karl on one side of the river and herself on the other, and though she ached to cross, she could not. And now she felt blinding anger with him, and that too had no sense.

The morning fog blurred the men and women and horses, all vague in shape, but the solid trees seemed to move, as she drank her tea. Once at the tiller she felt calmer.

"The Seafarer belongs on water, Mistress," Finnvid said. "Iron gets rusty ashore."

"And so does a crew," Lars said, smiling at her.

The day held another surprise for her. Making the right choice of The Braided River awoke some instinct in her, or perchance her grief was lessening. When Olaf said it would be a day for plain sailing, and the Varangian Sea was not far off, she knew it was time for her to do more than just hold the tiller. She squeezed Thora's hand for strength and called her men to her. She said she must learn everything about sailing before they came to the Varangian Sea.

"Everything, Mistress?" Finnvid said. "It takes years."

"Ay, I do not have years, before we reach the restless sea. Two by two, stand at my side at the tiller. Do not talk idly of the villages we pass, and the people you see doing their chores. Or of Karl. Talk to me of sailing. Anders and Per, we will start with you."

It proved to be wise. As long as she listened and learned, she could hold her grief in check.

Anders said he thought it magic that a boat could sail against the wind, and he taught her how to catch the wind first to one side, then another, then back, and on. When the sail luffed Per told her to swing into the wind. She could not be a captain without sea talk, so Sven taught her terms like "backen" and "weather-breeder". Olaf spoke of a "stiff breeze" and a "stiff blow" and a "whole-sail breeze", and all three were the same.

The Warrior Women stopped to talk with people at the farms, and Zeno translated to Inge, saying the Slavs in the settlements had seen many boats sailing downriver through the years, but never with a woman as captain.

"Tell them, in the north we are born on a boat," Finnvid said. "Tell them we learn to sail before we can walk."

"Except for your captain," Lars said, "who is learning fast."

By even Inge was weary, and ready to steer to shore. One night Lars startled her with his cursing.

"Inge, you are blanketing me--cutting off my wind. I need more berth to sail."

"I cannot learn it all in one day," she shouted, and was surprised with her anger at Lars, and the strength to shout. At her side Thora smiled up at her.

That night he was most helpful, and drew in the mud with a stick so she could picture her boat reaching and running, and how to angle the sail.

"Inge, I am sorry."

"For cursing today at me? It was naught."

"Nay, not that. If I had it to do over, I would not have accosted you at the waterfall on Gotland. I would have turned my back on your beauteous body. And one thing more, Ingeborg. I never heard anything about you and the arrow maker who came to your farmstead. I only taunted you."

She looked up at the stars and thought her serving folk were trustworthy, and did not gossip about their mistress. Ah, in truth Gardariki was a new land, when a Norse man apologized to a Norse woman.

"If you need help, Ingeborg, you have but to ask. Without Karl, I am wont to protect you."

She thanked him. Unspoken was the Swedish custom: a younger brother married his brother's widow. Custom, but not law, she thought, the tears coming unbidden.

One night around the fire circle the men sang her a song about a Swedish sailor: every drop of his blood was tar, every strand of hair was rope.

"That will be you soon, Mistress," Anders said.

On the last night the Warrior Women would be with them, both crews and women walked through the gray-green feather grass. A dirt road ran on and on, and all agreed the Steppes were without end. In the distance horses ran free, and Inge kept one hand on Volnir. She watched sheep put into a fold enclosed with whole tree trunks. A wattle-and-daub fence surrounded a farmstead of thatched log huts. Inge gasped.

Thora put her arm around her. "Modir, take heart. Soon we will be back at Breidal."

Thora thought that seeing the log hut brought forth the gasp. Nay. It was a sudden, profound thought. How foolish she had been--for weeks she had tried to interest Thora in healing, and the maid resisted, refusing to learn, glorying in her sword. Inge berated herself for trying to mold the maid--the maid who was born with the one thing a healer needed. Without it, the skills, the herbs and Eir's charms and magic were of no use. But with it...

Her Thora possessed a healer's calming, comforting presence. That night she surprised them all.

XXIV

The Swedes had sailed out of Pecheneg territory, and they were safe from now on. The Warrior Women would leave on the morrow, and that night Inge held a great fest around the need-fire. While they sat eating fresh game and curds and sipping ale, Thora stood where the firelight illumined her face and spoke a lay:

"The ships of the ground raced
through upright green Steppes spears,
over the ropes of sand, splashing.
Through froth the women came forth
girt with curved battle-snakes,
whirling in the Wheel of Freya.

The birds of the strings flew
but could not pierce the war-woof
of the women's ring-shirts,
while the snake threw its tail
in weapon-wound.

Felled by the curved point,
all life reft, the foe fled
to the cloak of green spears.
The women reddened the eagle's claw
full well as any man."

Zeno translated, and Inge thought the women got the gist.

Perchance in their land they had skalds who spoke kennings. The Women grunted and shook their heads and jabbered together, and the maid blushed. Half-dan looked at her with adoring eyes. Inge wondered if he knew what a treasure he had in the maid. He would soon enough, when she began traveling from hall to hall in Sweden, as a skald, reciting the lays she had written here in Gardariki.

Tears started from Inge's eyes, and she brushed them away. Later, when she was alone in her leather bag she would cry. For now she must take joy in a daughter who honored the Warrior Women with a poem.

One poem, but none about her mother, the ship captain. Inge felt her throat tighten. Ah, she was jealous! She took a deep breath, chiding herself. This skald chose her own subjects. Some day Thora would look anew at a mother who dared to be captain. How tedious it must be for a young girl to sit day after day with a grieving woman who cried easily, instead of with her betrothed. Soon, Inge thought, she must tell the maid to leave her side and sit with Halfdan. Soon.

The next morning while the Warrior Women packed up, Inge told Zeno to thank them. The northmen owed them their lives. Perchance someday we can repay you, Inge told him to say in Slavic. Zeno spoke, and the old woman looked at Thora, at Inge and back to the maid.

The look struck Inge as a blow to the stomach. Ah. There was a way to repay the Women. And the worst of it was that Thora would love to ride with them. Already she was climbing up on Volnir, her fingers twined in the small horse's shaggy mane.

"Thora! " Halfdan cried, grabbing her arm. She shook him off, swatted Volnir lightly on the rump and followed after the Warrior Women. Halfdan turned to Inge.

"Aiyiii! We must stop her."

Though his pain cut her, she said, "Nay, we cannot."

Thora rode off in their midst, turning only once, to wave at the edge of the Steppes. Inge grasped her amulet. Freya, she prayed. Could the maid just leave-- go, and never be seen by her mother or her betrothed again?

Ay, she could. And yet Inge understood the pull of Thora's desire: to ride with the wind in her hair, to learn swordplay from other women of like mind, to travel to secret places. And these hard-living women with leathery skins would love a young maid to cheer them, a maid with energy and skills, some untried.

"Mistress, stop her before it is too late," Anders said.

"Nay. Thora is old enough to decide for herself. We can only trust she will come back to us."

"And to Halfdan," Lars said, nodding at the youth standing with crossed arms at the edge of the Steppes.

"Mistress--I want to take Ingvar and Per and follow her," Sven said. "We cannot just let Thora go...when we find her we can talk some sense into her."

Inge nodded. Though they were strong runners, who knew if they could catch up with the horses? She watched them fan out, finding a path through the tall grass, and then run singly. She had to believe Thora wanted to be found. Lars drew her to him and let her lean against him.

"Go if you wish, Lars. I am poor company."

"Nay, nay. How can I leave you before I turn you into a good sailor? So we can sail our two boats across all the wide waters, forever."

Another time she would have smiled, but now it was all she could do to lean against a willow and slide down, her legs too weak to stand. She knew Lars was teasing her to ease her mind, for he too was not certain if Thora would come back. Once again she asked herself. Could the maid just leave? Ay. She could.

Inge told Lars that she captained her ship only until they got home. And then she would never stray. Unlike her daughter, she was not a roamer.

The day dragged. The sun seemed not to move. Though Lars brought out the hneftafl board, Inge had no heart to play, lost every game and cared not. Zeno brought her the reed mat and a handful of soaked reeds, but she seemed to have lost all skill, and at the end of the day she ripped what she had woven. She sipped the tea Anders gave her, ate a few curds, and fretted. She could not sit still, but dare not walk into the Steppes. What if Thora returned, and she was not here? If she went to stand with Halfdan, it would be no comfort for either of them.

Finally the shadows began lengthening. The men returned, dropping down to tell Inge they had lost the trail. In a muddy swale they had found many big hoof prints, and four small ones that must be Volnir's. But then they found no more path through the grass, on either side of the river. In truth, they had no luck at all. The river was shallow enough to ford.

Inge thanked them, and after they ate and rested, set all the men gathering and axing more wood for the fire, piling it high, so Thora would see it from far off. Halfdan stood, facing the Steppes, refusing the fish and curds Anders took to him.

"It is too dark for him to see," Anders said, "but he will not come to the fire. He listens for Volnir's hoof beats."

The crews gathered around the fire, and Inge heard the men echo her own worries: Thora was gone too long...at least they were beyond the Pechenegs... still there might be a stray archer...the Warrior Women would care for the maid, would they not?...put on more wood so the fire burns higher...if Thora gets lost... Volnir can be trusted...unless Volnir decides to stay with the big horses...nay, nay, Volnir was Karl's horse...Thora wore the amulet of Thor...he would watch over her...she was a pain in the arse, but she could handle the sword better than many men...I miss her...

Ay, Inge thought, they all missed her. How could she bear the long hours at the tiller without Thora at her near side? She could not. She struggled to empty her mind of foreboding, and lost.

She sent Gunnar to stand with Halfdan, but the smith came back, telling her the boy was wont to be alone. If she ever-- nay--when she got Thora back, she would not expect her to sit with a grieving mother all day, every day. It was most unnatural for a maid. Perchance Thora's own mother had driven her to escape? Inge looked at the solemn men, staring into the fire.

"Anders, can you play the flute?" she asked.

"Ay, Mistress, but do not ask me for music tonight."

Inge put her hand on his arm. "Play for us, and perchance Thora will hear. When naught else can help, there is a power in music. Every healer knows the power."

Anders thought she meant herself. Nay, she meant Thora. Inge took a calming breath. She alone had discerned Thora had healing powers. The Warrior Women would soon see it too, and had still more reason to keep the maid.

Anders could not play any rousing tunes, but he could manage slow songs. The music pealed out into the black beyond Halfdan's vigil, and Inge hoped the night breezes would carry the plaintive sound. A stray Pecheneg archer would hear it...nay, Inge refused to think of it. When Anders tired the men passed the flute among them and took turns sending forth the old music. Gunnar played songs they had learned as children, and all sang softly. Inge sat leaning against Lars, with his arm around her. No one thought of spreading the leather bags. Soon enough the music lost its charm, and they had nothing left to say.

"When Thora returns, we will not ply her with questions," Inge told the crews. "She will talk in her own time."

"But we will tell her how our Mistress worried over her," Finnvid said, "and how we all fretted. She is much changed since she came as a thrall. Perchance she should go back to her thrall-ways and obey you more, Mistress."

To Inge's relief all talked of her return. They too expected the maid to come back. Every leechwoman knew the power of thought…while we are waiting, let us picture Volnir coming into our fire circle, bearing Thora on his back, she told them.

Zeno said perhaps they were listening too hard, and Finnvid snorted and asked how could they do that? The fire turned to simmering coals, but when Hrolf brought over a pile of wood, she told him to save it for the morrow. The sky was becoming streaked with light. The men dozed, their heads on their knees, and Inge knew they could not stay awake. Some had been running all day. She too put her head on her knees, the only one awake. She missed Karl, she missed Helgi. She missed Thora.

She was the only one awake to smell the pungent, sweet-sour smell of horse. Softly she whistled Karl-Eirik's two-note whistle, and Volnir came to her. She stood and stroked the mud-coated flanks, the tangled hair. The horse had no rider.

If only Volnir could talk. Did the little horse escape from the others? Had Thora stayed behind, and sent him back with a swat on the rump?

Nay. Two figures walked toward her hand-in-hand. Inge's throat was too tight to speak, and she could only pull her daughter into her arms, all of her, except for the one hand Halfdan would not release.

Anders was the first to note their return. All the men jumped up, circling around the maid, and to Inge's relief, they asked no questions. Ah, they were a good crew.

Lars alone spoke freely. "Thora, if you were mine I would thrash you. How could you worry your mother so much?"

She kissed Inge's cheek. "I am back now."

"You came back to Halfdan?" Gunnar said.

She played with her strand of hair. "Back to my mother."

Inge thought the words the sweetest she had heard, and she held Thora tighter. Back, back to both of them. And though naught was said, she knew they must all keep close watch on Thora from now on.

* * *

Before they came to the port of Oleshie on the Varangian Sea, the men wanted to take down the shift and row in, and Inge agreed.

The quay was empty: no goods piled on carts, no stomping horses, no women selling bread and ale. Warehouses were boarded up tight. All Inge saw were men, sitting on tree trunks, idling away their time. Their two boats were the first of the season, scratched, the paint scraped, the iron work dulled and pitted.

"We will stay for repair and painting and tarring," she told Zeno to translate, "but we are unwilling to linger."

He talked to the idlers and told her, "If you pay them more, they will work faster."

"Nay, there are many men, and only two small boats. They are only sitting, doing nothing now."

Lars told her a shrewd trader like Karl-Eirik had taught her well. When the boats were rolled up onto the dock for repair, she took Zeno, Halfdan and Thora with her into the countryside. The shipwright's store is still closed, she told them, and they had found the only port in Kievan Rus where the customs trader sleeps as a bear in the den. With the protection money he would have asked, they would buy a fine sail. Outside a log hut two women were twisting the water out of a long, newly washed woolen bedcover. Inge knew the look of strong wadmal, and she opened Karl's purse, heaping a handful of gold coins on one woman's palm. The two stared. She knew it was more gold than they had ever seen.

Halfdan carried the wet bedcover to the dock and stretched it to dry. The next day Inge cut it into strips, and the crews plaited it over-and-under in a basket weave. Their fingers were thick and clumsy, but they managed. She found it pleasing to sit on a tree trunk spinning yarn to sew the sail, her feet on her beloved earth.

When the sail was up, it was not a soft red, but a dull gray. Another time she would be ashamed to have it above Karl's boat, but it was stout, and would serve.

The workers gathered to see them off. Inge smelled the tar and the iron in the paint. She held the tiller and let the boat drift back until they cleared the harbor, and then pushed it at an angle. The sail hung limp, and the men took out their oars while Sven whistled. Between each whistle he talked to the wind, "Come along, good breeze. Come now, happy wind."

"Shut up, Sven," Finnvid said, making sacrifice. "The breeze hates whistling and may well stop altogether." He scratched the mast with his fingernails. "This is the way to bring forth a breeze."

When they opened out into the Varangian Sea, Inge thought it was not these sailors' beliefs that brought on the stiff wind, but the long reach over such a vast sea. Not since the Baltic did they have so much sea-room with so much space. As soon as they left the placid Dnieper, the sail billowed. Inge held fast to the tiller as the men ran back and forth adjusting the stays. She looked at the long swell, the whitecaps cresting.

"I hope they have not untied the third knot, Mistress," Anders said.

"What third knot?" Zeno asked.

"In the north of Sweden, they can make fair weather, or can stop a ship in its course, by selling wind."

"That is absurd. Nobody can sell the wind."

"Ay. The wind merchants make three knots in a cloth they sell to a buyer of wind. Untying the first knot makes a breeze, the second a fierce wind, but the third, a wind so strong that ships have trouble."

"Zeno," Gunnar said, "in Skotland, too, the wind merchants have a ready market."

Zeno spread his hands. "You Norse will believe anything."

"The winds are contrary on this Sea," Lars shouted to Inge, "and I am wont to sail within sight of the coast."

They stayed so close to shore she heard a dog bark, smelled smoke, and the seabirds flew low around them. Ah, there was much rain in the air. She remembered last night's somber red sky, cloud-streaked, and how the men had fretted about it.

"I like it not sailing so close to shore, Mistress," Finnvid said. "The wind is too shifty. The thicket of trees onshore gets in the way of the airflow."

After daymeal the wind strengthened, and Inge felt the gusts through the floorboards. The clouds flattened and turned dirty. Finnvid told the crew to wedge the gear tighter. Lars steered close by, and she saw his furrowed brow. He was worried.

"There is an old seaman's saying," he shouted. "'A good sailor avoids a storm he cannot weather.' We would be wise to go ashore while we can. I will lead."

As his ship turned Inge heard two whistles and two arrows struck the deck of The Goldenbreast.

"Down!" Lars cried, and his men fell. Crouching, he turned the tiller and the boat came about and headed back out to sea.

"Unfriendly bastards," he shouted. "Most inhospitable. They cannot be Swedes. Inge, there is a second part of the saying: 'A good seaman weathers a storm he cannot avoid.'"

She had no time to ponder. With a bang there was a huge flash, and an enormous ball of lightning appeared out of nowhere, bouncing around her deck, striking the rigging, hitting the sea chests. The crew froze against the gunwales, their lips moving in prayer.

"Thora," Inge screamed, but the maid too was frozen in terror. Gunnar alone seemed able to act. He clambered up the mast, hammered in a strip of copper and flipped it over a gunwale into the water.

The ball lightning struck the copper strip, and vanished.

Inge was so weak she hung on to the tiller so she would not fall...they were saved! The Seafarer had not caught on fire. The copper had deflected the ball lightning and sent it out to sea.

The men gathered around Gunnar, pounding his back, thanking him, though the keening wind stole their praise. She wondered at which ale hall he learned the trick. It was the kind of thing that made the Norse the best seamen in the world.

The storm struck, and the drenching rain was so thick she could no longer see the top of the mast, or even her bow.

"Is it time to lash the tiller?" she called to Lars.

"Nay, we will try to outrun the storm."

The wind increased to a whine, and Inge held to the tiller with both hands, while the boat rose and fell. Spray filled the air and she could scarcely see Lars's boat. The sea hammered her hull, and streaks blew off the tops of the waves. One towered over them and fell, and The Seafarer shuddered, the decks awash. Finnvid bundled her shift around two oars and tied them at the bow to keep from drifting. Above all, she knew she must keep the bow lifting into the waves, and the boat moving.

A ship cannot drift away from trouble, Inge remembered Finnvid telling her. She sent a silent prayer to Freya, in the sea-storm form, Mardoll.

"Inge, we will sail under bare bones," Lars shouted, and she called to Ingvar to lower the sail. It seemed to her the boat dipped further, rose higher, ploughing the sea under a ploughman with elvist.

"We will capsize!" Thora cried out.

Anders put his arm about her, and shouted, "Nay, a boat with a stout keel rarely capsizes."

Inge knew there was more danger than the men would admit. A boat broadside to one fierce wave could get trapped in the trough, and they would all drown. She braced her body and held fast to the tiller. Above all they must not drift.

"Mistress, we are going too fast," Finnvid shouted. "It is unsafe."

The water was coming over the gunwales from both sides, over stern and bow, and Inge thought she could be no wetter.

"Lower the anchors to slow us," she called to Finnvid, and he dropped one, and Hrolf the other.

Finnvid cursed and struck the gunwale. "Mistress! The killick lines have parted. The stone anchors are at the bottom of the sea!"

Inge's throat tightened, and she felt fear as a lump in her chest. The workers ashore had exacted their revenge for low wages and quick repair. They had frayed the killick lines.

"Mistress, we must slow, or we are doomed!" Finnvid said.

She knew he was right. She could not control the boat much longer at this frantic speed. The men looked up at her as their captain, and she knew not what to do. Lars's boat had disappeared in the roiling sea, and she was alone, with no way to save them.

XXV

(" Mistress, we have naught as heavy as the killick stones to slow us!" Finnvid shouted as the heaving sea pitched the boat in all directions, and Inge braced her body against the gunwale, clutching the tiller. The high-pitched whine of the wind became pain in her ears. Finnvid's lips moved in prayer, and she saw the others too were praying to Odin--they were desperate.

Though an untried captain, somehow she must slow the ship. She dare not free a hand to touch her amulet, but she sent a quick plea for help to Mardoll. She looked at the raging sea.

"Ay, we have something almost as heavy!" she shouted, though the keening wind stole her words. "Ballast is all about us."

She cared not if the crew thought she was stricken with elvist, but with one hand on the tiller, used the other to point out what she wanted. Ingvar emptied six buckets and brought them. Thora untethered the animals from the mast and pushed them down in the stern. Inge pointed to Hrolf and Olaf and Gunnar to lay belly-down at her side. Ingvar emptied six buckets and gave each man one for each hand. Two, four, six--would it be enough?

With all the weight the stern was lowered, and much of the gear rolled to it. Inge showed the men how to drag buckets filled with heavy seawater behind them. Two, four, six buckets. Would it be enough? It was the same water that pounded her shoes and battered her legs as it sloshed through the boat.

Two, four, six. It must be enough. The men held fast to the birch withe handles, dragging water through water. Her heart pounded. If her scheme did not work, they would die at sea in a foreign land, as though they never lived. Her sacred healing, Thora's verses about Gardariki, the men's stories about Karl, all would be lost. Zeno knelt at the gunwale, his mouth open beseeching the White Christ for help. She prayed again, more fervently, held the tiller hard against her gut. When Olaf half-rose, she pushed him back down with her foot.

She looked at the horizon. Was it no longer jumping up and down as fast? The mad dance of trees on shore seemed to be slowing. Or was she seeing it as she wanted it to be, through the mist and blur?

"Mistress, your trick is working!" Anders shouted in her ear. "Our boat is slowing."

And then she felt change through the floorboards. The breeze did not die all at once but slowly, slowly it diminished so the pain in her ears was less. Now the movement of wild, mad trees on shore slowed to a stately dance. The horizon no longer jiggled.

The wind slowed enough that her crew heard her when she shouted how proud she was of their hard work--they had saved the boat and their lives. Gunnar turned over and told her nay, it was her idea that saved them. Anders said they would talk about her helming in every ale hall on both sides of the Baltic, and she found strength to shrug.

When the wind slowed to a freshened breeze she set everyone to bailing with the buckets. Two, four, six. It had been enough. The men bailed with cups, bowls, hands, helmets--all served.

"Once again we cheated Ran and her daughters waiting for drowned sailors beneath the sea," Finnvid said. "Our captain gave us no gold coins, so I never thought we were in danger."

The men laughed in relief. Our captain, Gunnar had said. Inge smiled. Ay, she had earned the title, and not merely because she had inherited the boat.

"Karl and Hervor built The Seafarer for bad weather," Anders said, and she heard his pride.

"A small boat rides as a chip of wood atop the waves," Per said and it seemed to Inge she could hear Karl saying it.

"I knew the storm would not last long. I heard no church bells," Zeno said.

If the crew thought Zeno a fool no one said so, caring only that the storm was spent. Though the water was still choppy the sea looked oily, and the crests not as ragged. Before their eyes the thunderheads broke into drifting clouds.

Inge stroked her beloved tiller. Who would have thought this storm would be a gift to her? She feared it would be their death, but she alone had thought of a way to slow the ship, with Freya's help. Inge touched her amulet, grateful. Zeno was right about using the skills of the weaving room at the tiller. Off their bow, they saw Lars's boat intact, his men too kneeling and bailing. The two crews waved, happy to be together on this restless sea. When Lars steered close by,

Finnvid told him how her plan worked. Lars was amazed. Only with great luck had The Goldenbreast survived.

"Ah, Ingeborg, I am wont to leap between the boats and congratulate you with a kiss," Lars said, tying the boats close enough to talk, "but I must oversee the bailing. Greek, who shot the arrows? They were good marksmen."

Zeno was always one to stop work and talk.

"The Bulgars live there--enemies of the Pechenegs, the Khazars, the Magyars and you northmen. There have been enough Vikings down this way in other years that the Bulgars fear you will capture them as slaves. Or worse, if you come peaceably, they will lose their daughters to your men."

Inge looked at her crew. Ay, they would turn a woman's head, sodden as they were.

"Word of the great lovers we are has preceded us," Anders said.

Lars agreed, smiling, and asked the Greek if there was no part of shore safe between here and Miklagard.

"None. We Romans have a name for this sea: Axenus, meaning unfriendly to strangers."

The captains decided to sail day and night, dividing the watches into airts, changing the shifts at morningtide and undernoon and the rest. On this contrary sea she kept her boat lashed to Lars's ship.

The boat and gear soon dried in the stiff breeze, and with the sail bellying above them, she told the men they must talk Greek. As their strong voices rang out she hoped the Bulgars ashore would think they were cursing them.

That first day she often fought the tiller, glad she had practiced steering on the calm Dnieper. Now she knew why her instincts told her she must watch Karl and the men, and learn to sail.

"The shape of the swell tells the strength of the current, ay?" she asked Finnvid.

"Ja. Fine helming can conquer any disadvantage, they say in the ale halls, Mistress. In truth, there is no change so swift the one at the tiller cannot react to."

Inge felt a sudden gust through the floorboards. She asked if this was like sailing around the tip of Skotland, and he said nay, those were real winds, not fair breezes like these. She smiled and gave him the tiller. She looked ashore and saw sheep grazing on the hillside. She longed to get off the rolling, pitching boat and dig her fingers into the spongy fleece.

And now that they were safe, the grieving once again took hold, and she could only sink to the deck until the wretched crying stopped of its own will. Thora's strong arms held her fast, and Inge said she had thought herself healed, but she was not.

"Modir, the Warrior Women told me it would be this way. It will not last forever. But I will be here."

Inge told her she doubted if she could survive this dreadful sea without Thora, and the maid said she did not have to try. Anders could not set up the cauldron to heat water on the pitching deck, but he brought cold borage tea, and Inge drank. When she recovered she asked Zeno why she smelled the stink of sulphur, and he told her salt from a southern sea flowed in and killed off all that lived in the water long, long ago, and the sulphur smell remained.

In the days to come Inge thought the gods favored their passage, for they had no more gut-wrenching storms, though the hard winds continued, buffeting the boats from all directions.

All day they sailed within sight of the coast, though far out, and at night when there was not a single wolf-fire ashore to guide them, she learned to use The Nail Star and The Guiding Star to steer. The night wind arose after solarfall, and Lars kept the boats lashed close.

Each night he leapt over the open water to talk to her about sailing. One night, when he finished telling her how the stars marked points on the horizon, he asked her if she thought it was time for him to settle down--to put his gold into land and cattle, as Karl had done. She said she could not speak for him. On another night he told her he felt no hurry to get back to Roslagen, to winter over with only Halldis for company. Inge told him his mother would be a good audience for his tales of sailing to Miklagard. Ah, she was lucky to be from a land where it was only custom, not law, for a man to marry his brother's widow.

One day she heard Thora ask the Greek when his outlawry would end.

"Never. It is for life. Your own is for six months, but mine is without end. But I will get back into Miklagard. I was a linen-weaver to the Emperor, and I learned many tricks in his service--dyes for hair and skin as well as cloth."

The men stopped their tasks to listen. Finnvid asked what he would do when he got inside the wall, and Zeno said Helgi told him Basil had a new Prefect who would not know him. Zeno would manage, Inge thought. He was wily. She urged him to tell them about the city, and he said it was a walled city with many gates, but the Norse were only allowed to use one.

"The most important thing to know is how to prostrate yourselves before the Emperor. All of you stand."

"Go to Hel's home, Greek," Finnvid said. "Show us."

Zeno sighed. "You cannot stay in the city longer than three months--indeed, they will billet you outside the city, at a settlement called St. Mamas, up the Bosphorus. It is just as well. You would never become devoted subjects of the Empire."

He stood, and motioned for them to stand back.

"I need room. The movement must be done smoothly to honor the Emperor. A lifetime of practice has enabled me to make an offering of myself, though no one expects you seamen to do it well."

It seemed to Inge his body was without bone. He fell forward so smoothly it was all one motion until his forehead touched the deck. He rose the same way, and his face was flushed.

"I will be happy to teach you."

"Never," the men shouted.

"Karl would not follow the Volga River because he would not bow to the Khazar leader," Finnvid said. "We can do no less."

Inge set Zeno to fishing, though the fish tasted sulphur-laden.

"Your crew is made of fools," he told her. "Ambassadors, you northmen, everyone, must prostrate before the Emperor and Empress. There is no death penalty, but there are ways of persuading the men to honor the Empire. You will see."

She knew the men were edgy from the everlasting sameness of the rolling deck, the same food, even each other. She asked Zeno to come to the stern and talk about weaving in the Empire. He told her about a pit loom, where the warp was stretched over a hole with moistened soil to keep the linen dampened, while he sat.

"I would like to sit. In Sweden we stand, and it is tiring."

"The Greek suffers from 'weaver's bottom,' Mistress," Finnvid said, and she told him to go to the bow and drop the knot line overboard.

One afternoon she found herself able to cry without collapsing and felt her grief was lessening, though they all gave way to it, now and again, herself most of all. Each time she hunted for healing runes. In the frothing water she took heart in the rune kaun, the rune of recovery. In Thora's blowing hair she found hagall paired with fé. Ah, life is a gamble, the first told her, but the pairing revealed that success follows hard work. In truth, the hardest work she had ever done was holding the tiller during the brisk winds.

Zeno said his people called these wide waters The Black Sea and Inge thought it aptly named, for black mists often rose from its surface. Each morning they woke to a fog, every ell of the deck and all the gear slippery with dew. "Summer fog will scorch a hog," Anders said, and the men laughed at the old saying, but Inge had a sudden attack of lonesomeness for her farmstead and Skulda, her sow. Yet for the first time she was able to hold back her tears. She was beginning to heal.

The men often talked of Karl, and she listened. Though some of the tales were fanciful, they kept him with her. Karl-Eirik will be in good company in Valhalla, Sven said. He was the best with bow and arrow. Finnvid said he had taught him everything he knew. They talked of the time Karl shot an arrow toward the sky, and they waited all day for it to return, and it never did. At even they set an arrow upright to mark the spot, marveling that Karl shot so high.

"Do you remember, we went back the next morning?" Gunnar asked. "There was the arrow Karl shot, its point stuck in the notch of the other. Ay, Karl was the best."

The farther south they traveled the more stifling the weather became, and their clothes became splotched with sweat. On this strange sea the wind did not cool them, but brought a stronger stink of gagging sulphur. Zeno told them they should thank God for the harsh winds that kept the pirates ashore. Later, in the months the Bulgars called the Clear Time, they would be attacked. Still, Inge knew even Karl would tire of this journey.

She often felt beset by anger, anger that he had put her in this fix. Though her mind told her he was only obeying his inner nature by not waiting for a convoy of nine ships, she was heart sore. Only with Thora did she feel any relief.

The maid sat close by while Inge steered and they talked idly of Breidal, or their journey, but the Warrior Women were not mentioned. In truth, Thora had told them she had returned for her mother, and Inge took it on faith. She knew time must work its healing from Karl's sudden death, but ah, it was slow.

Finally, Ingvar spied land ahead, and as they sailed near enough they saw the high stone wall, the beginning of the Empire, where Helgi was wont to hang his shield. Zeno was happier than they had seen him. He said the air already smelled better.

Inge turned the tiller so they sailed east along the sandy coast, and on this southern shore she saw more life--gray herons and black cormorants. And more beacon lights for signals. She thought the beacon-keepers ashore were sending word to Helgi about the passage of the two boats in code, so the Empire could not read it. She wondered about him. Did he think of her? Where would they meet again? In Miklagard? Nay, Helgi had been defeated here once.

She had to put him out of mind. At the entrance to the Bosphorus they came to the enormous Clashing Rocks, water striking them and falling in a torrent of spray.

"In olden times they would clash together," Zeno said. "Sailors were told to loosen a dove to fly between them. If it was caught they turned back, but if the dove got through safely, they waited until the rocks opened and got through. Fortunately for the sailors telling the story, the rocks just clipped the tail feathers of the dove, and they escaped with only a little damage to the stern."

The rocks would not close on them, Inge thought, but her ship could founder or scrape, and crack the wood. Finnvid stood with her, and although she held the tiller, he told her how to push it.

When they were through, she looked behind and saw Lars, too, had made it. She had not clipped their tail feathers. The next time she would try it without Finnvid.

Both shores of the Bosphorus were lined with high hills covered with small trees, and she wondered about their healing power. The river itself was fast-flowing. Inge had Olaf drop the sounding line, and he told her they sailed in shallow waters. The men took out the oars, and Gunnar teased them they had forgotten how to fit them in the oarlocks. Inge could feel their eagerness to reach the ale halls, with women to listen to their tales, even in halting Greek.

Zeno pointed out the names of capes of land and harbors, and she thought them fanciful: Harbor of the Wild Walnuts, one called Harbor of the Goats, and a small village called Peaceful.

Ahead was a huge chain across the river, and she told the men to hold back the oars. Zeno said they must stop and pay toll for using the Bosphorus, and she said it seemed most unfair--the gods made the river, but the Greeks were paid for it.

She chose a quay and steered in, The Goldenbreast following. Olaf leapt off to tie up on the tree trunk.

"Ingeborg, Finnvid and I will go in with Zeno," Lars said.

"Nay, I will go with you, without them," she said, smoothing her sulphur-stiffened pants.

"Inge! They will not expect a woman. And they will not talk Swedish, but Greek."

"Ay. Zeno has been teaching us for the whole journey, and now we will see how much I learned."

She swung down, and Olaf caught her. She led the way to the wooden hut, and Lars followed, cursing her stubbornness. Her gait had a sea roll to it, and she was no longer wobbly the first time on land, but getting her sea legs. Karl would have been proud.

Two things were found in every part of the world's wide waters, she thought: the stink of fish, and men who demanded money. In the hut two slight men resembling Zeno sat at a table.

"Tikainess," she greeted them in Greek.

The men looked up, astonished, but did not answer. They talked to each other and Inge understood enough of it, though Zeno had not taught her the word for "whore." She knew what these bastards were saying--they thought the Norse captain brought his whore for payment, and they would accept it, if both could bed with her at the same time, with Lars watching.

Inge felt her anger rising, and was glad for it. Lars removed the peace bands from his sword, and quickly she tossed a gold coin on the table--more than enough. Let the Greeks think she was a well-paid whore, one they could not afford.

She and Lars went outside, and the men followed. From her pouch Inge took another gold coin and gave it to the man at a wooden stanchion. He bit the coin, found it real gold, and turned the chain on the stanchion until it dropped. As the two boats sailed past the men on shore, they heard the grinding as the stanchion turned, pulling the chain back up. Zeno was eager to know if they understood her Greek, and she told him certain gestures and scrunched-up eyes meant the same in every tongue.

Now they saw more ships than they had for weeks, many small fishing craft with three-cornered sails. Inge put by her fears about Miklagard, and tried to share her crew's excitement to be this close. Men on other ships called to them and Zeno answered, happy to be home. Inge envied him, and then berated herself. Every leechwoman knew envy was most harmful.

"They have never seen a woman at the tiller, and they are surprised," he told her.

"Mistress, you are one to catch a man's eye, even though the sulphur winds have encrusted your eyebrows," Anders said.

Ay, the sulphur had encrusted her skin and clothes and hair and nails--even her Golden Cleft. She could have scraped the Jade Stalk of a toll-taker raw.

Zeno pointed out a cliff where the Empress Theodora had long ago made a home for reformed whores, though not all of them had liked it, and threw themselves into the sea. They must have missed the Norse customers, Inge thought, for no Greek she had seen was worth an early death.

When they came close to St. Mamas Inge gave the men time to brush and clip and comb and scrub. Lars's crew did the same. Finnvid trimmed his beard like Karl's. She asked Zeno if the Christians had any land spirits they would affright if they kept the prow post with its red glaring eye. His God was not afraid of anything he said. The prow posts stayed on.

"Zeno, we have been together many weeks, through hardships of all kinds. Without you, we would not have survived. When we see Helgi we will tell him your debt to him is repaid, and you are free."

He grinned. "How did you know about my debt to Helgi?"

She smiled. She did not, but suspected as much.

"In a way, Zeno, you are as adventuresome as Karl-Eirik."

There. She had said his name and had not dissolved in tears. Ah, in some strange way captaining Karl's ship had helped her grieve. And her words made Zeno happy.

He looked up at the hills. "I am going overland to the Golden Horn and make my way across the water to the city. If you need me there is a public bathhouse two blocks from the Palace, off the main street called the Divine Mese. I will be bathing every noon in warm water. It will be a delight."

"Do not let your bathwater become clouded with dye," Inge whispered, and he laughed.

She kissed him on both cheeks. He left, disappearing through the trees, and she was sorry to see him go, though in truth he was often an ass.

They docked and walked to the barracks at St. Mamas. Lars said they were as plain and grim as the soldiers' barracks in Danmork, though without an earthen fence. Four northmen were at swordplay in front of the weathered wooden building. Inge could feel Thora's yearning to unsheathe her sword and join them. When the crews hailed the four Norsemen in Swedish, all the men clasped arms.

Not until she and Thora were in a wooden tub soaking to their chins in warm water did Inge let herself think they had arrived, and safely. The bath was the best of her life. It seemed to her the stink of sulphur had gone through her skin into her blood. Lying in the water, she felt the rise and fall of the sea in her legs.

Now she could be a countrywoman, and walk her beloved earth. If grief overtook her she would not be at the tiller, but able to lean against a tree for strength, even a spindly Greek tree. She needed to feel herself rooted, the sadness drawn up through her body like water from the earth, going out through her fingers, to be rid of the weight of it. She looked up and saw Lars standing in the door. How long had he been there?

"Ingeborg, I am wont to wash your back."

She sent him away, though she would have enjoyed it. When she finally dragged herself from the warm bath, she and Thora washed their clothes and hung them on bushes to dry. Volnir and Bratta were hobbled, eating sweet grass. The bell cow's ribs showed. Inge thought Bratta needed to be back on land as much as she did.

Lars said there was an ale hall the Greeks called a taverna at the waterfront, where they could drink wine, and talk with the four swordsmen.

"Lars, emperors and kings have spies wherever talk flows freely. We need a hill far removed from everyone."

The crews carried not one but two casks to the hill. They sat, Thora and Halfdan without a jot of space between them. The swordsmen pointed out the towers and turrets of the Palace and the round domes of the many, many churches. Ah, the circle was ever powerful, Inge thought, chewing a grass stem.

The Swedes told news of home, and learned the swordsmen worked for the Emperor when needed. Basil was respected, even admired, but not liked, and needed to be closely guarded. He had many enemies. The swordsmen's leader was called Saemund, and the other three let him talk. Inge thought no one could doubt these four were Norse. They had the same fair hair and blue eyes as the crewmen.

Saemund pointed to a large torch-lit house, with many columns around a walled garden, not far from where they sat. It was here Basil murdered Michael the Drunkard with the help of Eudocia Ingerine, Michael's lover, now Basil's wife. Once again Inge thought she must keep Thora safe at her near side.

"Basil may be a murderer," Saemund said, "but he is smart. After he killed Michael, he crossed the Golden Horn to the city. He wanted to be within the Palace when news of Michael's death reached the court, or someone else would declare himself emperor.

"The head porter, a monk, had the key to the Chalke Gate, where the Emperor goes in and out, and Basil would have been stopped. But he went to a house bordering the Palace Grounds and kicked open a stone wall, and so gained entry."

Inge sipped ale and kept herself from shuddering.

"From then on nobody could stop him," Saemund said. "Basil's wife Maria was exiled to Thrace, so Basil could marry Eudocia. But the gods are punishing him. He was always with his son Constantine--in the palace, in battle, walking the Divine Mese, but Constantine is dead. Basil grieves day and night, and naught can help. He is much given to listening to the advice of an old necromancer, a man who claims he talks with Constantine."

Inge chewed a spear of grass, and thought she must convince Lars it would be unwise to linger long in Miklagard. She asked Saemund how Constantine had died. Saemund told them no one knew, but Basil had lost heart. Two of his last campaigns against the Arabs and Syrians had failed.

"The Empress Eudocia is the most beauteous of women, fair in face and form, like all Swedish women." He bowed to Inge. "They say she was gladdened by Constantine's death, for now one of her sons, Leo, is co-emperor. If anything happens to Basil, Leo puts on the purple boots and ascends the throne."

Inge hungered to talk with a Swedish woman, but not this one. Yawning and stretching, Saemund told them they would travel with the crews to Miklagard on the morrow.

"We leave in two hours. It is scarcely worth going to bed."

"That will be the middle of the night," Anders said.

"Ay. We northmen can stay in the city from 3 in the morning till 3 in the afternoon, unless we are Basil's bodyguards. This way we pose no danger. And we cannot go armed."

The room for Thora and Inge in the barracks was plain, but with a straw mattress, and both thought it luxurious. Inge woke feeling her breasts heavy with longing. Karl had made her come by fondling her breasts. In the dark she could no longer picture him, and it frightened her. If she could not see him in her mind's eye, he might vanish.

Once on board The Seafarer again she could remember him clearly--how he stood at the tiller she now held in her hand, how eager he had been to see Mikla-gard. Lars called to her from The Goldenbreast, and said he was glad to be back aboard with the world stripped to wind, water and sky, and wondered if she felt the same. Ay, she called back, surprised at herself, for it was true. The Bosphorus was ripply, and it was an easy voyage. She looked up at the darkened tree-covered hills and wondered if Zeno was safely back inside the walled city.

They steered past a huge rock Saemund called Midwife's Stool, and Inge said she had used one like it many times to help in birthing. Saemund was amazed: she was both a captain and a midwife?

"Ay, and a weaver and a leechwoman."

She heard the change in the song of the rigging before she sailed into the rough waters where the Bosphorus met the Golden Horn. The water was filled with boats, and she steered with care, past torchlights at bow and stern. The sail filled, and the crews listened to the swordsmen pointing out buildings, here a church, there a statue, up on the hill the Palace. In truth, seven palaces on the grounds, a city within a city.

Inge steered past a double harbor, every berth taken by deep-hulled ships of burden, while men on the quay unloaded bags by torchlight. Small boats scudded between fishermen's craft, barges and boats jammed even at this hour with people heading for the other shore.

She looked over at Lars. They had made it. Despite the attack by the Pechenegs, despite Karl's death, the portage, the storms, hard winds and cold rain, weeks cramped together on ships too small, they had made it. Thora could not hold still, as she pointed out this church, that house to Halfdan.

"Mistress, there were times I was unsure we would get to Miklagard," Anders said.

"Ay? My helming has improved, Anders."

"Nay, Mistress. It is not your steering, but all else."

"Anders, you fool," Finnvid said, "I never doubted we would arrive. Karl and Hervor built well."

Ja, Inge thought, but men were flesh and blood and bone, not wood and ironwork. Saemund pointed out The Fruit Pier where all Norse must dock, and she steered in.

"Miklagard is not so different from Dublin," Anders said, and though none disagreed, Inge knew each man was stricken dumb, overwhelmed with the size of this city--bigger than anything they could dream of, with more buildings, and higher and more beautiful. And Karl would see none of it.

She felt grief fill her throat so she could not breathe. She shivered and could not move, her body frozen, though in truth the air was hot and cloying. Lars gave his tiller to a crewman and leapt onto her deck. He held her tight, and neither spoke. Though she would fain be in Sweden, she must see the wonders of this city as Karl would have seen them, but with her own eyes, for Karl was beneath the mould. And she was alive.

XXVI

The men rowed in to the Fruit Pier, and Anders jumped ashore to tie up. Inge sniffed, and thought Miklagard close up was not beauteous. The air bore the familiar stink of rotting fish, gulls shrieking and screaming. A ragtag port, with bales piled high on the quay and stooped-over men carrying them on their backs. Whinnying horses pulled over-burdened wagons and sullen women hawked bread and meat and wine.

She saw no beauteous women, nor men to catch a woman's eye--none but ones she would not turn her back on, in a dark street.

Once off the boat the men formed themselves around the women in their midst, and Inge was glad for their protection. She held fast to Thora. They walked between huge piles of orange and red fruits they had never seen. Gunnar thought they might be the pomegranates and apricots that Zeno loved.

Saemund told them the furs and wax would not be safe in the boat, and they should be sold now. Inge looked at the warehouses, some of them four, five stories high. Which would Karl have chosen?

From her seapouch she pulled out the firestone neckring Helgi gave her. Her crewmen turned away, and did not hide their distaste. Despite herself, she loved the cool feel of the stones.

We must present a fine appearance to the trader, she told the men, so they do not think we come to him humbled and beseeching to sell our goods. Helgi's furs and wax are quality. An overlord would send no less.

A squat, short man approached, wearing the trader's shirt and a cloth wound round his head, a winking jewel in its folds.

"Can I help you?" he asked in flawless Swedish.

"Nay," Saemund said, hurrying them away. "He is an Arab trader," he whispered. "The Greeks will take offense if you sell to him. Your furs would go to the caliph, their ruler in Baghdad."

Inge saw the Arab did not like being rebuffed, but his face revealed nothing. He put his arms in his sleeves and watched them.

In the end they went to the warehouse Inge chose, though she did not tell them the rune fé was formed where two staves met over the door. Fé by itself was riches, and Karl had ever been one to strike a hard bargain.

Between Saemund and herself they settled a price in Greek. While her crewmen brought the furs and wax, she put the gold nomismas in a pouch inside her shift. The weight of coins was pleasing. She had added to it.

When they came out of the warehouse, the Arab was there again, telling them he hoped they made a good trade, and wishing them a good visit.

As they moved toward the city Saemund whispered that she should not trust a Swedish-speaking Arab, though traders befriended all men and knew all tongues. He is most wary of you, he warned her. Arab women never leave the house, let alone bargain for a price.

At the city gate they were stopped by an official who wished to know their names and purpose for coming to New Rome. Inge was glad she had asked Zeno to teach them Greek.

"I am Ingeborg Andersdottir, captain of The Seafarer and this is Lars Nilsson, captain of The Goldenbreast, and these are our crewmen."

"Captain? You are a ship captain?" he asked.

"Ay. A ship captain."

If enough men learned she was a captain, they would get used to it. With a pointed tool he scribbled some letters on a piece of thin leather and held wax over a candle to seal it. He said they would need it to get in and out of the gate. A city of many rules, Zeno had said.

They climbed a steep, twisting dirt path, poorly lit. When it opened out onto a street they saw it was as choked with people as the harbor was choked with boats. Inge wondered where so many came from. Was this a city where no one slept?

Saemund led them down a street, and they saw a group of people in rags gathered at an iron gate, grabbing for bread tossed to them, as the hens at Breidal grabbed for the grain Geda threw. Before the gate slammed shut Inge saw a garden with a spraying fountain and people dressed in finespun, laughing. She smelled lavender from a hedge, and felt homesickness strike her. Later she could weep and give in to it. Not now.

All along the way she heard the muted hiss of torches, and the soft splash of fountains, and chittering crickets, and she thought Helgi had seen none of this from the harbor.

She saw women in shifts that fell in soft folds, their hair in dark ringlets or coiled over their ears, white hands that did not hold a ship's tiller. She hid one red, chapped hand behind her seapouch and held Thora tighter with the other.

Saemund pointed to a tall white column and said it was the Column of Venus, said to be able to tell true virgins from false ones, and the Swedes laughed. How did the column know, Anders asked. Saemund had no answer. How Helgi would have laughed.

They walked past little shops and stalls selling candles, clay pots, bolts of fine-spun and people arguing over the goods with the owners. Papas with heavy gold crosses on their chests were arguing with ragged men. At stone benches people sat gesturing and arguing, and it seemed to Inge that arguing must be sport and gaming in Miklagard, so many enjoyed it.

They passed carts heaped with berries and round green fruits, and Inge's mouth watered when a man slashed one open and she saw it was pink inside. How surprised Karl would be.

Three men with close cropped hair swaggered down the street, and women ran up to touch them. The men's sleeveless shirts revealed huge arms.

"Charioteers," Saemund said. "Racers, admired and adored."

Inge saw dark-haired women gossiping around fountains as they filled their buckets, wearing homespun no better than thrall clothes. Dark-haired children chased balls and each other, screaming. Why were they not in bed?

The babble grew louder. They heard hoof beats, and Saemund pushed them to the side. Four abreast, huge white horses thundered past, their riders in leather armor and green plumed hats with a white feather. The high-stepping horses tossed their manes. Though she held her sleeve to her nose to keep from breathing dust, Inge knew Karl would have marveled at the enormous mounts.

"The pride of Basil's army--the Cavalry," Saemund said. "Basil came to the city as a stable hand and knows horses."

"And horse shit," Finnvid said, and they all laughed.

Now Inge saw why so many people spilled into the street. Their homes were stinking huts, piled atop each other in row after row on every side street, huts no bigger than her byre, with dirt floors and dogs running in and out. Even her cows lived better. She smelled rotten meat cooking, and felt queasy.

The people pressed closer, and the crowd surged forward. The Swedes were swept along with a mob, chanting, all headed the same way. Inge planted her feet in vain, and was shoved onward. She clutched Thora with an iron grip.

"We are headed for Saint Sophia, the Church of Divine Wisdom," Saemund shouted. "There must be a celebration."

The church was plain outside, but once through the doors at least it was quieter. Saemund said the Emperor must be in the Vestibule of the Warriors with his bodyguards, and led them through an open door.

Inge gasped. This one room was bigger than her farmstead and the Homefield and all the outbuildings together--so big she felt dwarfed. Would Karl have believed this? Hundreds of torches and candles and hanging oil-burning lamps lit the space. The dome up above was so high she could scarcely see it.

"Modir, it is floating!" Thora cried, and Inge agreed.

In the center was a large man with his fingers raised, looking down, and Inge thought it must be the White Christ. Up that high he would be above the stench of the people. Both women covered their noses with sleeves.

Inge looked about her at the walls and cried out, squeezing Thora's hand. The pictures seemed to move! Then she remembered Helgi telling them the flickering candles had this effect, and in truth there were hundreds of them. Gunnar pointed out a white column that appeared to have lace at the top, till she peered closer and saw it was carved stone.

Saemund came to them and said, "Look to your side, as we go up to the Gallery. The Emperor will be in the purple robe."

Inge thought he looked no different from the hordes of men on the street: his long face tanned, his beard curled and black. But his clothes were more beautiful than any she had seen: a purple silk robe with pictures in gold panels, and on his feet, purple shoes that made Inge smile: this Basil had little feet. The gold diadem on his black hair was trimmed with pearls, but not much finer than the ones she and Karl had worn at Birka.

She liked the helmeted soldiers standing behind him in leather armor much better. They held two-headed axes over their shoulders. Ah, she would know Swedes anyplace.

Saemund pointed out a column sheathed in brass. The hole in the middle was always wet, though no one knew why. There was no well beneath. The hole was said to heal eye troubles and above all else, make women fertile.

Then I must keep Thora away, Inge thought.

Women and northmen must go to the Gallery for church, Saemund said as they walked up a path with large, uneven stones. He led them down a long hallway to one alcove where he pointed out the Empress amidst her ladies, across from them.

Inge saw that Eudocia Ingerine was as fair as any Swedish woman. Her nose was straight but small: a woman whose mind ruled her heart. There was somewhat of a child about her, the way she let her women smooth the folds of her purple robe and pat the pillows on the marble sill to cushion her elbows. A woman used to mirrors, one petted and spoiled by a Swedish father.

In their own alcove Inge was disappointed. They could see nothing but the tops of heads below. Thora jumped up and down.

"Modir, I cannot see. Let me stand in front with Halfdan."

The others stood aside to let them through. Inge was loath to drop Thora's hand, but she chided herself for being over-watchful. Soon they would leave Miklagard, and it was Thora's only chance to see this church with all its wonders.

After two hours Inge thought one visit to the Divine Wisdom was enough. The floor, hard and cold, came up through her legs. The gold on the ceiling was tarnished. The smell of an herb she did not know rose to them, and made her sleepy. She had often dozed the night through, waiting for a lambing or a birthing, and so she passed the long dull hours. The crews and Saemund did the same, though twice Finnvid punched Anders awake when the younger man snored. Finally, she heard a movement like a huge animal stirring below, and knew people were leaving. They had much patience.

Thora and Halfdan came back to her, chattering on about the racks on the floor for old people to lean against. The swordsmen led them all down the rough stone path, talking of food and drink at a nearby taverna. They reached the bottom, and Inge thought she would die for one breath of fresh air. Thora and Halfdan giggled, and the maid whispered to Inge.

"Modir, the Greeks will not soon forget 'Halfdan was here.' He carved the runes into the marble sill with his knife."

Inge sighed. It had always been her way to take a thrall aside for a scolding or worse, and now she did the same to Halfdan. She took him away from the others, and told him he would be harshly punished if they found out who did it. She reminded him how the Greeks flogged and outlawed Zeno for bringing his extra woven cloth to market on an ass.

Halfdan promised to keep his knife sheathed, and they clasped arms on the pledge. Inge liked him. He did not naysay he had carved the runes, nor offer an excuse.

When she turned back to the crew she saw the horror writ on Anders's face and how stricken Finnvid looked. Her body turned numb.

"Mistress!" Anders cried out. "Thora has disappeared!"

* * *

Inge awoke to the dim light of her room at the barracks. She reached for Thora and felt only empty space. She struggled to remember, but she could not think.

"Cry. Scream if you wish, Ingeborg," Lars said sitting next to her on the bed. "This second loss is more than a woman should have to bear."

Inge felt the jolt through her whole body. Her daughter was gone.

It was the only thing she could remember. Somehow the men must have gotten her down to the boat, back up the Bosphorus and into her bed at St. Mamas, fully clothed.

Anders brought a cup of hot herbal tea, but she could not drink, even when Lars tried spooning it to her. She knew this time the crews thought grief had truly unhinged her mind.

One by one the men came in, their faces red, their eyes gleaming with lust for revenge.

"Though the Greeks will not let us into the city with our swords, I have the knife Helgi gave me, well-hid, to cut out the heart of the bastard who stole Thora," Lars said. He thumbed his knife and said, "The swordsmen let us borrow their grindstone."

"We will find Thora, Mistress, we promise you," Gunnar said, and Inge saw his teary eyes.

"And when we do, we will kill the shit who stole her," Finnvid said, "though killing is too good for him."

Only Hrolf and Halfdan were silent. Halfdan sat sunk in gloom, his whole body sagging, his hands hanging empty.

Inge tried to think. What would Karl have done to rescue the maid? Karl, who always acted wisely to spare his own men. Karl, who would know they could not save Thora without some of his own captured or killed. She felt swept by a wave of nausea.

"Stop!"

Lars stood. "Ay, we will stop talking now, bring back your daughter and take down some of the Greeks."

"Lars--"

"Inge, we will not be rash, but we have our minds hard-set."

She struggled to sit, too weak to stand. The men moved toward the door.

"Wait!" she said.

She was grateful now for the long weeks they obeyed her aboard The Seafarer, for they obeyed her now, and waited. She took a deep breath to calm her churning stomach.

"It is a big city, and you do not know where Thora is hid."

"We will find her, Mistress," Olaf said. "There are few blond maids in Miklagard."

"You cannot walk every street, looking for her. She could be behind any of the walled houses."

Her eyes met Halfdan's and she flinched from his pain.

"We must find where Thora is hid before we can free her," she said, shaky, but standing, holding fast to Lars. "Bring the swordsmen to the hill," she told Finnvid, and began walking with Lars's help.

She did not know what to do, nor how to do it, but she must move before this room stifled her. She must think of a plan to use the men's anger.

Atop the hill she leaned against a spindly tree, and sat. The sun beat down upon the towers and turrets of the Palace, the round domes of the churches. Somewhere in that city Thora was hid. Anders poured tea, and she forced herself to drink. She tasted meadowsweet blended with mint to soothe a distraught woman.

"In Sweden," Saemund said, "where everyone knows his neighbors, Thora could not have been easily stolen. But here...almost anyone could have done it. She was comely."

"Is comely," Inge said, biting her lip so she did not scream. She fingered her amulet of Freya. "Is comely."

"Ay. Is comely."

She picked up some grasses and began twining them.

"Who could free Thora?" she asked Saemund.

"The Emperor. And perchance, the Empress. Basil and his wife have been much estranged of late. They are rarely together."

Inge knotted the grass in a clove hitch. She could talk to the Empress alone. The Empress was a mother, devoted to her son Leo. The Empress would understand why Thora must be freed."In Miklagard husband and wife often intrigue against each other," Saemund said.

Inge began knotting a bowline. Then husband and wife would not work together. Basil would not naysay what his wife decided. Inge felt pain in her chest and knew it for fear. How could her Thora be gone? She had left her but a moment. Ah, if she only had that moment in church back.

"Though you should know," Saemund said, "even if we find your daughter, we may not be able to free her. We northmen are looked on with some dislike. Even the Emperor's Varangian Guard cannot help you. They have sworn allegiance to Basil. And like all Swedes, they keep their pledge."

Ay, the word "Varangian" meant "pledge," Inge thought. Her heart ached, but she must use her fear to think and plan.

"Lars, Zeno said he would be at the baths at noon. We need his help."

"Say no more, Ingeborg. I will bring him back, I promise you."

She watched him leave and knew he was glad to be escaping, to do something, anything. The gold pouch hung heavy around her neck. Gold speaks. Ay, she would spend it all and more, to get Thora back.

The swordsmen brought her lentil soup, and she ate a few spoonfuls. She lay down to rest, too tired to sleep. Anders stayed with her, and the others went to sit in the wineshops and listen for news of Thora.

When she saw Zeno coming with Lars, she sent a prayer of thanks to Freya. The Greek looked different--he had hair and it was brown. She held out her arms to embrace him, and his hair fell off. Another time she would have laughed. Quickly he picked it up and slammed it on his head, and told her he was sorry about Thora.

"You wear another man's hair?" she asked.

"An Arab weaves them for men who lose their hair, one way or another. They are most skillful. Rugs in particular."

Lars exploded. "Ingeborg, it is Thora we seek."

"Ay, Lars," she said. "Zeno, are these Arabs wealthy? Can the men afford many lovers?"

He sat, twining grass. "Indeed. Their religion forbids them to take in young Muslim girls, but they are drawn to women from other countries, be they Christian or Jew or..."

Inge felt her first twinge of hope. She remembered the Arab at the quay who wanted to buy their furs. They knew quality, these Arabs. She began twining a mat of grass.

"The swordsmen say the Emperor or Empress would be able to free Thora."

"Yes. Either would have the power, but first we must find her. This is not the time to say so, but I have always admired your weaving skill. You are as good as any silk weaver."

"Ingeborg--" Lars said, and she hushed him, for the beginning of an idea came to her.

"Zeno, can you get us silk?"

"No. Every bit of silk is rigidly controlled by the Prefect. A pity. But I will bring Turkey Red dye. The bright color will cheer you."

"Inge!" Lars cried. "Do not prattle about grasses and weaving and such. We must save Thora before..."

She chose longer grasses and continued twining. "Lars, you speak wisely. Zeno, can you come back on the morrow and tell us what you learn about Thora? And bring the dye."

She need not remind him she had saved his life. He agreed to talk with the linen-weavers, who were glad he was back. Some knew Arab weavers who might brag about an abducted maid. He left overland, and she thought how desperate their situation was, to rely upon an outlawed Greek who was back in the city illegally.

Yet while she was twining grasses, a plan had formed in her mind, and for the first time she was hopeful.

The men were at loose ends, and she put them to work, Sven to bring back iron pieces from the boat. Halfdan and Olaf gathered piles of wood for a blazing fire. Gunnar hunted down branches from the spindly trees. She drew a picture of a flower in the mud, and Anders went to find it. Hrolf hauled up the cauldron, filled with water, and the others brought buckets and sheep's fleece and her handspindle.

They were to work swiftly, she told them, for Thora's life was at stake. She drew a picture for Gunnar in the mud, and she bent the branches he brought till she found the best.

"He is making a loom?" Ingvar asked.

"Ay. A round loom," she said. "The circle is magical."

Lars told her the Norse were skilled at strandhög, stealing from beaches. They could be ashore and gone before anyone missed a bale of silk from the quay.

Nay, she said, thanking him. The silk would be closely watched, and she had lost enough.

Gunnar lashed the loom together and pounded nails to hold the warp. It was crudely made, and at her farmstead she would have thrown it in the shithole, but here she was grateful for it.

"One thing more," she told him after she praised his work. "I cannot weave without the helping runes."

On the rim he carved a bindrune of kaun, and áss. Together they formed the rune of inspiration, for she knew she must borrow the skill of the gods. It must be better than any weaving she had ever done, the best of her life. She warped with trembling fingers.

She set about dying wool in buckets of simmering water. From the taverna Saemund brought salt, to set color. Anders found leaves and flowers of the rose mallow, and from them she made a dark green. Gunnar soaked nails in vinegar, and a yellow-pink appeared. From her over-garment hem she unwound strands of woad blue--ay, the right shade, she hoped.

She spun yarn from Swedish fleece all night and when her arms ached so badly she thought she could never lift the spindle again, Zeno came to her room. He had heard a blond maid was stolen from St. Sophia for an Arab, Ibn-Mahdi, a dealer in fine rugs who served the Emperor. Thora had been added to Ibn-Mahdi's harem.

Inge knew then she could spin forever. Thora was found.

Zeno took the men to scrape lichen off the rocks along the Bosphorus, and put it in a bucket of boiling water. All the men pissed in it to deepen the color. When all was ready she added Turkey Red and Zeno said it was close to Imperial Purple, but she must keep it out of the sun, and it was not colorfast. He gave her black angora goat hair to spin, to set off the pattern.

The yellow from sumac smelled like new hay and made her lonesome, yet she knew she must not give way to sadness, but use all her energy.

Finally the spinning was done and the yarns dyed, drying on the thin spindly trees. The next morning she took a scrap of yarn from each color and tossed them in the air. When they fell she saw how the gods meant for them to be placed in the pattern.

She was not the best weaver in Roslagen, but she hated the tedium of plain weave and loved weaving patterns. Her fingers shook as she lifted her comb to beat in the first strand on the loom.

A small yellow bird flitted amongst the trees: Freya in bird form. She prayed to Freya to watch over Thora until they could rescue her. The bird winged south to Miklagard.

Inge took a deep breath and began on the border, in an old, old Swedish pattern from long, long before her mother's mother's time. Eudocia Ingerine might have seen a bit of Swedish weaving with it.

When she finished the border the hard part began. She wove until even, drank tea and wove on, by the light of the burning oil lampstands Saemund set in her room. Lars fed her curds and ale and bits of bread while she wove. She dare not stop.

The second night she thought her mother came to her and then turned into Thora, but when Inge cried out, the figure vanished. Her eyes burned, but she wove on. When her hands cramped she flexed her fingers, and wove again. When her wrists grew too heavy to lift, Gunnar put a board beneath to rest them, and she kept weaving.

On the third morning Lars found her asleep. He roused her, and she murmured that the weaving was finished. The men thought it wondrous. Miklagard was a city of beauty: golden pictures that seemed to move on the walls, stone carved to look like lace. Her weaving too, seemed to have life, but she was so weary she could not be certain. Halfdan thought it enchanting.

That day she slept and woke and slept and woke and took an herbal bath, with rosemary to calm her thoughts and lavender for cheer. She soaked her aching body, and let Lars wash her back, though she kept her chest covered with a cloth.

At 2 a.m. she put on her sky-blue pants sewn from her overdress. Helgi had said they were all the rage, and she must be in fashion to see Eudocia. She wore Helgi's firestone neckring. She put Karl's knife between her breasts. She was ready.

She let Finnvid take the tiller of The Seafarer in the dark journey down the Bosphorus. As she tied off her weaving from the loom, she thought of Thora, excited about holding Karl's weapon on the way to Birka. Thora's pride in slashing the glass-caster. Thora eager to practice swordcraft with Halfdan. Thora with eyes shining as she fought the Pechenegs. Thora reciting her poem about the river as a sword. Thora riding off with the Warrior Women.

Inge sighed. This daughter she had adopted to learn the healing herbs would never be a healer.

She tied off the last strand of weaving, and made her peace with the thought: she would take Thora as she was.

As Finnvid steered into the Golden Horn she took a deep calming breath. She would win the help of the Empress who could understand a mother's love.

She looked at the bales of silk in many shades on the quay, all with armed guards. Her own piece held the same blues and greens of the Northern Lights, the reds of the sun rising in the east.

The street was as crowded as ever. She saw Arabs with jewels winking from folds of cloth wound round their heads. Any one of them could be Ibn-Mahdi. She held fast to the seapouch with her weaving inside. She gave her pouch of gold coins to Lars and told the crews to sit and wait for her on a bench in the Hippodrome across from the Palace, and watch the charioteers at practice.

Lars took her in his arms and kissed her. "No empress could refuse such a beauteous weaving, Ingeborg."

But the sour-faced guard at the Chalke Gate could. He looked her up and down and asked in Greek if she was on the Empress's list of callers. Inge answered in Greek that he should look for her name. When he did not find it, she said she had a gift for the Empress, and he offered to take it to her. She refused, and he slammed the door.

Ah, he was the last man she would trust with her weaving.

Then she felt the heat and dirt and stink of the city, and she longed for her farmstead where there was green shade and a fjord, for cooling off. What would Karl do now? She looked at the northmen sitting in the Hippodrome, and thought she must gain entrance to the Empress another way. It would be easier for one woman to get inside the palace grounds than a horde of men.

She walked around the wall and saw it was well-guarded with soldiers atop, who called invitations to her in Greek, and she pretended she did not know the tongue, though she seethed inside. The only way to get in seemed to be the Chalke Gate.

Across from the Palace in a grove of gnarled trees she found a stout one to lean against. A group of men huddled beneath another tree, men with a fringe of hair around bald heads and gold crosses hanging over long dresses knotted at the waist--the Christian papas, making marks on sheets of thin leather.

One of them smiled at her, and she said "tikaines." Surprised she knew Greek, he squatted down, and she took out her weaving. All the papas gathered round and gasped, and she told them in halting Greek that she had worked hard to make a gift for the Empress, and the guard at the gate would not let her in. Her tears came unbidden, and the papas clucked their tongues.

"Neh, neh," they said over and over, and she remembered it meant yes, yes.

She wiped her eyes and thought the only thing left to do was storm Ibn-Mahdi's house and rescue Thora. Full sure the northmen would be killed. Her heart hurt so much she cried out "Nay!" and the papas patted her shoulder. One of them put down his reed pen and beckoned her to follow him.

He led the way through the Chalke Gate, past the sour guard who acted as though he never saw her. She was inside! She took a deep calming breath. She must let nothing stop her now. They walked through gardens bright with orange and yellow flowers, though they gave her no cheer.

The papa said Basil was saddened by the death of Constantine, and they were trying to interest him in collecting books, though Basil could not read. The papa ducked into a white stone building and came back with a fine leather box, jeweled and gilded. He opened it. Inside were fine pictures in gold and words scrolled and fanciful, unlike the straight lines of runes. So this was a book, she thought, and now her weaving looked poor. But her weaving had one thing the book lacked.

The papa stopped at a plain house with rounded windows covered with silk hangings. Through his gestures she knew he was telling her she must prostrate herself before the Empress. Would she take three steps and fall, if it meant saving Thora?

She must trust the gods would show her a way round this hateful bowing. The papa said he could go no farther. Inge thanked him. As she looked at the forbidding stone front it lurched, and the silk hangings swayed and the papa's kind face swam in front of her. She was faint with fear. Thora's freedom depended on her.

She took a deep breath and pictured Thora reciting her lays. One aside the hearth at Breidal, another in the dead of night, unknown to anyone but her mother, a third at Karl's graveside, a fourth about the Warrior Women. This daughter had a rare talent. Inge knew she must not let the maid live out her life in an Arab harem. She belonged with Halfdan, in Sweden.

Inge thought how she had grown to love this wayward daughter. And every leechwoman knew the power of love.

But love that was just thought, with no action, had no power at all. The heavy wooden door was not even an obstacle. The Empress was not locked in, a good omen. Inge shoved it with her hip, and it opened.

XXVII

Her mouth was too dry to swallow. At least no one was here to stop her. She leaned her hot cheek against the green stone wall to cool it. She smelled smoke, and thought for all their fine silk window hangings these Greeks had no smokevent.

The stairs stretched up and up, and she walked, clutching her seapouch. Who knew what awaited her at the top?

It was nothing more than a long dark hall lined with doors, some open, some closed, the rooms no better than the barracks at St. Mamas. Her foot scuffed a picture of three sheep made of pebbles. She saw the drooping ears, circled horns and fat tails of her own sheep, and took heart. For all their fetid city, these Greeks knew how to make pictures from stones, and would see her weaving was finely crafted.

She hurried on, before any one came and made her leave because she was not on the Empress's list. Her hands shook, and she felt a wave of dizziness as she walked to the door of the last room, and looked in.

Eudocia Ingerine was alone, asleep upon a purple silken couch, surrounded by purple silken pillows and hangings on windows and ceiling and wall. Ah. Her weaving would not be out of place.

The dressing table was littered with glass jars of all sizes, in blues and browns, brushes, trays, a burnt candle, four hand-mirrors and a larger one propped against a goldwood box. Inge set her weaving over the mirror and stood behind the Empress.

Eudocia Ingerine had three runes spread before her atop a carved wooden table. Did she want no one to know she made runecasts, and had sent her women away? Or did she doze, and her women thought it a chance to sneak off?

Over her purple silken dress she wore a purple cloak fastened with a jeweled clasp, purple slippers, and a diadem stitched with pearls. She stirred, and Inge's throat tightened.

Eudocia's eyes flew open and Inge marked a spasm of surprise, and then control returned.

"Goddag," Inge said, and felt calmer. She had used the right shade of woad.

"You are Swedish?" Eudocia asked in Greek, and Inge nodded.

Eudocia covered her runes with hands pale as ivory.

"Everybody must prostrate themselves before the Empress," she said and Inge heard the voice of a woman who craved power.

"You were asleep," Inge said in Greek, and felt Eudocia hesitate.

Inge saw her lips were indented at the corners, a sign she was somewhat uncertain of herself. A woman who loved power would not want to show herself for a fool. What if one of her women saw a stranger appear before the empress without prostrating herself?

To divert her, Inge asked if her father had taught her the runes. She told the Empress she had Swedish hair and eyes. Eudocia drummed her polished nails on the table and did not answer the question.

"My father talked of Swedish women, and now I see why. I have never seen one. Who are you, and how did you get here?"

Inge knew she must use the Empress's curiosity, and she told Eudocia her name and somewhat of the journey. And she thanked Freya for the Swedish father.

Eudocia asked how Inge kept her skin so fine, and she said she would get a jar of salve to the Empress, though the pork fat she used aboard ship would have to be mixed with lavender to get it past the sour guard.

"Do you know runes?" Eudocia asked.

"Ja. They are the key to inner mysteries. The runes are sacred--the very word means "secret", and they have meanings from the most earth-bound to the realm of the gods. If I can see the runes, I will know what they foretell for you."

The Empress removed her hand, but not before Inge saw she had changed logr so it was no longer reversed.

Inge frowned. "You cannot cheat the runes."

"I did not. Read them."

Inge saw before her a spoiled woman. "After I read them I will give you a runescript to help you."

Eudocia scooped them up and put them in the pouch.

"An Empress does not need help, Ingeborg. I see you do not like their message, and today I do not need your foretelling."

Both knew Eudocia could not change a runecast. Logr reversed meant the Empress was tempted to do a great wrong, but it would not go unseen. Inge spoke calmly and told her two of the runes often bore good tidings: madhr, advice could be trusted, if it followed bjarkan, Freya's rune of blossoming and ripening.

But in this runecast, bjarkan had been reversed, and this revealed a split between two people, and that the health of a loved one was troubled. Eudocia would not like to be reminded Basil was grieving after Constantine. Or over Maria, exiled to Thrace?

Inge smelled perfume, and a tall, bald man entered, prostrating himself, and she thought him clumsier than Zeno. Eudocia reached out her foot and he kissed her instep. Inge was appalled.

"You may rise," Eudocia said, and he got up on his knees.

"Oh, Glorious One," he said, and Inge heard his voice as high and reedy. "I fear for you when you are alone. Your women came to me and said you sent them away."

Inge thought he was tall, but had none of the strength of the northmen. His skin was as smooth and polished as oiled wood. His robe was a fine Turkey Red, but Inge marked a flaw in the sleeve. A flower was unfinished. Like a robe, a man too, was not perfect. Eudocia smiled, and Inge saw she hated him. This man had control over Basil that the Empress lacked.

"Theophanes, this is a Swedish woman who knew my father," she said, and Inge saw how easily she could lie.

He bowed toward the mirror. "An excellent likeness, oh, Great One."

Eudocia swiveled and saw the weaving for the first time. Inge thought her heart would pound out of her chest. They must hear it beating.

"Oooooh," the Empress said, and Inge heard the voice of a little girl getting a honey cake.

"I did not know you posed for it, Divine One," he said.

"Theophanes! She has captured me, down to the color of my eyes! How did she do it?"

Inge felt faint from the perfume, and dared not take a deep calming breath.

"You have many admirers who speak of you, Empress Eudocia."

"Pah, Theophanes, she does not tell us. Ingeborg, the likeness is beautiful, but why did you not use silk?"

"I had none, or I would have used it."

Ah, this secluded Empress did not know silk was carefully guarded. Theophanes's eyebrow lifted just a notch, and Inge saw he was unused to seeing forward women in the presence of the Empress.

"Leave us," she told Theophanes, waving him away.

He got up off his knees and Inge heard the creaking of an old man. He left, and Eudocia batted the air.

"Phew. I can only stand him so long, but he is devoted to the Empire. He is a eunuch, and the Empire is a eunuch's paradise. They are no threat. For a boy to be successful, it would be wise to make him a eunuch. Do you know what it is?"

"Nay."

"Their balls are cut off."

"Nay! But why?"

"There is a rule that a eunuch cannot be emperor, and so they are no threat."

Inge felt sick at her stomach. This Miklagard was a hateful place. Horses were gelded, rams and bulls, but never, never men. Never Swedish men.

"You could never do this to your son Leo."

"No, no. I love my son too much."

Ah. This Empress would be on her side. Inge felt hopeful. Eudocia could not take her eyes from the weaving.

"Now, Ingeborg, you are to make this likeness in silk for me. The House of Lanterns, the Empire's silk factory, is on the palace grounds. Foreigners can stay thirty days. Do you have a family, Ingeborg?"

Thirty days. Thirty days to find some way to free Thora.

"My husband was killed by the Pechenegs."

"You will find another. Greeks are drawn to foreign women."

Inge clenched her hands so she would not slap the Empress. She took a deep breath. Thora's whole life depended on this woman.

"Empress, there is an Arab rug dealer, Ibn-Mahdi, who serves you and the Emperor. He has taken my daughter, Thora, to his harem. I need your help in getting her back."

There. It was so simple. She would weave Eudocia her likeness in silk, and in return, the Empress would get Thora freed. Yet Inge's stomach burned.

"How fortunate for you, Ingeborg, that your daughter is in the harem."

"Nay!"

"But it is. You are a lucky woman. She will learn to read and write Arabic, play the lute, and most of all learn to please men. She will get a training she can get nowhere else in the Empire. And Ingeborg, if Ibn-Mahdi tires of her, she will become more marriageable."

Inge's palms felt sweaty. "Thora is betrothed to Halfdan."

"A Swede? She will forget him soon enough. I would be happy if my daughter was chosen."

Inge forced her voice to be calm. "But you have only a son."

"To my sorrow. But I do envy you, Ingeborg. Now I have one of these tiresome state functions to attend."

She clapped her hands, and three women appeared, to fuss over her. Inge's heart sank.

She had failed.

It had been a fool's thought to believe this Empress who tried to cheat the runes would help free Thora.

"Ingeborg, you look so sad. Come now, men do not like women who are not cheerful. If the silken likeness of me turns out well, we will meet again in thirty days and talk about your daughter."

Inge thought she had never been so miserable. Thirty days. Eudocia handed her the weaving, and asked one of the women to take her to the House of Lanterns and bring back the Overseer. When Inge said the crews were waiting in the Hippodrome, Eudocia sent another woman to tell them of Inge's great luck in being able to work at the House of Lanterns for thirty days.

"A great honor, Ingeborg, one worthy of your talents. You will find the food choice. The silk weavers eat as well as the Emperor, I hear."

Inge followed the woman through a maze of buildings and gardens, and she saw nothing, Her eyes smarted with tears. Could she weave a picture of the Empress that would suit? Could she weave in silk at all? And would the Empress keep her bargain?

She clutched her weaving and thought she had gained only one thing: she would not have to return to St. Mamas at three in the afternoon.

Time was her ally, and she must put every moment toward freeing Thora. She had lost a husband. She would not lose a daughter.

* * *

Every morning Inge entered the House of Lanterns, and it was like walking amidst flowing water. Lengths of silk in every shade of every color were set on racks to catch the luster of reflected light in the high, high room--and set to show the wealth of the Empire. Long ago Karl-Eirik told her Miklagard had hundreds of colors of silk, but nay, there were more.

Here was cloth of gold and cloth of silver, brocades, gold lace, patterned cloth with woven pictures, and silk so sheer it was all but invisible. In the center, placed so no one could miss it, was a fine robe of Imperial Purple, more costly than gold.

The workroom beyond was airy, and filled with looms where weavers sat or stood, the walls marked in warp measurements and designs. One whole wall held shelves of rolled-up sketches.

When Inge walked in with her woolen picture of Eudocia, the women gathered round and praised it. Good workmanship was applauded everywhere, and their smiles allayed her fears. The Overseer found her a place at one of the high north windows and gave her a tapestry roundel, already warped.

Here she could sit apart from the others. They were friendly, but she would have liked to drop them, homespun shifts and all, into her fjord to be bathed. At that, she learned she was lucky. The House of Lanterns was far from the dye works, with its stink of ash and sulfur and stale wine used to brew dyes.

The women were all thralls called slaves, owned by the Empire. Inge never thought she herself would be a slave. Her mother and father always had thralls, she and Karl had owned them as well. It was not possible to manage a farmstead of any size without them, but never did she think she would be one. These slaves responded to any kindness, and she resolved to be less sharp-tongued when she got home. There was no way for them to earn their freedom, and they were slaves for life, while she was only imprisoned for thirty days.

They adored their Empress. In the past some Emperor's wives permitted only themselves and their husbands to wear silk, but Eudocia allowed everyone at court to wear it, and ambassadors and senators as well, so there was plenty of work.

Silk-weaving was easier than Inge expected, and if Thora's life did not depend on her skill Inge knew she would find it joyful to choose the colors of spun silk-

-the right shade of blue for Eudocia's cunning eyes, the right red for her sullen, pouting lips. Inge smiled, and thought Helgi would have approved.

As the days wore on Inge knew her Greek had improved, so she understood all they said, and could answer. She seemed to be two people: one, repeating a Greek word with each strand of weft she beat in, the other fretting and scheming and lonely. Always she worried about Thora, learning how to play the lute and please men. And Inge feared that even if the Empress was delighted with the silken likeness, she might not agree to help free Thora after all.

The weavers' singing did not lift her spirits. The songs were the same mournful ones Zeno sang, and she missed the lilting music of her weaving room at home.

They worked from dawn to dusk, but the sun set earlier than in Sweden, and she had time to walk at even, exploring the grounds. She stood on a parapet overlooking the Sea of Marmara and looked for Norse ships, but all she saw were huge boats with two decks of oars and small fishing craft.

She felt trapped. There were underground tunnels out of the palace grounds, to carry the silk so it would not get rained upon, but they were boarded up in this dry season. She walked the gardens until the dusk blurred the flowers, and when it was dark she prowled the wall, feeling for the broken part into the house Basil had entered after killing Michael. All the stones were solidly in place.

If she felt helpless at even, her dreams left her shaken. In the slaves' dormitory she dreamed of Karl-Eirik: running down to the fjord to meet him, dancing with him in their hall to Per's flute, riding horseback with him on the hunt. Often she woke with a stirring in her Golden Cleft, and thought he came to her in dreams to take her from this hateful city and her worries.

She wondered if she dreamed of him out of guilt. If Karl had been alive, he would not have left Thora to chide Halfdan, but berated him in front of the maid. And so she would not have been stolen.

Gossip traveled as swiftly in the House of Lanterns as any place else, and the slaves knew of Thora's abduction. They could not imagine their daughters having the luck to be trained in an Arab household. The slaves came from the desert where they walked behind the men riding on camels, as they gathered fleece and dung for the cooking fire. In the House of Lanterns someone cooked and served them.

In truth, the food was good. Lamb, well-seasoned with mint. Fish in cream sauce, a table heaped with bread. Jugs of wine that made Inge lonesome for ale. Apricots in pomegranate sauce that made her think of Zeno. Almond cakes and dates. She ate to keep alive, but without pleasure.

Until the figs. While she wove she saw the Varangian Guards walking by the open window. She took heart from seeing the Swedes, though they could not help her.

But one day she found a ripe green fig on her bench and thought only a northman would throw it in the window: the rune naudhr was carved into the skin. Patience is necessary, the rune meant, and she ate the fig so there would be no trace. She carved kaun on the stone with her tapestry needle: kaun following naudhr had the message of new beginnings. She threw it out the window and watched it roll against an oak--not the summeroak of Sweden, but a tree a northman would know.

To her sorrow the stone was still there the next day. But she found another fig on her bench, this with the rune iss. Coming after naudhr it meant her problems were only for the moment, and would be sorted out. Inge felt lighter than she had for days. She had a friend.

The third day she found a fig with the best rune of all carved on it: logr. When it followed the first two runes it meant she must trust her own intuition.

She ate the fig and saw the women watching her. Nothing escaped their quick eyes. They teased her: a man had seen her weaving and been taken with her. She smiled, and kept on working. She had been there long enough to know which of the women were leaders and which followers, but not which were spies to Eudocia.

She trusted none of them, but if they told her where the figs grew, she promised to bring some to them on the morrow. She learned there were three fig trees on the grounds, and at even she set out to find them in the failing light. A northman might be waiting, as eager to talk Swedish as she was herself.

Nobody was at the first fig tree, nor at the second, and she felt a sharp disappointment. At the third, it was already dark, but she fingered the tree for figs and touched the wall behind it. A stone moved beneath her fingers. She reached and found another loose enough to wiggle.

She listened, but all was quiet. Ah. She had found the wall a murderous emperor had kicked apart to get into the Palace grounds. Basil's men must have put the stones hastily back in place. Inge listened, but all was quiet. She wanted no one to hear and come to see what she was doing. She pulled at the stones, and one fell out in her hand. Again there was no sound.

Gently she jostled out stone after stone, pausing after each to listen. Some were heavy, and once she dropped one and felt fear stab her, full sure someone would hear and stop her.

But no one came, not even a Varangian Guard. When she had a big enough hole she crawled through and fell into a house. What would the people say when they saw her break in? But it was deserted. Even the rats had abandoned it. She saw a crack of light, and felt for a door that pushed open.

She took a few steps and was on the street. She took a deep breath. Could it be she had escaped from the Palace? It was a shock to be back with dirt and noise, and a bustling crowd. She knew she might get caught up again in a mob, as she did on the day Thora was stolen.

Except then she had the northmen to protect her. Now she was alone--but armed. From her shift she pulled out her knife and tucked it into her belt with the blade for all to see. She looked straight ahead, and walked toward the blazing torchlight of the Hippodrome.

She was free! Somehow she would free Thora too.

People sat on the stone steps--eating, drinking, shouting at the children who raced up and down. The Hippodrome was crowded with acrobats, and men juggling balls, Greek soldiers in leather armor, men in striped robes and headdresses held on by a circlet of woven goat's hair. Beggars mingled with painted women. A man held a dancing bear on a leash.

In this city where no one slept, the Hippodrome was their great hall. Despite the confusion, she marveled at how alive the city was, how it had room for everyone.

Even a Swedish woman, she thought, tying her headdress tighter so no one would see her blond hair.

Under the watchful eye of a guard she went through to the street, and here were animals prowling in cages--striped, spotted, growling--and she wondered who got pleasure from looking at them.

The Palace windows gleamed, lit by many hundreds of torchlights, and she thought fortresses like this were walled, not alone to keep silk and gold in, but to keep the poor out.

She smelled the briny smell of the sea and was overcome with longing for The Seafarer and her crew, and for Karl-Eirik. She needed peace to think how to free Thora. She grasped the knife handle hard and left the lights behind, following a dirt road downhill, past a church with the mournful singing.

At the bottom she saw huge houses, high houses with no front walls--shells, open to the cooling night air off the Sea of Marmara. Lit by the moon, she saw each house was heaped with a different kind of fruit: apricots, peaches, plums-- the fruits the silk-weavers ate.

In one house the moon glittered on dark green fruits, piled almost to the ceiling. The same one she had seen on the cart her first day in Miklagard, when it was cut open and she saw pink inside. Her mouth watered. She looked about and saw no one.

She could not forbear to leave without tasting. Quietly she slashed one and ate, smelling the sweetness. The juice dribbled down her chin. If there was better, more cooling fruit in the Empire she had not eaten it.

Ah, if Karl was only here. She chose another for him. She wanted the best. This one...nay...that one...nay...ah, any one. They were all perfect. She stabbed one.

Behind her she felt the presence of someone before another knife thudded into her melon.

She whirled, pulling out her own sharp blade.

XXVIII

Inge felt her body tighten, and then relax, though she still held fast to her knife.

It was only a beggar in a tattered cloak, the cowl pulled close about his face--the city was full of them. But this beggar had tooled leather sandals, perchance stolen. She was glad she had given Lars her pouch of gold coins.

She pulled his knife out of the melon and set a piece atop, offering it to him. The knife had a jeweled hilt, and the fingers that took the fruit bore many rings. A most successful beggar.

"Welcome," she said in Greek, "to the melon house."

"You are trusting."

She heard the authority in his deep voice. As he devoured the melon she marked his teeth were better than most beggars, who often had brown stumps.

"Cut me another piece," he said.

She threw him a melon, and he caught it easily.

"I am not ordered about by any man. Have your knife back."

She threw it, and this too he caught easily. She slashed a piece for herself and ate it, watching him. He flipped his knife on his palm. She licked her lips, and cut another piece for herself.

"Christ Almighty," he said, "no man in the Empire would put up with you. You are insolent."

"Nay, I am not insolent, but Swedish. I would not ask a Greek to put up with me."

He pulled off his cowl. His beard was black and curly, his skin well-tanned. She had seen him before, wearing Imperial Purple on his small feet. The Emperor Basil had no right to be here. Like her, he was imprisoned on the Palace grounds. But unlike her, his guards might be close at hand.

"What are you doing here alone?" he asked.

"Eating melon." She handed him a piece. "I am happy to do for men, if I am not ordered about."

Her stomach felt queasy, but she took a calming breath and told him she was a silk-weaver at the Palace, in the city to make a silken likeness of the Empress Eudocia.

Basil grunted, and broke a melon in half with his bare hands. He would not know of her weaving, in this city where husband and wife intrigued against each other. He sliced her a piece.

"This far from the Divine Mese there is small pickings for beggars," she said, taking the piece of melon.

A smile crossed his face and faded. He wore an air of sadness.

"You know who I am. If you tell anyone I was here, I will have you killed."

"Ay? I like not to be threatened." She balanced her knife on her palm. "What if I throw my knife and kill you first? You are only human."

His face darkened with anger. "The Emperor is divine. I am the Chosen of God, the Equal of the Apostles, the Ruler of the World. And you, you are only a stupid foreigner."

"Nay, I am not! I am Ingeborg Andersdottir, captain of The Seafarer. I manage a farmstead with a hundred thralls. I have gold coins in a pouch, much gold buried at home, I have chests of fine jewels--"

"What is that to me? I have hundreds of ships, thousands of slaves and more gold than you could dream of. Jewels you cannot imagine."

She did not try to hold back her anger. "And what is that to me? You are a murderer who would not be emperor if you had not killed Michael the Drunkard and his uncle. You are hated and feared, but this I tell you--you fear revenge far more than your people fear you."

She was exhausted, horrified. She had been waiting for the right time to ask his help with Thora, but the time had passed. She watched his hand tighten on his knife.

"All I wanted was to get away, and I cannot even do that."

She pointed to the open door. "I am not keeping you here."

Basil threw back his head and laughed, and she thought how he was the most enslaved man in the Empire. No Greek would dare talk to him this way, but she was no Greek. She sat down on the melons and gave him a piece of fruit.

"It must be dull shit being the Chosen One, the Ruler of the World. Is there nothing to love?"

He shook his head and took the melon. "I loved my son. But he is dead. I love--I love waking up in the field to the fresh air, not like this stinking city. I love reviewing my troops and knowing that day we will conquer an enemy for the glory of the Empire."

Ay, and the glory of Basil. He had the same far-seeing eyes as Karl-Eirik. Not since Karl spoke of sailing had she heard a man speak so happily of work.

Basil shrugged. "I do not enjoy it any more without my son. But I like you Swedes--you make fine soldiers. I have some in the Imperial Guard, and they are loyal to me. All they need to prepare for battle is to sharpen their swords and axes."

"You go to war without sharpened swords?"

"By the Virgin, if that was all! The Palace travels with the Emperor. A hundred bottles of wine. Four ovens. Nets to capture fowls and wooden troughs for them to drink from. A portable bath with twelve bronze cauldrons and twelve heating machines to heat the water for my bath."

Inge laughed, and thought it had been too long since she laughed freely.

"All this to make war?"

"And more. Eight containers for rose water, perfumes, an earthquake chart, a thunder chart, fishermen to catch fish, books on dreams and omens and arms and fighting."

Books Basil could not read.

"No wonder the Swedes are such good fighters," she said. "The men do not take cauldrons to heat bath water."

She looked at him. It was easy to see why Eudocia helped him kill Michael. Basil was most attractive.

"Enough about the Empire. Tell me why you are in the city."

She began with Thora's sentence for Lesser Outlawy, talked of the journey and Karl's death.

Basil's face lengthened. "You, too, have lost. But you have a daughter. I envy you."

Her throat hurt, but she knew she must talk of Thora now.

"Nay. My Thora has been abducted by the Arab rug weaver, Ibn-Mahdi, for his harem. He serves your court."

Her mouth was so dry no melon could moisten it. She watched him chew.

"You are a lucky mother, Ingeborg. The Arabs treat their harem girls well."
Hatred swelled her chest.

"Lucky! Send your son to play the lute and please men." Anger choked her.
"You do not have a daughter and so--"

"Shut up! You will bring the monks from the church on us."

"Ay! Let them come and see you as you are. You want me to lose my child
too--"

"Mother of God, you have a temper. If you were mine I would thrash you."

Inge felt a lust to kill. She lifted her knife, and Basil grabbed the handle and
yanked it away. She picked up a melon and pitched it at his feet. He was quick
enough to pull back so the pink fruit only splashed his sandals when it cracked
open.

"Are you trying to break the Emperor's foot?"

She looked at him, and let the tears fall. What trick of Loki made her think
she would get help from this murderer? Yet it had been a fluke that they met, and
she must keep trying.

Basil sighed. "There was a time no one in the city would have thrown a melon
at me. I could walk the Divine Mese from one end to the other, and people would
talk to me, ask me for things, and a priest at my side wrote it down. Times have
changed. I no longer walk unless I am heavily guarded."

She knew she must be bold. "There is only one thing I would ask. Before I
began this journey, there were many things I wanted. But now, only one."

Basil wiped his mouth with his sleeve. "Ibn-Mahdi makes fine rugs. Eudocia
chose him herself. Ibn-Mahdi is the best."

"So is my Thora. Do you not see? If I lose Thora I lose everything. I will have
naught left."

In this strange land, what words touched an Emperor, or an Empress? She
had failed with both. Gloom covered her like a cloak. Basil put his arm about her
shoulders. Let him have his way with her. What did she care what happened?

"Ingeborg, you shall have her."

She pulled away, blinking. "Ay? Nay? Ay?"

"Yes."

She giggled and cried and giggled again, helpless to stop. She shivered, and
turned hot, and shivered again.

"Say it again--then you shall have her."

Basil smiled. "Then you shall have her."

Inge went limp in his arms, and said a fervent prayer of thanks to Freya. Dare she allow herself to hope?

"Say it again," she said.

He laughed. "Twice is enough. Come to the Magnura Palace tomorrow at noon. I will expect you."

Inge's mind whirled. Could she trust him? Basil had said, "Then you shall have her." Twice. An Emperor would hold to his word. Such a small thing for him, and her whole life to her.

"Now, Ingeborg, do you know how to do proskynesis?"

She felt giddy, and giggled. "It sounds like a sickness."

"No, no. Here I will show you. Everyone does it before the Emperor, even the soldiers in the field. You must do it before me when you come to the Magnura Palace."

He prostrated himself smoothly, and she thought it the first time any emperor prostrated himself before anybody, man or woman, Swede or Greek, or anyone else. He got up and she thought he moved like the wrestler he was, without effort, his body controlled.

"Do it, Ingeborg. Practice so you do it right tomorrow."

"Nay. It is easy. I will do it when I must."

She began climbing the mountain of melons. No wonder the Empire lost wars, if its soldiers had to prostrate themselves before fighting.

"Ingeborg, be careful."

"I am a countrywoman, used to climbing. I want to see the sea. I get as lonesome for it as you do for your field of battle."

Basil too climbed the melons easily, sure-footed as a man used to the outdoors. What torture it must be for him to be confined, she thought. No wonder he escaped to the melon house. The Marmara Sea looked inviting, with its moon-tipped waves and the soft lapping against the shore.

"Do you see the yacht tied to the quay?" Basil asked.

"That little boat? My Seafarer is bigger."

"By the Virgin's Robe, you are outspoken. Your ship is just bare boards, but the Emperor's ship is appointed with marble and gold and ivory."

They jumped down. Ah, but her ship would carry her and Thora away, and she would never return. She yawned.

"It is late, and I cannot weave if I do not sleep. On the morrow I must meet someone at noon at the Magnura Palace."

He nodded, and Inge wondered whether he would remember. Ay, he would. She would stand outside and scream and scream for him until he came out. In Greek she would scream, not for Basil, but for her Thora.

Together they walked uphill to the Palace, Basil with the cowl back over his head. They passed a wineshop and through the open door she saw blackened walls and ceiling, smoking lamps, men sitting at tables with wine and water bowls. Though he could not go in, Inge felt his longing. He talked to her as he would never talk to anyone but a foreigner. He stopped before the plain wall of a small church.

"I always knew I would be Emperor, Ingeborg. Signs were given to me, even as a child. When I came to the city I was determined to enter Michael's service and gain his attention, but I had not a nomisma. I lay down to sleep here, on the stone floor of this church. It was in ruins then.

"It is dedicated to Diomedes, the defender of truth, and while I slept he came to me and said I would be Emperor, the Ruler of the World. In exchange he asked me to take care of his church. Go in. I want you to see the inside. It is no longer in ruins."

It was empty, and at the front she saw one of the gold mosaics in flickering candlelight. She moved to the side to look at a statue and to her horror the eyes in the mosaic followed her. She cried out, and ran outside. Basil pulled her to him, and she felt quieted by his hard body.

She shuddered. "The eyes in the mosaic followed me--there is a man in there --trapped behind the wall--"

"No, no, Ingeborg. It is a trick of the artist. There is no man there, only God's hand in all."

Should she believe him? Ay, she could do little else. They passed a roofed street, with people sleeping right on the cobblestones, huddled together.

"I roofed this part so they would have shelter," Basil said.

So much gold on the church walls, and yet people were so poor they slept on the street. A strange city. They walked, Basil's arm about her, and she thought an Emperor was but a man who enjoyed being close to a woman. And ay, she enjoyed the closeness herself. They stopped at a corner of the Palace. He squatted and held his fingers laced.

"Step in my hands, Ingeborg, and I will lift you so you can climb the wall. Wait for me, and I will jump up, and then leap down and catch you."

"This is how you get in and out?"

He smiled. "One way."

She stepped into his hands and he lifted her easily, so she could scramble onto the wall. He put his fingers on a ledge of stone, pulled himself up, and fell easily on the other side. She sailed down, and he caught her.

"You are very strong," she said. "Most men could not do that."

Though every northman she knew could do the same.

Basil shook off his cowl, and she thought he was now free to go anywhere on the Palace grounds. It was as close as he got to freedom. They climbed from one pink marble terrace to another, past the tinkling fountains, past statues. She sniffed the flowers hungrily, and Basil told her it was jasmine. The Arabs made scent from it, and sold it to the Empire.

To take away the stink of the city, she thought, giving herself over to the beauty of the mild night. It had been weeks since she had been with one man alone, and she found it pleasing.

They passed many large white buildings, their doors open for air. Basil's guards stood watch, and she was happy to see many Swedes, their two-headed axes over their shoulders. Perchance one of them tossed the green figs, and so changed her life.

"I wish I had more Norse in my guard," Basil said. "They have a Grand Interpreter, so they do not need to learn Greek."

Ah, but they understood it, that she knew. He showed her a building where an empress kept a lover for twelve years, and she thought the emperor a fool, or else he cared not at all. One building had many beds, with one end propped up. Basil called it the Hall of 19 Couches, and here the court ate. Inge was amazed to think they ate half-lying down. Basil pointed out gold dishes hung by golden ropes from the golden ceiling, too heavy for servants to carry, so they were swung from one couch to another.

Inge looked at all these wonders, for herself, as well as for Karl. Ah, he would not have believed them. They passed the Chapel of the Virgin and Basil said he would show her the rib of St. Paul among the relics, but she said nay. One man's ribs looked like another's. In one Palace a fountain flowed wine, and she said in truth, this was the richest city in the world. Basil agreed but said it was often not rich enough. Sometimes they had to borrow silver and gold from the churches to impress a guest.

Huge trees stood around a building, the leaves longer than her arm. Basil said it was a date palm and one man did nothing but wait until a leaf fell so he could snatch it up and keep the grounds neat. Inge thought she would never let a thrall be so idle.

Basil pointed to one church with three domes and said his advisor, Isteles, talked with Constantine in heaven, and the boy wanted his father to build a church even bigger, with five domes. Isteles had studied in Ireland, and learned how to talk with the dead there. Did she know of Ireland? It was on the edge of the world.

Ay, she knew Ireland, she said, but did not tell him Karl-Eirik found their churches easy to attack, with much gold hid beneath the altars.

Basil stopped before one domed Palace and told her a golden tree with golden birds was inside. Would she like to see it?

She nodded, her grief freshened. So long ago Karl had talked of this tree. And now she was here, without husband or daughter. If she had known the price, would she have left home?

Basil led her inside, past tapestries and statues. From the far end of the room she heard birds singing. When they walked closer, she gasped. Each golden bird fluttered its wings, and each one was different from the next. She clapped her hands in delight. She saw a thrush and heard its flute-like song. She heard the klee, klee of a hawk, and found it. Here was the familiar rattle of the woodpecker, and ay, there it was.

Longing for Karl filled her. He would have loved this marvel.

Basil walked up to the Emperor's High Seat, with a golden headboard and canopy and footstool, and when he sat beneath a mosaic in gold, Inge thought this man gave off the power of an Emperor, though in beggar's garb.

On each side of his High Seat a golden beast's mouth opened and it roared, and she cried out. The eyes glittered, the tongues moved. Ah. The golden lions of Miklagard.

From his High Seat Basil smiled. "Do not be afraid. Close your eyes."

"Nay! I am wont to keep both eyes on the lions."

"They are not real. Close your eyes, and you will see the finest marvel of all in the Empire."

She lifted her chin. "I do not like to be ordered about."

Basil laughed. "Please, close your eyes."

She did. She had ever responded to a polite request.

"You may open them, Ingeborg."

She shuddered. He had vanished, as though he never had been.

"Up here," he called and she looked up and saw the High Seat had risen till it was just beneath the ceiling.

She was too dazed to speak. How did it get there?

"Close your eyes again Ingeborg, please," he said, and she did. "Now open them."

He was sitting before her. She blinked and cried out. Who would believe this? Loki's magic had traveled to Miklagard.

"When you go back to Sweden, tell them what wonders we have in the city," he said, walking her to the door. "We like your furs, your wax, your brave soldiers almost as much as your beautiful women.

"Tomorrow at noon, Ingeborg," he said, and he kissed her hair, holding her long enough she felt his hardening beneath his ragged pants. She wanted to linger in his arms, and pulled away. He was an Emperor, and she was a widow, still grieving.

Basil asked a guard to walk her to the silk-weavers' quarters, though she thought she could float. How could she sleep when Thora might be free at this time tomorrow?

That night her daughter's face appeared to her over and over in her dreams. Thora with her hair blowing on The Seafarer. Thora stirring the cauldron. Thora calling across the water to Halfdan. Thora carving. Thora reciting a lay. Inge was unsure how much she dreamed, and how much she wanted to see.

The next morning she could only nibble at the meal, and drink one swallow of the bitter black tea. She was edgy, and ripped as much as she wove. Before noon she left by the open window, knowing the women would think she was meeting a green-fig lover. She blessed them for never asking why she brought no figs from last night.

Her legs shook and her hands were clammy, as she walked to the Magnura Palace. In daylight it looked in need of repair. The doorsill was broken and the wall streaked with cracks.

A short Greek with puffy eyes stood in the open door. She liked not at all the way his lip curled when she said in Greek that she was there to see the Emperor Basil.

"Our Illustrious Emperor has canceled all appointments," he said, and it hit her like a blow to the stomach.

"Nay. We are to meet at noon."

Smirking, he said, "Look behind you."

She turned and saw a line of mules wending toward the Chalke Gate. They bore slings stuffed with fowl nets and wooden troughs and books. Nothing could keep her heart from breaking.

"The Emperor left at dawn," the guard said. "He is on his way to fight the infidels."

Inge sank to the ground. The last she heard was the oily voice telling her Basil the Ruler of the World would not return until he conquered the enemy.

XXIX

Inge sat in the window of the silk factory working at the tapestry roundel of Eudocia, worse off than before she met Basil at the melon house, before her hope had been aroused. With her tapestry needle she stabbed the Empress's pointed chin. She wished she could weave a scar on the smooth cheeks or a pimple.

Yet not all in Miklagard were thoughtless. A northman in the Imperial Guard had caught her as she fainted outside the Magnura Palace, carried her back to the House of Lanterns and brought her wine. She was most grateful to him.

But not to the Emperor Basil. In his joy of making war on the infidels, he had forgotten his promise to free Thora from Ibn-Mahdi. He was now miles beyond the city, and Thora was still an Arab's whore.

In Sweden, a man's word was his bond, but in Miklagard a man's word meant nothing at all. Inge chided herself. She should have known not to trust an emperor.

She chose pink, red and cerise strands of silk to blend for Eudocia's lips, and thought the chattering of the women would drive her mad. She was enveloped in sorrow, unable to share their excitement about St. Helena's Day on the morrow. She cared not a whit it was one of the four feast days a year when all state slaves were free from dawn to dusk.

She looked out and saw the fig stone still lay against the summeroak. She had found no more green figs on her weaving bench, and her unknown friend had disappeared. She felt sunk in gloom. She had no choice. On the morrow she too would be free from dawn to dusk. She must stop for Zeno at the public baths and meet the crews to plot an attack on Ibn-Mahdi's walled house and rescue Thora. It would take little to encourage them. They loved to fight.

As a leechwoman she could not take sword in hand, but must set the Swedes on the Arab and not reckon the cost, for cost there would be, in death and maimed men. Thora balanced against the two crews, one life against many. Was it worth it?

She was glad her mother was not alive to see her incite men to kill.

The next morning she walked out the Chalke Gate while the city lay swathed in fog. She saw one of the silk-weavers run up to a man and kiss him, while their children jumped about them. They went off to the Hippodrome, their arms about each other, and she was so envious she had to look away.

More people than ever crowded the street and the carts sold fancier goods on this feast day: carts filled with flasks shaped as acorns and birds, glass armrings and spoons. Potters, smiths, all hawked their wares. One cart was filled with green melons and she turned away, her stomach churning.

Lambs were being slaughtered on the corners of the Divine Mese, and poor, ragged people waited for a share. She passed men reading books aloud. She watched a procession pass, cavalry in white tunics and gold helmets, and behind them a canopy carried on poles inlaid with ivory, resting on the shoulders of six carriers. Ah, there was much cruelty in this city, and poverty and fakery, but much life.

She walked aimlessly. She had not recovered from the shock of a much-loved husband's death, and now she was adding to her grief. Not all her crew, nor Lars's, would live through an attack on Ibn-Mahdi.

At noon she waited on a bench outside the baths in the shade of a plane tree for Zeno. He was overjoyed to see her. He looked no different. A woven hairpiece did not grow. He and the crews knew she was at the silk factory, but he too was uncertain if Eudocia would barter Thora's freedom for a silken likeness.

He said the two crews knew she would be free on the feast day, and the men had sailed in from St. Mamas to the Fruit Pier. She sighed. Ah, if only she did not need to encourage them to be killed.

He chattered about the Emperor. That morning many candles had been lit in the churches and many prayers offered for his safety. Once again Basil had gone to save them from the infidels, though everyone knew he hated to leave his beloved city. Inge thought the only talent an emperor needed was disguising an outright lie.

A camel caravan passed, and she held her sleeve to her nose. She asked why Basil let Arabs like Ibn-Mahdi and this camel driver into the city and make war against others.

Because of his great heart, Zeno said, and told her he heard Thora was a favorite in the Arab's household. Inge stumbled, but he caught her before she fell. She forced herself to ask: what else had he heard?

Nothing else, he said, but it would be best to free Thora soon. These Arabs had "unusual" tastes when they bedded with young girls. Inge begged him to say no more.

She saw the masts of the two boats, and ran to embrace the crews amidst the bales of silk and piles of fruit, the raucous gulls, the horses and shouting drivers.

She cried. These men smelled Swedish.

She hugged Halfdan, and marked worry had added lines to the lad's face, and his smudged eyes told her he had not slept well. Lars jumped off his boat and kissed her, then held her out at arm's length.

"Ingeborg, the rich Greek food has fattened you up."

She teased him he was only trying to find an excuse to pinch her. Both crews climbed aboard The Seafarer and drank ale, and Inge told them about meeting Basil. Zeno was amazed. She said Basil must have some Norse in him, for he loved fighting as much as he hated ceremony.

She marked how restless the men were. They told her they had spent their time at St. Mamas, practicing swordcraft and aiming their arrows for targets Finnvid set farther away each day.

She did not want to talk of attack. She asked if Bratta and Volnir were well. They thrive pastured at St. Mamas, Anders said, but she saw the men cared about nothing but a battle.

"Mistress, they will never suspect us until we are inside Ibn-Mahdi's wall," Finnvid said.

She walked to the stern and looked at the Golden Horn, teeming with ferry boats, ships of burden, fishing craft, a barge with a blue and gold canopy.

"Say the word, Mistress, and we will fight to the death to rescue Thora," Anders said, and she heard the joy in his voice.

Zeno came to her. "I wish I could promise you your men have little to fear from Ibn-Mahdi, but the Arabs are superb soldiers. The harem women are well guarded."

"Ay. I am trying to think of another plan."

Behind her she heard the racket on the quay quiet down. People on other boats were pointing and talking to each other. The crewmen came to stand with her to look out at the Golden Horn. A ship was making its way under sail, the ship only bare boards piled with bales and goods, but the silken sails were the most beauteous Inge had ever seen--a desert scene at sunrise. A grove of palm trees, a pool of water only silk could show in its full shimmer, sand that took on warm pinks and reds, a circle of square black tents. And in the foreground lambs and kids that made Inge's heart hurt for the ones that were frolicking in Sweden now.

She suspected city dwellers like Zeno had a love for vast, open space. When water came from a mossy fountain and the sky was choked by smoke from countless cooking fires, it would be hard to remember they too were part of nature. She turned, and saw men and women still standing, watching. This sail touched some desire for beauty in them.

"Who owns that ship?" she asked Zeno.

"Ibn-Mahdi, I fear. He has a fine collection of art. How I envy the weaver who can do such work."

Ay, she thought. Envy could be useful. Ayiii! Envy could gnaw at a man until he would do anything to be better than another. The boat rounded the Palace wall and headed for the Sea of Marmara. Even when the sails were only a sheen of color they held the eye of every watcher on the quay.

She dug through the ship's gear and found her carved wooden bridal cup. She traced the carved bird set on a branch of the Tree of Life and thought the cup precious to her. But Thora still more precious. She ordered the men to stay aboard.

"I am going to see the Arab trader with the jewel in his headcloth. What is his name?" she asked Zeno.

"Al-Sina. I will come with you to translate."

"Nay, he speaks Swedish. Stay here."

She picked up her seapouch, jumped off and held out the cup for Anders to fill with ale. She saw Al-Sina standing in front of his warehouse. He welcomed her, and invited her inside. The shelves bore fine pelts. Al-Sina knew quality. She greeted him in Swedish and told him he had honored her the first day, by speaking her tongue. He said a trader dealt with captains from many countries, and he spoke ten languages.

"Ten!" she said and set the finely-carved cup on the counter. He looked at it, and a light glittered in his eyes and went out. In truth these Arabs knew quality. A man who knew quality would feel envy.

"I brought you a sample of fine Swedish ale," she said.

"Thank you, but my people drink nothing stronger than camel milk."

She marked his voice was as silken as his trader's shirt.

"Tell me, did you see the beautiful ship sails? I am a silk-weaver at the House of Lanterns, and I have seen much finespun, but nothing like these sails."

His face was bland, but again the light flickered and went out.

"It is the boat of Ibn-Mahdi, one of our rug dealers. His work is so fine he serves the Emperor Basil. Ibn-Mahdi is away, but perhaps you would like to buy one of his rugs to take back to Sweden?"

Did Al-Sina know Thora had been stolen by Ibn-Mahdi? She had to hope he did not. Perhaps they were enemies and did not talk together. She dare not lift the cup to sip, with her hand shaking.

"Nay, but my crew was much taken with the sails. Could we buy them?"

"No. Such beauty cannot be bought and sold."

"Ah. Perchance I can weave them myself. I am making a silken likeness of the Empress Eudocia."

She saw he did not believe her, and she gave him the woolen likeness from her seapouch. He took it to the open door and when he returned the light gleamed in his eyes and did not flicker out.

"You are a fine weaver. You have caught Eudocia's lovely face. You will be well paid for making it in silk?"

She shrugged. "Gold is nothing compared to the hope others will see my work, and want my services."

Dare she push him further? The purple had faded as Maurice predicted, but it gave the likeness a softness Eudocia did not have. His eyes shining, Al-Sina took the likeness to the door again.

"Our women are wonderful weavers, but I have never seen anything like this. Tell me--do you think you could weave a set of silken sails with pictures for me?

I am not merely a trader. My humble business has prospered, and I have a fleet of my own."

Her heart pounded. At the best, she had hoped he would ask for a banner in front of the warehouse.

"Not like Ibn-Mahdi's, of course, but different," he said. "Something like the desert scene, but better. Our people have a long history of fine art."

"Ay? I have seen none of it at the House of Lanterns."

"No, of course not, but we do. If you can weave the Empress's face--I would like you to do animals--a peacock, yes, a peacock with its tail spread on a sail. Perhaps a winged horse. And a unicorn, like the Christians put in their paintings. There is one in a chapel on the Palace grounds. Of course! You could use it as a model."

Ah. Al-Sina would not only outdo Ibn-Mahdi, but the Christians too. He could not conceal his excitement.

"Our people like designs of circles and triangles and interwoven flowers," he said. "On the border?"

She squeezed the cup handle, and turned toward the door. "I would enjoy weaving your peacocks and winged horse and interwoven flowers, but I have seen nothing like them at the House of Lanterns. I am sorry. Farvell."

"Wait! All these could be seen at Ibn-Mahdi's. I can arrange it. He is proud of his art, and would be flattered to see it on my sails. The pictures belong to all of us, in a sense."

Ay? She thought. Nay, Ibn-Mahdi would hate it. Now was when she must be most careful. She thought the light in his eyes would burst. She drained the cup.

"I promise nothing. But if I can look at the art, I will see. I must take along a linen-weaver to the Emperor who speaks Arabic. I will not be intruding at Ibn-Mahdi's?"

"Not at all." He pulled out a piece of leather and a reed pen from beneath the counter. "Here, you can make sketches on this. Bring it back, and we will discuss the sails. I will send a runner to tell them you are coming. You will find us Arabs hospitable."

She heard a sound like horses being gelded, one she had often heard from the House of Lanterns. Al-Sina bowed to her.

"Excuse me. When the muzzerin sounds, I must pray."

To her surprise he knelt in the middle of the floor facing east, and began to pray. So this was the reason for the dread sound. Other men rushed to join him and she left quickly, twirling her carved cup.

Now, all depended on a loving mother's skill. And luck.

She told the crews she and Zeno were calling on the house of Ibn-Mahdi, to see his fine art. They would get Thora out, one way or another.

"We will not be able to use our well-sharpened swords, Mistress?" Finnvid asked, and she heard his disappointment.

"Keep them close at hand, Finnvid. We will not get out of Miklagard without a fight."

"Let me go with you," Halfdan said. "You may need protection."

But she would not let him. Lars jingled her pouch of gold coins and said they could buy Thora, but she thought not. An Arab like Ibn-Mahdi did not lack money. She hefted her pouch, and told him to guard it until her return. Why was it heavier?

"Inge, in our spare time at St. Mamas I have gone every day to the wine-shop to gamble for you. The Greeks have a good game passing a ring beneath a blanket--"

"You gambled for me? With my money? Nay!"

"Ay, but I have doubled it."

She kissed him. "I should hate you, but I need your help. Zeno, we cannot stay in the city in late afternoon. Are fishing boats allowed to stay in the Bosphorus?"

"As long as they are outside the city wall."

"Good. Now, Lars, go to the Bosphorus with the two boats, drop anchor and lower your fishing lines. Once we have Thora we will signal you from shore. Then you row in to get us, and we will all sail back to Sweden."

It sounded simple, but she knew the men were not fooled.

"This I promise you," she said. "If Zeno and I fail, you attack Ibn-Mahdi with my blessing."

"Ingeborg, I have already lost a brother," Lars said, holding her, and she felt joy in his taut body. "Let me come with you."

She kissed him hard, and told him Ibn-Mahdi's men would be suspicious if she came with anyone but Zeno to translate the Arabic. She pulled Karl's knife from her shift. She would not be unarmed.

He thumbed the blade. "Sharp enough, Ingeborg." He put a boat-shaped brooch on her cloak and she saw it had a long pin sharpened to a point. "I hope you do not have to use either the sword or the pin. Your plan is fraught with danger."

"Ay. But I can do naught else."

"Inge, be most careful," he whispered and she saw his tears.

He pulled out the neck of her overdress and slipped the knife back between her breasts, nestling it in place. It was pleasing to have him touch her. When she had time, she must tell him so.

"Lars, do not follow me. Or let the men."

She kissed him again, harder, and felt the stirring in her Golden Cleft. Ah. She was healing.

"Lars, I have a hunger to eat fresh mullet tonight and celebrate leaving this stinking city. Now, tell me a signal."

He was unwilling, but after some coaxing he pulled her hand mirror from her seapouch, and showed her how the sun would flash a light if it struck it. Two boats out in the river would see it. Ah. Now she must rescue Thora before the sun went down. And if she could not?

She must try, with all her heart and will. Lars gave her the pass to the city, and she said she hoped it was the last time she used it. She and Zeno set off. She waved to Al-Sina, standing in front of his warehouse. She held the leather and reed pen up for him to see, though her hands were clammy with fear. He bowed.

She half-listened to Zeno as they walked between carts of spicy sausage and baskets of hazelnuts and mint and cumin, garlands of sponges.

"The cooks in New Rome are so discerning they know which side of the mountain the mint grows," he said.

"I care not. These Arab women follow behind the Arab man as if he is a king." She groaned and said, "I would hate this for Thora."

"Fear not. We will save her. These Arabs are not all bad." He talked on, and she knew he was trying to soothe her. He spoke of an Arab doctor named Al-Kindi, who had cured a wealthy merchant's paralyzed son with music. Al-Kindi fell from fame and disappeared, but he left writings in which he said there was a close connection between the body and feelings. He set forth new ideas: the importance of what we eat, the influence of the weather, how sickness can be spread by unclean water.

She felt like throttling him. "All these have been known by leechwomen in Sweden long, long before my mother's mother's time."

He stopped, and pointed to a high, well-kept wall and whispered, "The house of Ibn-Mahdi."

She felt weak with fear, clutching him so she did not fall.

"Before we go in, I must tell you, Zeno, how grateful I am you are willing to go along and translate."

"I am happy to do it. Thora and I are much the same."

Except that Thora's outlawry was for six months. His own was for life. Inge did not like to think how he would be punished if he was caught, and taken before Basil. She marked her fingers were trembling. How could she hold a reed pen? Could she even get in to where Thora was held? And how could she get her out of this walled house?

"Hope deferred maketh the heart sick," he said. "That is from our Bible. I know you have been heartsick over Thora's capture. But we will save her, and then I will disappear back into the city."

As they walked to the iron gate Inge saw the wall was higher than the one around the Palace. If she failed, she could do nothing but let the northmen attack, and all might be killed. Even that might be a waste, and Thora would live out her whole life amusing Ibn-Mahdi with the Arab's unusual tastes in bedplay.

She felt a chill pass through her body, and chided herself. She was a chieftain's wife still, though the chieftain was dead. Later there would be time to give way and be mawkish, but now all of her strength must be turned to the task at hand. It seemed her life in Miklagard was one of closed doors and gates--the Chalke Gate of the Palace, Eudocia's door, the one with stones she had loosened to escape the Palace grounds...

This was only one more, and it might be the last. She lifted her head high and held up the leather and the reed pen. The gate swung open.

XXX

Inge took a deep breath and strode into the courtyard. Strangely, she took heart from the clang of the shutting gate. She would not leave, unless she left with Thora.

An Arab in homespun with a simple, unbejeweled headcloth bowed before them. He talked in Arabic, and Zeno translated. His name was Giyath and word had reached him from Al-Sina of their coming. They were to follow Giyath for refreshment.

He led the way through a garden with a tinkling fountain, but Inge had no desire to linger. They entered a house built with heavy brick pillars holding up a brick ceiling, so strong she thought it would withstand the stars if they fell. This house was built to shield people from the glare of the sun. In here it would always be like the world at even--dusk, and cool.

The wadmal beneath their feet was thick, thicker than in Helgi's palace. She longed for him, but knew he would not be here in this city that had defeated him. Her eyes got used to the dim light, and she saw the wadmal beneath their feet had black and red flowers intertwined, most beauteous. Every ell of brick on floor and ceiling was covered with scrollwork in circles and triangles. Giyath led them through massive arches into a large hall.

He pointed to a tapestry that covered all one wall. Zeno cried, "Merciful God," and Inge gasped. Here was a whole city woven in silk! Houses, a flowing river, boats, camels, horses, wagons piled high with fruits, carts with charcoal cooking meat, a smith at work, a jeweler twisting gold, fountains, statues, people in finespun, strolling, while children played with balls. Inge knew even if she stood there forever she could not see it all.

At the bottom edge bronze braziers smoked lazily and perfumed smoke rose from the throat of bronze birds with jeweled feathers. All was wondrous, and Zeno breathed in the smoke, but it made her dizzy.

Giyath beckoned them to follow him to the courtyard where he spread cushions for them in the shade of a tree with pink flowers. A young boy brought dates and bowls of camel milk, and purple sticks set on trays of woven palm leaves.

"Suck the sticks," Zeno whispered. "It is sugar cane, and the Arabs are indeed generous--it is a six-knot stick. And appreciate the woven trays. They know you are a weaver."

Inge smiled, lifted the tray and nodded to a group of women twisting date palms. The sugar cane made her sick and the camel milk threatened to gag her, but she ate and drank, observing the Arab's hospitality, though her stomach knotted in fear.

"Ask Giyath," she said to Zeno, "what that woodenwork is, on the upper windows."

Zeno translated and told her it was called shibaah, a word meaning "network." It was made to fit together closely so no one could see into the women's quarters, but light and air came into each room, and the women could see out.

Was Thora looking down on them?

"Zeno, tell Giyath I am wont to look at the shibaah more closely, to use it in the sail for Al-Sina. It is wondrous, much like the Gripping Beast on The Seafarer's prow."

While Zeno translated she made herself sit calmly and eat the wretched dates.

"Giyath says he has many hangings and paintings far more beautiful for you to copy. And men are not allowed in the women's quarters."

"I am not a man. Tell him that."

When he did, the two men laughed together.

"Giyath says he can see that," Zeno said.

"Then there is no reason for me not to go," she said, and stood.

She was fearful Giyath would stop her, but it was Zeno who did. "I cannot help you there," he whispered.

Inge shrugged and looked at the Arab. He spread his hands.

"You can help by keeping Giyath busy," she told Zeno. "When I need you, be ready."

It seemed to her that her heart pounded as loud as her feet on the winding stone stairs, but she kept climbing. At the top a huge black man with a shaved head sat at a table, writing. Ay, only a eunuch would be allowed here in the women's quarters. She felt her quaking knees, and pushed them tight together. Smiling, she leaned the leather against the wall and began sketching him.

He looked up in surprise but did not stop her. With a few strokes she drew his large head, his brocaded robe, his pen. She finished and walked down the hallway. He called, and she turned.

All was lost--he was going to stop her.

But nay, he held out his hand for the picture--flattered. Someone had drawn his likeness. She shook her head and pointed to the blank space left on the leather and to the women's rooms. If she gave it to him, she had no excuse not to go into the harem.

He grinned and waved her through. She thanked Freya as she walked, for this skill in making likenesses was one she did not know she had.

She ignored the sharp pain in her stomach she knew was fear, and forced herself to look in each room on both sides of the hall. They were small and dim as a cowstall, with a mat on the floor, where small dark-haired girls sat, combing their hair or applying a brush to their eyelashes or staring into space. Inge had ever hated idleness, but she felt sorrow for these girls, trapped in their cowstalls till Ibn-Mahdi sent for them.

Thora was not in the first, nor the fifth, nor the tenth--what if she was not here at all? Inge leaned against the wall for support, and the sound of strange music came to her. The music-maker had no skill, for the playing was dreadful.

In the last tiny room, the smallest and dimmest of all, a girl sat on the mat wearing a blue shift, her blond hair piled atop her head, tied with ribbands. She did not look up or stop plucking the instrument.

After all these days, after the scheming and plotting and worry, Inge expected her daughter would jump up and throw her arms about her. But there was no rush of a warm embrace. Thora held up the long-necked pear-shaped instrument.

"This is an Arab lute, and I am learning to play. I saw you from up here. I thought you would come." She lifted her hand. "What do you think of this? I have my own room here--not like the hall at Breidal where I slept on a bench covered with stinking furs."

Inge's heart was breaking. "Keep playing, Thora. To cover our voices."

The maid stopped. "I am free here. I obey no one but Ibn-Mahdi, but I will keep on practicing."

She resumed the miserable plucking.

"I like it here, Modir. I am staying. I will never leave. The water is warm for bathing, scented with jasmine, not like the Dnieper."

Inge knew she had but a few minutes till the eunuch came.

"And Ibn-Mahdi, Thora? What does he ask in exchange?"

She smiled, and Inge thought she was still beauteous.

"I am learning much about pleasing men."

"You can use it to please Halfdan."

"Nay, I am learning the Arab stories, better than ours. Stories about lamps you rub to get anything you want, and rugs that fly, and jewels big as serving bowls."

"You can tell them to your child, Thora."

The maid stopped plucking and looked at Inge, her mouth hanging open like a thrall's--the thrall she had once been. Her face reddened.

"I am not with child! See, my belly is flat!"

"A leechwoman knows the signs, Thora."

"I am not with child. But if I am, there are ways..."

Inge forced herself to stand rigid, and not shudder. It was her grandchild Thora was talking about. Some of this hateful city had washed off on the maid. Ah, Inge thought, it had never occurred to her that her daughter would not want to escape.

"Thora, you have not told Ibn-Mahdi, have you, for you know he would murder your child. He would not have a blond baby grow up in an Arab house."

"Ibn-Mahdi loves me. I know he does. I am his favorite. He had to go away, but he will come back to me."

Inge hated herself for her cruelty, but now she needed to rescue Thora more than ever. A helpless babe in the womb was involved.

"He did not take you with him?"

"Nay. I must stay and practice my lute. Ibn-Mahdi likes my lays and he wants me to sing them to music."

"If he does not take you now, he will not take you when you are round in the belly. Not when he has a choice of a hundred others."

Inge felt the eunuch at the door before she saw him. Thora spoke to him in Arabic and he put his hand on Inge's shoulder. The hand was flabby.

But she was a countrywoman, and strong. She shook off his hand, and pushed him away. He fell with an "oof ", his head hitting the floor, knocking him out. Inge rolled him over with her foot.

"Modir, you killed him!" Thora said, jumping up.

"Nay, nay."

Inge took out her knife, blessed it for its sharp edge, and sawed free one of the silk lute strings. She pulled the guard's hands behind his back, bound him and sawed loose another string to tie his feet.

"Thora, undo your ribbons."

The maid did not move, but Inge snatched them from Thora's hair and stuffed his mouth and tied that too with a lute string she yanked out. Bound and gagged, he would give her time, if no one had heard the thump when he fell.

"Modir, I am not going with you."

"You cannot practice your lute. I have put the strings to better use. This man is their property. When they find him tied up in your room they will punish you."

Inge looked at her daughter, hair flowing loose to her shoulders like any unwed maid. But now one with child. Though the maid tried to hold back, Inge was stronger, and she pulled Thora after her, down the hall. When they reached the curved stair, she heard screams, and knew the eunuch had been found.

She must make a distraction.

Though it hurt her, she opened a brazier and pitched the coals onto the wondrous hanging of the city. In the dry air it caught fire easily, and the room filled with smoke. People poured into the room, beating on the flames. Inge saw the amazed faces of Giyath and the palm weavers and she ran, pulling Thora after her, through the massive stone arches out into the garden.

Zeno was waiting, and she showed him how to lift herself and Thora atop the wall and climb up, as Basil had done. She touched her amulet, thanking Freya that Zeno was as strong as the Emperor.

Soldiers with plumed hats rode their horses up to the gate, forced it open and rode in.

"They will see us," Thora whispered.

"Nay," Inge whispered. "No one sits on the wall. They will not think to look up."

Later, they would climb down, and get to the shore and give the signal to the waiting northmen. For now she held fast to Thora. Who would have thought the maid unwilling to leave?

"Modir, I hurt my ankle when you pulled me after you."

Thora moaned, and a soldier looked up at them and pointed.

"Run!" Zeno shouted, and slid off the wall. Inge pushed Thora down to the ground and once again pulled the maid behind her, through the crowd, keeping Zeno's brown hairpiece in sight. For once she was grateful Miklagard was choked with people to hide them.

"This way!" he shouted, turning down a side street.

The shouts were louder, and Inge heard hoofbeats. Zeno turned a corner, then another, led them through the open door of a house and out the back, while the people eating at a table stared. Inge heard Thora panting, and her own chest was heaving. Zeno took them in and out of a maze of streets and into a yard covered with brambles and thorn bushes. He bent, trying to lift one of the fallen headless statues that littered the yard.

"Help me," he grunted, and the women lifted with him.

Fear brings strength, Inge remembered, and another time she could not have done it, but not only their three lives were at stake. There was a babe in the womb. They moved the statue far enough to reveal a hole.

"Down here," Zeno said, and slipped in.

Inge heard a splash and pushed Thora after him, though she was unwilling. Inge knew there was no way she could lift the statue by herself and cover the hole. Full sure, the soldiers would follow, and they would be trapped.

The hoofbeats pounded closer. She jumped in, falling down, down into water and kept falling until it covered her head.

She flailed her arms and spluttered to the surface. She called to Thora and Zeno, and there was no answer. She was alone, up to her neck in icy water. It was altogether dark, except for a square of light where the soldiers could slip through and attack them, and no one would hear her cries for help.

* * *

"Modir," Thora called in a shaky voice.

"Ssst," Zeno whispered.

Inge thought their voices sweeter than music. She was not alone, and all three of them were alive.

"Stay away from the opening," he whispered, still softer. "Be quiet until the soldiers leave."

Inge floated, reached out and felt a body--her beloved daughter. Never had she loved her more. She looked at the square of light, and saw stars. They must be in a well, where anyone could see the stars that were in the sky, day or night.

The soldiers were sure to see the hole with the statue pushed aside. She heard their cries and felt for her knife. When they came down the hole she would slash and cut and protect her daughter as best she could. At least Thora was with her, though most unwilling.

The curses and cries above them died away, and Inge touched her amulet. She sent a prayer of thanks to Freya. They would not be raped.

"Zeno, where are we?" Inge asked.

"In the Cistern of a Thousand and One Columns. There are thirty of these beneath the city, where water is brought through pipes from the Forest of Belgrade, north of the Golden Horn. We Romans like our baths."

Inge bumped into a stone and felt it up and down, one of the columns. "You have a fountain on every corner of the city. As many as churches."

"Yes, but fountains would be useless in a siege. The cisterns were built so we could hold out forever against an enemy. With a safe water supply no one can conquer us."

Not even Helgi, she thought, as Thora nudged against her, teeth chattering. Ah, a jasmine-scented bath was not as much training for this cistern as the cold Dnieper.

"People all over the city raise trapdoors to dip into the cistern with a bucket," Zeno said, "and we can get out through one of these. We must look for moss along the ceiling. There will be the door we can push up."

Inge wondered how they could see without any light. She bumped into wood. Tracing it with her hands, she felt a boat.

"I would fain row a boat than swim," she said, pulling herself up. She squeezed water from her pants and helped Zeno and Thora climb in, both shivering. Inge felt the floorboards and found a pole. She gave it to Thora.

"Using it will warm you, my daughter."

Thora poled, while water in the bottom surged to and fro over their feet. There was a splash, and Thora whimpered.

"Modir, I was so cold I dropped the pole."

"We will manage," Inge said, though Zeno cursed. She reached out and felt a column. "We will push ourselves from one column to the next. This way we will all move and warm ourselves."

In this fearsome hole the only sound was the lapping water. In vain they looked for a spark of light. Inge peered, and thought she saw a gleam ahead. Her hands flailed empty air--they had gone beyond the columns.

"Paddle," she said, "toward the gleam of light," and they bent their arms into the icy water.

Hope could give strength as much as fear could. "Freya," she whispered, and to her joy she saw the goddess had not abandoned her. Atop a stone column a huge stone head of a woman rested on its side, with ringlets of mossy stone hair, and a broken nose.

"Modir--another one--," Thora said, her voice echoing.

"There is light so the two statues can be seen," Zeno said. "I will climb on the head of one, and see if a trapdoor is overhead."

He jumped up on the goddess's head, and Inge heard him scratching the ceiling. Inge and Thora huddled together, shivering, listening to grunts and groans and curses, and then they saw a blessed sliver of light that swelled to a yellow square.

"God is good," he called. "I found a way out."

Now her damp, cold clothes were of no moment, Inge thought, sending Thora up first, and followed. The house smelled sour and musty, but no one was home.

Once out on the street Inge felt a rush of joy, though she kept watch for soldiers on horseback. Zeno thought they would be safer walking apart, but Inge would not let go of Thora.

"Our clothes are drying, and there are enough people that we can blend among them," Inge said, "but we must get outside the city wall to where the northmen can see the flashing handmirror. And we must stay far from the Fruit Pier. By now Al-Sina will have heard what happened."

Zeno told her the only ways out of the wall were through gates, and he wished to avoid the Prison Gate. Inge looked at the sun hanging like a shield in the sky. They must get out by even, or the crews would not see a handmirror reflecting the sun. She held Thora fast with one hand and held the other up to her nose.

"Phew. What is that stink?" she asked him.

"The caravansary, where men bring their camels into the city, milk them and sell their fleece in the bazaars."

"Ay? How do the men and camels get in and out of the wall?"

He smiled, and she told him to follow them behind a house and keep watch. She ripped her linen shift into strips. She and Zeno quickly bound cloth over their hair and she tucked her plait beneath. Thora fumbled with her strip and Inge wound her headcloth. Ah, this maid was deft only with a sword. Inge held her for a quick hug.

"Modir, I am frightened," Thora said. "When Ibn-Mahdi finds me he will punish me--" Inge's heart burned. They must get out of Miklagard and far from Ibn-Mahdi. The Arab would think naught of punishing Thora, only one of many in his harem. He would use the maid as an example to the other girls of what could happen if they tried to leave.

Inge took a deep calming breath, and thought she must take heart. They were close to being safe aboard the ship. The only remaining hurdle was getting out of this stinking city.

Her daughter was paler than usual. Inge set them to rubbing mud into their skin so they looked dark as desert people. Zeno said he prayed they would pass, and led them to the caravansary. Men milking camels never looked up. Good. They had passed the first test. Inge felt a great longing for her beloved Brattahlid. Soon, soon, she too would be milking, but not these wretched camels.

When they approached the Camel Gate Inge felt her chest tighten with fear. To calm herself she told Zeno the camels were the ugliest beasts she ever saw: stiff-legged, lumpy necks, yellow teeth. He told her they were one of the meanest animals and never learned to love a master, as a horse did. She remembered Volnir's love for Karl-Eirik. To think Karl's name brought her close to tears, but she must hold fast to her common sense, and not weep.

"Keep your eyes down, Thora, so the guard does not see your eyes are blue."

The camel drivers led their beasts through in groups of ten, and the three stepped between two groups.

"Get behind me, like dutiful Arab women," Zeno said, "and gather fleece and dung, or the guard will be suspicious."

The fleece, but not the dung, Inge thought, picking the stinking fleece where it caught on a thorn-bush. The line stopped, and she forced herself to stand quietly and wait, while the guard jested with a camel driver. She kept her eyes on the tail of his headcloth until once again it was swinging. They were so close to safety. She must let nothing stop them now.

All went well until they got to the guard, and he cupped his hand around Thora's breast. She turned and faced him, fighting him off. Inge felt her whole body turn cold. He was looking straight at Thora's blue eyes in her dusky face. He screamed in Arabic, and Thora struggled. Inge was certain of only one thing. They needed another distraction.

She had no fine hanging or coals in a brazier to start a fire, and so she used what was close at hand. She kicked a camel in the leg, again and again. The startled beast bumped the next in line, and that the next until a bubbling roar filled the air. Suddenly, all the camels were running, the drivers behind them cursing in vain.

A camel stepped on the guard's foot, and he yelled. Another beast bit the one in front, and a third shifted his burden so it fell to the side and it got down on its knees. Though the driver took a stick to its flank, it would not move. The camels piled into each other, and all was a confusion of cursing and shouting men and roaring beasts with flaring nostrils.

Zeno led the way through the melee, and when the three were beyond the gate he ran. Now Inge did not need to pull Thora along. They ran until they were beyond the racket and at the edge of the Golden Horn. Inge pulled out her handmirror.

She dared flash the signal only once. By now word of their escape would be all over the city. Greek seamen in the harbor would suspect flashes of light from on shore and report to the Empire's soldiers.

Freya, she prayed, let one of the northmen look ashore and catch one quick flicker of light. This is our only chance to escape, or we will be imprisoned in this hateful city forever.

XXXI

Inge stood with her arm about her trembling daughter, both too drained to talk. The boats were thick in the Bosphorus, but they saw two of them had caught enough fish for one day. The crews pulled in their lines, took their places at the oar, and threaded their way to shore through the other ships. Inge thought The Seafarer was the most beauteous boat she had ever seen. The Goldenbreast, too, was a wondrous sight.

She put her handmirror back in the pouch and the three waded out and climbed aboard, Halfdan waiting to take Thora in his arms. Like herself, Inge thought, he would take the maid any way he found her.

Lars told them to lie down on The Seafarer's deck with the sail spread over them, hiding them until they were safely away. Through the boards beneath her body, Inge felt her beloved boat turn and head up the Bosphorus. The men grunted, rowing. Inge reached out her foot and touched her daughter. Thora touched back. Inge thought she could bear any hardship now.

Finnvid gave them no time to rest. "Do not move or talk, Mistress." She heard him jest with a passing boatman from his place at the tiller. "Ay? We will share in the reward?" he asked in poor Greek.

Inge felt the slap of waves and the rocking of The Seafarer as the fishing boat went downriver, and then she heard only the splash of waves hitting their own hull.

"Mistress, I am glad our sail is so large," Finnvid said, "for you must stay hid. Word of your adventures has reached the Empress Eudocia. She has set a reward of six gold solidus for your capture. When you are returned to her she will put out your eyes, for being disloyal to the Empire."

Thora cried out, and Inge shushed her.

"Only six, Finnvid? I am under-priced. In truth I like my eyes. I expect to see Sweden again with them."

Once back at her farmstead she would never, never leave. She would give over journeying to foreign lands to her crew.

"With the luck of the gods we will get away," Finnvid said. "We will dock at St. Mamas to pick up Bratta and Volnir."

She thanked him, for if Finnvid wanted to leave the animals behind she could do little to stop him from her place beneath the sail. She smelled the briny fish smell of St. Mamas, felt the boat bump the quay and then the ship heeled and righted itself, as the two beasts were goaded aboard. She heard Saemund wish them well, and the boat was given a hard shove back into the current.

Inge curled up tighter, while the beasts pawed the deck and snorted and finally settled down, tethered to the mast, as Anders soothed them. She comforted herself by thinking soon they would be safely out of the Bosphorus and she would have her hand on Bratta's teat, squeezing out warm sweetmilk. And never, ever would she eat another sickening, sweet date.

"We pay no customs on leaving Miklagard, Mistress," Finnvid said, "though I would be glad to pay for my freedom. As you would, I am certain."

"Ay, and they would pay to be rid of us. Their women liked us too well," Sven said and they laughed.

Inge marveled that Karl's men could always laugh, no matter how hardpressed.

"Strange. They are not lowering the chain for us, Mistress," Finnvid said. "It might be a trap to catch you."

"Inge, you are worth more than six solidus to me," Lars said, from The Goldenbreast.

"I am not wont to stop, Mistress," Anders said, and she heard the quaver in his voice. "I see the custom-takers standing on the bank, motioning us into shore. They will turn you over to the soldiers."

"I see only two custom-takers, Mistress," Finnvid said, "and the man at the stanchion. I can take three easily. Anders, give me my bow and a full quiver."

Inge despaired. Someone would die. Someone, but never themselves, these northmen believed. In her fear the smell of the wet woolen sail was sharp.

"They are not lowering the chain, Mistress," Finnvid said. "They will not let us through. I am steering in. We will kill the bastards and lower the chain ourselves."

She heard the twang of Finnvid's bowstring. She heard the men taking the peace bands off their swords. She touched the weave of the sail, the over-and-under weave she had woven a hundred hundred times...over-and-under...

"Finnvid, stop!" she cried out. "If they will not lower the chain, we will go over it."

The men all argued at once, and she had to agree it was a fool's thought. Yet sometimes only fools had a chance.

"Mistress, you are our captain but you can see naught from beneath the sail," Anders said, and again she heard the quaver.

"Ja, I am your captain. Now, Finnvid, sail close to the chain in the middle and tell Lars to follow, so the two boats are side by side."

The men grumbled and cursed, but they had always obeyed their captain, and they would now. Lars would not want her to do it alone. The crews slammed their oars on deck, and she felt the bump on the hull as Lars's boat pulled alongside.

"Now," she said, "steer as close to the chain as you can, and when you are there, all run to the stern, with Bratta and Volnir."

"Mistress!" Anders cried. "The bow will rise, and we will sink."

"The bow will rise, but just enough to clear the chain. Then all must run to the bow, and the boat will go over it."

"Mistress, it will be our death!" Anders cried.

"Death is certain if we do not try," she said, her voice sharp to hide her fear. "Unloose the beasts."

She heard the rumble of the chain as the bow touched it.

"Now!" she shouted and the men raced to the stern. The beasts stampeded, lowing and neighing. The ships were stout, but neither had been weighted so heavily at the stern, not even in The Varangian Sea storm. The boat began heeling over and Thora screamed and Finnvid swore and Anders cried out for Odin's help, and Inge's stomach lurched.

"Back!" she shouted and felt them run past her, the animals following. The boat twisted and righted, and she heard the blessed sound of the chain scraping the length of the boat from bow to stern.

They were over.

The ship rocked from side to side, and water splashed aboard and the men laughed with joy, joking with Lars's crewmen, who had followed her scheme and were also safely over.

Inge heard the clatter of oarlocks opening, and felt the surge in the boards as they rowed hard. She was too spent to think. She could only lie on the deck, soaked and numb.

Her plan had worked. They were alive. And she had not wondered what Karl would do, but thought for herself. Once again she proved herself a captain, and she was pleased.

Anders knelt at her side and lifted the sail, holding a cup of cold tea while she sipped, absorbing the strength in the healing herbs. Hrolf and Ingvar put up the sail. Inge stretched, glorying in being alive. Halfdan could not leave off holding Thora. He kissed her face round and round in the Circle of Love, and she giggled and wept.

"Are we safe?" Inge asked Finnvid, leaning against the gunwales. She had never been so weak.

"We are never safe, Mistress, but the farther we get from Miklagard, the less we have to worry. Soon we will be at the Clashing Rocks and then on to the Varangian Sea."

She looked up at the hills and found a spindly olivewood tree. She closed her eyes and imagined herself leaning against it, taking in its strength.

Her peace was short-lived. Like a cruel trick of Loki's a new threat arose. Ahead she saw a two-tiered ship with rowers on each level. The sun glinted off the armor of soldiers on the top deck. Its huge sail gave it speed. No one could doubt it was heading straight for their two boats.

"It is a dromon," Zeno said, "one of the Imperial warships. I am certain that in Basil's absence Eudocia has called it forth to attack us and get you back."

Ay, she and Zeno were both outlaws now. They would be a prize for any dromon.

"What will they do to us if we are captured?" Anders asked, and again she heard the quaver.

"The Empire is merciful," Zeno said. "The Empire does not hold with the death penalty."

But there is little mercy in blinding and cutting their balls off, Inge thought. She looked at her beloved crew putting on their chainmail and helmets, eager for a fight, their swords and their skills well-sharpened. But they were pitifully outmatched. The towering dromon was four times as high, and it had the advantage. It would be an unequal fight. She looked at Lars's boat and saw they too were preparing. It was so unnaturally quiet she heard the splashing alongside the bows.

Her heart hurt as she watched Thora tuck her hair under her helmet, the helmet with the nosepiece that tickled. Inge bit her lip. She wanted to order Thora to hide beneath the half-deck, but the maid would hate her. No one, not even a loving mother, could mistake Thora's happiness.

"Modir, I was born to fight. I will defend you, as I did at Birka, and with the Pechenegs. Do not worry, Modir. I will not let them take our boat."

Thora hugged her mother and held her fast, and Inge felt how slight she was to be fighting Imperial soldiers. Slight, yet strong. Inge wished she could weave a cordon of love around this daughter to protect her, though often love was not enough. After all they had endured, it would be unjust to die on their way back to Sweden. But she had seen little of justice in the world beyond her fjord.

"There are two of our boats, and only one of theirs," Anders said, and now the quaver was replaced by excitement.

"Ay, though the dromon is bigger we fight best when the odds are against us," Finnvid said, and Inge knew they believed it.

But fighting the huge dromon would not be like warring with a ship from Saxland or Frisia. This prow was covered with hides, and she wondered why. Mournful singing came across the water, and she thought their music loathsome, but it was soon drowned out by the sound of a thundering roar. The Greeks swung a fireball toward them, but it fell short and hit the water, yet did not sink.

"Hah! We are out of range," Finnvid said, "and the fools are wasting their firepower. But what is this?"

An orange flame came from the fireball, lay upon the water and did not go out--it grew stronger and spread, coming toward them. Lars and Finnvid swerved their boats, and it continued down the Bosphorus, still burning and smoking. Both crews stared after it. Inge felt fear prickle her neck and turned to Zeno.

"This is the wet-fire Helgi asked Karl to learn about?"

"This is it. It feeds on water, and does not go out."

Another fireball left the dromon and hit the deck of The Seafarer with a whoosh. The wood caught and the flames rose, crackling and snarling. Bratta and Volnir screamed and pulled at their tethers, backing away from the fire. Olaf and Hrolf unrolled leather bags and tried to smother it, but the fire burned on. Lars leapt over with another unrolled bag and all three pounded, but it was as though they fed the loathsome fire. The smoke stunk of grease. Inge heard a gurgling shriek and knew it was herself. She clutched her amulet. They would die on this river, not by drowning but burned to death by wet-fire.

"Zeno!" Inge cried. "Is there naught we can do?"

"Only vinegar, piss and sand together will put it out." He spread his hands. "We are in the midst of the river. Where would we get sand?"

"Inge, get vinegar," Lars shouted, yanking up the staves and disappearing under the half-deck.

"The hold is empty," she shouted, though she knew he could not hear her.

The furs and wax had been sold, the gold brocade and jewels given to the Warrior Women. They had no fine goods at all to barter for their lives with a dromon captain.

"Mistress!" Anders called and pointed where the fire had snaked to an iron plate on deck. To her horror it was melting. She had to do something, so she fumbled among the gear and found a cask of vinegar. She held it up to Zeno, but he shook his head. Piss aplenty they had, and vinegar but no sand. She moved toward the tiller and shouted she was steering ashore to find some, all the time knowing by the time they reached it their boat would be a cinder, sunken in the Bosphorus. And if they did not all burn to death Eudocia's soldiers would kill them when they went ashore. Or worse, take them hostage. The Empress would waste no time in putting out her eyes.

Out of the hold Lars's head appeared and then his hands, holding earthenware jars like the one Karl gave her so long ago.

"Gunnar! Anders! Olaf! Take these and dump them on the fire. Inge, pour the vinegar. Zeno, piss."

She felt a spasm of hope as the men grabbed the jars, tore out the stoppers with their teeth and dumped them, while she ripped out the bung and poured vinegar, and Zeno pissed. Per and Sven did the same, and three yellow streams joined the vinegar and the dirt flowing from the jars.

"Aiyiii!" Inge cried out. "The fire is dying! The jars hold loam from Breidal, but our soil has always had too much sand. For the first time, I am grateful."

Lars lifted himself onto the deck and kicked the staves back in place. He held her and together they watched the fire simmer to coals, leaving behind the greasy stench.

"We are saved," Inge cried.

Lars kissed her and said, "Karl did not know how long your homesickness would last, and so he brought many jars from Breidal, though as it turned out, he only needed to give you one."

She was giddy with joy. None of them would die on a burning boat in the midst of a foreign river. The men pitched the empty jars into the wet-fire and they floated.

"Eudocia!" Anders cried out, though the Empress was not within hearing. "We send you these jars as a message."

"Ay, you sent your worst," Gunnar said. A two-tiered dromon, and we fended it off, though it was four times the size of our two little boats."

Both crews watched the jars rock on the smoking, burning wet-fire on their way to Miklagard.

"I am glad Karl packed so many jars," Inge said. "He is helping us from the grave."

"Mistress!" Anders cried. "Turn around. The dromon is so close I can see the soldiers, their swords out, ready for attack."

XXXII

They all looked up at the dromon bearing down on them, but not yet was the huge boat close enough for the soldiers to leap aboard. They had a minute, maybe two. Inge looked at the messy gear. Was there nothing to help them?

Ah! She pulled out her seapouch of fleece and emptied it in the coals. With new fuel the flames leapt up, the men backing away. Inge grabbed an arrow out of Finnvid's quiver and rolled the tip in the blazing wool.

Grinning, he took it from her and shot for the dromon, and the men rushed to grab their bows and dip their arrows in flame, letting fly with a murderous howl. She saw her act gave the men heart, though the arrows that hit the deck were quickly put out. The ones that fell in the burning sea only added to the fire.

"More fleece," Finnvid shouted and Inge could but shake her head. She had none left. He scowled. The men scraped the last of it, and Finnvid shouted to them to make each shot count. With a quiet smile Thora took Anders's bow and hooked her fingers over his arrow.

"Bitch!" Finnvid yelled. "Give it back to Anders. Even if you are a captain's daughter, we have no fleece to waste."

As though Thora never heard she lifted the bow, pulled back her elbow, aimed, and loosed the arrow.

It hit the sail smack in the middle and a flame spread like a glowing stain. The northmen yelped for joy. In the racket, Finnvid pounded her back. Inge stared at her daughter. Where had she learned to shoot with such skill? Ah, the maid had many mysteries.

On board the dromon the burning sail was quickly extinguished and lowered, and now the Norse shot for the deck, with plain arrows, and less luck. Still, it gave them time, and heart, to stamp out the last of their fire.

The Greeks had another surprise. They whipped the hides off the bow and the Swedes stood, struck dumb. Here were lion heads turning, the open mouths spitting forth the monstrous wet-fire. Lion heads much like she had seen at the Magnura Palace, Inge thought, her stomach churning.

"To the oars," Finnvid shouted, and the men ran to their places. Both boats turned back downriver. The crews rowed with an elvist Inge did not know was in them, rowing for their lives, and were soon out of range. But going backward down the Bosphorus where capture awaited them. She joined Finnvid at the tiller.

"Mistress, I am hoping they will use up their fire-power, and then we can fight them like men."

"If you think they will use all their wet-fire, they will not," Zeno said. "The Imperial boats are well-stocked. The Empire has thousands of bottles of it."

"Where is it stored?" Finnvid asked. "If we can get some of it we can be on an equal footing."

"It is stored in the churches, where a merciful God keeps it safe."

Finnvid told him to ask his merciful God to help them, not the dromon, or the Greek would be turned into a eunuch.

All their faces were smoke-blackened, but the men were keeping the dromon at a distance. The lions spat fire now at their boat, now at Lars's, and it landed on the water as a flame that never went out but continued to grow, to their horror. The three boats continued twisting and turning and Inge smelled death close at hand. If it came to hand-to-hand fighting she knew Thora would be in the midst of a battle against impossible odds.

Though the sheets of flame pursued them, Finnvid and Lars were skilled helmsmen, eluding the wet-fire. Inge wondered how long they could bear the hard labor of it. Only one thing favored the Norse ships. They could maneuver closer to shore while the huge, unwieldy dromon had to stay in mid-river where it was deeper.

Inge sent a silent prayer to the goddess Freya. She saw the men's lips moving. Ah, they too were praying to Odin, Zeno to his White Christ. The gulls had been chased off by the smoke and noise, but she saw a sleek black cormorant stretch its neck upward, dive and disappear beneath the waves. Was it Freya in bird-form?

It seemed to Inge her prayer was answered, for she saw a small flame flicker at the waterline of the dromon. She grabbed Finnvid's arm. "Look!"

She was glad noise rent the air--the dromon would not hear a small flame crackling. It could not turn as swiftly as the smaller boats, and so it could not avoid the burning water as well.

"Fire was ever Karl's favorite weapon, Mistress," Finnvid said, and she laughed, foolish with this turn of battle.

Then she knew the goddess must have heard her prayer before she dove, for the wind caught the flame on the dromon and whipped it higher.

Zeno smiled. "The wind always comes up in late afternoon on the Bosphorus."

Her crewmen grinned. Inge looked over at Lars and marked he too saw the growing flame. The two crews rowed without pause, though the cords stood out on their arms and their clothes were pasted to their bodies with sweat, but now they rowed with hope.

Until Inge looked downriver. She saw a horde of soldiers at the customs house. The Swedes were trapped. Unless...

"Do they have any way to put out the fire on the dromon?" she asked Zeno. "Any vinegar or sand?"

"They would have no reason to keep vinegar or sand on board. It is an Imperial warboat. They sail close enough to the city, and the men go home at night to eat and sleep. We were lucky your Swedish soil has so much sand in it."

Now there was no stopping the fire on the dromon, as it rose higher. The Swedes watched the bottom tier of rowers coughing and choking in the smoke. One oar dangled, useless in the water, then two, then four, and then all of them. Inge heard Greek curses and Greek commands and Greek cries for help. The ship slowed, no longer able to steer without rowers and avoid the wet-fire on the surface.

The soldiers disappeared from the upper deck and there was much shouting and arm-waving, as the dromon swerved this way and that, out of control, straight into the sheets of flame.

All the while the wet-fire kept spurting from the lions' mouths so the flame grew around the hull, devouring the Greek ship. No one aboard seemed able to stop the wet-fire from coming forth, nor in truth, the dromon itself from sailing into the growing stretches of flame that covered the river in bigger and bigger patches.

The Swedes watched men leap, screaming from the deck, some able to avoid the wet-fire, some not. Inge turned away. She dare not stay to soothe the burned skin on these men, though she hoped someone on the dromon could help.

Finnvid turned the boat around and Lars did the same. Once again they were going upriver, and the men stared at the flaming dromon, now a confusion of men screaming and struggling to get to the gunwales, while some fell, some jumped, some were pushed, into the water.

They passed the burning ship and Inge turned away, northward.

"I will take the tiller before the Clashing Rocks," she told Finnvid.

"You are not weary, Mistress?"

"Nay. Freedom is heady. I have my eyes and I am filled with the energy ond to be free. Free! Aiyii!"

She raised her arms high, feeling better than she had in weeks. As Ingvar climbed the mast they saw their sail was unburnt. Their mast was whole. They could sail home. The men set the boat to rights, pitching over charred wood and gear. Already Gunnar was at work, sawing wood to repair the burned deck.

Had Freya helped them? Inge wondered. Zeno believed it was the White Christ. The Norse would claim it was Odin. Gunnar thought it was only the wind that always came up at even on the Bosphorus. Whichever, the Greeks' powerful ship had been turned against themselves. Inge reveled in the feel of wind and sun on her cheek.

"I was wont to point out the flame to the dromon," she said to Finnvid, as she took the tiller, "but they saw it soon enough."

Bratta lowed, and Inge thought no matter what, a cow must be milked, and she called Thora and Halfdan to get the bucket. He carried it for the maid and set it in place. In time Thora would forget the warm jasmine water of the harem.

"Mistress, we have room for Halfdan, but none for the Greek," Finnvid said. "Are we putting him off at the Varangian Sea?"

She said nothing, bent on steering through the Clashing Rocks without singeing her tail feathers, and saw Lars did the same. When both were safely through she cried out at the view of the Varangian Sea opening before them--fairer than any gilded Palace of the Emperor. They were alive and free.

"Toss Zeno off, Mistress," Finnvid said, and all the men agreed. "Or we will be stuck with him all the way home."

She looked at the Greek holding down his hairpiece in the wind. She told Finnvid they would have died many times over, without Zeno's help. He had taught them to speak Greek, got the oxen at the portage, helped them drag the two heavy boats, brought the Turkey Red for her weaving of Eudocia. He had gone with her to Ibn-Mahdi's. She told the men how he had boosted them up to the wall, led them to the cistern and found the trapdoor. He had helped them pass through the Camel Gate. And he alone knew the secret of putting out wet-fire.

She smiled, and saw the relief in his eyes. Nothing could be hid from eyes.

"I was glad to help," Zeno said. "Now I am thinking of becoming a Swedish weaver."

She squeezed the tiller hard, controlling her surprise. There was no way to protect him from the jeers and curses of the men, who turned on him. He was a linen-weaver to the Emperor, ay? In the Empire they did this better and that better. Why, then, would the Greek want to leave it?

The wind caught the sail, and the boat surged ahead. Inge's mind cleared. She should have expected he would not want to stay in Miklagard, where he would always be an outlaw despite a brown hairpiece.

"Zeno, you have repaid your debt to Helgi, and he would be glad to have you live at Konugard. You could be valuable to the overlord."

The Greek looked back at the fading city, now only a series of domed circles. "Yes, but I wish to become a Swedish weaver, in Sweden, not in Konugard."

She had not thought he would want to stay with them. Could she keep the men from killing him on the voyage home? He knew how they had treated him on the way downriver, and he would be expecting their taunts...but ay, he knew how to answer back...she could not keep them from teasing him, but when they got used to him...yet how would her women at Breidal like a man weaving alongside them? She turned the tiller and steered west, along the sandy shore.

"Zeno, my farmstead is plain, not large or beauteous as Miklagard. We have no braziers to heat the weaving room. And we live too far north to grow much flax for linen."

"I have woven enough linen. I would like to learn to weave with wool. And nettles. Perhaps I could teach your weavers patterns from New Rome, ones they could learn no other way."

She held the tiller with a lighter touch and pondered. He was serious about becoming a Swedish weaver. She had seen him making rush mats, and ay, he did know patterns altogether new to her. The women in the weaving room could learn much from him. And they would all have new designs from Miklagard.

She looked at him clutching his hairpiece. He turned away from the city wall, forward, as they were traveling. She made up her mind, though she had learned from watching Karl the art of bargaining, of exchange.

"Zeno, I will be happy to have you join my weavers. On our journey home you can weave rush baskets and mats and such for us to use at Breidal. And when I am not at the tiller, you can teach me new patterns."

He smiled, and she wondered if somewhere in Sweden there was a woman who could love him for his skill, and see more than a short, gap-toothed Greek with fake hair.

"Thank you. I will be honored to work for you. We can talk of weaving while you steer," he said.

"Mistress--" Finnvid began.

"Finnvid, Zeno stays," Inge said. "He will sail with us to Sweden and live at Breidal. If you find him a burden, you have ever been free to come and go. But not before the waterfalls. I will need your skillful helming."

"Finnvid, stay with us till Konugard," Olaf said, "and help Lars avenge Karl's death." He patted Finnvid's muscled arm. "We will need your good sword arm with that shit Helgi."

Inge thought between now and Konugard she must talk Lars into asking Helgi for wergild, and not revenge by the sword for Karl's death. The Warrior Women said Ilana sent word the Norse needed help. They only wished they had come to fight the Pechenegs in time to save Karl. Perchance Helgi could not be blamed for Karl's death altogether.

With Helgi she would have no problem--he liked all things Swedish and he had always listened to her, down through their many lives. But Lars would need persuading, and above all, her crew.

"Finnvid, stay until we are sailing up our fjord," she said, "and I give each man his share of gold. You have earned it."

He stared out to sea, but she saw his shoulders soften. He would stay. She would try to keep him separated from Zeno, though it would be hard on this small boat. She was still amazed the Greek did not want to return to Miklagard, but he valued his own head, though topped with another's hairpiece. Anders brought her a cup of cold tea.

"Mistress, what will you do when we get home?" he asked.

The stench of the wet-fire was no longer strong, and she took a deep breath. With her captain's seasoned eye she looked up at the gentle blue sky with sheep's wool clouds, down at the swell of the dark blue sea, and up again before she answered.

How would it seem to be back at Breidal without Karl? Her life with him was ended, and there was nothing she could do to change it. If she had tried harder to convince him to wait for the convoy, would he now be alive? Ah, who could say. The course of a man's life was set by his nature, and Karl had always been headstrong. The witch-seer's first two runes came true as foretold--a passage into darkness...a journey, part of which could not be shared...

She must not wallow in regret for what might have been, though her body still ached for his touch. The third rune, wyrd, was the Unknowable, and who could portend what it meant?

"Anders, you ask what I will do when I get home. I will jump off The Seafarer and kiss the earth of my farmstead and never leave. I will grow old watching my cows fatten. My sons will soon be home, and they will marry and I will dandle my grandchildren upon my knee."

Thora gave her a drink of sweetmilk and passed the bucket among the crewmen. One grandchild I will be able to love even sooner, Inge thought. A chill came into her body, and she pulled her cloak tighter. Could the babe be Ibn-Mahdi's? Fathered by a Greek, whose countrymen tried to kill them with wet-fire? How could it be loved in Sweden?

Inge chided herself. She was not altogether guiltless. She had been too busy grieving and learning to captain The Seafarer to see that Thora was old enough to need the Cup of Roots, to prevent a child quickening in her womb. The maid could not be expected to know...only a watchful mother...

Ah, done was done, and she must not stay mired in regret. Now there must be a hasty wedding to Halfdan, the bridal shift loose at the waist.

Gunnar turned the deck repair over to Olaf and sat next to Inge, carving in the days on the runestock.

"I know you must carve two bad days each month, Gunnar. One is when the dromon attacked, I trow. And the other?"

"When our captain was taken from us to become a state slave. All of us were at sea without our captain."

She smiled at him. Our captain. How sweet the words were to her. Our captain.

Lars steered close enough to talk. "Ingeborg, you are so young and beautiful at the tiller. You will marry again."

She shook her head. Could she ever find another like Karl-Eirik? She had been all the way to Miklagard, and there was no other like him. The happiness they shared the week on the Dnieper before the waterfalls could never be matched.

"I am unready to take on another husband, Lars. I was but fifteen when I married Karl, and knew naught of the world beyond my fjord."

And now she had seen enough of it. She was glad it was only custom, not law, for a widow to marry the younger brother.

"I can wait, Ingeborg," Lars said.

"Do not waste your youth waiting, Lars."

He laughed. "We both have time opening before us like the wide waters of the world."

In truth the wide waters were one, meeting and mixing. Her fjord was part of the Baltic, and the Baltic flowed into the Dvinna that joined the long Dnieper, and that ended in the Varangian Sea, connecting with the Bosphorus and the Golden Horn that blended into the Sea of Marmara, and that another sea, flowing on without end.

Flowing together, yet separate. She looked over at Lars, and thought him most fair. She felt a stirring in her Golden Cleft, and it surprised her, yet it was pleasing. For the first time in days her body was reminding her she was alive.

She looked at Lars again, standing at his tiller as she stood at the tiller of The Seafarer. Two captains with much in common. It was a long way back to Sweden, and the two boats must stay close together to survive.

Moving forward is our natural state, Karl had said. She looked at Thora and Halfdan, Zeno, her crew, and Lars. All faced forward. She too must face forward, flowing with the world's waters, together, yet separate.